The Soul City Salvation

Jonathan LaPoma

San Diego, California

ISBN: 978-0-9988403-8-3
Library of Congress Control Number: 2019920089

Cover design by theBookDesigners
Interior design by Polgarus Studio
Author photograph by Emilio Azevedo

For more information, contact info@almendroarts.com.
www.almendroarts.com
www.jonlapoma.com

Praise for *The Soul City Salvation*

"Jay is revealed to be an intriguing soul to follow, and LaPoma seamlessly depicts aspects of Jay's mental illness as well as his attempts to get successfully published. Along the way, the author effectively plays with the theme of control—specifically, Jay's lack of it, in both his classrooms and in his personal life . . . Readers who are looking for . . . a good character study of an educator yearning for more will be satisfied . . . A . . . highly readable tale of a struggling but well-meaning schoolteacher."
—*Kirkus Reviews*, Recommended Review

"A philosophical story of growth, insight, and discovery . . . that moves beyond the usual focus on young adults to consider an adult's evolutionary process . . . Readers looking for an introspective journey will relish *The Soul City Salvation* for its ever-changing evolutionary realizations which offer rich food for thought long after Jay's story concludes."
—Diane Donovan, *California Bookwatch*

"This book reminded me of two things; one—we are all on different journeys and two—we don't get there at the same time worse off the same way. I love how easy it was to relate to Jay, because he was human—he was imperfect, difficult, weary, sweet, hopeful, creative, loving, scared—everything in one . . . What he saw on the surface as anxiety turned out to be much more. There's a part in the book where he asks 'How long will it take to fix me?' and it tore at my heartstrings . . . This is not one of those books you can say will make you feel a certain type of way, and that's refreshing. It will however make you feel different things at different times."
—Dora Okeyo, Author of *The Crown of the Sea*

"**So honest that it hurts . . . I absolutely *devoured* this story!** It's one of those 'Just one more chapter!' books . . . that just emphasizes the realism of dealing with mental disorders. Healing isn't a linear path. And sometimes the things we do to try and better ourselves do more harm than good . . . *The Soul City Salvation* had me in tears as it hit me over and over again that other people think the way I do, and that, if it can be okay for them, I can survive too . . . **This novel preaches hope and understanding in these blasé fast times** . . . If you are looking for one of those books that deals with real issues, mental health, or slightly psychedelic self healing, *The Soul City Salvation* is definitely worth a read . . . **Jonathan LaPoma has insane talent.**"
—Audrey, *Warped Shelves*

*To Arne, Woody, and all the other Wild Men and Women
who save our lives, often without even realizing it*

All of humanity's problems stem from man's inability to sit quietly in a room alone.

—Blaise Pascal

Part I

Chapter 1

I'd planned to move to LA, but if you go to LA when you're already broken, you'll only be crushed into a thousand more pieces, so instead I ended up on my buddy Doug's couch in Soul City, CA. Doug was studying geology at the university there, and as little as I wanted to see him, I still filled his living room with boxes lugged from my car. It took me four days to hit the coast once I'd left Buffalo, NY, but I could've made it in three had I not stopped at a few national parks along the way. A snowstorm had covered most of the East in powdery white winter, and I didn't escape it until western Oklahoma. Despite the storm, the drive was easy. I had my tunes and Philip Norman's biography of John Lennon on CD. I also had the voice recorder I'd picked up the day before I left and spent several hours engaged in talk therapy with myself, trying to undercover the meaning of my trip—the meaning of my anxiety. The reason why, even after a year of teaching in one of the toughest middle schools in Miami, I still had problems looking people in the eye. Why my body shook when discussing my dreams. With the recorder in my hand, I assured myself that I was strong and smart and capable. That I would finally find the secret to unlocking my creativity and achieving my potential as an actor and songwriter and poet.

But, as usual, it was easy to talk about dreams and confidence and earth-shaking while blazing a hundred miles per hour through the Mojave Desert alone, blasting Grateful Dead and John Lennon's life story, but that was nearly impossible to do on Doug's couch. I arrived at 3 a.m. and woke around eight to Doug's laughter.

"Why the hell'd you bring so much shit?" Doug said, as he rummaged through one of my boxes on his floor. He picked up my dartboard. "You opening a dive bar or something?"

"Fuck you, man," I said.

"You'd better clean this up. My roommate will be back from class in a few hours, and she was pissed when she saw this mess."

"Christ, I got in late as fuck. What'd she expect?"

"For you not to be such a fucking slob. This is California, man, not some Sloan, New York shit-smellin' duplex by the train tracks."

"All right, all right, I'll clean it up after breakfast. Whaddya got to eat?" I unzipped my sleeping bag, rubbed the sleep from my eyes, and got up.

"Got a supermarket down the street," Doug said.

"Fuck this," I said.

"You're free to leave any time," Doug said.

"Not before I get a full refund. I paid Helena three hundred bucks last night to stay here for the rest of the month."

"The cost of living is high as fuck here. Get used to it."

I bought some milk, eggs, cereal, and bread at the supermarket, ate breakfast, and put all of my boxes in the corner of the living room beside Helena's turtle tank, which was filthy as hell. The whole place reeked of algae and turtle shit, and I couldn't see how a few cardboard boxes filled with my clothes, computer, TV, and other shit made the place any worse.

I went with Doug to the university that afternoon and marveled at Soul City as we drove toward the coast in his convertible. Even with a population of about six hundred thousand, the city, which was about an hour north of Hollywood, didn't seem crowded. In fact, many of the houses had front and backyards, and there seemed to be some breathing room, unlike Miami Beach, which was filled with high-rises and people everywhere. The natural beauty was spectacular,

and I stared at the bright blue ocean and sky and at the dusty-brown rolling hills littered with gorgeous Spanish-style houses, covered in orange-tiled roofs and clean white stucco walls. The night before had been thick with fog, giving everything this surreal, epic feeling, but during the day, the city was less dramatic and intimidating.

Doug introduced me to some of the other geology grad students, and a few of us went to the beach for dinner and drinks. It was hot that afternoon, and I was in a T-shirt and jeans, but once the sun set it cooled down quickly, and I understood why in movies, people in LA so often wore long-sleeved flannel shirts and jackets. February in California was nowhere near as cold as February in Buffalo, but it was still miles away from February in Miami, and I shivered as we wandered from bar to bar. At one point, I took off my shoes and stepped in the ocean, and it felt as if I'd fallen off the *Titanic*. Even so, there were surfers riding the waves.

"So, you're a teacher?" one of the geology students asked me. He was a tall guy, about Doug's height but much thinner. He was in his mid-thirties, a decade older than Doug and me, but he still loved to party and had gotten drunk on wine during dinner.

"Yeah, I applied to a few schools before heading out here and already have an interview for a subbing job next week," I said, still shivering.

"That's cool. I hear there aren't many teaching jobs out here now."

"Yeah, with the recession, I've heard they're cutting tons of teaching jobs and forcing people into early retirement. People keep telling me I'm nuts, but I'll make it happen. The sun set about an hour before I crossed into California last night, and the colors in the sky were so unbelievable, I just knew I have to be here."

"Good luck finding a place to rent on a sub's pay," Doug said.

"I've always been fine before, and I'll be fine again," I said.

We headed into a bar and got drunk on craft IPAs. The place was filled with surfers—flannel shirts, flat-brimmed hats, jeans, flip-flops. The vibe was relaxed, but this seemed more due to money than surf

culture. Soul City was an affluent area, and these people laughing and drinking eight-dollar craft beers were probably millionaires, or close to it. They had none of that work-two-jobs-to-afford-heat-in-the-winter Buffalo exhaustion in their eyes. None of that my-kids-could-die-in-a-drive-by-at-any-moment Miami fear. No, these people had their sun, their sand, their ocean-side mansions, and their plastic surgeons to keep them all young and pretty forever.

I felt uncomfortable around them, but I also felt that I wasn't so different from them. Were they smarter than I was? Harder-working? I knew that I too could someday shake the misery and exhaustion from my face and wear such an effortless smile. Someday I could enjoy the sun and sand as well.

"Yo, you shoulda seen this guy in high school," Doug said, pointing at me. "He had absolutely no friends."

But that day wasn't coming anytime soon.

I stared at the stars as Doug drove us home. So many songs had been written about those stars. Woody Guthrie had once found salvation in them. Others too: Humphrey Bogart, Marilyn Monroe, Paul Newman. Looking at those stars was nothing original. But now it was *my* time to do it. Now was *my* time to feel alive.

Helena must have rearranged my things, because when we got back, all my boxes were in a different corner. Doug and I decided to keep the party going, and I pulled two frosted glasses out of the freezer and poured us both a drink.

"These yours?" Doug said about the glasses.

"Yeah, I brought a set with me."

Doug laughed. "You really think of everything, don't you? That's pretty cool actually."

I smiled and we drank while talking about our time living together in Mexico after college graduation. I hadn't seen him since he'd left Lila to take care of his sick father, and we'd both been through so much in such a short time. His father got worse and then improved, and I got beaten down while teaching at an at-risk Miami middle school, learning so much about myself and how to hold a

professional job. I didn't think either of us would be able to survive California without the experiences we'd had. But I was ready now.

"Let's start a band. I've got so many more songs," I said.

"Yeah, I know some guys in the department who play guitar. I wanna play drums, though. I'm done with the bass."

"Works for me. You know anyone who can produce? With all the technology they got now, we should cut a few albums ourselves."

"With what money?"

"Money comes when you really need it."

"I hope to have plenty of that when I finish grad school."

"How much longer you got?"

"Another year, then I'm thinking of doing a doctoral program overseas, maybe in the UK or Switzerland."

"Damn, man, you *ever* plan on working?"

"Fuck you, these things take time." Doug grabbed another beer from the fridge and poured it into his glass, which was no longer frosted.

"Anyway, I should probably get to bed," I said. "I've gotta head over to the district office tomorrow to get my teaching credential to sub. If I get this job, I'll make a hundred and twenty-five bucks a day, which comes out to about two grand a month after taxes. I'll need to find a place that's under seven hundred so I can afford food, utilities, and my student loan payments."

"Good luck finding that out here. You'll definitely need a roommate."

"I'll make it happen."

We finished our beers and went to bed. The hum from the turtle tank's pump filled the living room as I stared through the window at the shadows of the distant mountains, stars above and house lights below. Miami was so flat it had depressed me, but these mountains were what I needed—to climb them and speak to the gods. I fell asleep quickly and woke the next morning to Helena dropping a coffee mug. I said good morning, but she hardly paid me a glance before sweeping up the mess and walking out the front door.

I looked at the beer glasses still on the kitchen table. Doug was right. Like an Oregon Trail settler, I had taken everything with me, never to turn back. Before leaving, I had told my mom goodbye and that she might not ever see me again. I wasn't sure if I'd meant that literally or figuratively, but I was sure that this was it—the trip I'd tried to make several times before but had always failed at. But this time I was going to succeed. While in Miami, I'd developed a taste for beach living and knew I needed to be around natural beauty in order to heal the tremendous pain inside of me. I didn't think I'd be able to heal this pain in Stand-Your-Ground Florida. But California was the Promised Land. California had saved so many others. It saved Jim Carroll when he went to Bolinas to kick heroin, and I knew it'd help me kick the darkness destroying my life as well. Every day still felt like survival of the fittest, and I wasn't fit. It physically hurt to talk to people. To stand for long periods of time. I needed saving, but I also knew now that no one would save me. I needed to do this shit myself, and deep down, I knew I could only do this in California. In the place where people practiced yoga and ate organic avocados and where so many of the tunes that had saved me had been written and performed. Where so many of the films that made me want to live for one more day had been shot. I needed to be here and be a part of it all. I needed to shake off the Darkness so I could finally write my stories and songs. To get close enough to my emotions that I could act. Direct. Publish my book. Start a band. Achieve my potential. I knew that the old me had to die.

But I wasn't ready yet for LA. Part of why I'd gotten into teaching was to get comfortable speaking in front of crowds. Telling jokes. Learning how to manage my emotions while controlling the behavior of the masses. I needed to teach for a few more months to prepare myself for auditions. If I walked into one now, I'd start stuttering and sweating and saying, "C'mon, just one more c-chance!" I needed to adjust to California living slowly, and then make my way south once my fears and insecurities had subsided. Once I felt a little more comfortable drinking beside millionaires in beach dive bars. Once I felt worthier of taking meetings on yachts or in Malibu mansions. Once I felt capable of speaking a complete sentence without trailing off and looking away. Once I finished reading Boleslavsky's *Acting: The First Six Lessons*. Then I would hit the auditions with a swagger and a tan. Plus, I needed to save up cash.

I headed to the district office and got cleared to sub. Because I had a New York State teaching credential, I didn't have to do much. I got fingerprinted and paid the fees and walked tall the rest of the day. Now I just needed to ace the interview.

Doug was playing keyboard in the living room when I got back. I headed straight for the bathroom, and the harmony he was playing seeped inside of me. While pissing, I came up with a melody, but I didn't share it with him. Instead, I pulled out my voice recorder, which I'd been carrying in my pocket, and quietly hummed the tune.

Eventually he stopped playing, and we made dinner: quesadillas and scrambled eggs. One of his geology friends came over, and we got pretty drunk while watching *The Office*. On his way back from a bathroom break, Doug started singing a song: "You got brains in your head so they called ya Doogie Howser. You got shit on your pants, now they call ya Dookie Trouser."

I got into it too: "That's Howser, and if you look at me wrong, I'll lobotomize your brain though you came in with a gallstone."

The geology friend mentioned something about stabbing someone in the eye with an IV, and we all laughed. Later, we went to a dive near the apartment and filled up on cheap beers. Some guy said something Doug didn't like, so we had to pull Doug out of there before they called the cops. I tipped the bartender well in the hopes that he wouldn't get pissed if I decided to come back.

The geology friend went home, and Doug and I stayed up late playing our guitars in his room. I didn't tell him, but I recorded the whole session and listened to it later while falling asleep on the couch. Most of it was crap, but there were a few harmonies that got stuck in my head, one sounding like the harmony Doug had played on the keyboard. The melody came back to me, and I added some words to the chorus to give it structure: "You hear 'em talkin' about that dookie—dookie—dookie on your trousers, oh yeah. Try to get away but the smell just won't let go." I sang that song in my head until I fell asleep, and it was still with me in the morning, stronger than the night before. No one was around, so I pulled out the recorder and added a first verse as I scrambled some eggs.

> *"As I was gettin' ready, I could see the distant city lights:*
> *blood on the left and fear up on my right.*
> *But who would call it pretty?*
> *Then again sometimes the stars will align;*
> *some will break through while the others will fail to shine.*
> *Well, I was lost, and I was found, but I'll get lost again.*
> *Oh, I was lost, but I was found, and I'll get lost again,*
> *Hear 'em talkin' 'bout that dookie . . ."*

I knew the chorus had to change, but I didn't have it yet. All I had was the silence—the silence I knew would engulf me once I took up a professional job again. The silence on the ride to work. The silence in the classroom as I ate lunch alone. The silence in my kitchen as I made and ate dinner alone. The silence of growing old and dying in my sleep, alone.

The silence . . .

> *"Hear 'em talkin' 'bout that silence—silence—it's only gettin'*
> *louder, fuck yeah.*
> *Try to get away, but the sound just won't let go."*

Holy shit! I had it! Was it California or was it me? The tunes had been coming fast since I'd started recording myself in Arizona, and I'd filled the recorder's first folder in only a few days. I started working on the second verse:

"Feelin' kinda heavy, well I dumped the beggar all my change.
One of us now's never ever gonna be the same.
Legs are moving steady, found a rhythm never thought was
mine to claim.
Today is all mine but tomorrow's up for debate—"

Doug opened the door, and I dropped the recorder trying to turn it off. I grabbed it quickly and stuffed it in my pocket before he could see what I was doing.

"Were you singing?" He dropped his backpack on the carpet.

"N-no, I think that was the turtle tank. It's making weird noises."

"You've been makin' weird noises, too. Helena's pissed. She says you keep waking her up, playing your guitar all night."

"You were playing too."

"Not all night. You gotta cool it with that shit. She wants you out."

"Fuck her. I paid her. It's not like I'm just crashing here."

"Yeah, she's been gettin' on my nerves. She keeps eating all my veggie burgers."

"Why don't we move out? I've got my interview tomorrow, and if I get the job, I'll have enough for rent."

"Dude, places are expensive as shit out here. This tiny-ass apartment is fourteen hundred a month."

"If I get steady work, I can make seven hundred a month happen. If you're already paying that much, why don't we solve both of our problems?"

"Yeah, well, whatever . . ."

I checked Craigslist, even though I knew what living with Doug was like. He alternated between insufferable asshole and caring friend, and his moods were getting more extreme. He'd been an asshole since high school, but there was some hardening in his ways now, as if he was growing tired of fighting against the rigidity of adult misery and was slowly letting it take over. He was about as talented a songwriter as anyone I knew, and if we could just get it together, we could start a successful band here, playing at beach bars and cliff-side porch parties, but I was growing tired of trying to pull him into my dreams. We'd played in a band in college, but after graduation, we never played with a group again, and I only had so much energy to try to convince him to see my vision for our future.

Still, though, maybe shit would fall into place here. California seemed to have an energy about it—a long, rich history filled with success and realized dreams. Plenty of broken dreams as well, but I'd been walking barefoot on the shards of my dreams for so long already that my feet were calloused and my heart sufficiently strong.

No, California was going to be about success and nothing more. I was going to make it here. Hell, I already had . . .

Chapter 2

I got the job, and Doug and I found a cheap two-bedroom place in a beach town south of Helena's apartment. The town looked to have been frozen in the 1960s and had a unique vibe, filled with hippies and motorcycle gangs and surfers and skaters and homeless kids hanging out on the beach, playing guitar, picking pockets, and making the whole place smell like weed, piss, and patchouli oil. The main strip ran along the beach, and surfers carried their boards past bars with dozens of motorcycles parked out front, and people were drunk and smoking cigarettes at all hours as they discussed stickin' it to whichever Man was currently bringing them down.

What drew me to the place, other than its strange energy, was that it seemed like the perfect spot to transition to street life if all else failed. Since childhood, I was always waiting for the bottom to drop out, when I'd finally end up crawling around the streets naked and barking at people, and Sand Beach seemed like the bottom-out capital of the world. There didn't seem to be much difference between the dreadlocked kids begging for change on the streets and the dreadlocked millionaires playing harmonica right next to them.

But something about the town's hippie feel made me get lost in the craters and valleys in my soul, and I didn't want to invite that kind of negativity back into my life. In Miami, I'd survived a year of teaching and resolved to continue to grow and develop as a person. I didn't want to start smoking pounds of weed and drinking gallons of beer again as I slipped deeper into the Darkness that had consumed my formative years. Things were relatively good now. I had the sun and a new job and I hadn't yet destroyed my health or mind. Perhaps I should have picked a better spot to live. But those squares up north in Snob Beach weren't my crowd either.

Plus, the rent was cheap as fuck here, mainly because of the chaotic buzz. The people in Sand Beach actively defended their way of life against becoming another soulless California beach town.

Doug and I got a small but nice house a few blocks from the ocean with a shared patio and some great neighbors, who pretty much all greeted us as soon as we signed on the dotted line. On one side of us was a retired gay couple who spent lazy afternoons getting high and tending to their beautiful garden. On another was a tie-dyed thirty-something CPA who wasn't shy about showing us the weed plants he was growing in his closet. The other two neighbors were thirty-something lesbians, and they lived closest to us. Our living room windows faced each other and were only about three feet apart, so it felt as if we were all living together.

Once we moved in, they all stopped in to say hi, and to bring us potted plants and food. We drank some beers and smoked herb on the patio, and then I went inside, plugged in my Strat, and let it sing a tune to my new beach community. There was a freedom in the energy here, and I felt aligned with it while rocking the blues as the sun shone through the windows. After a while, the CPA, Doug, and I walked to the beach for tacos and beer.

On the way home, we passed some early-twenty-somethings sitting on a couch and armchair in an alley behind their apartment. They said they were moving and that we could have all their stuff. They helped us carry it to our new place, and now we had the couch and armchair, along with a microwave, TV stand, and a coffee table. We bought them some beers and burritos, and we all got drunk as hell sitting on the patio. They were moving to a farm outside of Portland, and we wished them well.

My first subbing gig was for a fifth-grade class at an elementary school near the mountains. I grabbed my substitute ID at the main office, and a woman pointed me to the classroom: a trailer in the back across a dusty spread of asphalt. Though school hadn't started yet, kids were running around outside and having fun. Some chubby kindergartener ran up to me at the classroom door and said, "I ate a whole pumpkin this morning," and I said, "Oh my gourd!" as he grinned and ran away.

The teacher wanted me to pass out some worksheets during English and math, play a movie during social studies, and perform a lab during science. I'd subbed before and knew this was asking a lot—unless, of course, the kids were into it.

When the bell rang, I stood at the door and greeted kids as they walked inside. A few smiled and said, "Sub day!" One of the best parts about subbing was watching how excited kids got when they saw you. Your presence meant their day was about to get a whole lot better. But it also meant yours would probably get a whole lot worse, because even great kids might turn on a sub. The key was to get them on your side right away.

Once the students were sitting at their desks, I passed out their first assignment and addressed them. "As you can probably already tell, I'm not Ms. Mahoney, so I'd like to introduce myself. My name is Mr. Sakovsky, and I'll be your sub today. A little about me: I love history and music, and I recently moved here from Miami, Florida. Does anyone know where Florida is?"

A kid raised his hand, and I had him come up to the map on the side wall and point it out. "Great job! Okay, I can see that some of you are really excited, and I'm hoping that's because you're excited to meet me, just as I'm excited to meet you. I know that Ms. Mahoney has her class rules, and I have similar ones. I'm okay with you moving your seat next to a friend as long as you follow my rules."

"What are your rules?" a girl asked.

"That once you pick that seat, you stay there and don't get up unless you're told to do so. Can you do that?"

They said yes.

"Also, you have to talk quietly—no swearing—keep your hands to yourselves, be nice to me and everyone else in the classroom, and try your hardest with your assignments."

They agreed, but there were always problems throughout the day. As a sub, I wasn't trying to win teacher of the year. By letting them pick their seats and talk quietly, the kids usually saw me as pretty cool and wouldn't give me too much shit, which was the best I could hope for. You usually got the worst problems when you pushed too hard or were disrespectful of them.

I sat at the desk and edited my novel, which I'd finished writing before leaving Miami, and I intermittently stopped to walk around the classroom and correct student behavior. Elementary school was tough because you didn't get a break outside of lunch, which is why I preferred middle and high school, but it was my first day, so I took what I could get. Besides, subbing was great regardless, because you could usually get a lot of work done on side projects, and that day, even with a few obnoxious students, I was able to edit quite a bit.

At the end of the day, I left the teacher a glowing summary. "You have such a wonderful class, and I'd be thrilled to work with them again!" Subs lived and died on referrals, and if a teacher came back to a "your students are terrible!" note, they'd be less likely to request me to sub for them again. Project enthusiasm, confidence, and competence, letting teachers know you can handle whatever their kids throw at you, and you'll get asked back time and again, which is extremely important living in a place where a gallon of milk costs more than six bucks.

When I got home, Doug was hopping around the living room, scratching his legs. "Those fuckin' stoners gave us furniture covered in fleas."

"I don't see anything," I said.

"They're everywhere, and I'm fuckin' allergic."

We told our landlord, and he said someone would come out the next day to kill the fleas. In the meantime, Doug stuck his legs inside of an empty trash bag and tied it off at his waist. He'd claimed the smaller room and I took the bigger one, which was still pretty small, but I had to pay an extra fifty bucks a month for it. Rent was only eleven hundred, and the place was pretty clean, other than the fleas, so we were cool with its size.

We got drunk while watching my *Seinfeld* DVDs, then walked to the beach. Despite the bohemian vibe, Sand Beach concealed an aggression just waiting to blast you in the face the second you weren't looking. Some street kids started talking shit after we refused to give them money, and they followed us down the street. Doug got heated, and I had to stop him from dropping the loudest of the pricks. Doug was a mean motherfucker and could put just about anyone on the pavement, and those kids were lucky I was able to cool him down.

Some other kids smoked us up while we sat on the beach, and it mellowed out the mood. One of them had a guitar, and I played some Doors tunes as some of the others sang. Doug and I went home around 1 a.m. because we both had to be up early. I had another gig at a high school downtown, and though high school started about an hour later than elementary school, I still had to be up around seven. We got burritos on the walk back, played some more guitar, and went to sleep.

"How 'bout you sit on this dick?"

Sometimes when you tried to be cool with the kids, they weren't so cool back, and this punk gave me shit right after my "you can sit wherever you'd like" line.

"No, thanks," I said. "I'm afraid of needles." Saying shit like this was always risky, because it could escalate the situation, but usually once the kids heard you speaking their language, they saw you as one of them.

"Oh, shit, he just roasted you, Jose!" a boy in the back row said.

Jose mumbled a few swear words, knowing not to push back. After a few years of teaching, I got pretty good at shutting kids down with one-liners. Most teachers would get mad when students disrespected them, but the wiseass inside of me preferred to beat the kids at their own game. I felt subbing was great practice should I ever want to try stand-up. If I could stand at the front of a classroom and manage behavior with my words, I could certainly do it in a comedy club.

When the bell rang, I stood at the door and greeted the next class. Down the hall, I saw a group of kids giving another sub hell. Dude was tall and dopey and seemed the type to make a lot of empty threats and "who do you think you are?" comments. Some people weren't cut out for teaching, and when I'd watched him asking for his ID badge in the office that morning, I knew right away that this dude would have problems. The woman who gave out the badges was on her cell phone, laughing and chatting, while he stood there patiently waiting for his pass. I grabbed one off her desk and she gave me a dirty look, but Dopey just kept saying, "Ex-excuse me." Too many wolves in this profession to just stand there like a lamb chop.

When the bell rang, I addressed the class and put in the movie *Romeo + Juliet,* with Leo and Claire Danes. The teacher, Mr. Cisneros, wanted me to start the movie from the beginning for each class, but I didn't want to rewatch the same clip over and over, so I let it play where it left off after each new group came in. None of the kids gave a shit anyway. They talked and played on their phones or else slept.

I continued editing my novel and was making pretty good progress. It was a monster—almost two hundred thousand words, which was, like, three hundred pages on Word, single-spaced, so I needed to be making progress.

At lunch, I ate alone in the classroom. I saw the dopey dude sitting on a bench outside, trying to chat up some of the other teachers, but no one gave a shit.

During fifth period, I was making good headway again, blocking out the movie and bad student behavior, until it ended and "Exit

Music (For a Film)" started playing. Then the dark curtain descended and I got rushed with thoughts I couldn't slow: What the fuck are you doing in another school, Jay? Don't you know Bob Dylan was already the voice of his generation by your age? Don't you know Brando was already igniting the big screen? That Einstein had come up with his theory of relativity? You need to be in London! New York! Paris! Leave this place *now* and rush to Mexico City. Follow the footsteps of Kerouac. Burroughs. Stop wasting your time here with ungrateful kids. Stop pissing your life away in dive bars with other lunatics. You're gonna die soon. You gotta go now, now, *now!*

I saw the dopey dude subbing about a week later at a middle school a few miles north of Sand Beach. The kids weren't too bad, but they were still giving him hell. This time, I decided to join him as he ate lunch alone on a bench outside.

"I think I saw you subbin' at Irving High last week," I said.

"Yeah, that was probably me," he said. He was eating tuna salad and it looked as bad as it smelled. "Math."

"What?"

"I was subbing for a math class. You?"

"Oh, English. Those kids are pretty rough there, huh?"

"Children are a product of their environment." He stared at me with this look of deep reflection, as if he was going to say something incredibly profound, but then he looked away and I realized this was California and that was as deep as shit was gonna get here.

I grabbed the PB&J sandwich and Doritos from my brown paper bag and got to work.

"I'm Jay, by the way."

"Cody."

We shook hands.

"How long have you been in Soul City?" I said.

"I'm one of the few who was born and raised here. I graduated from Soul City High in ninety-three. You?"

"I'm from Buffalo, but the last few years I lived in Mexico and Miami."

"What were you doing in Miami?"

"Teaching. Thinking I was making a difference."

"And Mexico?"

"I went down there to live with a friend who was studying Mexico's most active volcano. Technically, I was there to teach English at a language school, but mostly I was traveling and blowing off steam."

"Hmm." He looked at me as if studying my very essence. "You seem to have a way with children."

"In a lot of ways, I feel like I speak their language."

"And what is your pedagogical philosophy?"

"I, uh—treat people how you want to be treated?"

"Very interesting. Simple, but interesting. I may have some use for you. What's your number?"

We exchanged numbers, and he saved my name as Interesting Jay. Something about that fascinated me; I wanted to know more about this guy, so I said "sure" when he asked if I'd call.

When the bell rang, we went back to our respective classrooms, and from across the blacktop, I watched a few of the kids who had been good to me earlier in the day give Cody hell. A girl was mocking the way he stood, leaning forward with her shoulders and head, as a group of kids laughed. Still, it didn't seem to affect Cody. I mean, he didn't seem to be loving it, but he didn't yell at them or anything.

That night, Doug and I had a cookout on the patio. We made cheeseburgers and veggie burgers and about ten of his geology friends came, along with all of our neighbors except for the CPA. We got pretty drunk and the older couple smoked us up. They brought some of their friends over too, and soon Doug and I were taking song requests on our guitars. The older couple, Ryan and Remi, loved Fleetwood Mac, so I played "Never Going Back Again" as they sang (it was too hard for me to play that song and sing it too). One of the geology students was a gorgeous woman named Diah, and we spoke for a little while, but she seemed really into Doug, so I gave up and let the night do its thing.

We decided to hit the bars, but Ryan and Remi and their friends stayed behind. Our other neighbor couple, Tuyet and Kelly, came with us, though, and they out-partied us all. They seemed to know everyone at every bar, and they were the life of the party. We tried to keep up but eventually had to go home after Doug got kicked out of a biker bar for pissing in the bathroom sink. Doug almost came to blows with the bartender, but Tuyet stepped in and de-escalated the situation. I was glad for that because I didn't want to have to explain to my next group of students why I had a black eye and a swollen nose.

I had a particularly rough day subbing at a high school, and, as soon as I got home, I stripped down to my boxers and lay in bed. I was always so fucking stressed, but that afternoon was worse than usual. The anxiety crippled me, and I could feel rivers of chemicals racing up my spine, twisting and clenching my muscles, turning them to stone. I tried to relax, but I kept replaying what happened that day in my mind. Kept seeing that shithead threaten to cut me after school because I told him to stop tackling people while playing two-hand touch football in gym. Kept seeing him and his friends charge me while the other PE teachers watched it happen. Kept seeing him motion like he was gonna hit me, and only then did another teacher step in and stop them from jumping me. Kept feeling my right hand in my pocket, squeezing my keys between my fingers, just waiting for shit to get ugly. Waiting to have to start puncturing tracheas and eyeballs. But it didn't happen that way, and I got to come home in one piece. Got to come home without having to talk to cops or doctors or lawyers.

I lay on my back, but I was so tense, you could slide a cell phone under my right shoulder and they wouldn't touch. All of my weight was always on my left side when I lay down, and on my right when I stood up, and nothing seemed in balance. Fear ruled my body and mind. All I wanted was to stay in bed, but I could tell just by the way he opened the front door that Doug was looking for trouble.

"Yo, it's such a beautiful day. You're going to the beach, right? You're gonna go to the park?" Doug said.

"No, I had a rough day—"

"You're such a fucking bitch! How can you waste a day this gorgeous?"

"Have you ever worked a day in your life?"

"Yeah, you know I had that job at Honey Baked Ham—"

"In high school . . . for one fucking Christmas season."

"Only *you* would move to California to spend your time laying in bed."

"A kid fucking threatened to stab me today, and he fucking meant it! Just leave me alone."

He mumbled some crap as he left my room. Fuck his beach day. That fucker was terrified of *his* fear. Terrified that I wasn't terrified like he was.

It made me reach for my phone and call Cody.

"Interesting Jay! How nice to hear from you," Cody said.

"Hey, wanna grab dinner or something?"

"Sure, there's a great Mexican place by my house."

I headed north to Snob Beach, and met the fucker at his cliff-side mansion. Christ, the dude was loaded! At dinner, I waited until the time was right to say, "I couldn't help but notice you're living like Steven Spielberg up there in your ocean-view house. What are you doing subbing like the rest of us chumps?"

"Well, that's actually why I asked for your number." He pulled his seat forward, put his elbows on the table, and smiled like an idiot kid. "Recently, I bought a school that went bankrupt, and I wanted to sub so that I could get an insider look at what goes on in a typical school, and also to meet wonderful teachers like you, who I hope will share my vision."

"And what vision is that?"

"I want to reform education. Change the whole paradigm. I spent the last decade of my life working in the biotech sphere, and I can't tell you how many days I've felt as if I were just throwing to the wind. I want to make a difference—just like you did in Miami. I want to save lives."

"Why not be a doctor?"

"A doctor simply patches people up. I want to give children the power to understand and follow their dreams."

"Well, I gotta say that I do share that vision."

"Join me."

"How?"

"I'm still working through the last of the bureaucracy and red tape right now, but we plan to open next month. Cody Cares Academy."

I almost laughed out loud, but I dug where he was coming from, so I held back. "That's a great name. Simple but effective. So, is this a public or private school?"

"Private, but I've met with a lot of benefactors who wish to donate to the school, which should keep tuition costs to a minimum—hopefully, zero."

"So, is this like a job interview or something?"

"No, it's a job offer."

"Thank you, but I'm going to have to think about it."

"From a teaching perspective, there will be minimal planning and grading, and the emphasis will be on making meaningful connections with students. You'll only be working with a small group each day, which means fewer behavioral issues, and you'll have the satisfaction of knowing you're making a difference."

"Yeah, that sounds great. I'll let you know my decision soon."

On the drive back to Sand Beach, I kept going back and forth on it.

You said you were done with teaching, Jay. You're already pushing it with this subbing crap, but taking a full-time position puts you right back at war.

Yeah, but I need money. It seems like a pretty easy gig: no planning or grading. Small groups. A ten-to-six schedule, so you can party every night. Play late with your band.

Would Dylan take this job? Fuck no! He'd hop a boxcar with his guitar, then change the world with his music. You came here to write. To make music. To act. And this is just another compromise. Every little compromise you make, you give away small pieces of yourself, never to come back. Think of how much of yourself you lost in Miami. You didn't even listen to music for the first eight or nine months you were there.

But Dylan was a genius, and his genius was at his fingertips. If there's anything like that inside of me, it's buried way deep down. Something about stability seems like the only way to mine it out. I need to stay put for a little while to give it some time to wriggle out of me. If I keep jumping from place to place, I'll lose pieces of myself too. I'll harden up when I need to be loose.

This guy seems like a lunatic. You wanna put yourself in the hands of more people who don't understand you?

He seems all right. He seems like he actually cares and wants to change things. When I first started teaching, I wanted to change things too. Maybe it's still possible. Maybe Miami was the fantasy and this is reality.

If you do this, don't blame me when you find yourself in a blinding panic on a random Tuesday night while making dinner. Don't blame me when you almost faint from stress while sitting in a laundromat on a sweaty Sunday afternoon. Don't blame me when you're stuck in rush hour traffic and the pollution invades your lungs and you can't fucking breathe. Don't blame me when you can't sleep at night due to the worries and demands and every other fucking horrible thing that comes with "professional" work.

I handled it before, and I'll handle it again. In fact, I'll handle it better now. Something inside of me needs this.

You need to go to LA! You're already twenty-six. If you want to act, your time is running out.

Ten months, okay? I'll get myself out of debt, use my health insurance to finally see a doctor and dentist again, save up a few grand, maybe meet some cute coworkers, and I'll be outta here before you know it.

Ten months? You sure?

Yeah, just ten. Look, I'll even pick the date: December 15, 2009.

That's just before Christmas. Better January 15.

Okay, January works. Wait, maybe we should push that to February. I'll get my tax return back and I can use it to buy an old RV or something. I can park it on Beachwood Drive in Hollywood, and be close to all the directors and producers and all that.

Okay, February 15, 2010, but not a single day later. All right?

Let's do it!

I called Cody two days later and told him I was in.

Chapter 3

I drove north of Snob Beach, and pulled into the Cody Cares Academy parking lot. The building looked like a standard California school: two stories with classrooms that opened to the outside rather than onto an inside hall like in Buffalo. But what *was* strange about the academy was its location. The back third of the school hung over the edge of a cliff about fifty feet above the churning ocean. Each time another wave hit, the parking lot and the school would shake. I figured this was probably why Cody had been able to buy the school so cheap.

Two other people stood nearby, and judging by their faces, this must have been their first day as well. Their names were Barry and Karla. Barry was a tall, muscular guy with drugstore looks, who had recently moved from Indiana. Karla was born in Monterrey, Mexico, but had lived in Soul City for the majority of her life. She was pretty with a hippie vibe—an authentic one though, not the modern California I-spent-ten-grand-of-daddy's-money-to-look-like-Janis-Joplin bullshit. Barry had met Cody while on vacation in Soul City. They'd shared a scuba diving boat; Barry wouldn't stop talking about how much he loved giant squid, and Cody wanted someone with that kind of passion to work for him. Karla had met Cody at a local film festival where she'd been working, and after seeing how cool she remained under pressure when one of the projectors broke, he asked her to come on board as well. So far, I was the only certified teacher.

We walked into the cafeteria where Cody and his vice principal, Camarin Kefana, greeted us and told us to take a seat. The school wouldn't open to students for another week, but Cody and Ms. Kefana wanted to give us plenty of time to get set up before the kids arrived. That day was the first in a series of orientation sessions. When the other two teachers arrived, Cody addressed us all.

"All right, all right. Welcome to our first day at Cody Cares Academy. We, uh, are happy to, uh—" Dude was sweating through his gray button-down. He gave Ms. Kefana a look and she stepped in.

"Thank you again for joining Mr. Sunders and I on our quest to bring the best possible education to the children of Soul City. We hired each of you because we saw something special in you— something unique—and we believe you'll be able to give our students something they wouldn't get from a public school education. We aren't interested so much in your teaching experience as we are in your general passion for living, and we know that passion will infect our students as well."

She went on like that, explaining that because it was a private school, we didn't have to stress over the kinds of things that public schools did—test scores, attendance numbers, dropout rates—but we did have to worry about where our money would be coming from, so our emphasis would be on customer service. Clearly this wasn't Cody's forte, but Ms. Kefana was about as magnetic, competent, and compassionate a person as I'd ever met. I felt comfortable around her right away, even though I felt uncomfortable about what I was supposed to be doing.

"Like many of you, I haven't been in teaching very long," Ms. Kefana continued. "I spent the last ten years working PR for an entertainment company in Los Angeles. I was making a lot of money but I wasn't making a difference. I'm ready to change that. I'm ready to start a new journey, and I'm thrilled to take those first steps alongside all of you."

Part of me felt like giving her a standing ovation, but another part was rocked by her words. I was starting a new journey as well, and it seemed likely to be long and grueling.

Cody Cares worked on the trimester system, so we'd get a month off every three months and not an entire summer like in Miami. Also, instead of having my own classroom, all the teachers would work in the gym, and a group of eight to ten students would alternate between teachers and subjects every half-hour or so to get them up and moving and to avoid losing their focus. And, we wouldn't stand and deliver in a traditional sense, but rather, we would play premade videos with the day's instruction, then pass out Scantron sheets and students would do multiple choice quizzes before moving on to the next station. All I had to do was start the video, make sure the kids were paying attention, then have them take the quiz and run it through the Scantron machine for grading. Then I would record the grades in my book, update student files, contact parents with progress updates, tidy up the "classroom," and go home. This system removed the hardest parts of teaching—planning, grading, and managing behavior—and I knew I could make it to February 15th with no problem.

Cody Cares served high school students, and we planned to cycle through all of the grades twice throughout the day, starting with our first group of ninth- through twelfth-graders in the morning, then doing the next group in the afternoon, with our lunch in between. As soon as each grade finished all of their courses, they would go home, and with only English, math, social studies, science, and an elective that changed each month, the kids would only be there for about two and a half hours each day. Cody claimed this was sufficient schooling, citing some bullshit study saying that when it came to learning, less was basically more, but I didn't care. He was paying us well, and I knew education was mostly smiles and bullshit anyway, so I suppressed my criticism and doubt, and smiled when Cody took us to lunch at a local Thai place.

I sat beside Karla, and we hit it off. She was smart but socially awkward, and I think we could sense that about each other. I was glad to hear that her teaching station would be next to mine. The other teachers were nice too, and I felt that we had a great team. Cody seemed to have found teachers who could make up for each other's weaknesses, and it seemed that he'd brought me on for my ability to relate to kids along with my easygoing nature. I'd grown up in a big family and played sports most of my life, so I was comfortable working with other people—always seeing *us* as a team that needed to take on the world together. But I wasn't comfortable staying organized and focused, while Karla seemed to have those skills down. She said her weakness would likely be classroom management, and I think that was why Cody put us near each other.

When I got home, Doug was on the phone with his mom, screaming at her to send "MORE FUCKING MONEY, BITCH!" I didn't need that shit, so I took a walk down the beach. Overall, I was feeling pretty relaxed because of the progress I'd made with my novel. Once I'd decided to take the job at Cody Cares, I quit subbing immediately so I could finish editing my book before the new gig. I'd printed the manuscript and gotten it spiral-bound at Kinkos before leaving Buffalo, and I went to Soul City University with Doug every day to work on it in the library while he went to class. I'd sit in a chair in the corner for eight to ten hours, stopping only to piss or eat a banana or an apple. Though it was thrilling to finally see my words in print, I knew many of them had to die, so I cut out significant parts of the story. I'd never taken any writing classes aside from general English courses, so I followed my instincts. Originally, those instincts told me to write every goddamned detail. I couldn't just walk up the stairs, I had to step on the first step with my right foot, then grab the banister with my left hand—describing the grains of the wood, of course—then take the next step with my left foot, and so on, rather than simply write, "I walked upstairs." I think a part of that was because I felt the story wasn't honest without explaining every detail, and I think another part was due to my own psychological baggage; I was always so focused on every minute detail around me, it constipated the motion in my own real-life story. I couldn't walk into a room without noticing how all the furniture was arranged, what all the people were wearing, what color the curtains were, how the carpet felt under my feet, what the temperature was, where all the noises were coming from. I couldn't shut that shit off, and it showed up in my writing. I struggled with whether or not to keep this level of detail in my novel. If this was how I thought, then perhaps it was best to write my stories this way. To invite others into my mind for a little while—after all, wasn't that the joy of reading? Escaping inside another person's brain? Experiencing life as they did? Wasn't *this* experience as important to the story as the characters and plot? In fact, *wasn't* this experience characterization and plot?

But the other side of me argued that this wasn't necessary, and that perhaps these thoughts weren't useful to readers. And, perhaps, they weren't useful to me, either.

After spending so many hours reading my own thoughts and seeing how inefficiently—and strangely—I processed information, along with my biases and the numerous things that pissed me off, I realized there was something wrong with me. I was always so overwhelmed with data. Information and sensations flooded every moment of my existence. How were authors like Hemingway able to cut out the fat and get right to the point? Hell, even Faulkner, with his ornate prose, was actually sharing relevant information. My detail was psychological vomit. Refuse.

Still, there was something calming about reading my own words. About having this thing that was so much a piece of me now out in the world. If I had a heart attack while sitting in that chair, someone could pull the pages from my hands and read them and know that I had truly existed. That I'd exist for all of eternity. Because I'd written something, I was now immortal.

Pretty girls would pass by, but I paid them little mind. Students walked by with food, but my stomach didn't grumble. I was in the zone, and four or five hours could pass so quickly that I wouldn't even notice. I didn't need breaks. When I got into something like this, my brain could focus right down to the smallest detail, and it was during one of those marathon editing sessions that I thought that perhaps genius was nothing more than the ability to focus on something so deeply that its connection to everything else came into focus as well.

But that focus seemed to come with a price. The chemicals raged and my muscles locked; I needed to finish this book soon so I could relax again.

When I finished it fifteen days later, I was so overjoyed that I took a stroll around campus and finally absorbed all the beauty surrounding me. Californian universities had a different kind of beauty than those on the East Coast. My alma matter, Conesus U, had the ivy-covered two-hundred-year-old brick buildings that hit you in the gut when you looked down on them from the top of the hill on Main Street and the sun was setting just beyond, casting the world in this warm, golden glow. Californian universities had a glow too, but it was brighter. Everything was bright greens and blues, with Spanish-style buildings and smiles on everyone's tanned faces. The women here were so gorgeous I felt unworthy to even walk outside, and their families had come from so many places where the women were so beautiful—Iran, Vietnam, Mexico, Brazil, Japan.

It was great to take in the sights. Great to be finished editing, even though I knew the book was still nowhere near ready for publication. Deep down, I knew it wasn't Kerouac's infinite scroll, but rather, infinitely pretentious. Infinitely impenetrable. Infinitely diseased.

I emailed the file to a few friends, and they humored me, pointing out parts they liked, then changed the subject when I asked for criticism. God, writing seemed similar to the Darkness inside of me. There was a light at the end of the tunnel somewhere, but I just couldn't see it. Maybe I would in ten years. Maybe twenty. Something about starting this new job made me feel that I was now working toward finding that light, and this part of me knew I had to keep moving forward no matter how loudly my brain screamed to burn it all to the ground, to escape to Europe to drink absinthe and wax poetic in Parisian cafes. Here was where I'd have to stay.

But feeling the warm sun overhead and listening to the waves crash against the shores made me feel that this was as good a spot as any to sweat out my disease.

On my walk home from the beach, I passed a house with clothes scattered all over the front lawn. A pretty woman came outside and dumped out some more.

"Hey, you." She picked up a red Polo button-down and walked toward me. "Here, try this on."

I put it on. It fit perfectly.

"Now, *that* looks good," she said.

"You having a yard sale or something?" I said.

"Nope, just cutting a piece of shit out of my life." She grabbed a bunch of shirts and handed them to me. "Here, they're all the same size."

"You sure?"

"Yeah, please, take 'em all. But hurry. He's coming back soon."

I grabbed as many as I could and headed home where I opened my computer and crossed "clothes shopping for school" off my to-do list.

When I got home after that second orientation day, Tuyet invited me for drinks. She was a tall Indonesian woman with thin muscular arms and a pretty face, and she was as extroverted as anyone I'd ever met. I think she was the reason why Kelly knew so many people, because Kelly was quieter, even though she still loved to party.

As we walked to the main strip, we stopped at least seven times so Tuyet could say hi to friends hanging out on porches or in front yards. Most of these people were friendly, but some were territorial shitheads who judged people based on how long they'd lived in Sand Beach. They all knew I was new, and a few dudes pressed me about it. Tuyet laughed each time as if it was nothing, but as a guy, I knew it wasn't nothing.

We walked down an alley and then through a narrow path between two houses and arrived at a small house on an ocean-side cliff. Out back, there was a huge porch and below that a pool, and there were twenty- and thirty-somethings everywhere, drinking and getting high. A punk band was playing on the porch as tattooed skaters and surfers thrashed in the pool. I watched the band as Tuyet walked around hugging everyone, telling them she was passing them her "goddess energy." I asked an older punk if I could grab a beer and he handed me a bottle of something delicious. I drank and admired the sunset. In Miami, the sun set behind you when you were staring at the ocean, but here it set over the ocean, and it was gorgeous.

Later, I went inside to piss and found people in the living room smoking meth and snorting coke. I pissed quickly and got the hell out of there. I could feel the panic gripping my back and throat and did my best not to breathe until I got outside. I didn't want a trace of meth inside of me, ever.

A helicopter circled overhead, warning us to "stay inside and lock your doors." Someone assured me this was normal in Sand Beach and, "No worries, bro."

An hour later, Tuyet and I arrived at a dive bar just off the beach, and she got lost greeting everyone inside. I sat on the front patio and watched the freak show. There was a short pier to the right, where street kids gathered to shoot junk and get high. I was always nervous I would step on a needle there, and besides, all the shitheads would talk crap and demand money and get aggressive. In fact, when I had my back turned to the beach, scanning the bar for Tuyet, a tall tweaker dude pushed me in the shoulder, and when I turned around, he got right in my face.

"You got a bowl?"

Before I could even say no, he screamed, "FUCK YOU!" and crossed the street. He approached three teenage boys leaving the beach with their surfboards, and when one of the kids shook his head at the "You got a bowl?" question, the dude grabbed him by the throat, swung him around, and tossed him headfirst into the street just as a car was passing. Luckily, the driver swerved. The driver got out and started beating the tweaker's ass in the street, and a few bikers came out of a nearby bar to join in. They carried the tweaker to the sidewalk so he wouldn't get run over, and the cops picked up his limp, bloody body about ten minutes later.

Tuyet was dancing closely with a woman inside the bar, so I went for some pizza. The pizza place had some great beers on tap, but I decided to cut myself off. It was okay to fuck around while subbing, but having a real teaching job was different. I couldn't go in there like a zombie every day. While walking home, some forty-something skateboarder almost smashed into me, and he gave me the finger as he passed by. I realized then that Sand Beach was the land of perpetual rebellious youth; I needed to get out of here fast.

Chapter 4

Karla helped me organize my section of the classroom/gym before the students showed up that first day. I was dressed in a shirt and tie and had my game face on. It was one thing to sub for students you knew you would be leaving behind at the end of the day, but it was another thing entirely to teach a group you'd have to see day in and out. I was nervous as hell, but when the first kid showed up and was cool, it eased me considerably.

"This school is so weird," he said, as he took a seat in my section and waited for the first bell to ring.

"Yeah, isn't it great?" I said.

He smiled.

"What brings you here?" I said.

"I was getting picked on really bad at my other school, so I wanted to try something new."

"Wow, it takes a lot of courage to say something like that."

"Does that mean you'll be giving me straight A's?" he said.

I laughed. "Sure, as long as you earn 'em."

I could see some of the other teachers speaking with the kids in their sections. Barry looked like a natural, chatting away without a hint of fear. Doreen Brinkley was already laying down the law, pounding her fist into her palm, and letting the kids know she wasn't fucking around. Karla seemed nervous but controlled. I could tell she was the silent but strong type, and her students seemed to respond to that. More students showed up, and when the bell rang, starting the day, they went to their first class/station.

"Hi, and welcome to ninth grade social studies. My name is Mr. Sakovsky, and today you'll be watching a video on ancient Egypt."

"That's boring," a girl said.

Though innocuous, her comment sent shivers through my psyche, and at once, my confidence vanished. "Uh, it's exciting, I promise."

"It's, uh, it's, uh . . ." she said, and a few students laughed. There were only eight of them, but suddenly I felt as if I was at the center of a stadium filled with rabid hecklers.

"Are we gonna have a problem, Ms. Davis?" I said.

"I dunno, are you able to play the video or are you too stupid?"

"That's it—get out!" I said.

"And go where?"

"Go sit in Ms. Ramirez's class," I said.

Karla must have heard me, because she gave me a look as if to say, "It's okay, send her over," which set me at ease.

The student, Brenda Davis, got up, muttered some crap, and sat in the back of Karla's class. Though I'd gotten rid of her, I felt as if I'd lost the battle *and* the war. Once I played the video, the other students paid attention, then they filled out their Scantrons and I ran off to the bathroom before the next group came over. I locked myself in a stall as a wave of panic rocked me. I felt like a character in some horror movie, and even though I'd already escaped the area where the monster was, I went back because I'd left something important behind, then got ripped to shreds.

I'm supposed to be an actor, not a teacher. I'm supposed to be at auditions right now. Instead, I'm locked in some stanky-ass bathroom, hyperventilating because I can't control a thirteen-year-old.

I rushed back to my next class before the bell rang and started the video. This group was pretty good, and I got through it without any problems.

At lunch, the teachers ate together at the table near Barry's desk. He already seemed to be a leader among us due to his easy nature and extraordinary intelligence. I, however, felt like a piece of shit. Cody had hired me for my ability to manage student behavior, but I was already failing. The thought of having to see Brenda again made me dizzy. She was *my* problem, not some teacher's I was subbing for. I couldn't leave an "everything went great today!" note on the desk and fuck off to the beach. I got a little boost, though, when Karla told me how great I seemed to be doing with the kids. I told her the same and thanked her for taking Brenda for that period.

After lunch, things were much better. The second wave of kids came, and then we had our free period. Some of the afternoon students stuck around to get extra help, and I worked with them at my desk. They were good kids. Most had come to Cody Cares to get away from the bullshit they'd experienced in other schools, and the only problem I had that day was with Brenda first period.

Even though I didn't have to yell at Cody Cares like at my school in Miami, my throat was shot, and I could barely keep my head up as I drove back to Sand Beach. When I got home, Doug hit me with the, "Are you going to go to the beach?" crap again, and I walked past him, locked my door, and spent the evening in bed.

That Friday, Doug and I went out with Tuyet and a few guys from his school. The day before, Doug's girlfriend, who lived in Mexico, told him she was pregnant, and he'd been drunk pretty much since hanging up the phone. He was half smiles, half rage, and it probably would have been best to have stayed in for the night, but that ain't ever happening.

We headed to the beach and hit the strip. We popped into a crowded English pub where a greaser-lookin' dude on guitar was ripping through surf-rock tunes with his band on the back stage, which was hard to see due to the size of the crowd. The drunk surf/punk energy gave the place an ominous vibe. There were some older bikers and hippie burnouts in the crowd, but most were young, flannel-covered surfers and skaters. We pushed through them to the bar and waited twenty minutes to order. They kept serving locals first, slapping their hands and dude-bro-ing one another. Sand Beach seemed to be about as authentic a Southern California beach town as could be, but even so, the whole place felt contrived. Everyone seemed to have their role and no one broke character. There was also this palpable aggression hidden just below the razor-thin "no worries, dude" veneer. Dudes eyed us, but Tuyet kept giving them the "cool the fuck down, they're all right" look, and they hung back. She was the tamer and they were the lions as we walked across the circus's main stage.

"Damn, there're some honeys here tonight," Doug said, and he was right. It was great to be surrounded by Latina women. "Why don't you man up and go get laid?"

"Need a few more drinks first," I said. I pounded my beer while watching the greaser rock the stage. I closed my eyes and imagined Dick Dale up there instead, but that era was over—if it ever even existed. After seeing what I had of California so far, maybe all that sixties hippie shit was fake too. But even if it was real, all that was left now was Hot Topic California. Abercrombie California.

A group of three college-age women kept looking at us, and Doug and I played it cool, pretending not to notice. A sun-shriveled middle-aged surf dude sitting one stool over started staring at me hard, and I did my best to ignore him, too, but I could hear him saying, "Yo, man. Hey . . . hey." I kept watching the stage until he waved his hands in my face.

"What the fuck is your problem?" I said.

He raised his shaky arm and gave me the finger.

"Yo, you must have me confused with the dude who gave you that haircut. I'd be pissed too if I ended up lookin' like a fuckin' hobo Kurt Cobain."

Doug laughed.

The dude studied me, then said, "You got a lady's lips."

"Yeah, and you got a lady's dick," I said. I got right in his face, but Doug pulled me away.

"C'mon," Doug said, and we walked toward the college women but stopped about halfway on the dance floor. We danced while casually checking them out. They still seemed interested.

"Which one you want?" he said.

"Both of the brunettes," I said.

"That's cool, I like the tall one anyway."

"Yeah, she—"

A guy about Doug's size squeezed through an opening in the crowd and approached Doug. He was all smiles.

"Hey, man, nice to meet you. You see those girls over there?" the guy said.

"Which ones?" Doug said.

"You talk to those girls, and I'm gonna fuck you up," he said, then started grinning. "Just kidding."

A few of his friends approached us.

"But seriously, if you even take a step in their direction, I'm gonna fuck you up," the guy said.

Doug pushed the guy so hard he crashed into some dancers, falling hard on his back, and I instinctively grabbed one of the other dudes by the neck and started backing him away. Doug got on top of the fallen guy, but a bouncer pulled him off before he could throw any punches. I dragged my guy outside while the bouncers were dealing with Doug, and when I let go of him, I pushed him into a truck parked on the street, denting the door. He got up and staggered over.

"You're lucky I don't beat your ass right now." He was dancing around like a prick.

I pushed him back into the truck, and he stayed down a little longer this time, rubbing his right shoulder and trying to hold back the pain.

The bouncers came out with Doug and pushed him onto the sidewalk. He got up and charged one of them, but I grabbed him first.

"They'll fuck you up. Let's just go," I said.

Doug calmed down, and we waited for the others to come

outside. Tuyet was the first to walk through the door, and she started giving us the slow clap.

"You two are ridiculous," she said, smiling.

The truck-dent dude skillfully ninja-kicked the air at me a few times, then he threw an awkward punch and almost fell over.

I pushed him down and started laughing. "I think this bitch must have studied the partial arts."

Even the bouncers laughed, and the kick-boxer bitch stayed down and rubbed his head.

Doug's geology friends made some shitty excuse to leave, and Tuyet, Doug, and I went to another bar. About an hour later, the college women showed up, and they came right over.

"You really fucked that guy up," the tall one said to Doug.

"He was sayin' some shit he shouldn't have been sayin'," Doug said.

"Where you guys from?" she said.

We answered at the same time. I said, "Buffalo," and he said, "Mexico." I gave him a "what the hell are you talking about?" look, but he ignored it.

"Oh, wow, you're Mexican?" she said.

"Yeah, my family's from Mexico City," Doug said.

"And the other half is from North Buffalo, where you were born *and* raised," I said, giving him the same look. He picked up on it this time.

"We're Mexican too," the two cute brunettes said. "You speak any Spanish?"

Doug said something in Spanish that I didn't care to translate, then he bought them some drinks. We moved to a booth, and Doug sat beside the tall woman, I sat beside one of the cute Mexicans whose name was Melissa, and Tuyet sat beside the other. We spoke as a group but eventually Doug and the tall woman started making out. I took Melissa to the dance floor, and we danced while kissing. The bar was on the second floor of a building on the beach, and I kept looking at the reflection of the bright half-moon rippling on the surface of the calm ocean. Recalling what it felt like to see that same moon rippling over the Gulf of Mexico years back, when I rode with my ex-girlfriend and her family to a party in Veracruz on Christmas Eve. Recalling how powerful it felt to be with someone I loved in a foreign country where every part of me was yearning and breathing and growing. But here in California, it felt hollow and heavy, as if I'd been here before and already knew all the secrets the bars and parties concealed. It was the same old shit, just in a brighter, sunnier, twice-the-price package.

I looked at Tuyet, who seemed to be trying hard with the other Mexican woman, but the woman clearly wasn't into it, so she got her friends and left. Melissa gave me her number and grabbed my dick, so I knew I'd be giving her a call.

While walking home in the cool, salty air, I saw a group of senior girls from Cody Cares coming out of a biker bar. I quickly crossed the street and covered my face so they wouldn't see me, and Doug and Tuyet followed behind laughing and giving me shit for "acting like you're Paul McCartney or something." I used to see my teachers at restaurants and supermarkets and Bills games all the time in Buffalo, but for some reason, it terrified me to be seen by my own students like that. If they saw my drunk, sweaty face, they might know all my secrets and then tell their parents what a deviant and a lunatic I was, and soon they'd be calling the superintendent by the thousands until she had no choice but to finally lock me up where I belonged. I came to California to act, and I acted every day at work.

I acted every day at home too.

We saw the shitheads from the English pub eating at a food cart near the end of the strip, and even though Tuyet was a force of nature, she was helpless to stop Doug from storming over.

"Yo, I got another hot dog you can munch on when you're done with that one," Doug said, grabbing his crotch.

There were four guys and two girls in their group. Though it was fifty-something degrees with a gentle ocean breeze, the women were in short skirts, and one of the dudes was wearing a sleeveless T-shirt, probably to show off his White-boy tribal tattoos.

"It doesn't look like you got much meat in there," one of the women said. Her friends laughed.

"Yeah, well, that's 'cause every dick within a three-block radius of you shrivels to a nub," Doug said. "You look like an ugly Uma Thurman."

Her friends laughed harder, and she shut up.

The sleeveless dude stepped to the plate, saying, "Fuck you," while giving us the finger.

"What's that, your reading level?" Doug said of the single digit he was holding up.

"The number of shirts you own with sleeves?" I said.

"The number of women you've seen today but *haven't* roofied?" Doug said.

"Your ranking in the Soul City Sex Offender registry?" I said.

Several passersby erupted with laughter, and the asshole group walked away, but not before I pulled out the piece of paper with Melissa's number and did the *Good Will Hunting* "apples" bit to the guy who'd started all that shit earlier.

On the way home, Tuyet showed us where a few of the assholes lived. No one seemed to be home, so Doug and I stuck a garden hose through an open bedroom window and turned the water on full blast. We ran home laughing, and I caught flashes of people sitting on porches and in front of bonfires and walking down the street, all shouting shit like, "Where you goin' in such a hurry?" "Shit, the cops are right behind ya!" "Looks like somebody's gotta take a dump." Their faces were a blur. I'd been running fairly regularly since moving to Mexico with Doug, and even though he'd been a record-setting long distance runner in high school, I was now able to keep up with him. But that night, I pulled ahead of him and far ahead of Tuyet as the earth and darkness vibrated and blended together. I trusted my legs to carry me through the void, over the potholes and shards of glass, and when I arrived home, I wanted to keep running. I wanted to keep my body strong and powerful. But instead, I grabbed another beer from the fridge, and Doug, Tuyet, and I kept the party going on the patio. I forgot that I'd texted Melissa until she texted me back: "Sure, that's not too far from my place."

When she came over, she told me she'd fuck me if I played some hip-hop, so I grabbed Doug's stereo and speakers from the living room, brought them to my room, and played *All Eyez on Me* while fucking her like a dog until the sun came up. I was so drunk I couldn't cum, and I kept hammering away until the condom split open. I didn't realize it at first, but I calmed down when I showed it to her and she didn't seem to care. She tried jerking me off but we both fell asleep before my nuts could get some relief. When we woke up, I grabbed my guitar and played her a song I'd written in Miami on one long, fear-filled school night. I straddled her naked body and didn't realize that was the first time I'd ever played an original tune for a woman until I'd finished playing it. As hollow and heavy as California was, there was something powerful in it, and I knew I was gonna make something big happen here that could only happen here.

I put the guitar away, and we fucked again in the shower. I was able to cum this time, and holy shit! I offered to make her breakfast, but she had to work so she walked home. Doug and I went to get breakfast burritos and while paying for mine, I remembered the broken condom. I didn't have the courage to call her, so I asked Doug to do it, pretending to be me, and ask if she had anything crawling on her lady-bits. He told me to fuck off, but when I kept pushing, he said, "Fine, fuck it." He made the call, and she said she was clean, and I knew after that she'd never be back.

On the walk home, I told Doug he looked like an ugly Uma Thurman, and we couldn't stop laughing. Sand Beach was about to be our kingdom. Those fuckin' sun-kissed pricks didn't know what was coming.

Chapter 5

At school, I overreacted again when a senior girl said, "There's no point in learning this crap." I told her, "You're fired! Get used to hearing those words," and she left school, cursing me out. I didn't realize I'd made a scene until I saw most of the other students, along with Barry and Doreen, looking at me. Karla pretended not to notice and kept right on teaching.

On the drive home, I had a long conversation with myself as I cruised along the beach. *This isn't Miami, Jay. This school is entirely different. Cody does seem to care, unlike the principal at Christopher Columbus Middle, who never spoke about anything but test scores and who never lent any classroom support. Every day in Miami, there were fights and kids telling you to go fuck yourself and kids talking their way through every lecture, but here, the kids, coworkers, and admins seem all right. They're on your side. Stop fighting back! You're in a safe place now. Just relax. The next time one of these kids gives you shit, take a deep breath and keep your cool like you always did as a sub. Do what Cody hired you to do, and be in charge.*

I apologized to the girl the next day, and I was pretty sure she was one of the girls I'd seen leaving that biker bar. *God, she's a person, just like me. Holy shit! Kids are people!* Over these years of teaching, I've had to develop thick callouses to protect myself from what I knew would destroy me in the classroom. But I've made it so far and haven't been run out of there yet. Why do you worry about all this shit that doesn't happen? You're constantly worried about going crazy and going broke and being revealed as a lunatic and a menace to society. You gotta relax, man. None of that shit has happened yet. You've been through a lot and you're still here. Just keep your head. You're here to help students. Don't make their lives any more difficult than they already are. Help them up, don't push 'em down.

So I resolved to help students like her in any way I could, and in doing so, I started to understand why I always felt so distant not just from my students, but from everyone. Something about kindness felt foreign to me. All my life I'd been shown that you need to beat people down before they get any funny ideas that life could actually be great. Before they try to knock you down. Get them before they get you. Don't ever let them know what you're feeling. Don't ever smile when you're happy. Don't cry when you're sad. Just keep building that wall between us and them. The minute you stop, they destroy you.

But Karen didn't want to destroy me. She wanted to graduate and become an architect, even though her mom wanted her to be a dentist. I wasn't able to get this close to any of my students in Miami because there were so damned many of them. There, I saw anywhere from 120 to 150 kids each day, all coming and going at the blink of an eye. But here, I worked with small groups and got to know students much better. I knew Karen had been bullied at her other school, which was why she enrolled at Cody Cares. This school slowed the pace of life just enough for me to start to catch up with the humanity that I felt was dying to grow inside of me.

After school one day, the vice principal, Ms. Kefana, sat by my desk and said, "I just wanted to tell you what a great job you're doing with the kids. They really seem to look up to you. More than one has told me they see you as like a caring older brother, and I get tears in my eyes thinking about it. Thanks for what you do here."

I couldn't believe it. In Miami I'd been a number. But Ms. Kefana meant what she said.

"Thank you as well. It's nice to actually work in a place that works, you know what I mean?"

"I do."

"You know, I've been getting this feeling since I started here, that maybe part of the reason I got into teaching was that I was a terrible older brother to my siblings, and I feel like I'm trying to make up for it by being nicer to other kids. Does that make sense?"

Ms. Kefana took a deep breath and settled into a comfortable position in her chair. "Jay, I'm gonna tell you something personal, but only because I feel that we're on the same wavelength with these kinds of things. Is that okay?"

"Absolutely," I said.

"Okay, well, I grew up in Guam and come from a large, crazy family—the kind of crazy family where everyone loves one another but they can't seem to live together, you know what I mean?"

"I know exactly what you mean."

"I thought so. So, anyway, I feel like I can relate to what you just said. Every teacher I've ever met seems to have emerged from some traumatic event or series of events that's expanded their ability to feel the world and has made them want to heal it."

"You know, thinking of all the teachers I've ever worked with, I'd have to say I agree with that."

"I can see a lot of pain in your eyes. I think you'd benefit from letting it out."

"W-whaddya mean?"

"I mean, have you ever considered therapy?"

"Do I look crazy or something—I mean, I-I—"

"No, not at all. Look, I've been through it myself and it works. I see a lot of myself in you and just wanted to pass it along."

I felt as if she were looking directly at the Darkness inside of me, and while it made me uncomfortable, I felt as if I wanted to tell her *everything!* I almost burst into tears. "When I was younger, I went to the doctor and he said I had depression. I mean, I couldn't eat. Didn't care if I drove off a bridge on the way home from school. I was eighteen. I don't think that's ever gone away, and I think it started long before I finished high school."

"You have nothing to lose except a lot of extra psychological weight."

"Yeah, maybe."

She stood up. "Wow, anyway . . . you know, I didn't mean to say any of that. You've just got this way about you. I think you're a healer, and I think that's why the kids like you so much and why Cody brought you onboard."

I said thanks even though I had no idea what she meant. I was born in Buffalo. In the world of ice and snow. There was no therapy there. There was beer and wings and football and if you don't like it, you can just leave! Go to bed hungry. Therapy is for pussies. I set foot in a therapist's office and I'll never be able to live it down. But being around her made me think that maybe I could be a different kind of man. A better man.

I caught a reggae show at a bar near my house that Thursday night. Doug wouldn't stop shouting at his girlfriend on the phone, so I went alone. I loved my work schedule, which allowed me to party on weekdays.

The band was great, and I chatted up several cute girls and got a few numbers and walked tall along the beach on my way home. I breathed the salty air and looked up at the stars. Even with the light pollution, they were usually up there every night—no chance of Miami rain or Buffalo snow. In Soul City, there were no threats from above, and I could stroll as I pleased without need of protection.

"Faggot!"

I stopped walking and looked around. No one else was on the street.

"Faggot!"

Down the block, a truck's passenger window rolled up. Though I was really liking this new job, I couldn't stop myself from walking over and knocking on the window. The guy got out.

"Why don't you say that to my face?" I said.

He smirked and before he could say anything, I punched him in the eye. He was big, but dopey and slow, and he was holding a bowl in his right hand, so he was probably even slower than usual.

"Oh, that's it. I'm gonna fuck you up!" he said.

I punched him again, and he dropped back and started dancing around, screaming about how he was gonna kill me as he inched further away. His friends got out of the truck, but I could tell by their energy they weren't going to step in.

"I'm gonna fuck you up! I'm gonna kill you!" The asshole kept jumping around and pumping himself up as his friends leaned against the truck and watched.

"Apologize," I said.

"What?" he said.

"Look, you fat motherfucker, I just started a new job that I actually like, and I don't wanna lose it for putting your homophobic ass in the hospital. Just apologize and I'll walk away."

He stopped dancing, looking disarmed. He turned to his friends. "If I say I'm sorry, will you guys make fun of me?"

They burst out laughing, and I started walking away, but he blindsided me with a shot to the eye, and I put him straight down on the sidewalk.

When I got home, I iced my eye and went to sleep. I woke up the next morning with a huge shiner. Doug laughed when he saw me. I thought about calling into work, but black eyes were nothing, I thought. I used to get them all the time growing up, playing basketball and football. A black eye doesn't necessarily mean I got into a fight.

When I got to school, I let everyone know I'd gotten elbowed while playing basketball and not to worry, and no one seemed to care . . . and no one seemed to believe me. Barry kept shadowboxing when he passed by, and Doreen asked me how the other guy looked, and a few of my guy students hummed the *Rocky* tune. Neither Cody nor Camarin said anything, but I knew they wanted to.

All of the other teachers were older than I was, including Karla, so I think they all just kind of saw me as their pesky little brother. On the drive home, I vowed not to get into any more fights. Which meant I'd have to stop going out on the weekends. Which meant I'd have to stop drinking and getting high. Which meant I'd have to start facing the demons in my head I'd been running from since the Evil invaded my brain when I was nine or ten years old.

Which meant I was fucked . . .

That night, Doug and I made pasta, and we watched *The Devil and Daniel Johnston*. Watching Daniel Johnston's slow descent into insanity rocked me. It'd been a while since the Evil Thoughts that haunted my youth had hit me like this, and when they came at me, they did so with extra force to remind me they would always be a part of me. Doug smoked a joint midway through, and even though I declined, just breathing the smoke caused me to start slipping away. Over the last year or so, I'd had a few bouts of drug-induced psychosis from weed, where I drifted way out there, suspending time and distorting reality, and I didn't think I'd ever really recovered from it.

I told Doug I had papers to grade and headed off to my room, but he said, "I thought you didn't have to grade at that school," and I said, "Oh, yeah, there are some, uh, essays I can't put through the Scantron . . ." I locked myself in my room.

How will I survive here? No matter where I go, the Thoughts return. It doesn't matter how well I follow the plan society has for me, I'll never be one of *them*. No matter how hard I work, it will never be hard enough. No matter how hard I try to become an actor or a songwriter, I'll never succeed. And even if I do, I'll just end up even further out there in Crazy World, with no real job or responsibilities to keep me in check.

I lay in bed so tight I felt myself rolling onto my left side. I couldn't escape the sound of Doug laughing in the living room at Daniel Johnston's misery. Of Tuyet and Kelly having an argument next door. Couldn't escape the smell of weed coming from the CPA's house and seeping under my door. Tuyet's mom was laughing at the TV in the back bedroom where she was staying, and her voice pierced the thin armor surrounding me.

I reached into my nightstand and pulled out the very earplugs I'd praised myself weeks earlier for not having had to use yet, and put them in my ears. I shut the window and rolled up a few shirts and covered the crack under the door, and I lay in bed shaking and sweating. When the Devil finished with Daniel Johnston, he was coming for me. Music, art, expression were all a portal to hell. You need to stop fucking around. Cody Cares is your new life. It's your only shot. You can't fuck it up or you'll have nothing left.

Chapter 6

After sixth period that day, we had a wellness fair in the cafeteria. There was a massage therapist, a chiropractor, a nutritionist, and a psychologist, and each had a booth where they passed out information and spoke about their services. The massage therapist was giving free massages, and Doreen was the first in line. Barry struck up a conversation with the chiropractor, and they were laughing in no time. Karla grabbed a pamphlet from the nutritionist's table, but she shook her head and walked away when the nutritionist asked her if she had any questions. Camarin spoke with the psychologist and encouraged a few students to ask questions.

I hung out in the back corner and Karla came over with her pamphlet.

"You don't want to get any information from anyone?" she said.

"I'm not really into all this New Age hippie California crap. All the aches and pains in my life have always been resolved with an ice pack and an ACE wrap."

"I tried therapy once, and it was helpful, but I stopped going after a few months."

"I don't see how talking about your problems solves anything. Honestly, I think talking is the reason so many people are miserable. We should be *doing*, not flapping away about all our misery and heartaches and all that."

"I see your point, but when you talk about your problems in an environment like a psychologist's office, it gives them legitimacy and affirms your suffering."

"I prefer to get really, really, *really* drunk. That's Buffalo therapy." Karla laughed.

"People just need to stop whining about their problems," I said.

"You play basketball, right?" she said.

"Yeah, why?"

"If you sprained your wrist while playing basketball, then told your doctor what happened and where it hurt, would you consider that to be whining?"

"No."

"So what's the difference?"

"Bah . . ." I walked away from her strong point and approached the chiropractor's booth.

"Hi, I'm Dr. Tom. What's your name?"

"Jay."

"Pleasure to meet you, Jay."

We shook hands.

"Would you be interested in an adjustment?" he said.

"Oh, n-no, no, no thanks." I backed away from the booth. After a lifetime of burying my demons way down deep, I was terrified of doing anything that might shake up my insides and send them rushing to the surface.

"It's okay. How about we have you hop up on the scale instead?" He pointed at a scale that had two separate places to put my feet.

"What for?"

"This will determine how well your body is aligned."

Even though I knew my body was horribly imbalanced, I wanted to confirm it, so I said, "Sure," then took off my shoes, and stepped on.

The doc read the digital screen, then smiled and said, "Hmm."

"What?"

"Let's try this again. Can you step off then step back on? Make sure you stand up straight and aren't leaning to either side."

I did as he said, and he smiled even wider this time.

"Everything okay?" I said.

"I'm sorry for smiling, but it's just that I've been doing this for seventeen years, and I've only seen one person with higher numbers than yours, and he was almost four hundred pounds."

"What's that mean?"

"The first time you stepped on the scale, it showed you were fifty-five pounds heavier on your right side, and the second time, you were fifty-seven."

"That's bad?"

"Anything more than five pounds is considered bad—well, I don't like to use words like 'bad,' but it's not optimal, let's put it that way."

"You know, I get incredible aches and pains even when I'm sitting or lying down. When I stand, it feels like my right leg is a peg leg. Like it can't move, and it's just supporting weight. My knees ache and my back is always burning."

"You might be the most imbalanced person I've ever met. And, frankly, that fascinates me. I'd love to find out how you got this way and help you to gain your balance."

"Yeah, well, it was nice talking to you. I've gotta go do some grading now."

"Oh, I thought you didn't have to grade in this program?"

I hurried back to the corner where Karla was still standing. One of her students stood beside her, reading a pamphlet.

"It seemed like you two really hit it off over there," Karla said. "What were you talking about?"

"Just—just finding balance and all that."

"You should give it a try."

"Naw, I'm good." I rubbed my lower back. Now I was even more aware of how badly it always ached.

"Why don't you get a massage?" Karla said.

"I got one and it was great," the student said.

I was always flooded with anxiety in situations like these. It wasn't so bad when I was behind a desk and had a teacher's script in hand, but the second you took all that away and I had to fall back on my own judgments, witticisms, and charm, I hardened up like dried concrete. No part of me wanted to talk to any more of these "healer" lunatics—or even any of the other teachers besides Karla—but all the energy in that cafeteria kept pushing me in every direction away from myself, so I just laughed and said, "I guess it couldn't hurt," even though I'd never gotten a massage before, and if anyone from Buffalo heard that I had, they'd never let me come back. Regardless, I walked over and got in the chair.

The woman dug her elbow into my back and after a few minutes she was laughing just like the chiropractor.

"What?" I said.

"It's just that, I've been doing this for six years now, and I've never seen anyone as tense as you. Not even close. Your muscles feel almost like bone. You must be filled with stress. Sorry for laughing."

Goddamn it.

I was almost in tears when I got out of that chair. Camarin was still talking to the psychologist, and she waved me over, but I practically sprinted to the men's room. I locked myself in a stall and started weeping as the waves rocked the school harder than ever before.

When I got home, Doug was screaming at his girlfriend on the phone again, so I walked to the beach. On the way, I saw two homeless people fucking in the bank drive-through as a driver in line beeped and screamed out the window, "It ain't a fuckin' sperm bank, assholes! Go make a deposit somewhere else!" They were ass naked and looked to be in their fifties, and I didn't know whether to laugh or leave California and never come back.

When I got to the beach, I pulled a beer out of my backpack and poured it in a disposable cup. It was illegal to drink on the beach here, unlike in Miami where I'd regularly gotten shitfaced while watching the Tropical East Coast Freak Show. I got lost staring at the waves and imagining all the water between here and Australia, but then I heard more screaming, and when I turned around, the homeless guy, still ass-naked, was running over the tops of parked cars and shrieking while shaking his ding-dong at passersby.

A frog hopped near me on the sand, stopped, looked at the naked man, and then looked at me. It kept giving me this "follow me" head-jerking motion, but when I looked away to watch the cops put the naked man in their cruiser, then looked back to the sand, the frog was gone.

Beyond where the frog had been sitting, a group of street kids looked to be shooting up under the pier. A helicopter flew overhead, and I could have sworn it was warning us, "Return home and never come back." Surfers were a hundred yards into the ocean, floating above twenty-foot great whites, one of which had bitten a woman in half a few months ago. Bikers revved their engines and drunks celebrated in the bars at all hours and street kids begged for change and pissed and shat on the sidewalk. At home, Doug was probably still screaming at his pregnant girlfriend. Tuyet and Kelly were probably arguing about the latest chick Tuyet had fucked. The CPA was probably so high he couldn't get off his living room floor. Who cares if I'm the tightest, tensest guy in the history of the world? Who cares if my muscles are bone and my brain is mush? Who cares, who cares, who cares?

Cody Cares!

Ha! The fucking fool. All those fucking idiots aren't saving shit—just watering down the education system. They can have all the wellness fairs they want. They're all as fucked up as I am. Doreen is such an egomaniac she can hardly function. Karla quivers when she has to call parents. Barry does all he can to avoid answering questions because he knows he's a fucking fraud. At least I admit I'm a mess.

But do you? You ran out of that wellness fair pretty quickly. I didn't see anyone else doing that—not even the kids, who'd been bullied their whole lives. Maybe you're the most fucked up of all of them.

In the distance, I swear I saw the frog sitting on a cliff above the ocean, and even amidst all the chaos, it looked to be watching me.

I drank another beer, then headed home. Doug was still screaming, but at his mom now for "MORE FUCKING MONEY! GIVE IT, GIVE IT, GIVE IT, YOU CRUSTY OLD BITCH!"

I crawled deep inside my bone-muscles, into my silent place, far away from the screaming and smashing and helicopter warnings, and finished my six-pack and passed out on my cold air mattress in my bedroom at the edge of America but at the center of the world.

Chapter 7

I woke up around 3 a.m. to Doug playing guitar in the living room. He'd plugged his acoustic-electric into my amp and was playing something so beautiful, I still couldn't believe it came from him. He'd written the tune in college one night while we were high, and every time he played it, it reminded me of how much time had passed between then and now. Reminded me of how many people and roles we played on any given day. How something so beautiful could come from a person who hurt people like he did. How the everyday friends we eat, sleep, and shit beside can achieve genius at various, fleeting moments of our lives, and how we so often forget about this genius until it rocks us at 3 a.m. on a school night when we need to sleep, but now all we want is to grab our guitar, and head out into the powerful, pulsating night, betting everything on our dreams and knowing, just knowing, that our genius will guide us in the right direction and someday everyone will see what we've accomplished and lavish us with praise and tell us how we saved them with our song or theorem or novel. It reminded me of how love can be the same. How we can hold love in our hands for a brief moment as it rages through our body and soul, only to slip out again no matter how hard or little we try to stop it. It reminded me of how heroin was such a short distance from me here. Meth and crack too. All I had to do was lift my window, reach out my hand, and let it be filled with a pipe and a lighter or anything else I'd need to wander off into that night forever.

I grabbed my recorder and turned it on, doing all I could to preserve that moment of genius. After Doug finished the song, I put the recorder in my pocket and went to the living room, and Doug and I jammed and sipped brews until Tuyet came over and said, "Uh, guys, it's 5 a.m. Some of us gotta work, you know?" We apologized and unplugged and went to sleep, but not before I'd captured a few hours of late-night/early-dawn magic on my beer-stained recorder. I had enough material there for two albums, but as much as I wanted to create those albums with Doug, I knew that would never happen. By now, I knew all of his "yeah, sure, man. I know a guy in my department who has the equipment" promises were crap. He'd been giving me those for years but then bobbed and weaved like Ali when I pressed him to follow through.

I got a few hours of sleep and woke up with a throbbing hangover. The black eye was gone, but the dark bags under my eyes weren't much better. I got through the day without the kids giving me too much shit, but when Ms. Kefana came to speak to me again at the end of the day, I realized that I couldn't hide anymore. All my life, I'd surrounded myself with people who couldn't see me. But Cody could see me. Ms. Kefana and Karla could see me. Probably Doreen and Barry and the others too. Maybe everyone throughout my life had been able to see me. Maybe people were a lot more observant than I gave them credit for.

"Is everything all right, Mr. Sakovsky?" Ms. Kefana said, sitting in a comfortable position in the chair by my desk.

"Yeah, yeah, whaddya mean?" I shuffled papers and tried to avoid her eyes.

"Nothing in particular. You just look a little pale."

"I'm a Buffalo Polack. It's gonna take me a little while to catch up to all you beautifully tanned Californians."

"Okay, well, just know that the door to my office is always open."

"Uh, okay, thanks."

She got up and walked away, and I realized I was fucked. In Miami, I probably could have shot H in the school bathroom and nobody would have said shit, but at Cody Cares, I was under a microscope. There were only so many times Ms. Kefana would "chat" with me about black eyes and hangover sweats before Cody showed me the door.

Doug and I made pasta again for dinner and watched *Entourage* while we ate, and I had this overwhelming desire to grab my stuff and head down to LA that night. But I did the dishes and headed to the beach instead.

A few weeks earlier, I'd joined a songwriters' group where people played songs and the rest of the group critiqued them, and one of the members, Winston, called me that night in a bit of a panic.

"Hey, Jay, I'm in your hood right now. I got a show tonight and our opening act isn't here. Can you cover for him?"

"I, uh, don't know what to play," I said.

"Play that tune you played at the meeting. That one about the villain."

"I'd need to grab my guitar."

"You can use mine. Just come quick! We need someone to go on in ten minutes."

I started sweating badly. If he'd given me more time than *now, now, now!* I might have refused, but I got rushed with a wave of confidence and gripped it with everything I had.

I walked into the dark, smoky bar, the only light coming from a front window overlooking the ocean. Winston called me over and showed me the stage where I'd be playing. There was a good-sized crowd but they were quiet. I got onstage, sat on a folding chair, tuned the guitar—even though Winston told me it was good to go—and strummed it a few times to warm up. My college band with Doug played for much bigger crowds, but this was the first time in about four years I'd gotten on a stage like this—and the first time I'd done so alone. Rather than start with the song Winston wanted me to play,

I picked the one my band used to open with, Roy Orbison's "You Got It," relying on muscle memory and nostalgia to bring me through.

I wasn't much of a singer, so playing a tune by a guy widely considered to be one of the greatest singers of all time probably wasn't the best idea, but I tried to make it my own. The crowd was cold, but a few people sang along, and I was glad when the song was over. There were few feelings more isolating than playing songs into a dark void of a room, where the shadows of people absorbed your confidence and pride, and it reminded me why I'd imploded while playing with our group in college. I couldn't take the pressure of it then.

But now, after a year of teaching, and hurling knowledge into dark voids where students did much worse than simply ignore me, I felt more prepared. I played "Villain" next.

"They say you only write what you know anyway.
Then how do I explain about yesterday?
I know you, you know me, neither one cares,
You only come to my house when it's in need of repair.
Villain, what have you done with my mind?
Meaning, let's put these stranded thoughts on ice."

No one seemed into it aside from Winston, who was singing along to the left of the stage. I played one other original tune, then got off the stage. A few people applauded, and Winston and his band set up and rocked the room. Everyone was up and dancing after only a few songs. I knew I wasn't a strong singer or guitarist, and I needed a band behind me to generate the power of my tunes. I'd written several songs where the bass or drums played significant roles, and I couldn't express myself properly alone. I wished Doug would come up there with me, but he had a kid on the way, and even before the kid, he'd turned me down so many other times.

But Winston didn't, and he told me he wanted to jam sometime. His band was getting pretty big in Soul City, and they played this eclectic mix of rock, folk, and funk. I hoped someday I'd get to jam with them as well.

I stayed for most of Winston's show and got a few more phone numbers from cute women, one of whom invited me back to her place. She lived in a huge apartment on a high ocean-side cliff with her windows facing the mountains, not the ocean, and all four of her roommates were out, so we fucked all over the kitchen and living room and on one of her roommate's beds. The condom broke again, and I pulled out right when I felt it happen, then jerked off on her stomach and tits. I'd broken quite a few condoms over the years, and it was freaking me out.

She invited me to stay the night, but I had to work the next day, and after playing that unexpected show and fucking for an hour, my mind and body were confused and exhausted, and they craved something familiar. Still, it felt great to get onstage again.

That Friday, while Tuyet, Remi, Doug, and I were at a rooftop bar happy hour, Doug told me he needed to go to Mexico for a few weeks. "She won't fucking shut up about it," he said, and after that weekend, I had the house to myself. I spent that first week writing and recording songs, and the second week, my friend Ian came to visit.

Ian and I'd lived together in Miami, but he'd stayed there when I moved to California. He was still bitter about it.

"Yo, you just abandoned me in the American Tropics," he said over beers on the patio.

"Dude, move out here. It's even more beautiful, and as fucked up as it is, it's nowhere near as fucked up as Miami," I said.

"Yeah, maybe, but I kinda like working in the ghetto. Nobody gives a fuck what you do."

"They actually give a shit here, trust me. My boss keeps riding me about my organization and penmanship and all that crap. I feel like I'm back in school myself. As long as I didn't kill anyone at Columbus Middle, I was free to do as I pleased, but here—man, I'm fucked. Maybe I should head back with you."

"Nah, look where you are. Cali is gorgeous."

"That it is. Still, there's something missing. I was hoping being a few hours from the border would make me feel closer to Mexico, but I don't. It's still so far away. Everywhere I look is America."

"I'll bet a lot of where you look in Mexico also looks like America by this point."

"Fuckin' A."

"How's your writing coming?"

"I've been spending most of my time teaching and writing songs."

"So you stopped with the book?"

"I finished editing it a while back, but it still needs so much work, I don't think it'll ever see the light of day."

"Kinda like our screenplay."

I laughed. "I can't believe you lost the file. We spent months working on that thing."

"It was probably for the best. That script sucked, I'm sorry."

"Yeah, I imagine we could do a whole lot better now."

"I'm sure."

"So, why don't we?"

"Whaddya mean?"

"I mean, Doug's gone, along with all his negative energy. The house is relatively quiet. Let's write a script while you're here."

"That's nuts."

"Why? This is California, man. That's what you do here."

"Yeah, I guess we could. We've done crazier shit."

"Like that road trip to New Orleans?"

"Oh god, that was a nightmare."

"You know, I Googled that place we stayed in, and the cops shut it down because it actually *was* a crack motel."

Ian laughed. We finished our beers, went down to the strip for some burritos, and planned our script. Usually it was as hard to drag him into my dreams as it was Doug, but for some reason, he was all about writing this thing. We decided to write a TV series loosely based on our year teaching in Miami, and we gave it the working title *Tropical Teaching*. Neither of us knew shit about screenwriting, so we spent about an hour looking up how to format and write one and all that but gave up when it got too complicated. Instead, we handwrote it in a red notebook, laughing our asses off as we came up with characters and ridiculous situations, often based on real events. When I was at school, we both continued writing—he at my place, and I while kids were watching their videos—and compared notes when I got home. We wrote four episodes in two days, and came up with the series arc—both characters ending up in California and becoming successful actors/writers.

By the end of the week, Ian and I had finished the entire first season and were halfway done with the second. I told him to stay but he had to return to work. I drove him to the airport and hoped I'd see him again soon.

On a Tuesday after work, I met Winston and a few other songwriters at a bar east of Snob Beach that offered weekly open mic nights. This was the third or fourth week in a row that we'd gone, and we loved it. Winston was probably the best of us in both songwriting ability and performance. He was a strong singer and guitar player and his tunes could be weepy and hopeless or swingin' enough to get everyone on their feet. Stephone was a local who wrote darkly humorous folk tunes, mostly about insights learned doing seemingly mundane day-to-day tasks. Jadia had been born and raised in Fortaleza, Brazil, and she played bass and sang soulful pop songs whose melodies bounced all over the room. People couldn't help but dance the moment she started playing, usually having one of us accompany her on guitar.

There were a few others who came out, but that was the core group, and that night, Stephone started us off, playing a song where he realized he needed to break out of his everyday routine after having an anxiety attack when he reached for a hand towel that was always hanging on his stove, but wasn't there that day. Winston went after that and played a thoughtful song about an alcoholic who stops drinking when her three-year-old daughter pulls on a tablecloth, breaking a bottle of wine on the tile kitchen floor. The girl cuts herself on the shards of glass, and the mother realizes she needs to control her life. I played a song that I'd finished writing while the other two were onstage, and it was about a guy who's having a peaceful night until his estranged father calls him out of the blue, sending him into a tailspin of memories and shame and hopeless thoughts. After, Jadia sang about a bus ride she'd taken from Fortaleza to Manaus and all the people she met along the way. Her voice was extraordinarily powerful, and she'd spent most of the last ten years touring Latin America and Europe with her band. She had quite a big following already, and I knew out of all of us, she probably had the best chance of becoming a real star.

While she sang, I sat on a stool and leaned against the bar, Winston to my left and Stephone to my right. We were all in awe of Jadia's range. When she finished, she walked over, and we gave her a standing ovation. She pulled up a stool beside me, and she and I wrapped our arms around one another, and then the four of us drank and laughed and said thank you to people who came over to compliment us.

At one point, Jadia kissed my cheek and rested her head against mine, and I couldn't remember any time recently when I'd felt happier or more at peace. I'd been searching for my crew for so long, trying desperately to pull reluctant people into my dreams. But these people were moving in the same direction that I was, and I didn't have to pull or push them anywhere. I felt honored that they saw me as an equal.

Jadia invited us back to her place south of Sand Beach, and Winston and I went over, while Stephone went home. We drank a few beers and listened to some tunes, but when she broke out the bong, I started feeling the same way that I had while watching *The Devil and Daniel Johnston*, and I booked it outta there without even saying goodbye.

Chapter 8

While making dinner one night, I started thinking about my right peg leg and couldn't stop. It held so much tension, and no matter how I shifted my body, my knees and back and shoulders ached. My neck was always tense, and my head leaned forward and throbbed with dull pain. I decided to stop chopping carrots and microwave a pizza instead.

I sat on the free flea couch and ate while watching *Entourage,* but when I leaned over to grab another slice of pizza from the coffee table, I felt a sharp pain in my back. I realized I couldn't ignore this pain any longer. I checked out Dr. Tom's website, but seeing his smiling face made me think he already knew too much about me, so I looked up another chiropractor who had almost entirely five-star reviews on Google. Doctor Vinny!

I called and left a message, and his receptionist, Bonnie, called me the next day during school. The kids were watching a video, so I stepped outside and set up an appointment, then headed over before school the next day. The office was clean and well organized, and Bonnie was cute as hell. She took my info, then had me lie on a massage bed while waiting for Dr. Vinny. I could hear him speaking with another patient.

"Yeah, this will take the tension off your nerves, which will allow you to breathe much easier. Just follow me!" He had a clear, powerful voice like an old-time carnival barker. Soon, I felt a hand on my shoulder, and when I turned, he was standing above me.

"C'mon back. Jay, right?" he said.

I'd almost fallen asleep and was a bit groggy. "Oh, uh, yeah, yeah."

"Nice to meet you. We're going to start by taking some X-rays of your back. Right this way."

I followed him to a back room, and he instructed me to take off my shirt, put on a gown, and stand in front of metal plate. He took a few X-rays, then let me lie back down on the massage bed while he studied the images. About fifteen minutes later, he called me into a room.

"Okay, see here." He pointed at the X-ray. "Your spine is curved, and down here, see the spacing between your lower vertebrae?"

I leaned in closer and said, "Yeah."

"You've already got the damage of a sixty-year-old man."

"Holy shit . . ." I felt dizzy, as if I was finally paying for all the abuse I'd put my body through after decades of lifting and tackle football and driving through elbows and forearms on my way to the basketball hoop. Through all the fights and snowmobile wipeouts and the time I fell twenty feet out of that tree in my backyard and landed on my back. This was finally the moment they'd warned me about in health class. Now, I was finding out I had AIDS after a lifetime of shared needles and raw-dog boning.

"You've got scoliosis," he said.

"What's that?"

"It means your spine is curved."

"Is it curable?"

"I'm afraid not, but we can improve it."

Again, I was flooded with emotions. All the times I'd felt heavier on one side than the other. The times my knees burned at basketball practice when everyone else seemed fine. The hours I'd lifted in the weight room, feeling my left side growing twice the size of my right. The years of knowing something was wrong but never having an idea of what that was. Now I did: scoliosis.

He had me turn my head and twist my back as far to the right and left as they could go, and he said, "Wow, you've got the range of motion of a seventy-year-old man. I've been doing this for twelve years, and I've never seen anyone this tight. You're like a block of wood!"

I lay on his table and he did his manipulations, which took a ton of pressure off of my back, neck, and knees, and I walked out of there knowing full well why my high school buddy, Ryan, had told me never to go to a chiropractor. "It's addictive, man, trust me."

When I got to the car, I called my mom, almost on the verge of tears, and she said, "Your father has scoliosis too."

"How come no one told me? How come no one figured this out before? Do you know how long I've been suffering?"

"You always seemed fine. You were such a great athlete."

"Dad's always complaining about his back and knees. I'm gonna be fucked up just like him."

"You know he's such a drama queen sometimes."

"Wh-why didn't anybody do something?"

"What could we do?"

Exactly.

This was *my* problem. It didn't matter if it was passed down from Dad, and from his dad before him; it was infecting my own body and no one could take it away. At least now I knew what it was. At least I could see a hint of light through the Darkness. I thought about calling in sick to work but drove there anyway, and almost cried when I heard one of my ninth-grade girls randomly telling another student that she had scoliosis. How the fuck can this fourteen-year-old know this much about her own body when I don't know shit?

By lunch, I was feeling much better. I was amazed that I could counter a horrible doctor's office visit by immersing myself back in with the herd, and I was laughing again with Barry in no time. Karla brought cookies and I ate a few, even though I was trying to watch my weight. I'd only worked out a few times since moving, and now I didn't want to reverse what I'd accomplished with Dr. Vinny, so I figured I shouldn't start lifting again until he could straighten me out. Yeah, it was bad to have something like scoliosis, but after a quick Google search, I found I was in good company, which even included some Olympic athletes.

While eating dinner, my phone vibrated on my coffee table, and an unknown number came up. For whatever reason, I knew it was the psychologist from the wellness fair at work. She'd kept giving me these looks, and when I answered and confirmed that it was indeed her, I didn't know whether to be glad or creeped out.

"Sorry to call you like this, but you left your number with the massage therapist, and I thought maybe I'd ask you out to dinner."

It took guts to cold-call someone like that, and she was sexy as hell, so I said yes. The next night, we went to a Greek spot near her house, and she gave me her life story; I could see why she followed the career path she had. She'd lost a kid and a husband and recently a kidney, and I kept shaking my head and telling her, "Wow, I'm so sorry," as I devoured more hummus and pita bread. She was about ten years older than I was, which was cool. I loved older women. They knew exactly what they wanted and were much more likely to want to fuck with the lights on. We went back to her place, then her bed, and she unbuckled my pants as I grabbed a tube of hand lotion from her nightstand. She lubed up her right hand and worked my dick and balls as I buried my face in her tits. She applied the right amount of pressure and had perfect rhythm, and soon my whole body erupted. I squirted all over her sheets and thighs and even hit myself in the face near my right eye. A good hand job felt better than any BJ or even the tightest pussy.

"So, tell me about yourself," she said, as she wiped herself down with some tissues.

"Whaddya mean?"

"I mean, I've told you all about me. What's on *your* mind?"

"I, uh, I gotta go grade some papers . . ." I got up, squeezed the last of the cum through my dickhole, and took off. It was a fucking ambush! I shoulda known. She called me the next day, but I didn't answer. Fuck her and her, "So, where does it hurt?" questions.

Chapter 9

Doug came home a few days later.

"Whoa, you got married?" I said as he showed me his ring.

"It was the right thing to do." His face was half misery, half elation.

"She movin' here?" I said.

"No, I'm going there. I'll be moving out next month. Hey, you mind paying more for this month's rent? I figure I wasn't here for most of last month, so it's only fair that I shouldn't have to pay as much *this* month."

"That's not how this shit works, man. I can spot ya some cash if you need it, though."

"Yeah, that'd be great!"

We headed to a Brazilian bar near our house, and he told me all about the baby and the marriage and all that. They'd done a civil ceremony and would be having a full celebration in December. "You gotta be one of my groomsmen!" he said. I didn't know how I felt about returning to Lila. I hadn't been there in almost two years—since breaking up with my ex, Mariposa. I'd planned to marry her and live there, but shit didn't work out. We hurt each other, but she hurt me a lot worse. Even so, I was willing to give it another try. As crazy as she made me feel, I was madly in love with her. Every part of my DNA still ached to be near her. To smell her hair and skin. To wake up beside her. We'd been off and on for almost two years, but that last off was permanent. I hadn't believed it would be, but it was, and I didn't want to go back to the town that was filled with memories of her.

Still, I said, "Of course!" and bought the next round. Early in the night, an enormous dude was swaying around, and he bumped into me a few times. Nothing intentional—he was hammered, and he apologized.

Doug wouldn't let it go, though, and when the dude went outside for a cigarette, Doug followed him. I knew what was gonna happen and tried getting Doug to cool down, but soon he was asking the guy for a cigarette. When the guy grabbed one out of his pocket, Doug karate-kicked the shit out of the dude's chest, and he shouted in horror and sprinted down the street. Though he was huge as fuck, he looked like a tech nerd who spent all his time playing video games and jerking off to episodes of *Baywatch*.

While walking home, we saw the dude sitting on a sidewalk bench.

"I should say sorry," Doug said to me.

"Yeah, you can't attack people like that," I said.

Doug walked over and the guy screamed, but when Doug stuck out his hand and said sorry, the guy said don't worry about it. But when the guy got up from the bench, Doug punched him twice in the face, cutting open his eye, and then he kicked him in the knee. A man from a nearby house came out with a baseball bat and started screaming he was gonna call the cops.

"Let's fucking go, man!" I told Doug, but he wouldn't leave. He apologized again. The big dude got up, wiped the blood off his face, and started crying. I hated Doug. I hated how quickly he alternated between helping and hurting, often doing both at once. The big guy ran away again, and I stared up at the bright, full moon as Doug shouted, "I'M SORRY! HEY, YOU FORGOT YOUR HAT!" The baseball bat guy demanded to know our names, and when I said, "Warren Moon," he actually laughed out loud.

Doug kept telling me he wanted to find the big dude and apologize again, but I convinced him to come home. When I shut and locked my bedroom door, I realized I never wanted to talk to Doug again.

Cody had been doing a great job of recruiting new students, and each of our periods had grown by one to four kids. We didn't see much of him because he was always out recruiting, but he'd pop in from time to time to tell us all how special we were and how much he indeed cared. When he was there, he and Camarin would eat lunch with us, and we'd talk about our successes with students and tell jokes and talk about what we did in our free time. Because the school was new, we were all creating its culture on a daily basis. Cody began one morning by making a group announcement that, "I care about all of you!" and soon, that's how he started each day. It was cool to be a part of something that was evolving before my eyes. To be a part of the history of a place from the beginning. Soon, we'd need new teachers, and I'd get to welcome them to this culture and explain this history, and it made me feel useful.

I also developed some rituals, and just as I'd done as a sub, I greeted each student as they entered my classroom. I'd cooled down with my aggression when kids back-talked me, and learned new strategies to neutralize poor behavior by watching how Karla and Camarin dealt with it. Even though they had separate styles, both had supreme control of any group they were speaking to.

Camarin radiated confidence and compassion and you couldn't help but know she really cared about you, and because of it, you didn't want to give her any shit. She was great at making small talk and giving earned compliments and making cute jokes that would get everyone laughing.

Karla wasn't as personable, but she had that quiet strength. She knew what she was talking about. You knew she was fair and controlled, and something about that control permeated the classroom.

I felt honored to be working with both of these women, and

from observing them, I was learning how to become a better man. I wanted to be like both of them: confident, competent, compassionate, creative. I didn't want to fight people anymore. I didn't want to ice down black eyes and patch up bleeding skin. I didn't want to filter more alcohol through my exhausted liver. I didn't want to feel extreme fear every time I turned left when I'd planned to go right. I wanted to tell them what they meant to me, but how could I do such a thing? All of my previous friendships had been built on casual bullshit and insults and pissing contests and shame. But I felt that I could be around Camarin and Kayla without having to insult them before they could insult me. That I could stumble in conversation and they wouldn't call me out. That they weren't trying to push me into the spotlight just so they could highlight all my faults.

No, I could work quietly beside them and feel the love they radiated and do my best to learn how to do the same.

At lunch, Doreen brought in her hairdresser, Juliana, and introduced us. "Jay, don't you think Juliana would like to try that new Vietnamese place that opened up on the corner? Maybe you can take her."

"I brought my PB&J," I said.

"What are you, four years old? Go try something new." Doreen gave me a few awkward winks that I didn't pick up on.

"I-I'm already halfway through my sandwich . . ." I held it up to show them how I'd already bitten off the crust, which was my signature move before going in for the center.

"Fine. Juliana, let's go," Doreen said. The two left and Barry and Karla started laughing.

"What?" I said.

"She just tried to set you up on a blind date," Karla said.

"Really?"

"Yep," Barry said.

"That's weird," I said.

"Yep," Barry said.

Before leaving that day, Doreen laid into me about how, "I

brought that poor girl all the way here and you just reject her like she's a piece of trash . . ."

That weekend, Doug and I went to a party in Ensenada. One of the Geology students had a ranch there, and I drove down with Doug and a really cute woman from his class. This was the first time I'd been to Mexico since my ex and I broke up, and even though we'd lived in a town much farther south, below Guadalajara, her face was everywhere I looked.

Doug helped me navigate the Tijuana highways, and after a few hours we were drinking beers on the ranch. There were about thirty people there, grilling carne asada, tossing horseshoes, dancing under the desert moon. We brought two twelve-packs and worked through the first quickly. When I went back to the car to grab the other twelve-pack, I started the car and popped *The Man Who Sold the World* into the CD player, blasting "The Width of a Circle." Mick Ronson rocked the hell outta that tune, and I was really getting into it when Doug slipped into the passenger seat beside me.

"Dude, Corona's pissed as hell right now," he said.

"Why?"

He laughed. "I called her fat."

"No shit she's pissed."

"Let's hit the town. Fuck this place."

"How far is it?"

"Like ten minutes."

"Fuck it."

I cranked the engine and let Bowie guide our way into the night. I parked my car, which still had New York plates, on the main strip, and we got lost popping in and out of bars, pounding drinks and dancing. We hit a few strip clubs and dropped a lot of loot and made plans to drop a dude who kept following us down the street.

"I'll elbow him in the face and you take out his knees."

But before it came to that, we got in a Jeep filled with women, and didn't notice there were a few guys in there too until after we'd taken off, and we ended up at a bar where all the guys were wearing these small bags over their shoulders that looked almost like purses. I left to find an ATM and one of the guys ran after me saying it wasn't safe to walk around there and that he'd escort me. When I came back, Doug's face was white, and he said, "Yo, we need to get the fuck outta here. I just saw some shit. We need to leave *now!*"

We took off through the back door and ran for the car, which was a few miles down the road. I kept asking him what he'd seen, but he said it was better I didn't know. I woke up the next morning on a couch at the ranch, and I could definitely hear people fucking in the other room. A little while later, Doug and the cute girl we'd driven down with walked out of that room and into the kitchen. They cut some papaya and made some eggs, and we ate and took off. It was dark by the time we got back to Soul City, but it'd been dark inside of me the whole trip.

Soul City Times wrote a glowing article on Cody Cares, and we got a surge of new students. Cody hired a few new teachers and had them set up in the gym with us. It seemed like great news until Cody started going crazy about organizing our workspace. "A clean space is a teachable space" or some shit, and he came down hardest on me. I wasn't exactly the most organized dude and had crap all over the place, but so did all the best teachers I'd had in high school and college. Despite the mess, I knew where pretty much everything was and could reach my hand into a pile and pull out what I needed, so maybe I *was* organized but just not neat. Either way, Cody wasn't having it.

Karla could see I was struggling, so she helped. I never knew where to put anything. When someone gave me a paper or book or whatever, I'd usually just set it down wherever there was space and it would sit there forever as my brain worked on overload trying to remember where everything was. Karla's area was neat and color-coded and all that, but that shit suffocated me.

Karla made me a filing system and showed me where to put

everything, but I knew it wouldn't be long before I'd be a disaster again. Still, I thanked her and bought her lunch, then went out with Doug that night and got wasted.

Chapter 10

When Doug moved to Mexico, I decided to find a cheaper spot. I couldn't afford the rent for a two-bedroom, and even though I hated moving away from Tuyet, Kelly, Remi, and the others, maybe I didn't. When I found my new spot on the second floor of a two-story apartment building close to the main strip, a part of me didn't even want to meet my new neighbors. One offered to help me move my dresser upstairs, but I said no thanks. The CPA and Karla's brother were helping me already, and I didn't want to owe this guy anything.

Before Doug left and I moved out, we threw a big party on the patio. We all got drunk, and some of us went to the bars, and Tuyet promised she'd still hang out with me all the time. I got laid again that night, but I think the woman was on acid or something because she kept staring at me with these big black eyes as she rode me, almost as if Earth below us had faded away and all that was left was darkness and light, and she was one with it all.

My new place was even bigger than my spot with Doug, and it was all white: walls, ceiling, carpet. I imagined getting rid of most of my stuff and keeping it open. I wanted room to breathe. The guy told me, in a thick Polish accent, it was $965 a month, but after listening to him go on and on about how he'd escaped from the Soviets in the sixties, I told him I was a history teacher and, "Won't you come tell that story to my class?" and he knocked twenty bucks off the monthly rate.

That first night, I unpacked only what I needed, then got drunk alone and played guitar. The songs were coming at me fast, and I recorded them as quickly as they came. Since moving to California, I'd been going through the most potent songwriting period of my life, and that first week in my new place was the most potent of all. I got everything at once—harmonies, melodies, lyrics—while before, I'd usually have to work on each piece separately. The tunes were haunting and driven and hopeless. I filled all five hundred spots on my recorder, and I bought another with twice the memory, and filled that in a month. Being away from everyone—being able to lock my door and strip down naked and chant as I moved from room to room without anyone watching—opened me up in a way I'd never been opened. Even so, it felt as if there was still a steel door covering the best of it all. I squirmed and writhed and maneuvered my body to let the songs snake their way out, but still the tension and hopelessness and fear concealed the best parts of me. I knew if I could just unlock it—if I could look clearly at the songs rather than squeezing them out of my mouth like wet turds—I could write anything. I realized that was what must have set Dylan and Lennon and Jim Morrison apart from the rest. That they could access that energy at will. That they didn't just dip their feet in the river from time to time but that they were actually inside the river, and it was flowing through them, from them. I felt that I was near the river and there were moments I could dip my foot inside, but I wanted to do a cannonball into the deepest part and let it wash over me. A part of me thought that maybe drugs would open this world up to me. But the other part knew Karla and Camarin were right. I needed to go directly at the Darkness.

Still, though, the Darkness seemed to be the driving force of my work. If I hurled it all out in some therapist's office and replaced it with light, what would be left of me? Just some cornball teacher putting left foot after right every day until retirement. Maybe Karla and Camarin were pushing me in that direction so I'd be more like them. Happy? Sober? Organized?

Who the fuck knows? Who do I trust?

Things were going well with the chiropractor. Dr. Vinny was straightening me out. I could feel it in my back and knees and even my face. When he cracked my neck, it made my skull sit better on my spine, and it took the pressure off my jaw and cheeks, and my face was losing a lot of the tension. For all these years, I'd felt like a hideous, amorphous blob, but now my cheeks narrowed and eyes brightened. My body felt more energized and my joints felt more hinged. More than writing the world's greatest song or poem or book, my biggest dream was to sit on the couch with my back straight and my shoulders and head aligned. Where I could lift my right arm to grab the remote without having my entire left side lock up to balance me out. I could feel it now. Feel how twisted I was. My left hip was at least an inch higher than my right. My left shoulder was also about an inch or two higher than the right.

My body still felt horribly out of alignment, but it was much better than before. I didn't want to run or ride my bike or work out for fear I'd put myself back out of alignment, and this fear was growing. I worried that maybe I'd slip in the shower and fuck up my spine. Maybe I'd sleep wrong and undo all the progress I'd made. I began controlling my movements, careful not to do anything to disturb my spine or muscles. It terrified me to think that maybe now I was bringing a new form of insanity into my life. But my brain had been dealing with insanity for decades. It could handle more. Allow my body freedom. Allow me to run and jump and swim and fight and fuck correctly for the first time. Allow me to feel what I must have felt when I was a child. Before the horror had flooded my brain and disfigured me forever. Allow me to breathe. To sleep. If I could choose only one word to describe my life, it would be "desire." If I could have a second, I'd choose "exhaustion." Total fucking exhaustion. And the border where this desire and exhaustion met was extremely volatile, and this volatility was destroying my life.

One night after a session with Dr. Vinny, I decided to try out the bathtub at my new place. I lit some candles, played *Sea Change* by Beck, and lowered myself into a bubble bath. It was jasmine or lavender or some other girly crap, and I'd been embarrassed to buy it, but once I got it home, I didn't have to worry about anybody, Doug especially, busting through the door and giving me shit.

Since starting with Dr. Vinny, it seemed the straighter I got, the more the tension shifted to new areas of my body. It was as if to straighten my back, I had to tighten up the side of my left thigh and my right hamstring. It was almost as if I was pulling down a spring, and while it felt unbelievably incredible to walk more upright than I ever had, somewhere deep down, I knew that spring would release sooner or later, and I'd be even more fucked than before.

Maybe relaxing in the tub would even things out, though, and it did help. I put a towel behind my head and closed my eyes. My new neighborhood was right in the heart of the Sand Beach party zone, and my neighbors pumped the bass. Even so, I focused on my breathing. I felt as if there were a person trapped inside of me—that my insides were a maze I couldn't escape and the more I tried to relax and solve the grand riddle, the more the answers eluded me. The deeper I breathed, the more the anxiety flooded me. It didn't want me to relax. Relaxation seemed to be the enemy. If I relaxed, maybe the Evil inside of me would escape. Maybe I'd created this maze to keep it all inside.

I could hear my neighbors screaming in celebration. I knew they were chugging and smoking and grabbing each other's asses, and even though I did all that same shit, I always felt as if I did it in a separate space. That even if we were in the same bar or house party, I was partying alone, behind high walls, separated from the pack. When they partied, they seemed to be having fun. When I did it, it only caused me to feel further away from everything and everyone, including myself. When I drank and smoked, I was only traveling deeper within. I wanted to be able to let loose and dance and enjoy myself. I wanted to be young and have fun before I got too old and couldn't anymore.

Just breathe. Relax. See what happens. Maybe there is no Evil down there. Maybe it's all a trick. Maybe the nuns and priests and godparents tricked you into thinking you were Evil so you wouldn't get away. Wouldn't be able to enjoy life. Try it. What have you got to lose?

So I did. I tried breathing out the tension. I imagined it, like a dark cloud, moving from my feet through my legs and groin, up my stomach and into my lungs, and I exhaled it. The bath got cold, so I turned the hot water back on. This breathing thing was doing the trick. I imagined the Darkness passing through the maze, solving the riddle, and a few times I felt as if it was getting close to escaping, but I knew that was an illusion. The maze only wanted me to think I was getting close to freedom, because then it rearranged itself, with narrower tunnels and new twists and turns. It was as if the maze was the size of North America, and I could see no more than what was directly at my feet, and I was running blindly in all directions, bumping into walls, and not realizing how big it all was. Not realizing even where I was going.

After a few hours, I felt really loose. My joints, shoulders especially, felt warm and hinged. When I lifted myself up, my shoulders dropped down toward the tub, and I knew I'd have to do this more often.

Holy shit! Don't let that thought in. The moment you realize how beneficial relaxing in the tub is, the more you'll obsess over it. Soon it'll go from being this one-time thing that helped you to a mandatory part of your daily routine that'll dominate your schedule and cause you to panic if you so much as step into that tub a minute late.

No, no more baths. You can take a three-minute shower, wash your hair with Prell and skin with government-issued soap.

This is why you can't live alone, Jay! This is why you need Doug. The second you get soft, you'll slide away forever. Go, run back to him! Go back to Mexico!

But he's with his wife.

Fuck! It's all changing. Everything is changing. How'd I let it come to this? I was supposed to be in LA, acting. I was supposed to have my face all over billboards and on TV and the Internet, and she'd see me and realize how much she loved me and come back to me.

You fucked it all up with her. You can't go back to Mexico. Don't you see? If you find another girlfriend, you'll just fuck it up with her too. You told her you needed to go to LA to chase your dreams. That's why you left. That's why you both cried. You invited her to come but she wouldn't. She had school . . . she had that other guy. Mexico is a closed door. So is Doug. This is your new life now. This big empty apartment with noisy-ass neighbors and a funky smell.

Chapter 11

I went straight from work to Soul City Bar and Grill for their weekly open mic night. Winston, Stephone, and Jadia were already there. I'd brought a change of clothes but forgot the socks, so my feet were sweaty and disgusting. When Jadia hugged me, she didn't let go for a few seconds. Due to the chiropractic sessions, I was feeling better-looking than ever, and I was glad that she rubbed my back and put her hands on my sides, feeling my body in the best form it had ever been in. Her touch sent good chemicals racing through my body, and I wished we could've gone to a private place where she could touch more of me.

I went first that night and sang a song I'd written about a guy who, after breaking up with his girlfriend, asks her not to expose any of their secrets to her friends until he's had a chance to skip town. To be away from the "bomb before it goes off." I could tell that one got to some people because more clapped than usual, and Jadia wiped tears from her eyes when she told me how good it was. I ordered a drink and was just getting cozy with her when Barry walked through the door with his wife. I ran across the bar and closed my guitar case; I felt if he saw my guitar, he'd somehow know it was mine, and then he'd fuckin' know *everything*. He'd have all of my secrets and that bomb would go off right while I was sitting there on that barstool. I didn't want him to see me. To see Winston or Stephone, and especially not Jadia. So I grabbed my guitar and snuck out the backdoor.

Fuck, this place is tainted now. I'll have to find someplace new.

The panic gripped my chest and throat, and I had to wait about fifteen minutes before starting my car and driving away.

A song producer, who'd heard my song about the bomb going off and got my number from Winston, called saying he wanted to record it with a few session players he assured me were "the best of the best." I told him I'd have to think about it. In my vision, I would attract the right musicians to start a band with me, and we'd create our own style and sound before recording any tunes. I felt that playing with session players was jumping the gun. But after a long talk with Winston over a few beers, I decided to give it a shot.

I went to the producer's house, and he brought me to his garage, which he'd turned into a studio. He showed me the equipment we'd be using and introduced me to the bassist and drummer. I went to a booth and played the guitar part first. Between takes, I played "The Wind" by Cat Stevens, and the producer's face lit up.

"Damn, that was beautiful. Play that again," he said.

So I did.

"Let's record that next," he said. "You're on a roll, Jay."

I got off the stool, put my guitar away, and told him thanks but no thanks. Until I could write something that caused as strong a reaction as "The Wind," I had no business being in a recording studio.

I woke up one morning feeling incredible. My body felt more aligned than ever, and my shoulders were sitting well on my torso and my head was sitting well on my neck, and I felt trim and muscular and energetic. My cheeks were sunken and eyes were bright, and I walked into work with a smile on my face for probably the first time since starting at Cody Cares. I walked around giving everyone the wink and, "A lovely morning to you." If Doreen had brought me another blind date, I probably would have bought her half the Vietnamese place's menu.

During first period, I played the video and sat at my desk, thinking about how I could improve as a teacher. I watched Karla, who as usual was going over the important points from the video before handing out her Scantrons, and I decided to do the same. Only, I did it in the Mr. S way. "So, who can tell me some facts about George Washington?"

"He was the leader of the Continental Army," a girl said.

"Good. Anything else?" I said.

"That it was a myth that he had wooden teeth," a boy said.

"Yes, which is a great thing because it's hard to get rid of termites with floss," I said.

Some of the kids laughed.

Karla must have heard that too, because she smiled. It was great sharing a space with other teachers. Traditional schoolteaching has to be one of the loneliest professions. But at Cody Cares, we worked together as a unit. One of the hardest things for me while teaching in Miami was knowing when I should correct a kid's behavior. I always second- and third- and millionth-guessed every little thing I did, but here, if a kid was acting up in class, the other teachers would sometimes wave the kid over, and they'd sit out the period with the other teacher's group. This removed a significant amount of stress from the job, and observing how the others handled such issues gave me a better idea of how to deal with them myself.

I drove home, basking in the California sunshine and thinking maybe now I was finally ready to head south and try to make it as an actor. I was looking and feeling better than ever. I'd have to hit the gym for a few weeks first and work on my tan, but after that, look out Hollywood!

When I parked my car, I checked my phone and saw a voicemail from Brian the producer. "Jay, look, I think we should talk about your song. You got some talent, but it seems you're running away from—"

I deleted his number.

That night, one of my neighbors from the apartment complex next door plugged in an electric guitar and played as what sounded like fifteen people sang along. This continued until at least 3 a.m.— them shouting the lyrics to "Wonderwall" and "Faith" as I lay there millionth-guessing myself for the millionth time.

I can't sleep with those fuckers shouting. But what can I do about it? Only a fucking loser would go over there and say something. This is Sand Beach, man. The angsty adult-youth capital of the world. If there's one place on Earth that this shit is permitted, it's here. If you say something, you're essentially taking sides against California. Against your dreams. I mean, you're a fucking guitarist. What kind of a hypocrite would you be to tell him to unplug and shut the fuck up? Hell, you and Doug kept Tuyet and Kelly up a few times doing the same thing. Besides, you're too much of a pussy to go over there anyway. Just lie there and pretend that you like it. Pretend to smile. Breathe in the salty air and pretend that this is what you wanted all along. There's no sleeping in California. The only dreams you get here are the ones that get crushed out on the hot, bright streets.

I woke up the next morning feeling significantly shittier than the day before. When I got to work, there were no winks and "hey, how ya doin'?" smiles. No jokes after the videos. No laughter. My head was killing me and I hadn't even drunk the night before. At lunch, the thought of talking to people sent rivers of anxiety up my back and into my brain, but I sat with the others anyway. Doreen kept going on and on about this new shoe store near her house, and I wanted to bash my head against the table.

After last period, I brought my Scantron quizzes to the grading machine, but Doreen had messed with some of the settings and it had stopped working. She'd finished grading all but two of her quizzes, so she gave me the "sucks to be you" look before walking away. Everyone else was already done grading, while I had a stack of about ninety quizzes that I had to get into the book before leaving. I panicked, remembering all those days in Miami when I stayed two, three, four hours after school, grading and sweating and cursing myself for picking such a thankless profession. As Barry and Doreen and finally Karla left for the day, I still had seventy quizzes to get through. I started getting dizzy and almost all at once, the tension that had coiled inside of me released, and I writhed and trembled as my muscles strained and locked, twisting my hips and spine and contorting my body into a new puzzle I knew would be even more difficult to solve. It was a violent reaction, nearly causing me to fall out of my chair, and it terrified me to know I had no control over it. Since starting my sessions with Dr. Vinny, I'd been feeling the tension growing, and my body must finally have snapped. The better my body felt, the clearer I was able to think. When my spine was straight and hips aligned, I was able to feel happiness. To understand difficult concepts in science and math. To write songs with much more power and purpose. But after that chain reaction, my brain felt as strangled as my body. I couldn't concentrate on grading. My back and legs and neck ached. I wanted to walk straight off the cliff and fall head-first onto the jagged rocks below. I stood up and paced the room before punching the absolute shit out of the bathroom door while screaming, "FUCK!" at the top of my lungs. No one else was around—just me inside all of that empty space. The waves were rocking the school harder than ever before and my reality shook and pulsated.

I can't do this again. I can't put myself through this. This is what happens when you try to improve yourself, Jay. This is what you get for thinking you can escape Satan's grasp. He has you and he always will. You don't get to be like Barry and Karla, smiling and going home to your pets and talking about your weekend camping trips. You get the bar alley brawls. You get the bottles broken over your head and the drunk car crashes over the bridge. You get the needles sticking out of your arm under the Sand Beach Pier. You get rashes on your dick and scabies eating your skin and the eternal highways to nowhere. FUCK YOU FOR TRYING, YOU FUCKING PIECE OF SHIT! I FUCKING HATE YOUR FUCKING GUTS! KILL YOURSELF! KILL YOURSELF! KILL YOURSELF!

I sat on the floor of the men's room and wept. I'm going to die. If I don't kill myself first, I'm going to die soon.

That night, the neighbors on both sides were having loud parties, and my brain couldn't handle it. I headed down to the pier and walked it to the end. There was no one else out there, and I felt I was walking out into the ocean alone. I spread my arms and embraced the cool, salty breeze. The waves rolling in from the deep sea gently rocked the pier. I looked as far into the darkness as I could. A frog hopped along the wooden guardrail, over fish guts and bird shit, and stopped about three feet from me. Again, it gave me this "come with me" gesture, but I got lost staring into the darkness and when I looked for it again, it was gone.

The parties died down around 4 a.m., and I was able to get some sleep. Where do I go to find silence? Where do I go to find peace? Any direction I turn, I find myself deeper in chaos.

The only direction left must be within.

Chapter 12

"Oh, you just had a relapse," Dr. Vinny said, laughing and patting my back. "Happens all the time."

"But this was a violent reaction. I haven't recovered even after a week, and it seems my muscles have locked me into a new position that chiropractic can't correct. My body is playing chess with me, and this shit's Deep Blue, and I ain't even fit to carry Kasparov's pawns. This feels hopeless. I'm confused. Furious. Exhausted."

Dr. Vinny gave me the same confused look that a thousand other doctors had given me. It was this "I don't know what to tell you and I have other patients I need to help so I can buy that new boat so please fuck off" look. "Yeah, I-I don't know exactly what you're talking about, but let's get you on the table, and I'll fix you right up," he said.

He did his manipulations, and I walked out of there feeling worse than when I'd come in. The receptionist, Bonnie, smiled at me and asked when she'd see me again, and I misinterpreted her meaning.

"Oh, would you like to maybe get dinner or something?" I said.

She blushed. "No, I mean, like, when will you be seeing Dr. Vinny again?"

"I, uh, I'll call you about that."

Karla, Barry, and Doreen bought me a cake for my birthday, and we ate it at lunch. The other teachers came over to sing to me, but they went back to their desks right after. Barry, Karla, Doreen, and I always ate together and hung out and bullshitted during our free period. The other teachers were nice, but they kept to themselves, and I didn't know much about them. But Barry and Doreen were just as weird as I was. Karla, too, and it was nice that they'd do something for my birthday. Cody and Camarin even came over to give me a gift, a pen set shaped like golf clubs, which I knew I'd never use but still thanked them for anyway.

I still felt horrible after the relapse and it seemed that the maze inside of me was even bigger now and the light that had once guided my way was now blown out. I was forced to wander blindly over hot desert sands and freezing tundra plains, bumping into cacti and the edges of glaciers and the bottoms of jagged cliffs, using my hands to feel the way, hoping I'd soon arrive at a place where I could see. Where I could breathe.

When I got home, I ignored calls from Tuyet and Remi, and I microwaved a pizza and watched *The Office*. Later, I gave in to the urge and listened to "Indian Summer" on repeat. It was my favorite Doors tune, but I usually avoided it. It had the power to ruin me. It made me want to race back across the border and search for Mariposa and beg her to take me back. To rush down to LA before I was ready, and snort so much cocaine and shoot so much junk I'd lose myself forever. To fill the bath, warm my veins, and turn the water and tub and floor red.

But it was my twenty-seventh birthday, and I was still alive, so I played the song on repeat for an hour, maybe longer, as I moved about my empty apartment crying, speaking to people in my head, singing the lyrics, making strange noises, repeating nonsense words and phrases sixty, seventy, a hundred times before I was so exhausted I had to stop. I was lost in memories and dreams and nightmares. Lost in a way I couldn't have gotten lost if I was still living with someone else. But here, alone, surrounded by empty space, it all came out.

In the morning, I realized that by making it to twenty-seven, I'd make it to twenty-eight too.

Karla invited me to spend Thanksgiving at her house with her family. After the relapse, I was growing more reclusive, and told her no, but then I imagined myself eating a microwaved pizza alone and being haunted by the sounds of neighbors celebrating with their families, so I changed my mind. Being stuck in a house with strangers was hard enough if I was drunk, but doing it sober was nearly impossible. I never knew what to say, and if I opened my mouth too quickly, I might start saying shit that made no sense: "Tobey, Tobey, Tobey Tendahs on the tippadah moon." I had no idea why I had so much nonsense at the tip of my tongue, but it seemed there was more of it now than ever before. I think that by loosening up my muscles, all the Darkness and depravity was coming to the surface, and I was terrified to think of what I might do or say in front of someone I respected so much.

But when I got there, everything was fine. I did have an urge to shout and repeat, "PUNCH BOWL!" when I saw the gravy bowl, but I held it in and shook all the aunts' and uncles' and cousins' hands like a normal member of society. Karla had a gorgeous cousin named Tina, and Karla set me a place next to her at the table. I didn't talk to her, though, because I knew I looked as hideous as I felt, so I spoke with one of the aunts instead, telling her about a trip I'd taken to Guanajuato while I was living in Mexico, and she was impressed that I knew so much about her country.

Karla gave me some turkey and mashed potatoes to take home, and I thanked her. Lately, I'd been having a hard time finding energy to cook. There was so much noise in my brain that when I tried to relax enough to remember how to defrost chicken or where I left the black pepper, I'd get overwhelmed, and the best I could do was pop a pizza into the microwave, turn the dial, and go cry and shake somewhere until it was time to eat. I ate everything on the coffee table I'd brought from my old place with Doug. I'd brought some of the free flea-furniture too, but bought a new futon and upgraded from my air bed to a real one. Whenever I ate dinner, I watched DVDs on the thirteen-inch TV my dad had given me before I left Buffalo. Doug had offered to sell me his big TV at a cheap price, but I didn't want it. I didn't want comforts or luxuries. I needed flea-furniture and microwaved pizzas. I needed to stay tough. Hard. Look where softness and stability was bringing me. To near madness. I was losing my mind, and it was worse than ever before. At least before, I didn't have a job or responsibilities. Having to get up each day and head to Cody Cares filled me with such stress, I didn't know how much longer I could hang on.

But the thought of having some film producer tossing me a million dollars filled me with even more stress. If I had nothing but time and money, maybe I'd finally wander to some far-off corner of the world, wrap myself in the Darkness, and drink myself to death—a dream of mine when I was younger. To flame out. Go down like all the greats. An eternal sacrifice in the hopeless search for purity.

Soon it was winter break and time for Doug's wedding. I wanted to be in great shape in case Mariposa actually meant it when she said she'd like to see me while I was there, but due to the relapse and everything else, I'd been exercising as little as I could. Instead of getting bigger, I was getting skinnier, losing muscle, and my cheeks were hollowed out and my skin was sickly and pale. My Mexican friends, who I hadn't seen in a few years, noticed right away.

"You got cancer or something, Jay?"

I told them I was on a diet to lower my cholesterol, and they left it alone. When I arrived, Pedro was at the bus station waiting for me. I'd flown from Soul City to Guadalajara and taken a bus to Lila, and finally arrived about fifteen hours after I left my apartment that morning. He dropped me off at the cheapest hotel in the city center, and we met the others at Doug's fiancée's parents' house for a party. Something about being in Mexico relaxed me, and I felt some relief from my growing insanity. In fact, I was smiling and laughing again, even with Doug acting like an asshole. He demanded that I leave my hotel in the center, which I actually liked, and stay with the other guys at the most expensive hotel in town. It was a forty-dollar difference, but, "C'mon, you're making all that money now teaching." Yeah, I'm fuckin' rolling in it.

After the party with abuelita and the tias, the guys went to a bar. Doug's brother, Roberto, and our mutual college friend A-Bomb came along, and our buddy Herb, who lived in Lila, met up with us, too. Even Billy Bern was there. He'd been on tour with his band, which was still selling out shows all over the US and Canada, but he made time for his best friend's wedding. We got absolutely hammered, filling the table with empties and talking about old times. Everybody had stories about Doug, and no one had thought he'd ever get married.

"I'm glad you emailed me, Jay," Herb said. "This nut over here didn't even tell me when the wedding was."

"Really?" I said. "Maybe he just got busy and forgot."

"Yeah, maybe. Or maybe pretty Paz doesn't want me ruining her big day."

"Could be, but I mean, look who the fuck she's marrying. How much worse would it be for *you* to show up?"

We laughed.

"You doin' okay up there in Soul City?" he said.

"About as okay as I've ever been. Why?"

"I dunno. Just something different about you now."

"I-I don't know what you mean . . ." I hoped that by trailing off I'd make him move on to a different topic, and he did.

"You think Pedro will look pretty in his dress tomorrow? Heard he's one of the bridesmaids," Herb said.

"Yo, keep it down. You know he speaks fluent English, right?" I said. Pedro didn't seem to be listening, though. He was lost in conversation with A-bomb.

"Just better make sure he doesn't pop anything into one of your drinks. I see the way he watches you," Herb said.

"Relax, old man. You gotta chill with all that shit. The world's changing, homie," I said. It was indeed changing. Changing all the time. I could feel a big change coming for me that was gonna knock me straight on my ass—if it didn't end me entirely.

While walking to another bar, I spoke with Billy.

"Doug played me one of your songs. It was pretty fuckin' good. You ever think about recording?" Billy said.

"You know, I actually worked with a producer on recording one of my songs, but it didn't come out right, so I pulled the plug," I said.

"Well, I produce too, you know. You should come on down to New Orleans sometime and record with me."

"Whoa, thanks, that'd be great!" I said, even though I knew I never would. Playing music was like ripping off your clothes and jumping up on a table, shouting, "Hey, everybody, look at me!" and it was easier to do it in front of strangers than in front people who knew so much about you. Who knew your history. Your brothers, sisters, and parents.

We closed the bar down, took cabs back to the hotel, and passed out. A-Bomb and I shared a room, and we spoke a little before bed. I told him I was hoping to see Mariposa while I was here, and he said, "That might seem like a good idea, until you actually see her." A-Bomb had been with me in Mexico when I met Mariposa and I felt closer to her by being so close to him. After breaking up, I'd had to cut her out of my life. I blocked her email and erased her number from my phone, but the closer I got to this trip, the easier it became to face her. I'd unblocked her email and let her know I was coming, and she seemed excited. Before passing out, I asked A-Bomb if I could use his computer, and I checked her Facebook page, which I hadn't done in over a year. Her hairstyle was so different, and her clothes and everything. She looked older. Like a different person. I scrolled through a few of her pictures, bracing myself in case I saw one of her sitting on another guy's lap or something, but there weren't any like that.

In the morning, Herb took us out for breakfast, and we started drinking early. I killed a few caguamas, or liter bottles of beer, before lunch. Paz invited us to her place for dinner, but by then we were all so hammered, we skipped dinner and headed to another bar and then to a strip club. The taxi driver tried charging us five times the price, and I told him in Spanish, "I lived here for over six months and know you're fucking us, cabrón," and he gave us the normal rate. I didn't care so much about paying an extra buck or two—it was the principle. Lila had saved my life. It was a sacred place to me. I wasn't just some gringo tourist drinking and pissing all over the place.

Inside, a group of strippers were on us in a hurry. One sat on my lap and kept reaching under my shorts and grabbing my semi-hard dick, and I could see the other strippers doing the same with the rest of the guys. Herb warned me they'd be charging for this shit, but I told him we were partying and not to worry. He didn't have the cash, so he bounced. Pedro, Kike, and Doug took off, too, so it was just A-Bomb, Billy, Roberto, and me pounding beers and chanting, "AZUCAR! AZUCAR!" as she climbed the twenty-foot stripper pole and twisted and twirled her way down. Soon, she and Roberto disappeared into a room. A few strippers sat at our table, and I translated our conversation. When they found out Billy was famous, they said they'd meet us after work.

Roberto came back, shaking his head about how much he'd dropped to fuck Azucar, and we went to a karaoke bar. Billy's biggest song was on their playlist, and he gave the small crowd a killer performance for free, but no one knew who he was. While heading to the bar for a beer, some guy pushed Roberto so hard he fell back onto me, and I went after the fucker, throwing a few wild punches and falling on a nearby table, spilling drinks all over the guys sitting there. One got up and straight lumped me, and we took off before the cops showed. When I checked myself in a mirror, my eye was a bloody mess. The strippers actually did show up at the hotel, and we chilled in Roberto and Billy's room. I went back to my room to check my email. Mariposa hadn't written me, and I knew she wouldn't. I fell asleep while the guys partied in the room next door. In the morning, Roberto was bitching about how he'd spent all that money to fuck Azucar at the strip club, when he could have fucked her at the hotel for free. That's life, homie.

While getting ready for church, I realized I hadn't packed my dress pants. A-Bomb had an extra pair, but they were a few sizes too small. I took a deep breath and put them on anyway, and we headed out the door. Though I was one of the groomsmen, Paz asked the photographer to exclude me from the pictures due to my huge-ass shiner, which was still dripping blood. I sat next to Billy in church, and we cracked each other up making jokes about how they dipped the Body of Christ in the Salsa of Christ here, and he stepped outside because people kept giving him dirty looks. I looked around and noticed Herb wasn't there. He wasn't at the reception either, which was at a ranch in the country. When I asked Doug about it, he said, "Yeah, he couldn't make it," then walked away. We got drunk as hell at the reception, and a few women introduced themselves, and I spent most of the afternoon with one who was quiet and pretty and told me no when I asked her to come back to the hotel later on.

That night, we went back to Paz's mother's place and had a few more drinks. Doug had recently bought one of those new smartphones, and he recorded himself farting. He hooked the phone up to his car's stereo, and he, A-Bomb, Billy, and I cracked up as we drove around the city on his wedding night, listening to his farts on repeat. Paz was in the car, too, but she wasn't laughing, and when she told him to turn it off, he turned it up, then increased his speed. He got on the highway, and zipped around cars, speeding faster and faster into the darkness. The more his pregnant wife begged him to stop, the quicker he drove. We told him to cool it, though, and he dropped down to a normal speed.

We went to the beach the next day, and the day after, we left. Billy and I were leaving Guadalajara around the same time, so we took a bus together to the airport. As we cruised past the volcanoes in the distance, I wanted to scream, "MARIPOSA!" I'd squandered my whole trip getting wasted and listening to farts and getting rocked in the face and cheering on strippers. The next time I came back here, I would have to do it alone.

Billy and I hung out at the airport. When he opened his computer, he almost threw it. Doug had changed his wallpaper to an image of a large, muscular guy sticking a dildo up his ass, and I could see it was fucking with Billy's head. After he changed the wallpaper to something normal, I asked him if I could check my email; Mariposa still hadn't written to me. I did, however, get an email from Herb letting me know that Doug had given him the wrong address for the wedding and how he was "done talking to that piece of shit, and you should be, too." My flight left before Billy's, so I said goodbye and straight panicked the moment I sat down on that plane. The thought of going back to that empty apartment haunted me. But the thought of returning to a house filled with guys like Doug haunted me even more.

Chapter 13

I couldn't stand the silence of my apartment, so when Winston invited me to Slab City for the weekend, I said yes. He picked me up, and we headed southwest to the desert. There was a musical showcase that weekend, and it would likely draw talent from all over Southern California. It was my first desert trip, and I was excited to see the mountains and sand and cacti. From my place in the passenger seat, I was free to observe the natural beauty we passed, and I got lost imagining what all those adventurers before me had felt traveling through that same desert as they chased their dreams to the coast.

Winston's band had a huge following now in Soul City. He felt he was getting too comfortable with his sound and wanted to try something new that weekend, which was why he left his guitar behind and brought an accordion instead. We passed through the mountains and arrived in Niland, a desert town east of the Salton Sea. We stopped at a diner for dinner, then drove past Salvation Mountain and into Slab City, known as the last lawless place in America. The concrete slabs that scattered the area were left over from an old military base; squatters had moved in and made it a place of pure freedom of expression. They'd built a stage where people could perform, and we set up camp a few hundred yards from it.

I'd underestimated the January desert chill, and Winston loaned me a few more layers to keep out the cold. We practiced some songs while we drank tequila, and then we headed for the stage. There were about forty other people there, some locals, some musicians who'd come from as far away as Seattle. I sat on a couch in front of the stage as I sipped tequila and watched some of the best talent I'd seen in a while. This was definitely the kind of place where you could take off your pants and no one would give you a second look. After a few bands rocked the stage, Winston and I got up there and played one of his original tunes, then one of mine, and finished with "Tuesday's Gone" by Lynyrd Skynyrd, which sounded great on the accordion. It was one of the best audiences I'd ever played for; people seemed to get lost in our songs as they swayed and closed their eyes and nodded along to the music. After, Winston went to sleep in his tent, and I hung out with one of the bands. They had an RV behind the stage, and we ate hot dogs and drank cans of beer. It was freezing, literally, almost dropping into the twenties. I hadn't felt that kind of chill since leaving Buffalo, and shivering out there on my nearly one-year anniversary of heading west reminded me of all I'd left behind, and how far I still had to go to feel warm.

The singer, Dan, gave me his number and said we'd have to jam sometime. He liked my sound and was always up in Soul City, and I said, "Absolutely!" then went to sleep. Even with a sleeping bag, the cold, greedy earth was stealing my warmth, and I welcomed the sun in the morning. On our way home, Winston took a picture of me in front of Salvation Mountain, and I looked drained of all energy.

We were making great time on the highway, then suddenly hit a patch of traffic that seemed to come out of nowhere.

"Accident?" I said.

"No, immigration checkpoint," Winston said.

"What the hell is that?"

"They stop everybody driving through to check their citizenship and to see if they're smuggling anything in from Mexico."

"How the fuck is that legal?"

"Nine-Eleven fucked this country up in ways we'll never recover from."

When the prick asked me for my citizenship, I felt like telling him to fuck off, but I said, "US and A," and we kept going. I asked Winston to hang out at my place, but he needed to get home, and I was alone again.

I thought about calling Dan to see if he wanted to jam, but I figured I'd probably be leaving Soul City soon for LA, so what was the point? Anyway, Doug was back in town to finish up his grad program, so I wasn't on my own anymore. We went out on a Friday night, and while playing billiards in the back room of a bar, Doug got angry at a friend and pushed him through a window. The friend got cut up, but nothing lethal, and we took off running before the bouncer knew what was up. We ran back to the friend's place, and his girlfriend screamed and started crying when she saw him.

"C'mon, you're being a little dramatic, aren't you?" Doug said to her.

"You fucking destroyed his face!"

She kicked us out and took him to the hospital, and on the walk to another bar, Doug went on and on about what a bitch she was and how he wasn't gonna pay the bill and all that, and I told him I didn't feel well and went home.

He tried calling me the next day, but I didn't pick up, rereading Herb's words in my mind: "I'm done talking to that piece of shit, and you should be, too." Over the next week, Doug called and emailed and texted me, but I didn't respond. I felt terrified not to answer, but for some reason I continued ignoring him. I knew he'd blow up and come looking for me. Maybe he'd kill me. But he didn't know my new address, thank god! Still, I'm not safe. He'll find me. I need to lie low for a while.

I stopped going out unless it was necessary, and if I did leave the apartment, I wore sunglasses and a hoodie. Too many times now, I'd told myself I'd had enough of that shit, but seeing that dude's face all cut up and bleeding like that had been so horrible, I knew I had to stop. If I kept picking up that phone, I was gonna get cut up like that one of these days—or cut someone else up. If I kept going out with Doug, they'd find my body below the cliffs.

It was strange ignoring him. It was almost as if I had to sweat him out of my system, and in doing so, I learned that maybe it was possible to sweat out other things as well.

That Monday, I called Dr. Tom, the chiropractor I'd met at the wellness fair months back, and he told me to come in the next morning. I gave him the X-rays Dr. Vinny had taken, and he said, "Jay, these have got to be the worst X-rays I've ever seen. You can't see anything."

He took a full back X-ray, including my hips, and showed me that my spine was almost perfectly straight, confirming that I didn't have scoliosis. "Your problem is your muscles, not your spine. For whatever reason, they're holding on to a tremendous amount of stress."

"Can you help me?" I said, almost in tears.

"Yes, but I think you would also benefit from seeing an osteopath and a psychologist."

"I-I come from a world where if you show any weakness, you get knocked right on your ass—or worse . . ."

"I get it, Jay. Just give it a try."

I thanked him and left and set up a meeting with the osteopath who had the highest rating on Google. After examining me, he gave me the "I've been doing this for over twenty-five years, and I've never seen anyone as tight as you" bullshit.

"Can you help me?" I said.

"Not until you get rid of that stress."

"But that's why I'm here!"

"Sorry, I can't help you."

I tried another, and he said almost the exact same thing, except it was thirteen years. I went to three others, and the same fucking thing. I did the math and figured that in over one hundred years of regularly seeing patients, no one had ever seen anyone as bad off as I was. When that last doctor showed me the door, I felt as if the world had officially turned its back on me.

I went back to Dr. Tom, and told him what happened, and I asked him again if he could help me. "Yes, I can."

"Do you promise?"

"I do."

"You're not gonna just give up?"

"I don't give up on anyone."

"Are you sure?"

It went on like that for an uncomfortable amount of time. I was almost in tears, and I started telling him things I'd never told anyone. How my dad used to beat the shit out of me. How he screamed all day, every day. How bad of a temper I had. The times I'd hurt people physically. And he just sat there listening to it all, and then said, "Jay, I don't think the problem is with your body. I think it's with your mind. I strongly recommend you try behavioral therapy." I said no, and that I just wanted to try chiropractic again and that it almost worked last time, and as long as Doreen doesn't fuck with the Scantron machine again, I should be fine this time. This time it will work, I swear!

He said okay, but repeated that we probably wouldn't make much progress until I was able to release all that stress.

After work that day, I took a bath, which had become a mandatory part of my routine, just as I'd feared, then hit the strip alone with the intention of drinking myself into oblivion. When I got to a bar, I ordered a strong drink, pounded it, and ordered another. To my left, a tall skinny guy was yelling at the beautiful woman sitting next to him. I didn't hear all of it, but it was something about her looking at another guy. She stared straight ahead as if she'd heard it all before. I was surprised no one stepped in, and then, when he got up to use the bathroom, I sat in his seat. Normally, I had zero confidence with women, but something about the situation set me right at ease.

"Are you okay?" I said.

"Yeah." She continued staring straight ahead.

"Fuck that guy. I know I don't know you, but no one deserves that." Flashes of Doug screaming at me broke through my mind; it was much easier to give advice than to take it.

"I can't," she said.

"But how do you feel sitting there and taking that shit?"

She didn't respond. He came back from the bathroom, and when he saw me, he screamed at her, "GET THE FUCK HOME RIGHT NOW!"

I stood and told him she wasn't going anywhere, and he backed right out of there with this look of fear in his eye, even though I didn't even raise my voice. I sat down, bought her another drink, and after a few minutes, she gave me her life story. Her name was Nima, and she was from Iran. She came from a broken household, and her traumatic childhood experiences inspired her to write and direct a short film loosely based on her relationship with her mother, and it placed in some huge film festivals and even won one of them, but she was so creatively blocked after winning such accolades that she left Hollywood and headed north to hide out with her boyfriend in Sand Beach, hoping for inspiration to strike her again.

"You're obviously an incredible woman. There's no way all those festivals would be honoring you if you were a hack. You gotta get away from all that negative energy. Let's go take a walk."

She said okay, and we walked to the beach, and when the moonlight hit her face, I couldn't believe how beautiful she was.

"What are your dreams?" she said, as we walked toward the pier.

"I want to act, and I want to start a band. I've also written a book."

"Really? What's it about?"

"It's about a guy who runs off to Mexico after graduating from college, and he's suicidal but he finds something in Mexico that makes him realize he wants to live. It's part love story, but it doesn't end so well."

"It usually doesn't. Well, I'd love to read it."

"Oh god, it's a mess. I've spent so much time editing it, but it's nowhere near ready to be seen."

"That's the best time for me to take a look."

"Okay, okay, well, I'll email it to you."

"How about you show it to me now?"

"Uh, yeah, okay."

We took off our shoes and walked through the water, then she grabbed my hand and started running up the sand and onto the sidewalk. I didn't know why she was running, but she was smiling and laughing, and I didn't want to ruin her good time, so I followed. I showed her my apartment and flipped on my computer and let her read my novel while I poured us wine and microwaved a pizza.

"This is really good," she said. "It's so full of emotion."

"I think I'm fucked in the head." I handed her a glass of wine.

"That makes two of us."

She kissed me and we ended up in the shower, her riding me while I looked across my new apartment and watched the clock above the kitchen sink. I couldn't believe that I had my own place with a door that locked and a working clock that I'd not only bought, but put a battery into and set to the correct time and hung on the wall, and with a bathtub where this gorgeous woman was fucking my brains out. Maybe having my own space wasn't so bad. Maybe if I filled it with love instead of rage, shame, and jealousy, I could avoid having to go down the creativity- and confidence-killing route of therapy.

We finished in the shower and then went to bed. We woke up in the middle of the night, and she started rubbing her bare ass against me, and I lifted her right leg and entered her from behind, and she asked me if I'd ever been in love. I said yes, and she said she'd never been. I asked her if she still believed in love, and she didn't answer. I did, I told her, and you should too.

I let her move in, violating the terms of my lease, but fuck my landlady. She was the definition of a prick. I went with Nima to get her things, and her ex begged her, please don't go! But she was done with his shit, and I was proud of her as she walked past him, even after he dropped to his knees in the grass like a little bitch. For once, it was nice being the strong guy and not the coward.

I gave her my spare key, and we played husband and wife,

making dinner together while listening to music and sipping wine. She played me tunes by artists I'd never heard before, my favorite being "A Postcard to Nina" by Jens Lekman, and while listening to that song and chopping carrots and celery, I already knew she was my Nina, and when I called her that, she gave me this knowing smile as if the script were already written and we were just playing our roles until the credits and music and lights came on and everyone, including us, went home.

Nima pulled out the cutting board that slid into a groove under the counter, and covered it with cheese and figs and nuts that "go great with this wine. Here try," and we ate them while sitting on the futon and listening to Cat Power and the Arctic Monkeys. I lay in her lap and she dropped figs in my mouth, and I almost forgot how badly my back had been hurting since that relapse. Nima brought something into that household that I'd never had before: class. Grace. Charm. I liked seeing the spider plants she'd put all over the apartment. I liked eating chocolate with wine and hearing stories about her trips to Sweden and Denmark and how those societies functioned so much better than the US, and I wanted to hear more and more and more from her. She knew everything about world politics and economics and I knew she was far out of my league, but it didn't even matter because we'd already laughed together. We'd already made love. She'd already read my work and told me how much she enjoyed it. We'd already shared so much in such a short time. I knew we'd never fall in love, which was exactly what made everything so easy.

When the stew was ready, we ate, and it tasted unlike anything I'd ever made. Nima introduced me to spices like cumin, turmeric, and celery salt, and I vowed to never microwave another pizza again. We lit incense and fell asleep to music and held each other the whole night. How any man could scream at this gorgeous woman was beyond me. How any man could push her away was insane. But I pushed people away as well, and I needed to stop. I needed to find a way of giving people like Nima a home.

Of giving people like me a home.

Chapter 14

One of the teachers was fired for doctoring his students' grades, and Cody clamped down on the rest of us. Cody decided he'd only hire certificated teachers from now on, and he hired someone to put all the quizzes through the Scantron, which meant less work for me, but we also had to start showing Ms. Kefana our grade books each month to be sure that the quiz grades matched the grades we'd marked down. It wasn't a big hassle, but a hassle nonetheless. The grader was a recent college grad who was cute as hell. She made a lot of excuses to talk to me, citing problems with the machine or wanting me to double-check grades, which might have seemed like a part of the job, but after a few weeks of observation, I noticed she wasn't asking any of the other teachers to help her with any of that. Doreen kept telling me I should ask her out, but I had Nima. I hadn't told anyone about Nima for the same reason I hadn't told them I wrote songs or anything else about my personal life, but when I went to the Vietnamese place with Karla for lunch that day, I opened right up.

"Oh my gosh! Yes, I know who she is. She won the Canada Film Festival," Karla said.

"Yeah, she's incredibly talented."

"You know, I'd be happy to introduce you and Nima both to the director of the Soul City Film Festival."

"What do you mean, both of us?"

"I mean, I know what you're doing here. Don't get me wrong, you're a great teacher and all, but you've got 'I need to get to LA as fast as possible' written all over your face."

"You think Cody knows?"

"People are a lot smarter than I think you realize."

"Yeah, I'm learning that. Well, I think she'd be happy to meet him."

"The festival is coming up. I'll show you both around."

"Thanks. Hey, why'd you quit the fest?"

"I love film, but my real passion is working with kids. It took me a little while to figure that out, but now that I have, I'm satisfied."

I started laughing.

"What?" she said.

"It's like we're moving in opposite directions."

She smiled.

"Whaddya think about all the changes around here now?" I said.

"Change is a part of the environment."

"But really, though?"

"I think Cody's been gaining a little bit of an ego since they published those articles. I kinda hope it passes, and he goes back to normal. The school isn't perfect, but ego will take us in the wrong direction."

"Yeah, one of the reasons why I took this job was because he wasn't a prick. I don't deal well with pricks. If I'm not the biggest asshole around, I go straight after every cocksucker who looks at me wrong."

"My, is this your out-of-school language?"

"Sorry, my dad was a sailor and my mom is Lindsay Lohan."

Karla laughed out loud, and I took a bow.

Once the school started gaining popularity, Cody cashed in and rented vacant classrooms to companies like Starbucks, Subway, and Baskin-Robbins, and even to a few doctors and dentists. He used the extra money to spruce up the place, fixing the floors and leaky ceiling and paving the parking lot. I wasn't a fan of him whoring a school out like that, but it did enable us to offer free tuition to lower-income students.

It was also nice to get ice cream between classes.

I found a parking spot, and Nima and I walked a few blocks to the Soul City Theater. I wore a suit jacket and my work shoes, and sprayed myself with just the right amount of cologne, and Nima was in a flowing white dress with her hair done up, revealing her dangling earrings and putting her gorgeous face on center stage. Walking with her downtown, past all of the people on bikes and walking in and out of bars and restaurants and bookstores, made me finally feel as though I belonged there. She wrapped her arm around mine, and I stopped walking and hugged her, whispering in her ear how beautiful she was.

We met Karla out front, and she gave us two VIP passes that we put around our necks, then she led us inside. The ceiling was at least a hundred feet above and decorated with colored glass that the strong afternoon sun passed through, warming us and covering us in soft greens, reds, and yellows.

"He's a little busy right now, but he'll see you after the film," Karla said, leading us upstairs and into a hall. We passed a long line of people as we walked into the theater. Nima wanted to sit in front but I told her it hurt my neck and eyes to sit so close, so we moved to the second to last row in the back. Both Nima and Karla had been going on and on how this film was winning awards all over Europe and how the director was probably going to win an Oscar, and how talented and famous he was, especially in Barcelona where he was from, but I'd never heard of him. Still, I loved Spanish film, so I was looking forward to checking this one out.

People packed into the theater, filling every seat, and the lights went out, and the opening scene was one of the most powerful pieces of filmmaking I'd ever seen: A young boy ran through the streets of Madrid, introducing us to the city from his pace and perspective. It reminded me of my trip to Madrid with some friends in 2005. We'd arrived on New Year's Eve, ate our twelve grapes in the Puerta del Sol, and took a road trip through southern Spain and into Portugal, then back to Madrid.

I got lost thinking about the trip, but the assholes sitting behind us wouldn't shut the hell up, so I started flooding with anxiety. Usually, I pretended to ignore that kind of shit, but with Nima's arm on mine, I felt the strength to turn around and say, "Hey, will you two stop talking? You're pullin' us outta the film."

It was an older man and woman, and the man leaned forward and said, "Yes, yes, is a good film, no?" He smiled and sat back, and didn't talk again.

Nima nudged me with her elbow and smiled, and I tried to get lost again on the streets of Madrid, but the portal had closed. Once the anxiety floodgates opened, I was usually done for the rest of the day. I sat there waiting out the end of the film, and when it was over, the audience gave it a standing ovation.

The festival director, Brian Dalton, stood below the screen and spoke into a microphone, letting us know that the director was here and for him to come down, and of course he was the guy I'd shushed. He spoke a little about the film and how it was inspired by his own childhood, and I got lost again thinking about how there'd never be a film made about my childhood because nothing dramatic had happened to me as a kid. I'd played basketball and got straight A's and fought with my brothers and sisters, and my dad screamed at me, and there was nothing about it worth discussing. But when I was in Mexico, important things happened. I learned to choose life over death. I found love. Inspiration. But I didn't have a childhood like this guy, filled with yearning and life and experience. I didn't run away from home and survive by stealing and hustling and convincing girls to share their beds with me. As much as I felt filled with stories, and as much as I loved film and wanted to create one someday, I knew I didn't belong here. The second I'd start telling a story, it would vanish, just as my thoughts on Madrid had vanished when this Oscar-level director started chatting behind me. As rude as he seemed, he had serious talent. I didn't. The only reason I'd been able to finish writing my book about Mexico was that I'd lived the story and had written about what I'd done and seen, even though I'd made up most of the characters and plot. But to create some story out of the blue, like *Jaws* or *Lord of the Rings* or whatever else seemed impossible to me.

To my left, Nima was in awe of the director's presence, leaning forward and smiling and applauding. She even raised her hand and asked a few questions about camera angles and types of film used and all that crap, and all I kept wondering was if they sold beer at the drink stand outside.

After, we exited the theater, and Karla introduced us to the festival's director, Brian Dalton.

"It's a pleasure meeting you, Nima," Brian said, pretty much ignoring me. "I loved your film. I wish you'd submitted it. This theater's got such incredible projectors and sound . . ."

They got lost in each other's eyes, talking about lighting and open and closed form and mise en scène, and when Karla called over the director I'd shushed, I decided to head to the drink stand and hope for the best.

They did indeed sell beer, and I bought two, pounding one quickly and taking it easy with the second. People kept introducing themselves to me as if we were at some college freshman orientation, and while it was nice for directors and actors and producers to hand me their cards and think of me as a serious artist, I was terrified they might start asking me about lighting and "film versus digital" and all that stuff Nima was always going on and on about, and then they'd know I was a hack. A hanger-on. The boyfriend. And they'd kick me out of their club forever.

As I rounded the corner to use the bathroom, I almost ran right into the director. He hardly even looked up and continued down the hall with Nima, holding her arm as she'd held mine earlier, and as they walked away smiling, I knew that was it. She was never coming back. Soon she'd be giving speeches of her own and accepting her Oscar and smiling for a brief moment while thinking of the house we'd shared together for the blink of an eye before realizing I was a duck and she was a swan.

I found a producer about my age who liked to drink as much as I did, and we sat on a couch and shared stories about partying, and he gave me his card. He and a director he'd worked with needed a ride back to Sand Beach, so I found Nima and drove us all. When they got out of the car, they said they'd call me to work on a project, and Nima glowed as she told me, "Those guys won at Tribeca. You should work on that relationship."

But I had no idea how to work on any relationship, and it only made me feel more hopeless. It was better not to get business cards and talk with future movers and shakers. Just stay on your futon and eat a microwaved pizza while imagining yourself holding an Oscar. There were too many steps between me and that Oscar. Hell, there were so many steps between *Nima* and that reality, and she was light-years ahead of me. When we got home and undressed and lay together in bed, I felt like breaking up with her. Kicking her out. Certainly she'd do a lot better without me. I talked a lot of crap about getting away from teaching and being a star and all that, but the second I entered the star arena, I folded like a shirt at JCPenney.

But none of those people you spoke to seemed all that different from you, Jay. Yeah, they knew all that technical crap about film, but when you were telling that producer stories about Mexico, he seemed fascinated. He said he wanted to do a feature on them. Maybe you already *are* one of those people. They treated you as if you were. Don't they say fake it till you make it?

But I'm so sick of faking everything. Faking teaching. Faking being a boyfriend. Faking that I'm happy and not completely terrified all the fucking time.

Nima rubbed her hand down my stomach and grabbed a handful of dick, and I flipped around, got her on top of me, and we licked each other until we both came. She turned away from me and fell asleep, and I knew we'd never be close again.

Part II

Chapter 15

At lunch a few days later, I told Karla that Nima and Brian Dalton were getting together for dinner that night.

"Yeah, he kept going on and on about how great she is," Karla said. "He really supports her."

"Yeah, *supports*," I said.

Doreen tried setting me up with a woman she'd met at the supermarket, and I wanted to scream.

That night, I ate a burrito and watched TV alone. Nima came home later than she'd said she would, and she just looked . . . happy.

"I'm moving to LA," she said, as a smile burst across her face.

"Oh . . ." was all I could say.

"Come with me." She walked over and kissed my cheek.

"I, uh, gotta teach—"

"You hate teaching. Let's go. Now's the time."

It wasn't, though. For her, maybe, but certainly not for me.

"Yeah, probably," I said. "But, you know, I just signed that one-year lease a few months back."

"Break it."

"And it's a pain to set up the electric and Internet and all that again."

The light in her eyes went out, and all she said was, "Oh . . ."

In bed that night, she said, "Matt really wants to work with you, and I say you do it. Do whatever he wants. If he wants you to move sandbags, move sandbags, and smile. That's how you move up in this business. Start from the bottom and work your way up. You can learn while doing."

"Yeah." I rolled over and went to sleep.

A week later, she was gone. I couldn't even open the cabinet, seeing all the spices she'd bought. I gave away all the spider plants except for the one in the bathroom. When she left, she ripped a hole in me that I fell into hard, and even though she kept calling and asking me to move down there with her, it only made it worse. Soon, she'd stop calling. It made me hate LA. Made me hate my dreams. Made me miss waking up with her hair in my face. Made me miss missing her all day at work. Our dreams consumed the reality of our love.

Weeks after the film fest, I was still exhausted from talking to all those "yeah, bro, it's a genre-bending film unlike any you've ever seen" people, and I knew this wasn't normal. Other people had energy to do this shit on a daily basis. If one festival could destroy me like this, how would I ever survive taking meetings and calling an agent and going out to lunches and for drinks? There was only one way to get back to Nima, and that was directly through the center of me.

The neighbors in the apartment complex behind mine were having what sounded like a frat party one weekday evening, and their music and screaming shook my walls, windows, and brain. I took a mandatory bath, but I couldn't relax with all the noise, so I cut it short. I microwaved a burrito for dinner but my stomach was killing me, so I threw it out after only a few bites.

Doug called for about the twentieth time since I'd gotten off work that day. He'd been calling and calling over the last few weeks, but I never responded. He left voicemails, and I knew that if I listened to them, I'd end up wandering back to him, so I deleted them before I lost my resolve.

I shut off my phone and headed to the beach. I didn't know what I was looking for—I just knew I was looking for *something*—

and I followed my instincts, leading me along the sand and then to the cliffs near the pier. I passed the tweakers and junkies, took off my shoes, and walked along the smooth rocks sticking above the ocean. I rounded a corner and heard a man's voice and saw lights flickering inside of a small cave in the cliffs. I was terrified, but something about the voice soothed me, so I continued walking along the slippery stones until I was at the entrance of the cave. The inside was lit up by candles set in holders attached to the walls, which dripped water.

"Ahh, I knew it was you," the Frog said, sitting on a boulder. He had a deep, relaxing voice and a calm demeanor.

"How'd you know?" I approached him.

"Who else would it be?"

"Whaddya mean?"

"I mean, I've been watching you and waiting for you to visit me since you moved here with that bonehead friend of yours last year."

"You know about him?"

"I've watched that guy get into so many fights it makes me dizzy. So much aggression. You're not like him, but I knew it'd take you a while to find your way over here. I tried showing you the way a few times, but you weren't ready yet."

"Ready for what?"

"To drop the significant weight you've been carrying since you were a kid."

"What weight?"

"You know what weight. Here, take a seat." He pointed at a smooth boulder beside him shaped like a chair; it had an indentation in the center for my ass and back, as if millions of others had sat there since the beginning of time.

Immediately, I knew what this was and didn't hold back. "All these fuckers out here. All these assholes and phonies and meatheads and shit-talkers. They're killin' me. There's no place on this Earth you can just go and relax, ya know?"

"I do—"

"And they expect you to hold a job and fight traffic and work and work and work until your back bends and your knees ache and you keel over and they just dig a hole and toss you in, no chance at ever finding love or enlightenment. Everybody just leaves you. Or they stay put and *you* leave *them*. They go up, you go down. You go left, they dash right. I think the drugs and drinking have rotted my brain. I think I've hit the point of no return. But what even is return, ya know? What am I returning to? Where have I *been*, ya feel me?" I went on and on like that for a good ten minutes. I knew I wasn't making any sense, but it was almost as if he could understand everything, and when I stopped talking he said, "Well," and smiled.

I wanted to smile, but I was in it now. The point of no return. I was well beyond casual folksy smiles and platitudes about the weather. I *was* the weather, and I hadn't even begun dumping monsoon rains.

"I've heard this story a thousand times," he said.

"What story?"

"Your story."

"So, there are other people like me?"

"You could fill the Rose Bowl with 'em."

"So, I'm not alone?"

"Not anymore—that is, not if you don't want to be."

"I don't. Nima's gone, and Mariposa's gone, and Mom went away one day to work and never came back even though she did, and Dad was gone even as he sat right there in front of me."

"You were abandoned as a child. All that you're saying is related. You jump from point to point, raising your voice and cursing out all the 'phonies' and 'posers' and whoever else, but your real beef started at home when you were a kid."

"But my parents were always around. I mean, I was lucky—"

"You just said your parents weren't there even when they were."

"Oh, I was just bullshittin' you. I mean, words don't really mean anything."

"Words can do far more than you know."

"I talk all kinds of shit."

"I believe you. Tell me more about your childhood."

"What's to tell? I had a normal and happy childhood. Nothing crazy. I played basketball and got good grades and had a big family and my parents loved me, and even though my head was filled with chaos and panic, it was all my own fault. I was never good enough for God or the priests or whoever, and they punished me for it."

"I need to hear more about this."

So I told him. As I spoke, I got deeper and deeper into it, until he rocked me with the truth I'd always been searching for on all those long, sweaty, desperate US highways and dusty Mexican roads, and now on this drug-infested beach. "You're the victim of severe child abuse, and on top of it, you've got obsessive-compulsive disorder, along with general anxiety, panic disorder, PTSD, and major depression."

"What the fuck? You're not listening. I said I had a *happy* childhood."

"Jay, you just described a horror story to me. You call getting beaten by your father while your mother turned a blind eye 'a happy childhood'?"

"Hey, fuck you, man! You don't know shit."

"You told me yourself."

"I had great parents! See, that's the fuckin' problem with this country. Everybody wants to blame someone else."

"How did your father's aggression make you feel?"

"Shitty. I mean, it's probably why I'm always getting into fights."

The Frog gave me a knowing look. "See?"

"Whoa…" Instantly, I got rocked with this feeling of tremendous relief but also tremendous shame. Honor thy father and mother!

"It's okay, Jay. Your parents can love you and still hurt you. You can love your parents and be angry at them. Let the feelings come and don't judge or censor them."

So I did, and they hit me hard. "Y-you said OCD, right? But, I'm, like, the messiest person alive. They're always on my case about it at work."

"OCD has nothing to do with organization. It's a brain disorder that's quite similar to autism. Whereas most people are able to turn off their stove and faucet, then lock the door and head off to work, someone with OCD gets stuck, obsessing that if they leave the stove on, planes will drop out of the sky, cities will burn, their families will get into horrible car accidents, and they'll compulsively check it fifty, a hundred, a thousand times, while singing certain songs or counting to a certain number, until they feel some temporary relief and they're able to walk away. But the OCD never walks away. The more you perform these compulsions, the greater control the OCD has over you. The only way to stop it is to stop performing the compulsions and deal with the anxiety head-on, which sounds easy, but to someone with OCD, it's like asking them to chew with their ear or smell with their armpit. It seems impossible. And life then seems impossible, which is probably where your depression comes from. You've been self-medicating with the booze and the pot, and the constant travel gets you out of your head for a time, until it catches up and you start getting nervous again and need to flee. Really, it's all quite common for people with your disorder."

I didn't say anything. I was overwhelmed that this Frog could know so much about me, see so many truths, after only speaking with me for an hour or so. As much as I wanted to curse him out and tell him what a dumbass he was, I knew he was right, and I burst into tears. "I'm such a bad person. I've done so many horrible things. I've hurt everybody. Carolynn and Diane and Nima and Mariposa and Mom. I'm alone. I deserve to be alone. I don't know how I even have a job."

He handed me some tissues. All my life, guys would call me gay or a fag if I cried or looked like I was about to. But the Frog was cool with it, and I felt comfortable to let it all out. I felt a tremendous release of tension in my shoulders and lower back, and my brain felt warm and calm, despite my tears. I'd spoken with so many charlatans and phony healers and quacks, who'd thrown me out of their offices because I couldn't relax enough for them to help me relax. I'd searched for so many panaceas and secret elixirs hidden in nature's mystery, and had always come up short. I'd tried drugs and booze and fucking and fighting, but none of it worked.

But an hour with the Frog made me feel closer to myself and to the world than I ever had before. It seemed like a miracle.

"How long will it take to fix me?" I said.

"Years. Maybe a decade. Maybe more. You're right. While I've seen many people with anxiety disorders, yours is particularly bad. Quite frankly, I'm impressed at how well you function in society given what you've been through. You've never had any medical help, taken any medication, or had any assistance from your parents. The fact that you're even alive right now is incredible. You should be proud of yourself. There are so many healthy people who can't hold a job, yet you're doing it with a significant handicap."

"I feel pretty good right now. Are you sure it'll take years?"

"Raise your arm."

I did.

"How does that feel?" he said.

"When I lift my arms or legs or whatever, parts of my body have to tense up in order to balance me out. If I want to raise my right arm, my left thigh and shoulder and neck get so tense, almost like they're wood or bone."

"And what's that telling you?"

"That it's probably gonna take years to get the tension levels low enough for my body to function correctly."

"I'm willing to put in the time to help you heal if you're willing to do the same."

"I-I'm moving to LA soon to be an actor. Maybe we can do a few sessions until I leave though."

"I really think you should be on medication. I'm going to send you to a psychiatrist."

"Oh, no thanks. Any drugs other than weed freak me the fuck out, and even weed has been too much for me lately."

"How do you feel right now?"

"Better than usual."

"And how do you feel usually?"

"Exhausted. Exhausted doesn't even begin to describe it. My brain always feels like it's being strangled. I have horrible aches and pains all over my body. I'm constantly flooded with anxiety. I mean, I can fucking feel it cruising up my back, and it tickles my armpits and flows into my brain. My feet hurt. My eyes are so sensitive to light I get headaches when I walk outside. My stomach is always in knots. I feel like I can't even taste food or smell smells. Nothing excites me. I'm fucking pissed off all the time. I mean, I'm fucking furious. I'm worried maybe one of these days when I get into a fight, I'll just keep punching and punching until I've punched shards of skull into the concrete. I guess I feel like I'm already dead, and it gets worse every fucking day."

"You have no idea what normal feels like. The healing journey isn't like a marathon. You don't run and run until you cross a finish line and it's over. You're going to slowly heal, having successes and failures along the way. The successes will keep you moving forward, and the failures will teach you more than you've ever learned from anyone else in your life. More than I could ever teach you. All of that exhaustion you speak of can go away forever. You can get sleep and feel relaxed and not get flooded with anxiety, as you say. You have no idea what good feels like, but once you do, you'll never go back."

I left there filled with emotion. Guys weren't allowed to feel emotion, but speaking with the Frog legitimized my suffering in a way that made me feel worthy of experiencing everything swirling around my insides. Having the Frog on my side made me feel more manly for having experienced these emotions, not less. I probably couldn't have done this in Buffalo or Miami or maybe even Mexico. But California seemed like the spot for healing, and as much as I wanted to run screaming down to LA, I knew I was in Soul City for the long haul. I knew that the only way to unlock the actor inside of me was to free myself of the tension keeping the best parts of me hidden inside. I also knew I'd be at Cody Cares for much longer than planned.

But as much as I wanted to act and play music and write, I wanted to be able to sit on that stone in the Frog's cave and be able to lift my right arm and have my body balance itself naturally. To be able to use this beautiful vehicle of a body for the first time. It became as bright and clear a dream as any other. To walk down the street and feel okay. To step on Dr. Tom's scale and have it read zero, showing my left and right sides in perfect alignment. To lie on my bed with both shoulders touching the mattress. To fuck without feeling like it was a chore.

The whole night, I had that sick feeling in my stomach that you get when you find out your girlfriend is cheating on you and you know you have to end it. But this feeling was so much stronger. It wasn't as though I was breaking up with a woman, but with my reality. After allowing the Frog's words to spiral deeper inside of me, I realized that I'd been obeying—worshiping—a whole series of constructed myths and false truths since I was a terrified kid, and I knew I needed to break up with them. I knew I had to break up with the philosophies that pushed me out onto all those highways. That had always told me I was never good enough. That I was too stupid or ugly. That made me worship Daddy God and Mommy Goddess. That made me absorb all of the world's suffering in a desperate attempt to filter it through me and turn it into pure, driven energy. To solve all the world's problems. To sacrifice myself for my family, who felt like anchors pulling me underwater.

I had to break up with all of that. Let it go. And this literally affected every aspect of my existence. I realized that my "truths" and emotions were tied into every part of my life, from how to turned on the kitchen faucet to how I opened the front door. How I hung the towels in my bathroom. How I shot a basketball and made a turkey sandwich. Everything was tied to some memory—to some reality and emotion that I needed to let go of.

Remember when you were a kid and you watched Mom hang the towels after doing the laundry and you always thought it was so silly to dry something that would get wet again soon, and maybe this was why she was always so sad, because she dried things that were made to absorb wetness? Remember when Dad warned you to be careful when working with electricity right before he shocked himself fixing that light switch, and you always flinched turning on any light? Let it go. He should have cut the power to the right spot. It wasn't your fault he screamed and carried on about how shitty of a helper you were. He did that to himself.

It was easier to let go of the Dad memories and emotions than it was with the Mom ones. I'd died for her so many times throughout my life. So many times I would have given everything just to make her happy. You can't die for her anymore, Jay. She makes her own decisions. She can walk through that door anytime she wants, just as you did. She didn't say anything when you told her goodbye forever. She didn't run outside and ask what was wrong and listen to you. She just turned around, went back into the kitchen, and you headed into the blizzard, pushing through until you arrived in paradise.

Everything had an emotion, and I needed to erase all of them and start over. Hit the reset button. Start completely new. All I'd known was wrong. "Suck it up" was bullshit! "Be a man!" was another hollow, dangerous slogan. "There's nothing wrong with you!" "You think you got it bad, take a look at those starving kids in Africa, then see if you're still complaining." But, Dad, I had monsters in my head. Real monsters, and I know that now. God's world has always made me feel like the Devil. But the world of science has shown me that it's just a disease and not me. *I'm* not the problem. I'm gonna beat this. I'll do whatever it takes, but I'm gonna feel okay. I'm sorry, Mom, but I need to let you go. I'm sorry, Carolynn and Diane and Rebecca and Jeremy and Dan. I might never be able to speak to you again. Dad, you fucking lunatic! I should punch you in the face. But I'm done with you, too. Done with all of you. Here in the California sun, I'll finally find my family.

I had trouble sleeping at first, mind racing to Buffalo and back, but when I did sleep, it was of better quality than usual, and I woke up in the morning feeling somewhat refreshed. The sick feeling stayed with me all morning, and I continued to break up with my cereal and milk and car shifter and all the cars I passed on the highway and the way I parked and how I pulled the door handle to walk into Cody Cares. When I saw Karla, I wanted to tell her everything, but she was busy talking with students. I screamed at her with my eyes, letting her know what had happened, but what could she know from a look? You have to stop believing you're somehow magical because of all this. You have to stop believing the fantasy that others see you as a god because of it. It's just anxiety. It was just bad parenting. You give Karla a look, and she might simply think you're hungover. You need to be okay with being alone with your misery and stop dragging other people into it, romanticizing it and them in the process.

The kids came in, and I greeted them as usual, but I was so emotionally drained that I had a difficult time smiling, or showing any emotion at all. I felt like a zombie, moving twice as slowly as usual, yet a hundred times more aware of each step. A girl laughed when I missed the "play" button on the DVD player, but instead of instantly reacting, I had an epiphany. I could feel the anxiety and chemicals rush up my spine, and I realized that I needed this anxiety, almost as if it were a fuel enabling me to participate in everyday life. My natural speed was so much slower than average that I must have developed the anxiety to help me cope. When someone spoke to me or asked me to come over or handed me my change at the hardware store, the anxiety shocked me into responding at an appropriate speed. But rather than speed through a response to this girl, I tried to relax and let the fear flow through me. I realized that part of the reason why I always felt so out of control was that anxiety was calling the shots. That when those chemicals raced up my spine and I blurted out some response, I was only doing it to get through the moment without anyone thinking I was crazy. Without them laughing at the speed of my inner processor. And after so many decades of responding this way—of the chemicals being in total control—I had no idea who I actually was without it calling the shots.

Maybe this is why some people are able to respond so well under pressure. *They're* in control, not the fear. I rarely gave myself time to think before I responded, but I tried it that day, and I decided not to respond at all.

"Wow, is everything okay, Mr. S?" the girl said, getting more laughs from the class.

I said nothing and imagined the anxiety river stopping. I experienced several life-changing breakthroughs during that video on French philosophy's influence on the American Revolution, rearranging how I saw myself and the world around me. I thought about writing song lyrics or poetry, but I knew this was something I needed to feel and not write down. I knew that if I wanted to truly heal, I was going to need to slow down the pace of my life and to stop trying so hard for everything. That if I kept jumping from town to town, bar to bar, fight to fight, I'd never find the life inside of me. I could feel that new life down there, and it was growing stronger with every "yes" I said when I meant yes, and "no" I said when I meant no, and so when I told that girl I was going to call her mother if she didn't knock it off and then she called me a jerk, I calmly picked up the phone and passed it to her as her mom screamed loud enough for the whole class to hear.

But something about those screams also got inside of me. Suddenly, I saw myself in all those kids' faces. It made my heart ache to think how many of them were going back to parents who called them stupid or fat or lazy. It terrified me to think that if I continued down this healing path, I could no longer deny my responsibility to protect these kids, and all the others. That I was training to be a superhero. To be like Ms. Kefana or Gandhi or Martin Luther King Jr. That maybe, someday, I really could save the world.

But not today. Today, I needed to rest. I knew Karla could see it in my eyes, and when some of my second-period boys called me a zombie, thinking I couldn't hear, Karla told them to knock it off.

Karla, you have no idea what you're doing for me right now. I needed someone, and you sensed this and helped me, knowing exactly what to do. You just *knew*. How are you so powerful? How are you so smart? I want to be like you, Karla, and I'm so glad I get to work beside you. To watch you in action. To learn from you. To grow alongside of you.

Nima had called me the night before, but I waited until lunch to call her back. I stepped outside and told her about my meeting with the Frog, thinking that she of all people would get it, but she said, "That's crazy. There's nothing wrong with you. You're just being lazy. Call Matt and tell him you'll help him with his short. Go carry those sandbags."

I told her that carrying sandbags would kill my back, but she didn't understand what I really meant. She said, "If you wanna make it in this business, you need to break your back." I told her I wasn't breaking my back for anyone anymore and hung up. I'd had enough of the you're-not-a-real-man bullshit people were always shoveling on me whenever I told them about the pains in my neck and knees and heart and soul. Whenever I shed a tear, and they backed toward the door. But Karla wasn't like that. Neither was Ms. Kefana. I knew I could tell them everything, unlike Nima, who had seemed so wise and compassionate before. I knew then I would never join her in LA. I needed to find someone else to share my dreams with.

Earlier that day, some of my senior boys had made dick jokes, and instead of laughing, I'd said that the jokes were "inappropriate," making me feel as if I were some fifty-year-old nerd teacher. They looked at me strangely, as if to say, "I thought you were one of us, man?" but I was tired of playing a role and told them to knock it off. I always thought that the only way to stop the kids from turning on me was to show that I was one of them, but maybe being one of them was my problem. I didn't want to be an abused kid anymore.

I continued breaking up with reality when I pissed and when I walked to my car and checked my mail at my apartment and turned on the light in my living room. The sick feeling was still with me. It made my jaw weak, as if I was going to puke at any moment, and I was dizzy and confused. Though I knew I shouldn't, I Googled "anxiety medication" and read the horror stories. Being a hypochondriac, it was best for me to just take what I was prescribed and not ask about side effects. Once I knew them, I'd be sure that my liver had been damaged or that I'd had a mild seizure when I sneezed or that my hands were trembling and I was losing control of my muscles, and reading about all the horrible shit that happened to people who'd taken anxiety meds terrified me. More than anything, I was terrified of seizures. The thought that at any moment I could fall to the ground and start convulsing uncontrollably was worse than anything other than schizophrenia or a stroke, and it meant that I'd never again have autonomy over my life. I wouldn't be able walk upstairs or drive a car or backpack through Europe without the fear always in my brain that I'd lose control again.

Also, I was horrified by the fact that, if I took one of these medications, I wouldn't be able to drink. I'd been drinking heavily since high school and had tried to stop several times, but it was useless. I needed alcohol; that was a simple truth.

The next day after work, I waited until it was dark before I headed back to the cave. I could have sworn people were following me, watching me as I walked along the wet boulders and looked for the firelight leaping out of the darkness. Once they knew what I was doing, they'd drag me into the street, douse me in Everclear, and set me on fire, cheering and condemning my soul to Hell—Tuyet, Kelly, Remi, and all the others joining in.

I told the Frog about the research I'd done on anxiety medication.

"It's far riskier for you to continue without it," he said. "You mentioned feeling as if you'd gone crazy as a kid. Don't you want to get away from that?"

"D-don't talk about all that."

"Why not? I think that you've experienced psychosis several times in your life—"

"I'm not crazy!"

"I didn't say you were. And what's 'crazy' anyway? I'll bet some people with schizophrenia would tell us *we're* the crazy ones."

"I don't wanna talk about that. All my life, my greatest fear was that I'd slip into insanity. I've never heard voices or anything, but I've felt as though I was floating away so many times, especially on drugs."

"Look, your stress levels have been so high that, I believe, they've caused you to wander over into the other side a few times. But look, you've always come back. Honestly, I think someday you might see this as a wonderful thing. You've seen things most people never have. Things like this have the ability to make us stronger and more compassionate in ways that others might not understand. It's probably why you're so good with troubled kids."

"Am I gonna go crazy?"

"If you were going to go crazy—and again, I hate that word—it would have happened long ago, when your OCD first came on. I feel horrible for that poor little kid who had no one to help him. You must have gone through so much darkness and pain."

"Y-you have no idea." I wanted to tell him about the Dark Thoughts, but knew that if I did, he'd probably tell the others where I was and laugh as they lit me ablaze.

"Your parents should have taken you to a psychologist immediately."

"Yeah, but there was something in it—something beautiful. When the thoughts first came on, it felt as if all the knowledge of the world was now mine. I felt . . . infinite."

"Tell me more."

"No."

"Why not?"

"Who the fuck are you anyway?"

"I'm a friend."

"Ha! I got a lotta friends. Friends who left me passed out in alleys by dumpsters or out in the woods. I don't need any more friends."

"What's wrong?"

"Say I tell you something that's not so cute. What happens then?"

"Whatever you say stays here in this cave."

"Oh yeah? Whatever I say, huh?"

"Yep, that's how it works."

"So, what if I say fuck you? What if I call your grandma a dirty fuckin' whore? What if I pull down my pants and slap you across the face with my dick?"

"Go ahead, whip it out. I've seen it all."

"You're a fucking little bitch. Maybe I should just step on you, huh? You think anyone would care? You think anybody would give a shit if they walked by a pile of frog guts on a rock?"

"Probably not."

"You're not scared?"

"Of what?"

"That I'll do it."

"Again, if you were gonna do it, it would have happened a long time ago. So let's start there."

I shut my eyes and the thoughts rocked me hard. Visions of horror and madness ripped across my eyes, and I was sure he could see everything. "What if I killed somebody?"

"Did you?"

"I dunno. Honestly, I don't know. Since we last spoke, I keep getting these visions of a body lying in a burning pile of garbage way up on a mountain. I'm just a kid, but I'm watching this body burning. And my dad is dumping on more gasoline."

"Did this actually happen?"

"Honestly, I don't know. Maybe I killed someone and my dad covered it up."

"Our psyches are extremely powerful and can help us repress some truly terrifying things. Do you believe it happened?"

"When I was a kid, I got really spooked after hearing about this redheaded boy who lured a kid off to the woods and crushed his head with a rock. He killed him and buried him and it haunted me. I mean, it fucking haunted me. I kept obsessing that I was gonna do the same. I hurt some kid really badly after church one day. Maybe I killed him. You think that's possible? You think that's why I'm so fucked in the head?"

"Jay, if you killed some kid after church, it would have made national news. I never heard anything about that. Did you?"

"No."

"The whole city would have been talking about it."

"What about the body in the woods?"

"That body is a symbol. Let the image rise to the surface and breathe it out. Your dad didn't cover anything up other than your illness, and that body he was burying was you. The gasoline is figurative. He was feeding the flames of the guilt and horror killing you."

"Sometimes when I'm walking along the cliffs, I feel like if I just let down my guard, maybe I'll start pushing people over the edge. Maybe, when I'm driving, I'll just turn onto the sidewalk and mow people down."

"How does that make you feel?"

"Horrified. Straight horrified."

"Do you want to hurt someone?"

"Of course not!"

"Well, you won't."

"How do you know?"

"Because all of this is a symptom of OCD. They're called intrusive thoughts, and they make you obsess over disturbing and horrific things like killing kids or pushing people over cliffs."

"Does that make me a psycho? I mean, am I, like, a serial killer or something?"

"Not at all. People who have intrusive thoughts never act on them because they, like you, don't want to hurt anyone, unlike psychopaths who could hurt someone and feel no remorse. It's all a common symptom of your disease."

"So I'm not a killer?"

"Sorry to burst your bubble."

"Oh my god . . ." I almost passed out. These Dark Thoughts had haunted my life since they came on when I was nine or ten, and I always thought I'd grow up to be Ted Bundy or Jeffrey Dahmer. Once, I watched a documentary on murderers in prison, and some of them spoke about how they'd obsessed over killing their victims, and I knew I'd be in there with them someday. How can you focus on high school English or asking girls to the prom or working at Taco Bell with those kinds of thoughts tormenting your brain?

Suddenly, I was filled with rage against my parents. How could they have let this happen? The Frog mentioned that all of this was treatable, and if they'd just taken me to a psychologist, I would have known I wasn't a killer. Those motherfuckers!

I felt even more weight off my shoulders and cried again. Everything I knew was wrong. I knew I was in this for the long haul now, and that I'd have to sacrifice my last bit of youth in order to truly heal. I could no longer deny this. In two sessions, the Frog had shown me things about myself that no one else in twenty-seven years of life had shown me. How could I have gotten this far without knowing such simple but powerful truths?

As I walked home, I felt even sicker than last time. The first meeting ripped off the bandage, and now we were cleaning the festering cut, and it stung like hell. We'd removed the lid from my psyche, and the ancient evil began making its way to the surface. On that walk home, I found myself screaming at demons in my head, arguing with my parents, crying out loud. People must have thought I was insane, but they were probably used to seeing this kind of crap at the beach. Maybe this is the real reason why I moved here. Why I felt I needed to be *here* so badly. Maybe it wasn't to smooth my transition to street life, but rather, to smooth my transition to reality.

Chapter 16

I practically ran home and locked the door behind me, and I got rushed with horrific images of gargoyles and monsters and bloody screaming demons. I found myself stalking memories through my apartment, playing out scenes in my head, talking to myself and responding and flailing my body around, falling on the floor and leaping back up, and continuing on. Something deep inside of me knew that this pain was a punishment for my sins from a previous lifetime. Karma was evening out the score. For years, in dreams, I'd had flashes that I was some Wild West outlaw in a past life. That I, like Billy the Kid, had found a way to rationalize killing. That it was "all *their* fault! I *had* to kill them!"

But now it was catching up to me. Those rationalizations had infected my innocent childhood soul, making me identify with criminals and lowlifes and scumbags at the deepest levels of my being.

But if this truly is karma, perhaps I can make it right. I need to let it all come to me. Don't hold anything back. Feel all the pain. Listen to the criticisms of all the demons and saints. Accept responsibility for your sins. Know—really *know*—that what you did was wrong. It's the only way to salvation.

I was terrified to move in this direction. Terrified to let down my guard. I'd built so many fortress walls inside of myself, but the only way to heal was to knock them down and let come what may.

Standing and sweating and screaming in my bright bathroom and looking in the mirror at a hazy image I had of myself, I knew I had to make peace with death. That knocking down these walls could finally cause me to go insane. But I couldn't keep them up any longer. The other way wasn't working either. The other way might cause me to actually hurt someone in a bar brawl or a drunk-driving accident or by chanting at them to "CHUG! CHUG! CHUG!" until their face went purple and the life passed from their eyes.

So I stood in that bathroom and let it all come up.

Had I really seen a body? Did I kill someone? I'm so sorry! I'm so, so sorry. I don't want to hurt anyone. I want to be good. I promise, if You grant me forgiveness, I'll make something of my life. I'll discover how to understand my suffering and show others how to heal as well. I'll be an instrument of Thy peace, Lord! Let me heal. Give me Your worst. I can take it. I can take it now that I'm a man.

After lord knows how long, I moved to the bedroom and lay in bed, curled in the fetal position and shaking and crying and sweating. I probably looked like a heroin addict, days after his last fix. I hallucinated and spoke to myself and after several hours, I was able to fall asleep.

When I woke up in the morning, I felt ill—but it was a good kind of ill. The kind where I'd passed something terrible through my body, and now it was time to heal. Thank God I never smoked meth! Thank God I never shot H! I felt as if the good and evil inside me were on a scale and both weighed the same. With track marks on my arms, however, the evil might have had a little too much weight, tipping the whole thing over into the Darkness.

But I woke up in the bright Soul City sunshine, waves crashing onto the shore a few blocks away. The birds chirping overhead. I could hear them that morning.

I wanted to tell Karla everything. While lying and shaking and crying in bed the night before, I'd felt that she was there with me, bringing me tissues and water and rubbing my back. Camarin too. She was the one who'd convinced me to get help, and even though she wasn't there in body, she was with me in spirit. I felt her strength inside of me, guiding me along.

I had a hard time getting ready for work, and I forgot my belt and chose mismatched socks, and some of the kids laughed when they saw this, but Karla stepped in again. I felt even more like a zombie that morning, and was breaking up with even more of my reality. I didn't think I'd be able to continue working in this shape. But at one point, Ms. Kefana came over between classes and told me what a great job I was doing, and how happy she was to work with me. That made the scales tip even more into the light, and I knew that with her and Karla beside me, I could continue to work while taking such a dizzying emotional journey.

In fact, when Ms. Kefana spoke with me again after school, I told her all about it—minus the stuff about serial killers and crushing kids' heads with rocks, of course—and like the Frog, instead of cursing me to hell, she just smiled and said, "Welcome to the club."

I spent the afternoon and evening in bed, shaking and sweating and getting rocked by more hallucinations, and only pulled myself away to piss and heat a can of soup for dinner. I knew the Frog was right. I'd have to try medication, but even though I wasn't yet ready, I began preparing for it. The whole "no alcohol" thing seemed impossible, so I decided to go at it with the same energy I'd gone at training for basketball when I was younger. I'd do an hour on the treadmill, then spend another hour running suicides and seventeens, then I'd jump rope and do plyometrics for another hour, and finish it off with pushups, dips, and pull-ups. I tried not to think of how many minutes or reps were left, and instead focused on my breathing and form. I focused more on the process and not the product.

So, that Friday, I shut off my phone, locked my door, emptied my fridge of beer and cupboards of liquor, and tried to go one night without drinking. I'd gotten drunk on pretty much every single Friday for the last ten years or so, but with all these changes inside of me and the Frog and Camarin and Karla on my side, I felt as if I could actually take a night off now. I sat on my futon watching

The Office, but my mind was elsewhere. The voices in my head screamed, GO! GET OUT THERE! THEY'RE ALL PARTYING WITHOUT YOU! GO! SHE'S THERE, TOO! THE LOVE OF YOUR LIFE IS WAITING TO MEET YOU, BUT YOU'RE TOO MUCH OF A PUSSY TO MAN UP AND FIND HER! HURRY! IF YOU DON'T GO, I'LL MAKE THE EVIL HAUNT YOU SO BADLY YOU WON'T EVER BE ABLE TO SLEEP AGAIN!

Holy shit! The Frog was right! I'm terrified of being abandoned. Part of why I need to drink so much is the fear of missing out. That everyone is on the boat and if you don't get there soon, it'll set sail without you and never come back. If you don't get out there, you'll miss all the jokes and fun and you'll miss out on meeting the love of your life. On meeting your band. You'll stay alone forever.

The Frog was also right about hypervigilance. I kept checking the windows and door, jerking my head involuntarily and feeling my body screaming at me to GET OFF THIS FUCKING FUTON! GO SEE WHO'S OUT THERE! A KILLER? A FRIEND? Maybe this was why I lived in such a world of fantasy. I was always expecting the best and worst waiting around every corner. I was always ready, and it exhausted me. Maybe it was why I always felt so paranoid. Why even when I was alone in a room, I always felt someone else was there, watching me. Judging me.

I let the urges and screaming voices come and tried to understand them as best I could, and I learned more about my alcoholism that night than ever before. After a few hours, I realized that I *could* make it the whole night without running out to meet Tuyet and Kelly and the others at the bar, and I tried it again the next day. I woke up feeling nervous that I'd give in, but by around dinnertime, I still hadn't taken a sip. I hadn't yet turned on my phone, and I hadn't gone outside at all, not even to check my mail. I knew if I opened that door, I'd race off to the bar. After eating PB&J for dinner, I pulled Kahlil Gibran's *The Prophet* from my bookshelf. I'd bought it weeks earlier when Tuyet and I had stopped into a bookstore near the beach. She'd wanted to buy more incense, and of all the books, I knew I needed *The Prophet*—I just didn't know why.

I made some tea and played Cat Stevens's *Tea for the Tillerman*, and after the first page, I knew this was what I'd always needed. I devoured the book, understanding it on the most profound of levels, feeling Gibran's wisdom, love, and compassion filling my entire being. My eyes dripped tears as the music and poetry tipped the scales even further into the light. I finished the book and knew I'd not only be able to stop drinking for that weekend, but that I was going to have the power to change my entire life as well. I believed in the power and beauty of words. Gibran's words had such an effect on me, and now I had the responsibility to learn how to spread that same message with my own. I felt weak and all-powerful at once. I was able to see. To breathe. To release.

But this release had side effects. All of the changes in my brain were also affecting my body. The Frog said that when the OCD first hit me as a kid, it overwhelmed my brain so much that my body took on the stress, and even after all these decades, it was still deforming me enough to make doctors think I had scoliosis. My hips and spine were twisted and body listed to one side, and to the naked eye, scoliosis was a valid conclusion. But as I released the guilt and shame and anguish from my mind, my muscles started behaving strangely. They'd become accustomed to operating in such a tense system, and I was beginning to see that they *needed* this tension. My body felt confused, and I was dropping things and bumping into doorframes and lamps and my hand-eye coordination was crap, so when I woke up in the middle of the night, choking on my own spit, I knew this was the price to pay for healing. For a few seconds, I couldn't breathe—my lungs felt full of water and a dark, ominous feeling spread from my brain through my chest. I knew I was dying, but when I'd first started this healing process, I'd made my peace with death, so I didn't panic. I was prepared for it. I said goodbye to my parents and said, "Hello, God, if you really are up there."

After such a beautiful evening, listening to Cat Stevens's music and reading Kahlil Gibran's words, I was ready. Ready to take this profound knowledge with me to my next life. To some distant planet in another galaxy. I'd already cut my earthly ties, and I wasn't afraid to go. I'd been a fool to think I'd make it past twenty-seven anyway, and soon I'd join my heroes in this other world. Come, Death. Take me. It's okay. I won't fight you anymore. I'm ready. I truly am.

But after about ten seconds, I started coughing, and continued coughing, clearing my lungs, and after a few moments, I was certain I was going to live. But I also knew that if I went back to sleep, I might not survive another time. I'd already died so many, many times in my life that I knew the only way to go was forward. The only thing to do was sleep. My only regret was not yet having published my book. Not yet having produced the hundreds of songs playing nonstop in my head. Not yet having acted in some beautiful film like *The Motorcycle Diaries* or *Eternal Sunshine of the Spotless Mind*. That night, I realized the only way I could ever create something so beautiful was to let it all go. To stop holding on to it so tightly. To sacrifice my need to create in the hope that doing so would allow me to overcome the creative and spiritual blockages inside of me. Just like with the hypervigilance, I realized I never stopped pushing myself to create a masterpiece, and I needed a break. I needed to realize that John Lennon and Marlon Brando and Stanley Kubrick were as great as they were because they lived in the flame and were still able to sleep and eat and create. But I was trying so hard to be them that all of my energy was on my surface, beaming from my lips, shining from the top of my head, and it needed to go deeper. I imagined creativity again as that Great River, flowing deep inside of me, and what separated me from all of the greats was that they were living in that river, breathing underwater and never leaving it, and I was living on land, behind a high wall, and every so often, I climbed that wall and took a peek at the Great River, and I knew that if I could climb down the other side of that wall and jump into that water, I could finally unlock my creative potential. But there was no other way down than to fall, and it was too high up.

So, my only option was to destroy that wall. And now I knew

that the way to destroy that wall was to walk away from it. To go inside the house and make dinner and do my laundry and grade papers and call my mother and brothers and sisters. To stop climbing and sweating and straining and to have faith that if I were truly meant to be in that river, the waters would rise, flowing over that wall and into my house, and soon, I'd be in there with all the others. Dylan once said that all of his songs already existed before he wrote them. Stephen King said that his books are artifacts he uncovers from the earth. I knew my songs and poems and books already existed, and I needed to let them find *me*. The only way to do that was to go back to sleep, trusting in my body and believing in life over death. If death took me, that was okay, but if it didn't, it was going to have to take the worst parts of me, so new life could grow.

On Sunday morning, I felt invincible. I'd made it through Friday and Saturday without drinking a sip of alcohol. The possibilities felt endless. I knew that by making it through that one weekend, I might be able to do it again, and that confidence allowed me to make it a week, then a month, then a few months. Nine years later, I haven't been drunk once.

Chapter 17

I felt lighter when I walked into work Monday morning. Cody sang the Cody Cares song, and we started first period. As I played the video and sat at my desk, I realized there was no way I would have been able to undergo such a profound change if I was still working in a public school. At a public school, you had to be *on* all the time, which would have flooded me with so much anxiety I'd never be able to relax enough to get to the root of my problems.

But at Cody Cares, I could breathe. Think. Smile. I didn't believe in fate, but I did feel that I was exactly where I needed to be, which felt a little like fate. It seemed that "fate" might simply be the ability to finally see one or more of the solutions that were always surrounding us. That our unconscious already knew these solutions and was simply pushing us along to the places where we could see them, too. My unconscious had pushed me along so many roads, and now here, in Soul City and at Cody Cares, I could see many solutions I'd never been able to see before.

It seemed the better I felt, the more I began living for the long-term rather than the short. For most of my life, I'd simply been trying to get through the minute, the hour, the day. But now, I could see beyond those short bursts and imagine myself existing in the future. Sure, I'd had dreams of acting and writing and all that, but these dreams had always felt like clouds of smoke that could be blown away at any moment. But with a solid foundation under my feet, I could think now about dinner that night. What I would do on the weekend. Think about 403b's and using my health insurance and taking my car to the mechanic. I started thinking about actual steps I could take to get down to LA—but not anytime soon.

Now, you need your rest. Now, you need to continue to heal. See where this takes you.

One of my ninth-grade boys made a crack about me being scrawny now, and even though he said he was joking, I took it to heart. I hadn't been to the gym in months. To heal, I knew I was going to have to sacrifice my body. My muscles were so tense and body so misaligned that in order to run or jump or lift heavy weights, the anxiety would have to kick in and keep me balanced and moving. Running or even turning my head too quickly flooded me with such anxiety that I didn't want to move. Also, I began to realize that the strange aches and pains I'd felt in my feet and ankles and shoulders and knees throughout my life were due to this lack of alignment. It was probably also why I put one foot far ahead of the other when shooting a basketball, and why everyone always said the baseball danced around the air when I threw it.

If I wanted to heal my body, I had to let it go, just like the music. Just like my family. Just like my friends and everything I'd ever known. But this made me terribly self-conscious. Though I'd always felt deformed and hideous, my body still often got attention, and I didn't realize what a part of my identity this was until I had to let it go. I panicked, thinking no woman would ever speak to me again. I panicked, thinking there was no way I'd ever land an acting role if I had a gut. If I wasn't athletic, then what was I? Growing up, I used to beat on kids in football and basketball who went on to become state champ quarterbacks and point guards. While they moved ahead, I plateaued, and I didn't know why, but now it seemed that due to all the stress, my body couldn't develop as theirs had. If I ever wanted to achieve greatness, I needed to hit the reset button and allow my muscles to go back to neutral, allowing me to build them back up again in a more balanced manner.

I knew this was the start of another long journey I'd maybe never see the end of, and so perhaps I was throwing away my athleticism forever. I already knew that in order to heal, I'd have to sacrifice the rest of my youth. But, with the power of the Frog and Karla and Camarin and Cat Stevens and Kahlil Gibran now on my side, I knew it was worth it. Someday I'd be swimming in that Great River as an ugly, shriveled old man, filled with endless beauty and vigor.

After lunch, Karla approached my desk. "Hey, Jay, I couldn't help but eavesdrop on your fifth period today. I didn't know what a terrible person Christopher Columbus was."

"Yeah, he was one of history's worst monsters. I think we should reconsider our approach to discussing him, focusing on perspectives that paint him in a more honest, yet still appropriate, manner." Another thing I'd picked up on: My vocabulary had changed. I was using words now like "appropriate" and "approach," which had always sounded so nerdy and dry that I'd rather punch myself in the nuts than use them. But now I was sounding like all of *them*—and I liked it. Also, prior to this great change within me, I had always spoken as quickly as possible to return to the safety of silence. But now that I had more time to think about my words, rather than force, "Yeah, that shit just ain't right," through my pie hole, I'd go with, "I agree. It just isn't appropriate." I'd even bought a book to help develop my vocabulary, and I would read it and do the activities in my downtime at work. The stillness inside of me opened up a whole new series of intellectual possibilities, and I was excited to explore areas I'd had difficulty with before, mostly due to abstractions in the material. I could remember names and dates and definitions with ease, but I always had such difficulty with theories and philosophies. But now, I wanted to learn about government and economics and law, and I bought textbooks and read them compulsively.

I wanted to cram as much knowledge into my head as I could to make up for all the brain cells I'd killed in bars and at house parties and on endless highways to nowhere. Now that I was on the path to somewhere real, I realized that the better I articulated myself, the more people respected me—at least, people in professional settings like Cody Cares. In the past, the person who punched the hardest or chugged the fastest or fucked the most women was the most respected, but Cody would never slap me up because I lumped some furious parent in the parking lot. Though I'd always felt as though I had no discernible physical form, people really could see me, and they formed opinions of me based on what on what they saw and heard. Growing up in a world where white was white one day and white was black the next, I'd never really thought much about what I was saying, but here, people seemed to care. If I gave an opinion on something and changed it five minutes later, people had a right to think I was nuts, even though this was how everyone spoke in Buffalo. I knew I needed to pay more attention to what I was saying along with why I was saying it.

I was still spending most of my free time in bed, shivering and shaking and sweating and talking to myself, but it wasn't as bad as before. In fact, that night I got the great idea to write Mariposa an email explaining everything that was happening with me, ending with me begging her to call me on Skype so she could see my eyes and know I was serious, but I deleted it before I could hit "send."

That email loosened the writing gears, but I decided against trying to capture these changes with poetry or song lyrics, and instead started keeping a daily journal. My goal was to catalog these changes in a factual and rational manner so anthropologists could someday read it and have a better idea of the day-to-day life of someone going through such a change while living in a culture that didn't understand or respect the healing journey. I got a lot of ideas for this journal during my nightly bathing sessions, which I resumed once I started spending less time shaking and shivering in bed.

As I ate dinner, I heard the neighbor to my left slam a window, and I got rocked with anxiety. The neighbor to my right slammed a cupboard as the neighbor to my left tossed what sounded like a beer bottle in the trash, making a loud thunk that traveled through the wall as if it wasn't even there.

Holy shit! Why haven't I heard these sounds before? They've been here all along. Don't think about them. If you do, you'll end up like you were as a kid, obsessing over every little noise, stuffing your ears with earplugs and screaming at the neighbors to shut up! This can't be happening now. Not when you're doing so well. The sweating and shaking sessions aren't that bad now. You're supposed to be feeling better.

It seemed that as soon as I felt better in one area, another dark area presented itself, driving me into panic. I left my burrito on the coffee table and paced in my bedroom, but the neighbors in the building next door were blasting Limp Bizkit and screaming like assholes. I shut the window and put earplugs in my ears and turned my fan on high to drown out the noise, but it was no use. I could hear the bass notes and their high-pitched laughter, and the walls began pulsating and tipping toward me.

I practically ran to the cliffs, but the Frog wasn't there. FUCK! I walked along the pier to its end, staring at the dark waves rolling in from the edge of the world, and contemplated jumping over the edge.

Do you understand now, Jay? Do you see what you've done by talking to that stupid Frog? You've ruined yourself, and you can never go back. The only way forward is over this ledge. Go ahead, take a step. If you turn around, you've got a decades-long journey ahead of you filled with the kind of torment that drove you onto this ledge just now. There's no music or poetry or perfect body waiting for you. By the time you finish this journey, you're gonna be a lonely old man. I mean, look at you! Everything's changed. You've stopped living for the moment, and now you're living for retirement. You keep going in that direction and you're never gonna be remembered.

I walked along the beach for another hour or so, and thankfully it was quiet when I got home. Still, I kept in my earplugs, stayed away from the walls, closed all the windows, and blasted my fans. I knew I wasn't going to be able to stop doing all of this until I discovered why sounds caused me such torment, and the answer to that question seemed so buried under my twisted-wooden muscles and molten-lead blood that it was going to take years to discover. Suddenly, the entire town felt as if it were right on top of me, connected to me, and nothing I did could push it away.

When I went to work the next morning, the school was much closer to home than usual. I tried not to think about it and walked inside. All of the random sounds sent panic twisting up my spine. Barry clicking his tongue while he talked on the phone; Doreen stapling papers; Ben in the back listening to music; Karla tapping her foot against her desk; the cell phone place across the street blasting music.

"How are you this morning, Mr. S?" Ms. Kefana said with a smile.

"I-I'm good." I turned away and set up for the day, trying to hide my panic. The sounds overwhelmed the hell out of me, but my muscles began to squeeze, twisting and contorting me in strange new ways, and after about an hour, I felt better. I realized then that the squeezing was my body's way of easing my mental stress—just like the Frog had said—and I knew that I'd remain tight and misaligned until I found and healed the source of this stress. I also realized that when my muscles squeezed like this, I'd get confused and irritable and sensitive to light.

Worse than the sounds, however, were the Evil Thoughts, which had been creeping up from my deepest depths to finally reach the surface. The Frog had said this would happen, so I tried to roll with it, but when a parent stopped in with his ninth-grader to let me know the kid would be out for a month due to a serious medical issue, I was hit with an overwhelming urge to scream something like, "YOU SICK LITTLE BITCH! YOU WEAK LITTLE PUSSY! YOU'RE GONNA DIE! YOU'RE GONNA DIE! YOU'RE GONNA DIE AND WE'RE ALL GONNA LAUGH!"

I tried to keep my mouth shut so the words wouldn't slip out, and just nodded and made random affirmative sounds until they left, and then I raced to the bathroom and poured sweat.

Remember, these are just intrusive thoughts. You don't believe these things. You like that kid. He's a great fucking kid. Remember how many times you've helped him after class? The times you patted him on the back and told him how smart he was and how lucky you were to work with him? Focus on that. Don't focus on the ugliness.

I started crying against the bathroom door. All my life, these intrusive thoughts had screamed so many hideous things at me that I'd thought I was a killer, a psychopath. They made me think that I was simply acting every day, smiling at people and saying hello, when really, I was imagining their faces being eaten by insects. These thoughts had made me believe that I hated my siblings and parents and friends—at times wanting them to die. All the guilt and shame and horror I'd been holding inside all these years. How badly this had traumatized me. But where do the thoughts end and I begin? Am I a good person haunted by these thoughts or is there some truth in them? Do I really want that poor kid to die? Do I really hate him? Do I want terrible things to happen to people? Is this why I feel so distant from everyone? Is this why I always feel as if I'm underwater?

You gotta stop with this all-or-nothing bullshit, Jay! Have you ever killed someone? Have you ever pushed someone over a cliff? Of course not. You help that kid every day. You want him to succeed. That should be enough. Forget all this fire and brimstone. Just let the thoughts come and go, and keep helping these kids succeed in school—and give yourself a fucking break, will ya?

When I left the bathroom, the gym seemed surreal, and it took me a second to adjust to reality. Karla was standing halfway between our classes, telling two of my girls to be quiet. When she saw me, she smiled, passing no judgment. I smiled at her and wanted to scream, "KARLA, DON'T YOU KNOW THAT YOU'RE SAVING MY LIFE RIGHT NOW? DON'T YOU KNOW THAT YOU'RE SAVING ME WITH YOUR KINDNESS?"

I could have screamed the same at Camarin all the times she sat with me and calmly helped me organize my workspace, even when I felt lower than dirt.

After school, I thanked Karla for watching my class and she said, "Don't worry about it. You've done the same for me so many times."

I thought about her words, and they were true. I *had* helped her so many times as well, but it had never seemed to be enough for me. I hated having to rely on people, and I felt that I should be helping her a thousand times for every one time she helped me. Why?

Maybe it's because none of the people who were supposed to help you ever did, and now you feel you don't deserve help. Maybe it's because when you allow someone to help you, it reminds you of how much weaker you are than everyone else.

Holy shit! Another epiphany.

"How are you feeling?" she said.

"Oh, uh, I-I'm fine."

"I thought maybe you had the flu or something. You look a little pale."

"Yeah, I think it's going around."

"It's Doreen's birthday tomorrow. I'm going to get her a card now."

"Let's get a cake, too," I said.

"We've already got a Fudgie the Whale in the cafeteria freezer."

"That's great! Well, I'm gonna take off now. See you tomorrow."

I walked tall through the parking lot. Maybe you don't look so bad after all. Hell, she thought you had the flu. Maybe all the horror and trauma and shame stop just below the surface. Yeah, a few kids called you a zombie, but no one's telling their parents that you should be fired. Locked up. Sent off to the loony bin. Camarin and Cody keep telling you how great you're doing. Barry asked you to go golfing this weekend. Doreen keeps trying to set you up with random women. Maybe you're doing a lot better than you realize.

Maybe most people are doing a lot better than they realize.

I had another epiphany. After each breakthrough, I could feel my brain's chemistry changing. At first, I'd feel relaxed, but after, I'd get even more nervous than before—usually a day or two after. Then, when the anxiety had subsided, I'd feel so much better than before, allowing me the strength to be rocked by the next epiphany. It was a cycle, and the breakthroughs and anxiety had been overwhelmingly powerful at first, but they were now starting to level off. The sick feeling never left me, and I knew it wouldn't go away anytime soon, but it was easing up. I'd been in a relationship with my thoughts for so much longer than I had been with any woman, and it would take years to ever feel okay. I loved my thoughts, even though they caused me so much pain, but I had to let the negative ones die.

As I drove home, it seemed as if the traffic lights and street signs and pedestrians and cyclists were being pulled toward my car. In fact, someone's sunglasses hit me in the cheek, so I closed my window and drove slowly. When I got home, I walked upstairs and looked at the Sand Beach skyline, and Cody Cares seemed only about a block away, shaking as the waves crashed into the cliff below it. I tried not to think about it and went inside.

While taking a bath, I could hear my neighbors blasting German techno and chanting, shaking the walls. A helicopter flew overheard, warning us all to "STAY INDOORS!" and I wasn't worried about violating that order. I tried to relax, but the chaos was too much. I started to get out of the tub when I heard voices in the living room—I knew those voices! Two of my tenth-grade boys were raiding my fridge. "Yo, he got any ketchup?"

I slid back into the water and tried to hide. They grabbed some leftover takeout and walked off.

The chanting next door got louder. "CHUG! CHUG! CHUG!"

"Hey, Mr. S, come dance with us!"

I turned and saw two twelfth-grade girls dressed in clubbing gear standing in my kitchen. "Yeah, c'mon!" She started walking toward the bathroom and the other followed.

I grabbed a towel and covered myself while screaming, "GET OUT OF MY HOUSE!" then I shut and locked the door. They knocked and called my name, and the roof overhead ripped off the building. The cop in the helicopter shined his light down on me. "PERVERT! COME OUT WITH YOUR HANDS UP! IT'S

ILLEGAL TO BE NAKED IN YOUR OWN BATHROOM!"

I dropped the towel and raised my hands, but the helicopter flew off, and the girls were gone. I ran to the front door, locked it, and went back to the bathroom. I got in the tub, turned on more hot water, and was so exhausted, I fell asleep. I could have sworn a woman was standing above me and shouting in my ear, "Get up!" but when I woke up, I was alone.

The next morning, Cody Cares was right at the end of my driveway. I didn't even get in my car—I just walked into school. Cody sang his song and the day started, and at the end of final period, a large man stormed over to my desk and towered over me.

"You Mr. *Ass?*" he said, looking ready to rumble.

"I-I'm Mr. *S.* Can I help you?"

"So, you're the dumbass that failed my son?"

I could feel the blood rushing from my face, and I started getting dizzy and confused. Every part of my being was telling me to hit this dude in the nose then run like hell, but that would never be an option again.

"I didn't—uh, w-who's your son?"

"Karl Robeson."

"I don't think I, uh, failed him."

"Well, what grade'd you give him?"

"I can't remember. I'd need to check the book." Normally I would have caved and changed the grade, but something in me was done taking shit from cowards like this. But I still had no idea how to stand up for myself.

"Are you an idiot or something?" he said.

"I-I can't possibly remember each student's grades . . ." I fumbled for my grade book but looked up when the other teachers started singing "Happy Birthday" to Doreen, who was all smiles. She cut herself a piece of Fudgie the Whale while I continued hunting for my grade book. Seeing them celebrating without me made me feel totally abandoned, and with that dude staring me down, I wouldn't have been able to find a blade of grass on a fairway at Augusta National.

"What's taking so long?" he said.

"I-I just . . ." I said.

"Excuse me, sir, is everything okay?" Ms. Kefana said, smiling.

"No, this idiot doesn't know shit," he said.

"I'm sorry, sir, but this is a school, and we don't allow language like that in here," Ms. Kefana said.

"I'm sorry, but this idiot needs to tell me why he's failing my son."

"Sir, the students take quizzes, and we give them the grades they've earned. Mr. Sakovsky hasn't failed anyone."

"That's a load of bullshit," he said.

I pulled out my grade book, and he grabbed it from me, but Ms. Kefana snatched it from him.

"Gimme that! I'm gonna change my son's grade to something he shoulda earned," he said.

Ms. Kefana held the book away from him and said, "I'm sorry, sir, but you need to leave."

Barry and Karla came over, and the guy took off.

"C'mon, let's get some cake," Ms. Kefana said to me. She put my grade book on my desk and walked toward the table in the middle of our classrooms.

I was shaken up by the whole thing and felt dizzy when I stood. I ate a piece of cake but couldn't taste it, and it sat like a rock in my stomach.

At the end of the day, Ms. Kefana approached my desk. "How you doing, Jay? I know you've had a rough day."

I checked to make sure no one was in earshot. "How do you guys do it so easily?"

"Do what?"

"When that guy walked in here, right away I froze up. But you and Karla and Barry were so calm with him. How do I get to be like that?"

"It's much easier to deal with a student who's out of line than it is a parent. Parents pay our bills, so we can't be unprofessional with them, but we also can't let them push us around. You just need to stay calm and controlled. Stick to the facts. I simply told him that his language was inappropriate and that he'd have to leave if he spoke like that. Don't get caught in an argument. Let them know where the line is, and if they cross it, then you can ask them to lower their voice or watch their language or whatever."

"That might work for *you* guys, but I think people like that can see I'm different."

"You're not different. I simply told him he was crossing the line and that he needed to stop."

"When adults call me names like that, I believe them, you know? It's like it goes straight down to my marrow and bone, and I don't even know how to respond other than to give them everything they want and apologize for being so dumb."

"Jay, no matter what you may think, people have no right to talk to you like that. People say things like that to me all the time, too, but I know I'm not an idiot, so I let it bounce right off of me."

"Yeah, thanks . . . Hey, can I observe you interacting with parents to get some tips on how to do it?"

"Absolutely! In fact, I've got a meeting with a fairly—oh, how do I put this nicely?—completely irate mother tomorrow. Feel free to observe as much as you'd like."

"Thanks."

I left work that day knowing I was an idiot, just like that guy had said, and seeing how easily everyone else dealt with him made me feel like even more of one. I'd wanted to hit him, but it was so much harder to say, "You've crossed the line. There's the door, sir." Camarin was more of a man than I was. I needed to watch her closely and learn.

Chapter 18

Soon the semester was over, and we had a month off, which I badly needed. I'd barely been keeping it together and wanted to spend at least a week in bed, but no matter how hard I tried, I couldn't keep the kids and parents and cops and Sand Beach party animals from walking through my apartment, sitting on my futon, shitting in my toilet. When I got in the tub, the helicopters would fly overhead and shine lights on my dick, and kids would go through my fridge and cupboards, then disappear until they were hungry again. I'd wake up some mornings with a raging boner and the walls would be missing and neighbors would be taking pictures of my schlong and posting them online. Every time someone hit a softball at the diamond down the block, the ball would rock me square in the nuts. Sometimes, when I'd get home from work, I'd find stop signs and mileage markers attached to my back and legs, and I'd panic, knowing someone would get killed in an accident and it'd be my fault. Cody Cares was so close now that my apartment shook each time that cliff got hit with another wave.

That first week of break I received a book from Nima. On the title page, she'd written, "I miss you and your stories. I hope to read your book soon." I went online and searched for the best screenwriting books for beginning writers, and bought *The Screenwriter's Bible* by David Trottier, *Story* by Robert McKee, and *Making a Good Script*

Great by Linda Seger. I used to get such bad headaches when reading assigned books for school that I rarely got through any of them. I loved to read for fun, and I'd gotten through *The Prophet* with no problems, but if I had to read something mandatory, I shut right down.

But Nima was down there in LA making it happen. She'd finished writing a feature-length script based on her short and was looking for a team to put it together, so I forced myself to get through *The Screenwriter's Bible*, which explained story structure along with how to format a script. I knew nothing about acts and character arcs and all that crap, and felt that at twenty-seven I was already too old to learn something new. But once I got into the book, I realized it wasn't that bad. I finished it in a week, pushing through the headaches, and I outlined a story, then started writing the script.

I'd had a story in mind for years but had never written it because it seemed impossible. But now that I'd read this book and had written and edited a novel, I knew that if I just started writing the script, sooner or later it'd be finished. I called it *The Silent Protest* and based it on the road trip Doug and I took after college graduation, driving from Buffalo to Seattle to LA, and then back home. I created a fictionalized plot and characters, but the places they stopped and emotions they felt were pretty true to real life. It was about two guys who learn to look inward as a way to incite a rebellion that would end world suffering. I bought a computer program called Final Draft, which made formatting a breeze, and once I started writing, it all came out. From teaching myself how to write a screenplay to having an edited copy, it only took four weeks.

Though I was amazed at the speed at which I'd written the script, I knew it would likely be the only one I'd ever write. I mean, what the fuck else did I have to say? I couldn't whip out story ideas like Charlie Kaufman or William Goldman. All I had was my one screenplay and my one book. I thought about sending the script to Nima, but I was too embarrassed, so I printed a copy, put it on my dusty bookcase, and forgot about it.

With the script out of me, I felt more distance between myself and Soul City. Softballs weren't hitting me in the nuts anymore, and I hadn't brought home a single stop sign the entire time I'd been writing. But then again, I hardly left the house. Since starting my sessions with the Frog, I rarely left the apartment other than to go to work or to buy groceries.

Spending all that time in the apartment made me well aware of all the sounds and smells around me. The place had always smelled like a combination of mold, mildew, and cigarette smoke. The building was supposedly smoke-free, but maybe the last resident had puffed cigs with the door and windows closed or something. Either way, I'd gotten used to it, but the more I heard my neighbors slamming cupboards, blasting the TV and stereo, talking loudly, and dropping empty beer or wine bottles in the trash, the harder those sounds were to ignore. I felt as if the sounds were attached to me, attacking me, violating my personal space. The Frog said I had misophonia, which was an emotional reaction to specific sounds, no matter how faint, and that this was due to my OCD. For years, I'd tensed up as a means of ignoring those sounds, but now that I was feeling looser, I'd lost my defense mechanism and the sounds were tormenting me. This was probably the worst part of my OCD, because it made me feel as though I had no control over my environment.

Ever since I was a kid, I'd always had a thing with sounds and couldn't sleep if I heard my brothers snoring or neighbors talking or my dad watching the TV downstairs. I'd worn dirty earplugs every night, but they tore the skin in my ears, causing them to bleed and sting, and when I got old enough to drink, I used the sauce to kill the noise, giving my ears a break.

But suddenly I found myself cramming earplugs back in my ears and keeping them in whenever I was home. I even put my earbuds between an upper fold in my ears and the earplugs, holding them in place, as I blasted the sound of a waterfall, which I played on repeat. Even so, I'd still hear the bass notes from neighbors' speakers and the *THUD* of wine bottles hitting the bottoms of garbage cans and the slamming of windows and it all weighed so heavily on me that, at times, I felt I couldn't breathe. If the neighbor to the left slammed a cupboard, I'd spend the next few weeks on the right side of my apartment until the right-side shithead would throw a party or play loud video games, and I'd wander back over to the left for a time. The old lady downstairs would have her grandkids over and they'd scream so loudly I could hear them through the floor, earplugs, and waterfall. The neighbors in the building behind my apartment would party all day and night, blasting Limp Bizkit and Papa Roach and Kid Rock, and I wanted to kill them. I didn't know how I could go on. It enraged me that I'd begun this process with the Frog. Yeah, maybe before I was tense and furious and drinking myself to death, but at least I wasn't putting my ear to my apartment walls every time I heard someone fart. At least I hadn't been avoiding the bathroom because my neighbor slammed his shower door, causing me to jump and run to the other room.

I was losing my armor, which had grown thick as alligator skin over my soul. The Frog said I'd never had any boundaries growing up—that I had always been forced to obey the dogma of all the tyrants around me—and as a result, I had no idea who I was or how to read my emotions, and I absorbed every bit of shame and anger and ignorance thrown my way, making all of this my identity of zero. He told me that the only way to shed the alligator skin and develop real boundaries was to listen to my thoughts and understand them and what I truly wanted. To listen to my emotions and not suppress or judge them.

The alligator skin had a necessary role in your life, Jay. It protected you when you were weak and vulnerable. But it also dulled your senses. Cut you off to life. Served as a barrier between you and everyone else. Caused you to push people away and to get them before they got you and to hit hard and fast and run away. Caused you to hurt your brothers and sisters and to believe kids deserved pain. Caused you to distrust your emotions, making you addicted to chasing the highest of the highs and lowest of the lows to compensate for all the feelings you couldn't feel. But with solid, healthy boundaries in place, you can protect yourself from the shame and anger and abuse, giving that small child inside of you a safe place to grow and develop and feel.

But each time one of those cupboards slammed, it slapped that little boy in the face, and this made me wish I'd never spoken with the Frog. Made me realize the enormity and peril of this journey. That a handful of sessions wouldn't be enough. That this was going to be a lifelong thing. An entirely new way of being. I hoped I hadn't cursed myself to a new form of Hell. Hoped the Frog really knew what he was talking about and wasn't just another slick-talking tyrant looking to control me. Now I could see why so many people would go their entire lives without ever asking for help. Maybe asking for help was the biggest risk a person could ever take.

Still, knowing I was able to finish that script with all of the other bullshit weighing on me made me think that maybe there was a way for me to grow beyond the fear and become the person I'd always known I could be in those moments of inspiring silence staring through bus or airplane windows at the Mexican countryside, or cruising along American highways and believing that I could someday write the soundtrack for a lifetime.

I knew the Frog was right, but I also knew I wouldn't feel strong enough to fight back against those neighbor-noises anytime soon. I knew they'd have their way with me for years. Knew that anyone anywhere could destroy me with a lack of respect and consideration. Made me realize how little any of us gave a fuck about our neighbors. How it was all ME, ME, ME! and NOW, NOW, NOW! How hopeless it felt to ask them for help.

Even on the cold Southern California winter nights, I kept my fans running for the white noise, and I played the sound of the waterfall as I slept and kept my earplugs in at all times, and after spending my entire month off hidden in my apartment, only leaving to buy groceries, take out the trash, and take late-night anxiety walks along the beach, the skin in my ears had opened up again. Maybe I had to go backwards in order to go forward. But there was so much horror back there that it made forward motion feel impossible. I knew there was so much more I'd have to face—that the worst of it was still deep down in there. I told the Frog that it felt as if I was peeling back layers of an onion. I'd peeled back that outer layer in those first few sessions, letting the reality of my situation come crashing in, and I'd peeled back the next layer or two with my intense hallucination sessions in bed. I was terrified of whatever was in that core—in the deepest parts of me. If it was powerful enough to cause such a strong reaction in the outer layers, what would happen to me when I reached the center?

I still hadn't met any of my neighbors, and intentionally so. At my other place, I'd been happy to spend the night on the patio sipping drinks with Remi and Kelly and Tuyet, but here I didn't want anyone to even look at me. I just wanted to sneak into my apartment, lock the door, and hide out for another week or two. Going down to the laundry room caused me such stress, it almost wasn't worth doing. We had one washer and one dryer for forty residents, and while most people were pretty cool about quickly doing a load or two, there were others who'd hog the machines all day, leaving their clothes for an hour or two between cycles. Sometimes people skipped me in line. Before, I might have laughed it off, but now everything felt so personal—as if I *had* to fight back. But if I started fighting, maybe I'd light their clothes on fire. Maybe I'd toss their clothes in the dumpster. Maybe I'd piss on their stuff in the dryer.

It was better to close the door and walk back upstairs and sweat and curse and peek through the slats in the blinds to see when they were finally heading back down to the laundry room. To see if they had another load in their basket or if now I could finally clean my clothes.

The second or third week of break, Barry invited me out for drinks with him and Karla. He called a few times, but I didn't pick up. I kind of knew what he was calling about and didn't have the skill or energy to come up with an excuse on the fly, but when he texted me,

"Hey, we're down by the beach," I texted back, "Sorry, I'm in LA for the week. Have fun without me though!" I hadn't been taking any calls—not from my mom or dad or friends or Winston or Nima even. I felt that if I spoke with anyone from my old life, they'd find ways to shame me back into the person they were comfortable with me being, and soon Doug and I would be tossing people through windows again. I'd played so many roles throughout my life, acting differently with each person I spoke to, reading them and determining how to please, and I couldn't do it anymore. Some people wanted me to get hammered with them. Some wanted me to absorb the shame and guilt they believed I should feel after running so far away from home. Some wanted to remind me of what an asshole I was. This whole healing thing felt so fragile, and even though the sounds and everything tortured me, I couldn't go back. Back was worse than forward. I had to pull myself out of the cycle of shame. I had to imagine all the horrible things people were saying about me for not picking up the phone, and let it all fall to the ground. Just as I'd had to make peace with death, I also had to make peace with isolation. Maybe I was better alone, anyway. I mean, as shitty as I felt in that apartment, I felt more in control than ever before. Every time I'd gone to a bar or house party or whatever, I'd found myself doing shit I didn't want to do and saying shit I didn't agree with. I'd respond when guys called me "dawg" and "bro," and I hated those words. It was as if we all stuck in a cycle together, and I *needed* to pull away from it. Using that "bro" language would keep me forever running on the treadmill to nowhere.

I only answered the phone when my friend Silas called. We'd grown up together in Buffalo and had spent most of our free time playing basketball and lifting and talking about life and our dreams. He'd always been able to see the best in me, so I figured that answering his calls would bring me further along the healing path instead of pushing me off of it. He'd moved to California after high school, and there were a few years we didn't speak with one another. He joined the Marines and went off to war, while I crisscrossed the country searching for answers to the questions that haunt so many young people searching for their place in the world. We'd had a falling out before he left Buffalo, but now it was as if we'd never stopped talking. He was living in Austin and was one of the bigger hip-hop artists there, and we talked about following our dreams and building empires and getting together again soon. I told him I was in bad shape, but he said, "Can't be any worse than when we were kids." And he was right.

Still, when he said he'd visit, I hoped he wouldn't. I felt that just by leaving my apartment and hanging out with someone my age, I would find myself back out in bars, drinking so much I'd forget everything I'd spent so much time learning. I would fall off barstools and get into fights, and I would never write another script again. I felt that any step backwards, even a millimeter, would be enough to destroy everything I'd worked for. Everything had to be forward, with all my strength.

Chapter 19

esides the script, another good thing happened over that break. While browsing a social media website for travelers, I met a woman from Mexico City. She'd liked some of my pictures from Mariposa, and she said, "De nada" when I thanked her. Her name was Carolina, and she was the vice president of an insurance company and lived in a penthouse in Condesa. I thought maybe someone was pranking me, but after a Skype session, I saw that she was real and just as beautiful as her pics.

I made an excuse to end the Skype call quickly. While writing messages, I could think about my responses, editing out all the dorkiness and nonsense, but in real time, I stuttered and kept looking away from the camera. I knew my pain was written across my face, and exposing it to her felt more uncomfortable than showing off my twig and berries.

After that, I figured she'd never talk to me again, but that didn't happen, and seeing her messages day after day despite how shitty I felt gave me the courage to tell her what I was going through. She said she knew someone with OCD and didn't seem fazed by it. I wanted to discuss other things—happy things—but the Darkness was such a part of me that I couldn't avoid it.

I didn't tell her everything though. I didn't tell her about the hallucinations or the shivering and sweating in bed. I didn't tell her that I'd been shitting in plastic bags on the far side of my apartment because my neighbor had slammed his shower door one day just as I was squeezing one out. I didn't tell her I'd covered my back windows with aluminum foil because the glare from my neighbor's TV shone through at night, and I'd obsess that I could hear it even if the volume was on mute, so I had to block out the light and pretend I lived on a cliff over the sea with no neighbors in sight.

I'd never be able to tell a woman everything, because it was already hard enough finding someone when all was well. Whenever Carolina and I spoke, I wanted to tell her all the disturbing details that weighed down my fingertips and tongue. I obsessed over it, but I had to stop myself, and I realized that even now I was acting. Always acting. Always omitting and editing. No one could love the real me—*if* I could even figure out who that was. So I gave Carolina what I could, and she probably did the same with me, and I told her I'd visit her when I felt better. She didn't feel safe coming to me, and it was better not to invite her into my foil-wrapped reality anyway.

I was terrified to return to Cody Cares, but after the first day back, it wasn't so bad. In fact, after so much time off, I actually felt better than before. I didn't have any panic attacks and wasn't getting strong urges to say terrible things to the kids or parents. When the sick student returned from the hospital, I smiled and told him I was happy to see him, not once worrying that something horrible would slip out of my mouth. Karla told me I looked rested and that "it's too bad you were in LA. We had a lot of fun at the beach. You should come out next time."

I smiled even though I wanted to cry. This was going to be such a long, lonely journey. I wanted to tell her everything, and say please don't give up on me if I reject you. Please don't take it personally. I can't be anywhere near alcohol. I can't be anywhere near anyone who might call me "bro."

While contemplating this, I had another breakthrough. I'd always felt that I didn't deserve love or respect or friendship. I always screamed, "Yes!" whenever someone asked something of me, no matter how much I wanted to scream, "No!' and now I knew that was because I felt so unworthy of their attention that I was terrified to lose it. Ignoring calls and avoiding people, especially people I cared about as much as Karla, helped me to understand this.

There was something else about her that caused a stir. Working beside her day in and day out, I felt drawn to her, but I didn't know what to make of it. In the past, I probably would have asked her out months ago, but that didn't seem right. We worked together in a professional environment, and I respected how great of a teacher she was, and I was beginning to realize that maybe it wasn't okay to ask out women I worked with.

I didn't want to make Karla or any other woman feel awkward. I also liked being able to resist the pressure and see these women as coworkers and maybe friends. As a man growing up in the US, I'd faced considerable pressure from both men and women to always be fit and witty and confident and charming, and I liked the idea of being able to relax and just focus on my job. And it seemed that the more I stopped trying to charm them, the more women approached me. Maybe this was the key to finding success in love. After all, it seemed to be the key to healing.

The dating world seemed to be changing anyway, and with all the online dating and social media sites, there was less pressure to approach women in person, which was great for someone like me. Hell, Carolina probably only spoke to me because she hadn't yet seen me in real life, bumping into doors and dropping glasses and stumbling through conversations. In my condition, maybe this was my only chance to find love—to allow a woman to get to know me from afar, so that when she finally did meet me, she'd be willing to overlook my awkwardness. Despite the million reasons not to, I still believed in love and couldn't give up on it. Speaking with

Carolina online and having that professional buffer zone between me and Karla gave me enough breathing room to stop trying so hard, which allowed me to see women as regular human beings and not unapproachable goddesses who could kill me with a frown. All that pressure to be powerful and confident and handsome and rich—to swagger up to them like Cary Grant—all it ever did was put up a wall between us. I just wanted to feel close, even if it meant I'd never get another date again.

And I did feel close to Karla. To Carolina. Maybe someday I'd feel close to myself as well.

It surprised me that I could have such breakthroughs while teaching. That these thoughts could race through my mind, changing me and giving me an entirely new perspective on the world all while I discussed the Civil War or Reconstruction or whatever. That every fiber in my being was changing, yet to the students, I still looked like the same boring teacher.

Before lunch, I got an email from Doug. "Yo, Stonkey the Donkey, what's up with your phone? You forget how to answer it or something? I need to get my end table. Lemme know when I can come pick it up." I started shaking, cursing myself for opening the email. This is why you've been deleting his voicemails, you fucking idiot! Now he's got you. Don't you see? He's smarter than you. There's no escape.

Oh, c'mon, don't be such a bitch. He just wants his table back. Give it to him, shut the door, and tell him to piss off.

But then he'll know where you live! Then he'll start coming by whenever he wants. Plus, do you really think you'll be able to shut the door on him? He'll put his foot inside and muscle his way in. He'll tell you to come out for a drink and "Yeah, my wife's got this cute friend at work. We should go out to dinner together, the four of us." And you won't be able to say no. He knows how to work you. He knows your insecurities. Besides, all this "healing" shit's hopeless anyway. You think you're really gonna make it to the finish line? Don't be fucking naïve. You were born in Buffalo. Your dad filled vending machines and Mom was the school lunch lady. Who the fuck do you think you are, huh? Once Jimmy and Tony and Michael and Matthew all hear about it, they'll never let you live it down. They're gonna call you a SoCal fag and say how much you've changed and all that crap. Don't you see? No matter how many miles away you run, Buffalo is still on top of your shoulders. Just answer him. Tell Doug you'll go out for drinks. Tell him to bring some China white and a razor to slit your wrists.

I wrote Doug a response that I didn't send. At lunch, Barry was going on and on about how he'd tried surfing over the weekend and loved it, and Doreen kept telling him, "At your age, you're gonna break a hip," even though he was, like, forty. When they both finished, they went back to their desks, and Karla and I were alone. She started laughing.

"What?" I said.

"I was reading Yelp reviews of that bar we went to in Sand Beach over break, and I read one from a woman who said something about how she met this guy from Buffalo there, who was living with another guy who studied volcanoes, and they were both talking about how they lived in Mexico and played music, and she said she and her friend were going to go home with these 'cute guys,' but one of them got into a fight and they got kicked out. I wonder who those guys could be?"

My face was red. "I, uh, h-haven't gotten in any fights . . ."

"It's okay, I won't tell Cody. We'll let him continue to think you play in a rough basketball league."

I thought about making a joke about Bill Laimbeer being the league's commissioner or whatever, but I didn't have the brainpower to put it all together. Karla's comment reminded me of what I was fighting against, and I was glad I hadn't sent the email. I had another breakthrough sitting there with Karla. I realized that I wasn't as strong as I thought I was. I'd rationalized that maybe seeing Doug wouldn't be all that bad and had almost sent him my new address, but hearing a respected colleague's summary of our typical night out made me realize how fucked up I still was. That sending him an email would be weakness. A part of me wanted to self-destruct. It was easier that way. I had the weight of a city and a country on my shoulders. I was trying to break out of so many cycles of shame that it felt impossible. The cycles inside of me. My looped thinking. The cycles of social interaction in beach bars and parties. The cycles of shame I felt talking to professionals at work, who lived in clean, organized houses and had spouses and kids and entire cupboards filled with dishes and mixing bowls and blenders and shit. The cycles of shame I felt within my family, needing to play the roles of the asshole, the instigator, the blind messiah. The cycles I'd felt living in Buffalo, always rooting for the underdog and the long shot while sitting in freezing dive bars and drinking my life away. The cycles I felt as an American, feeling superior to all other nations. Needing the best of everything. To constantly BUY, BUY, BUY! To spend my whole life at the gym, so I'd have perfect abs and arms. To whiten my teeth. To style my hair. To drive the best, cleanest car on the road. To make more money than I'd ever need and hoard it away, letting it grow until I was the richest! The sexiest! The smartest! The strongest! Never show fear! Men never show emotion. Stay in the cycle! Stay on the treadmill! You're going nowhere, dawg, just like the rest of us. You'll never write your masterpiece. The only role you'll ever play is that of Jay every day as you drag yourself out of bed, fight through traffic, smile at parents and students, and tell admins how wonderful it all is.

I practically ran to the beach cave after work.

"I got it!" the Frog said in his full baritone. "Just leave the table at your old place."

"Yeah—yeah, I guess I could do that." A spring rain shower poured outside the cave, but that hadn't stopped several Sand Beach weirdos from following me. I'd lost them climbing on the rocks and hoped they'd gone away, but I could hear their voices: "Where'd he go?" "He was just here." "We'll get 'im!"

"Just drive it over after work—" the Frog said.

"No, too bright then. I don't wanna see Tuyet or the others. They'll force a bong on me, and soon I'll be running naked and bloody down the beach. If I go back there, I'm gonna lose all the progress I've made."

"That's not possible. Now that you've seen the truth, that can't happen. It's impossible to unknow what you know."

"Yeah, I guess so."

"Drop it off tonight."

"Okay. That's a good idea. He just . . ." I stared at a candle on the wall. "He knows how to manipulate people. He doesn't care about the table. He's just trying to fuck with my head. He knows what's up. He knows I'm pulling away from him."

"I'm glad to hear that. That is, I'm glad to hear you're making that connection."

"I've been making a lot of connections lately. When I piss, when I microwave a burrito, while watching TV, while teaching."

"They'll slow down soon enough."

"Sometimes I feel like I'm going crazy. You sure all this won't cause me to become schizophrenic?"

"You're not a schizophrenic. Stop worrying."

"Sometimes I feel like people are watching me, you know?"

"It's your PTSD and hypervigilance. You're always expecting disaster around every corner."

"There usually is."

"You're catastrophizing again."

"I had this friend in college—a really smart guy. You know, like, so smart his feet didn't touch the ground. He did acid a few times and went nuts, and everyone just . . . forgot about him. I think about him all the time. It's like he lives inside of my brain now. Like, I gotta die for him in order to live. Does that make any sense?"

"It does."

"He was a regular guy, just like me, until he wasn't. It still haunts me as much as it did when I first saw him screaming about aliens stealing his thoughts. We had to call the cops, and they took him away, and a part of me went away with him and never came back." I started crying.

"The acid likely unlocked a latent case of schizophrenia in your friend. It might have happened sooner or later without the drugs."

"So, it could happen to me too?"

"Well, no more than it could anyone else. You've never had any symptoms, which at your age you likely would have already experienced. While I wouldn't recommend someone with your stress levels to try psychedelics, even if you took them, you probably wouldn't end up like your friend."

"I feel like I've got no control. Like, at any time, the wind is gonna blow a whole vial of acid right down my throat, and it's gonna fry my brain, and I'll wander off forever."

"That's a typical symptom of the disease you *do* have, OCD. Relax and repeat after me: I'm fine."

"I'm fine."

"I'm safe."

"I'm safe."

"I'll be okay."

"I'll be okay."

"Good."

"I'm feeling a little better since writing this script. I feel lighter almost, like it'd be easier to write something new now. It's almost as if the better I feel, the more I can write, and the more I can write, the better I feel. It's like two separate journeys are blending into one."

"They *are* one. Just think of what you'll be able to accomplish when you finally put your anxiety into remission."

"So, all of this is curable?"

"Yep. The OCD isn't necessarily curable, but with treatment, you can knock it down so low you won't even notice it. I recommend you read a book called *Brain Lock*. It'll give you a better understanding of your OCD."

He'd had me read two other books, *Facing Shame: Families in Recovery* and *The Drama of the Gifted Child: The Search for the True*

Self, and I'd devoured both the same as I had *The Prophet*. It was almost as if I'd already had all of this information inside of me, but the books and sessions with the Frog helped me uncover it. I made a crack that if I ever wrote a similar book, I'd call it *I Think . . . I Hate Them*, and that got him laughing.

Outside, the voices grew louder. They must have heard me say that, because they were shouting shit like, "HONOR THY FADDAH AND MUDDAH!" and "HOW COULD ANYONE BADMOUTH THEIR DEAR OL' MA?"

"You sure you don't hear that?" I said.

"It's your paranoia," the Frog said.

"Yeah, yeah, probably." Regardless, I didn't want to leave when he said time was up. I snuck out of the cave and climbed up the cliff—which was pretty dangerous—rather than walking back down to the beach, where I could still hear those threatening voices. The cliff grew higher and steeper, and I felt through the darkness with my feet and hands for solid gaps in the slippery rock, and climbed to freedom. When I got to the top, I sat at the cliff's edge and stared up at the bright full moon, high above the ocean. It seemed that my entire life had been like that climb, reaching into the dark, feeling for something stable, only being able to see the faintest bit of what was directly in front of me. I couldn't see where I'd come from or where I was going. I didn't know how long it was to the top. I just knew that my muscles burned and mouth screamed for water. But now, after all I'd been through with the Frog, I could see a little more of that cliff than I could before. I could see that it actually *was* a cliff; before, I'd just felt the burning in my muscles and the ever-present exhaustion, but now I knew I was on a journey, moving through the chaos toward *something*, but what that something was, I still didn't know. I caught my breath and then pulled out the small notebook and pen I'd been carrying with me for the last few months and wrote something:

A Mother's World

It's dangerous living in a mother's world.
I walk outside at any time of day
and the world is celebrating mothers.
Kisses on Monday,
hugs on Tuesday,
red roses on Wednesday.
A standing ovation for the one who sacrificed so much for us
ungrateful bastards—
and it's not just the little girls
or kind older women
honoring dear old Mom,
but also the guys in the gutter
along the Sand Beach pier,
who'd rather crack a bottle of whiskey over a skull
than take an ill word on dear ol' Mum.
"She had more heart than you ever will!"
he shouts, as the bleeding bum he struck rises off the street,
centers himself, and takes another shot to the head.
"You got no heart!"
And I watch as the masses crowd around
as the fallen bum again rises to his feet.
He pulls himself up on a stone breaker wall and stands proud and tall—
after all, we all love a good comeback story, almost as much as we
love Mom—
and says, "I wasn't talking about your mom, I said it about my own."
The crowds let out a GASP!
and quickly overtake him,
ripping at cloth and skin 'til there's nothing left but bone.
And right then I think of poetry
but wait until the rabid crowds disperse.
They're still hungry for blood,
so I walk along the boardwalk

and stop under the pier
and find a nice dark spot
and pull out my journal and pen,
but I hesitate before writing a word.
And for the first time I realize that,
I think I hate poetry,
but what alternative is there
living in a mother's world?

When I got home, I locked the door and microwaved a can of soup for dinner. With all the noise in my head, I wasn't watching much TV. It was too much stimulation, so I ate in silence while trying to slow and make sense of my thoughts. I went over my game plan for bringing the table to my old place. I'd wait until midnight, then I'd lift it over the fence, place it down gently, and drive like hell outta there. I couldn't use the gate because it creaked, and I figured it might be best to park in the alley so no one saw my car.

Jadia called, and I made the mistake of listening to her voicemail. "Hey, Jay, we haven't seen you at open mic in a while. You still in Soul City? Anyway, we're getting together tomorrow night and—" I hung up and deleted the message, cursing myself for listening to it. I hadn't picked up my guitar in weeks and felt that my rhythm was gone and would never come back. I had no control over my body anymore. I'd never been a great singer, but now I probably wouldn't be able to carry the simplest tune. I opened my computer and took comfort in seeing that Carolina had written to me. "I got the raise! I'm so happy. I'm going out with my friends tonight to celebrate."

I responded: "That's great! I'm really proud of you. You definitely deserve it. Have fun tonight and take lots of pictures! Your face is so beautiful when you're happy—when you're sad too!" I hoped she'd respond and distract me, but she didn't, so I removed the junk mail from the end table, wiped it clean, and went over my plan one more time.

I waited until midnight and then executed everything perfectly, and when I got home, I felt a much stronger barrier around myself than before. I'd even left Doug the pot and set of bowls we'd bought together in case he tried asking for those next. This was an act of war, but with the Frog on my side, I knew I could win.

Chapter 20

An angry mother had been calling me on a near-daily basis, screaming and swearing, calling me a dumb shit and moron and con artist because I wouldn't give her son credit for a class he hadn't completed before they moved to Sacramento. It got so bad that I'd shake every time I heard the phone ring. We didn't have caller ID, so I never knew what would happen when I answered. Karla knew about the calls, and she'd eavesdrop and tell me what a nutcase the woman sounded like, but knowing she was a nutcase didn't help me. I believed the mom when she said all those terrible things about me. I'd never taken up Ms. Kefana on her offer to let me observe a meeting with an angry parent, so when she asked me if I'd be the teacher representative at a meeting one afternoon, I said yes. I knew it'd be useless to learn new strategies for the same reason it was useless to leave that end table at my old place. People like these angry parents and Doug were the only ones who truly knew me. Yeah, Karla and Ms. Kefana knew me, but they only knew one part of the story. I played my role of teacher pretty well, but the real me was an even bigger piece of shit than all of those angry SOBs said. Seeing Karla and Ms. Kefana smile and tell me how great I was almost made me respect them less. Made me think that maybe they didn't really know what the fuck was up, even though they'd seen all my black eyes and hangover sweats.

Maybe my issue with dealing with psycho parents was that, unlike Karla and the others, I wasn't interested in saying "Sir, you've crossed the line," then showing them the door—I wanted to fucking destroy them. But in a formal, intelligent manner, using logic and lawyer language, shutting them up and proving to them what colossal pieces of shit they were in a way that couldn't blow back on me. But when they started yelling at me, my brain switched off, and all I could think to do was start swinging. Only a pussy would show them the door. I wanted to show them the door to Hell. I wanted to step on their necks so hard they'd never speak such trash to anyone again. I wanted to dominate them, not enforce some weak-ass school rules. I lived by the rules of nature. The rules of the desert. The rules of the highway and the bar alleys. After all I'd seen, I wasn't showing anyone the door.

We usually held parent meetings after sixth period, during our free time. The mother and daughter came in, and Ms. Kefana and I greeted them, and then we moved to the wrestling room in the back of the gym where Ms. Kefana took all of her meetings. There was a long wooden table with wheeled chairs surrounding it, and I followed Ms. Kefana to the far head of the table. Both Mom and daughter looked more burned out than pissed off, and they both wore dirty, food-stained clothes and had unwashed, uncombed hair.

"Thank you for coming in toda—" Ms. Kefana said with a smile.

"Oh, don't gimme that bullshit," Momma said. "You're lettin' my daughter fall behind. She says all her teachers don't give a shit about her and give her dirty looks an' all that because of the stuff goin' on in her head."

"I'm sorry to hear that. What's going on in her head?" Ms. Kefana said. I took mental notes, observing Ms. Kefana recognize and affirm the parent's frustration and ask a question to gather more information and defuse the situation.

"She's been feelin' hopeless . . ."

Oh god! What have I gotten myself into?

". . . I think she got a few wires loose or sumpin and she can't focus on her work."

Every part of me wanted to run out of that room.

"Sweetie, would you mind stepping outside for a sec?" Ms. Kefana said to the girl.

The girl nodded and went outside.

"I don't mean to startle you, but it sounds to me like your daughter is experiencing depression, and I think it would be a good idea to have a therapist evaluate her," Ms. Kefana said.

My brain was swimming, and if anyone even so much as asked me my name, I might have started babbling and screaming and taking off my shoes and throwing them. I was filled with confusion and rage and wanted to pound my fists on the table, but I didn't know why.

"My daughter's not crazy!" Momma said.

"Crazy is a relative term. I can recommend a therapist . . ."

The meeting continued like that, and soon it was over. Despite her initial concerns, the mother said she'd contact the therapist, and when she left, she was significantly less upset.

I thanked Ms. Kefana for letting me sit in on the meeting, then went back to my desk to put grades in the book, but there was no way I could concentrate.

Why refer the girl to therapy? It's not gonna do shit anyway. She's gonna be depressed for the rest of her life. She'll never get married or have kids or follow her dreams. She'll end up living under the Sand Beach pier, hustling for change to buy smack. She's cursed, just like I am.

Man, you know that's bullshit. Maybe therapy *can* help this girl. Maybe if they get to it early enough, she can have a real life.

Fuck her! Why does she get to have a life and I don't? Why didn't anyone ever do any of this shit for me?

And there it is! Another breakthrough! Maybe this is part of why you feel as if this job is like rolling a rock up a hill each day, only for it to roll down the other side again. Why you feel as if real teaching and learning are impossible. When you were a kid, learning was chaos. A bomb had gone off and you were trying to collect as much information in the smoke and screaming and bleeding as possible.

Learning felt hopeless. The future felt impossible. What does any of this homework even matter when kids' heads are too filled with dynamite to process any new information?

But that's always seemed like bullshit. Kids *can* learn. These kids *are* learning. You learned. If it comes easier to them because they have therapists and counselors and teachers who are actually listening to them, then that's great. So what? So you slipped through the cracks. You're on the right path now. And what's more is that you put yourself there, not your mom or dad or teacher. Take a deep breath. Everything is okay. Sure, therapy wasn't a thing when you were younger. No one got tested for autism or OCD or bipolar disorder. We were all just "undisciplined" or "lazy" or "stupid." But you can't take that out on the younger generation. Things should always be improving. Help them improve. Don't wallow in misery because no one helped you.

I realized that if I was going to succeed on my healing journey, I was going to have to acknowledge that others deserved to heal as much as I did. That I wasn't the only one suffering. That help and hope *were* possible. And that maybe someday I could provide it to others. My growing awareness of my own struggles made me much more aware of those of others, and I felt as if I could smell anxiety or depression or panic in people, even if they'd pushed it way down deep. I thought Karla was depressed. I could see it in her eyes—a deep exhaustion—and hear it in her voice. I wanted to be there for her as well.

Observing Karla and Ms. Kefana gave me more ammo to use against angry parents, but I knew it would be years before I ever felt as comfortable talking to parents the way they did. It pissed me off that these asshole parents treated me like this while I was so vulnerable. I wasn't asking for anything more than a little respect, but even that was too much. It was this kind of disrespect and abuse that had put me in this situation to begin with, and it pissed me off to think *I* was the one who needed to change. But a part of me still craved revenge, and was it really all that bad?

Look, man, if you stay stuck in this kind of thinking, then these assholes win. You gotta let this shit roll off your back like Ms. Kefana does. You saw how cool she acted when that mother ripped into her. You're right. *You* gotta change. You gotta learn how to be healthy and happy in spite of all this shit—and not because you want to rub it in anyone's face, but because it brings you peace and happiness. Work toward peace and happiness, not revenge. The next time someone approaches your desk with a face full of rage, do what Ms. Kefana did. Tell them you're sorry for the situation—even if you're not—listen to their concerns, and tell them you'll do what you can to help them. Stick to the facts. Don't instigate. Smile. You're representing the school, not yourself. Their anger is directed at the organization, not at you. Don't take it personally. You're not a lightning rod for the world's abuse. The next time that mother calls to scream at you, tell her that you've heard her concerns and that there's nothing you can do for her and that she can speak with your boss if she'd like. Trust that Ms. Kefana will have your back. Trust that she won't fire you. Don't hide the abuse, worrying everyone will finally see what a fraud you are. Be a professional and deal with the situation according to the standards of Cody Cares.

I did my best to stick to this game plan, but it was easy to talk about plans when no one was screaming at you. But after a few successes, letting parents know that I'd heard their concerns but there was nothing I could do to change their kids' grades or drop the charges for lost textbooks or whatever, I started to feel an even stronger barrier around myself. I told myself that in times of desperation, just look around you and see how the other professionals are handling their situations, and in time, you'll be like them. I told myself to trust in the process. Trust in the good around you. You're in a good spot now. The adults you see every day are strong and compassionate. You can be like them. You couldn't be like the adults you saw growing up—always hurting and yelling and miserable. But you *can* be like Barry. Dude's always smiling, never says a bad thing about anyone. He's happy trying new things like surfing or Vietnamese food. If you have to speak with him about something important, he'll listen and not cut you down. Learn how to trust. It doesn't make you any weaker—in fact, it'll make you stronger.

I knew that sitting through any more meetings like that would probably bring up the same feelings, so I'd have to let all this go if I was ever going to be a real adult—a professional teacher who could actually help kids rather than seeing them as a nuisance and a threat. I had to protect them if I ever wanted to protect that little kid inside of me. All my life, I blamed that kid for not being strong enough to fight all those forces of negativity surrounding me. For not being strong enough to beat the demons in my head. But I would never think that any of my students were weak for not being able to do the same. I'd think it was *my* responsibility to help them deal with it all, just as it had been the responsibility of the adults in my young life to help me—except they hadn't. You're allowed to feel angry about this, but let that anger go. You'll only pass it on to these kids. You'll only keep that kid inside of you small and terrified. Be good to kids, and you'll be good to yourself.

On the drive home, I watched the sun setting over the ocean, filling the sky with oranges and reds and yellows. All of these changes were overwhelming, but like the Frog said, I couldn't unknow what I knew. When I got home, I started humming a melody that had been stuck in my head all day, but I didn't think to record it until I was reaching into my freezer for a frozen pizza. I grabbed my newest recorder and continued humming. This was always the most dangerous part. When the song was in my unconscious, it could come and go as it pleased, and I could whistle and hum it while grading lessons or weaving through traffic or taking a piss, but once I realized that I wanted to record it, I had to act fast. Once I became aware of the song, it could disappear, and when I turned on the recorder and it didn't start, I yelled, "FUCK!" By the time I put new batteries in, the song was gone.

I microwaved my pizza and watched *Seinfeld,* and after, I decided to watch a movie, but like with the recorder, I had to act fast. There was a small window of time for me to pick one and start it, or I'd start going through my entire collection, obsessing over which one I really wanted to watch the most. That process could take an hour or two, and I'd spend the whole time sweating and cursing myself. I put in *Y Tu Mamá También*, but I only got about ten minutes in before I had to turn it off. That film had been one of the things to inspire my move to Mexico years ago, and I hadn't watched it since. Now, I had to add it to my do-not-watch list. I was stuck in Soul City. Stuck at Cody Cares. Stuck inside this dark, shitty apartment, and stuck on this healing journey. I couldn't relax my mind and let it take me away to inspiring places like I could when I was younger and less encumbered. The thought of traveling or starting a band or acting or getting high or feeling free only made me panic. I had to ignore all of that. Winston had texted me a week earlier, asking me to join him on a road trip to San Francisco, and the thought of getting in his passenger seat and closing the door felt like locking myself up in prison. It made me think of how taking another cross-country road trip would be impossible. How I no longer had my coping mechanisms, and I would never make it past the state line. Made me realize how vulnerable I was now, had always been. That the whole hippie thing was a way to escape the rules inside my head. That I had to pretend not to care about anything because I'd spent so much of my childhood worrying about everything. Controlling everything. But the worry followed me along that entire trip, and it tortured me in so many ways I never wanted to feel again.

As crazy as I felt now, shitting in plastic bags and jumping every time a neighbor closed a door, I was doing infinitely better than before. I didn't respond to Winston. I felt that if I did, he'd find a way to convince me to go, or maybe he'd ask me to open for him again at a show, and the Darkness would wrap around me so tightly, I wouldn't be able to breathe. I knew that sooner or later, friends would stop contacting me, but if the Frog was right, there was something incredible waiting for me at the end of this journey, and I needed to get there. Maybe I'd end up in the Great River, swimming beside Dylan and David Bowie and the spirits of John Lennon and Bob Marley and Jimi Hendrix, but the only way to get there was to go all in. But unlike any of my other journeys, I wasn't going to go anywhere other than deep inside my own heart, mind, and soul.

The panic hit me pretty hard, so I took a walk to visit the Frog.

"It makes perfect sense," he said. "No one ever helped you the way you're expected to help your students, and it's only natural that it'd be difficult for you. It might even make you resent them." He took a sip of tea. It was a chilly, foggy night, and the lights from ships passing in the distance looked like bright dots on the dark ocean.

"I don't even know why I'm doing it. It's just, something in me feels like I *have* to teach, you know? Like I've been institutionalized, and there's no way I could do something free like start a business or be a lawyer or make a living acting onstage. All of that would be too selfish. I've spent my whole life in classrooms and that's where I need to die. Sacrifice myself for kids, and as much as I hate it, I can't get away. I want an office job where I can just zone out and think about my music or come up with screenplay ideas, but I *have* to teach. It almost feels like a command from God."

"You're playing your role, just as you did when you were a kid. You felt it was your job to save your family, your town, and your country. Now you're saving the children, and—like with the OCD—because of your religious background, everything is fire and brimstone. Heaven and Hell. There's no in-between. With you it's all or nothing, which is common in abused children. Some abused kids go the route of zero, getting into crime, drugs, drinking. Others become perfectionists, workaholics, caregivers, and protectors of righteousness and morality. You feel you need to die for students just as you once felt you needed to die for God."

"I stopped believing in all that shit over a decade ago, but it still has such a hold on me. I still feel God inside of me, judging me. Criticizing me. Giving me orders. Threatening me with Hell. How do I get over it?"

"It'll take time, but I think as your OCD lowers, so will the absolutism of your thoughts. You have an overdeveloped superego because you essentially had to raise yourself, and you need to recognize any thoughts that order you around and tell them they're no longer necessary. Look at you now. Look at what a great job you're doing. You're writing books and screenplays. You've worked full-time as a teacher for years. Tell that critic inside of you to shut up. It has no right to bully you, and once that voice gets weaker, you'll be able to do whatever job you want."

"Yeah, I hope so. I wanna get down to LA, but that doesn't seem like it'll happen anytime soon. In the meantime, I'd like to try to explore as much of my creativity as possible. Maybe I could write a few more screenplays, so that when I decide to move south, I'll have already built up a reputation. People will know my work and be more willing to give me the chance to act or direct."

"Sounds like a plan."

"I just wish I could get away from all the noises at my apartment. They're driving me nuts—I mean, like seriously nuts. What do I do about that?"

"Well, in situations like these, I'd say it's best to use good psychology. Maybe start by introducing yourself to your neighbors and bringing it up after speaking with them for a few minutes about other things. Or you could write a note asking them to go easy on the cupboards and to lower the TV, and tape the note to a bottle of wine and leave it on their doorstep."

"I can't do any of that."

"Why not?"

"Because that's what squares do, man. I can't tell somebody else what to do. Hell, I'm a songwriter. If I told someone to lower their music, wouldn't that make me a hypocrite? Would Lemmy ask his neighbor to lower the music? No, he'd smoke some meth, then go over and jam."

The Frog laughed. "Maybe, maybe not. You think Lemmy never got upset at anyone? You think he never told someone to shut the hell up? Maybe he'd march right over there and punch his neighbor in the nose. Or maybe he'd bring his bass over and jam like you said. Either way, you're dealing with some significant psychological issues and would it be so much for your neighbors not to scream at four a.m.?"

"I don't know . . ."

"You deserve the right to stand up for yourself."

"Yeah, but I've woken people up before."

"So, don't do it again. Problem solved."

"It's just—you can't do that. It's already hard enough out there. It's a lot harder when everyone turns on you."

"Again, you're catastrophizing. Doom and gloom. What if they say, 'Sure, sorry about the noise' and you're able to get some peace? What about that?"

"I-I just can't do it."

After, I headed down the normal way rather than climbing up the wet cliffs again. How do you ask for what you need from an apathetic world? Hell, how do you even *know* what you need from such a world? And how do you live with the repercussions of asking for help? When you ask most people for help, they make you pay for it. Plus, why do I deserve peace and quiet? Why do I deserve to heal? No one else is doing this shit. None of my friends in Buffalo have this luxury. Michael is hanging drywall. Matthew is working at a gas station. Tim is fighting terrorists in Afghanistan. What fucking right do I have to ask people to lower their music when Tiptoe Tim is getting shot at right now? What kind of pansy-ass bitch does such a thing? Is this what your life has come to, man? Are you gonna start wiping your ass with rose petals and going to get pedicures? Where do you draw the line?

And let's say you do decide to say something; how do you even get the words out without stuttering? Without pissing your pants and shaking like a kid? No, you can do all the shaking you want inside your own home, but the second you step out into the world and do that shit, you're gonna get beaten down hard. Besides, there are so many noises coming from all sides. How do you know where they're even coming from? What's causing them? Just like when trying to pick a movie, you're gonna get lost trying to figure out which noise to go after. You're gonna get lost listening to every little step someone takes. Just go home and go to sleep and forget all this shit about noises. The world controls you. You're its bitch.

I fell asleep relatively quickly that night, but even with the windows closed, fans and waterfall music on, and earplugs, I kept waking up to the neighbors screaming and blasting music until the sun came up.

Chapter 21

As shitty as I felt leaving the house, I joined a screenwriting critique group. We would read a different writer's script each month and spend the two-hour meeting giving feedback. The first script I read was so horrible I could hardly follow it. Some shit about ninjas in space and time traveling and all that crap, and it was an absolute disaster, but since I had no idea what my role in the group was, I mostly just checked for typos. At the meeting, we sat in a circle and everyone gave their feedback about plot holes and character development and I sweated more and more the closer it got to my turn to comment. I let the group know I had no idea what I was supposed to be doing, and went on a tangent about how to fix a particular dialogue passage, saying something like, "It's okay, we all fail sometimes," and not even realizing how insulting that was until the next person started speaking and it was too late for me to apologize. I felt guilty that they'd chosen my script, *The Silent Protest*, to critique next month, given how useless my feedback had been, and I was also nervous as hell to hear what other people would say about my writing.

When the day came, I bought a green tea at the café where we met and headed to the back room. I'd worn a dark shirt and baseball hat so they wouldn't see me sweating. I said a few awkward hellos to people and took my seat. Though I'd already burned my tongue, I kept taking nervous sips of my tea, and soon the meeting began.

The first guy, who'd started the group, said that he wasn't sure why I didn't set the story earlier. To him, the backstory was more important than the road trip these two guys took. I told him, "It's about their redemption *from* that time." He paused for a moment to think, then said, "No, no there's no story there."

The next woman said that there was too much vulgarity and that "people don't use so many curse words in real life." I felt like calling up Doug and having her speak with him for a few minutes to see if she'd change her mind. Some of these fuckin' Californians live in a hermetically sealed, ocean-side bubble where everything is white bread, red wine, and pink roses. But then she also said, "Real men don't talk like this—about their feelings and dreams. You should watch *Die Hard* to get a better idea of how men *really* speak." What she was really saying was that a man can run around a building shooting people while telling them to fuck their mothers and this was cool as long as he didn't mention how anxious it made him feel.

The next woman, the oldest person in the group, said that she thought the story was wonderful, going on and on about how well I'd developed the characters and that she felt the first guy was wrong about wanting me to set it in the backstory. "That past has happened and they're trying to deal with it the best they can by moving forward toward their dreams and fixing the wrongs they see in the world, not realizing that they need to fix themselves first." Her name was Rose and it was nice to hear someone affirm what I found beautiful in the story.

The others gave me some good feedback, and the guy I'd unintentionally insulted the previous meeting smirked as he said, "This is an R-rated movie packed in a PG-13 script." The dude got a chuckle from the group, and he patted himself on the back and soon the meeting was over. I thanked Rose for her comments, and a few others walked over to congratulate me as well. Rose said mine was the best script she'd read from the group, and that "Most of them submit *Indiana Jones* or *Lethal Weapon* or *Pretty Woman* knockoffs, and it was nice to read something new for a change. Try not to worry—most people don't like what they can't immediately understand." Some of the others, who'd gone along with the herd during the meeting, were now saying they agreed with Rose. Were they lying now? If so, why? If not, why'd they change their minds? As they hung on every word Rose said, I made the realization that groups like this had more to do with politics than critiquing art.

For days after, I contemplated the feedback. Some of it was useful, but I still didn't agree with most of it. But some of these writers had had their work produced into films. Some had written shorts that had gotten into the Soul City Film Fest. Who was I to think my opinions were better than theirs?

Regardless, I stuck to my instincts and made some changes to the script, rewriting several scenes and tightening up the overall character arcs, and decided to submit it to a few screenwriting contests. I looked for contests that might judge psychological, character-driven dramas like mine favorably, and submitted to those with the lowest entry fees.

I let Carolina know how things had gone with the writing group, and she said she was proud of me for putting myself out there. We'd been in near daily contact for months, and things were getting more serious. But the more serious they got, the more I started obsessing about testing her from every angle—as I'd done with Dr. Tom and the Frog. Testing to see how sincere she was. How compassionate. I wanted to pummel her with questions, pushing her in every direction to see if she could stand up to the bully inside of me. To the obsessions and fear and panic. This was at the tips of my fingers during every one of our conversations, and I realized it had probably always been at the tip of my tongue every time I'd spoken with women before— this desire to push her away while simultaneously begging her to stick around. Hoping that she'd just *get* what I needed and give it to me without thinking I was crazy or strange.

Again, it was already hard enough finding someone in today's fickle dating scene, but it felt impossible while fighting the wars I was waging in my head. But something about Carolina felt safe. Familiar. I'd pushed her a few times already, and she'd stuck around. I let her know about what the noises from neighbors did to me. I asked her if she shared walls with anyone in her apartment. A ceiling? A floor? I asked her if she could hear people talking in other apartments. What do you do if people slam cupboards? Shit like that, and I studied her responses—not so much because I cared about the layout of her dwelling, but because I wanted to know on an unconscious level if she was really on my side or not. If she could relate even slightly to my torment. And she did—slightly.

Though I had a month off in July, I knew I wasn't yet ready to see her, so I told her I'd come in December. I was still spending an hour or so in bed every day, and the thought of sharing a small hotel room with someone overwhelmed me—no matter how much I cared for her. I needed to be at my best. Plus, I hadn't worked out in over a year, and I was disgusted when I looked at myself in the mirror. Better to push it off until December . . . or maybe March . . . or maybe never.

Chapter 22

After watching Cody's interview on *Good Afternoon Soul City*, the principal of a charter school in the desert invited Cody to speak at a staff meeting about ways to boost student enrollment. Our numbers had been growing, mostly due to the TV and newspaper ads Ms. Kefana had created, using her PR background and connections. But the more work she did, the more Cody took credit for it, and on his TV interview, which Ms. Kefana booked, Cody said shit like, "Kids and parents are drawn to strong leadership, like the kind I've established at Cody Cares, which is the reason why our numbers are up."

Cody went to the desert with a smile and came back with a cowboy hat and cowboy boots, and he started wearing this getup to school on a regular basis and saying shit like "Howdy partners!" and "Let's saddle up!" Karla, Doreen, Barry, and I thought it was ridiculous, and even a little disturbing, but it was nice not being the weirdest person in the room for a change, and when Cody was throwing around lassos and screaming, "YEEHAW!" it took a lot of pressure off of me to act normal. I always thought people could see the insanity and fear in my eyes, but after asking Camarin a few times how I looked, she said, "Totally fine; stop worrying." Even on my worst days, other people seemed oblivious to my troubles. I started to realize that most people were so self-consumed they probably didn't think much of me, and even if they did, something else would soon win over their attention, and they'd forget they ever saw me in the break room, breathing through a panic attack and repeating nonsense words. And with Cody doing his cowboy shit, he was winning a lot of attention.

I began to realize that the warm feeling I got whenever Karla was around was more than just respect and admiration. It hit me one day while watching her coloring with one of her ninth-graders, who came from an abusive household. Karla had been spending her free time at the end of each school day with the girl, tutoring her or just hanging out and talking, and that day, I heard the girl ask Karla, "Can I go home with you today?" Karla looked too overwhelmed with emotion to respond, and as a tear dripped from her eye, I wanted to whisper in her ear, "Karla, right now, in this very moment, I'm falling in love with you. Right now, as you're saving this girl's life, you're also saving my own."

I sat at my desk to put grades in my book, but I had to wipe my tears away quickly when Barry came over to tell me about a fish he'd caught on the Sand Beach pier the day before. "You gotta come out next time," he said. I nodded and said, "Y-yeah, sure, sure, yeah, of course," like I always did, even though I hated those invitations and hated knowing he'd been on my turf. Years ago, I would have jumped at the chance to hang with him, drinking beers while catching fish and telling jokes, but now the thought of anyone entering my personal space terrified me. I almost wished no one would talk to me. It would be easier that way.

I'd accept Karla's invitations, though. It was easier for me to share myself with women, and even though Barry was a standup guy and would probably listen if I told him everything, I still couldn't. You can't do that shit with guys. But with Karla and Camarin, the neglected and terrified boy inside of me didn't have to play a role that kept his voice so small it couldn't be heard. All this confused me and made me realize that I was learning more about how to be a better man from women than from men. Thinking back, it was Mariposa's love in Mexico that had made me choose life over death, and now it was Camarin and Karla's love helping me to better understand what life truly was. The thought of watching Karla taking care of our kids someday, reading to them, laughing with them, teaching them how to ride bikes and bake cookies—it made me smile. It made me want to stay in one place long enough to reap what I'd sown. I'd been scattering seeds all over the world for years. There were weeds of me growing along so many Mexican highways and underneath stools in Buffalo dive bars and in the asphalt cracks in Sand Beach alleys and on the boulders near the pier. It was time I stuck around long enough to watch these pieces of myself grow.

A song came to me after Barry wandered away, and even though it was risky to open myself up in such an environment, hearing Karla and her student giggling had me wide open already. I took the small notebook out of my pocket, turned away from Karla, and wrote:

How do I tell you I love you,
when you're standing so close to me?
The vastness of your beauty, I
need a further perspective to see.
How do I tell you I love you?
How do I tell you just what I need?
How do I tell you I love you,
now that you're so far away?
As I paint the curves of your body
and the shadows of your face.
How do I tell you I love you?
How do I tell you when I can't see?

As much as I wanted to capture the melody in my voice recorder, I knew that would be pushing it, so instead I tried to burn the melody into my head, repeating it over and over as I put grades in the book, so I'd be able to recall it when I got home that day.

"Everything okay?" Doreen stood above my desk, scaring the

crap outta me. I shoved the notebook into my pocket and capped the pen, accidentally stabbing my palm with the tip.

"Oh, yeah, yeah, I'm good. What's up?" I said.

"Careful with that thing," she said about the pen.

"S-sorry, just a muscle spasm or something." In truth, since starting my sessions with the Frog, I'd been having weird muscle spasms on a regular basis. Sometimes while standing, my knees would jerk forward, causing me to almost fall over backwards, and my face was always twitching and my hands dropping things.

"You do your monthly grade book meeting with Camarin yet?" she said.

"Not yet. You?"

"I had mine last week. Everything was perfect."

"Just like you."

She smiled. "Don't worry, Barry hasn't done his yet either. He's working on his homework to clear his credential. Have you started your program yet?"

"What do you mean?"

"In California, you have five years to take classes to clear your credential. Luckily, the school pays the bill, but it's still a lot of work. You should start your courses soon."

"You gotta be kidding me! I have to do more school?"

"Yep."

"Why didn't anyone tell me? I've been down to the district office like five times since I moved here."

"You're pretty much on your own with things like this in California. Sink or swim."

"Well, I'm Jack Dawson right now."

She laughed. "What were you writing?"

"Oh, uh, just recording some grades . . ."

"In such a small notebook?"

"I gotta go, uh, talk to Camarin about something." On the walk to Ms. Kefana's office, I was overwhelmed with fear at the thought of having to go back to school. I hated school; as a kid, I'd always gotten terrible headaches trying to pay attention to my teachers, and I was constantly filled with anxiety and self-doubt. The clock is ticking now: In four years, you need to be rich and famous and done with this teaching bullshit. You're not going through all that learning crap again—at least, not in a school, with rules and expectations and teachers using words like "appropriate" and "approach" as they punish you for tapping your desk in patterns of fives or for having facial tics, telling Mom, "He has absolutely NO self-control! He should pray twenty Hail Marys tonight and beg Her forgiveness for his terrible behavior." No, fuck all that. You gotta stand up for that little kid now, Jay. Give this Cody Cares thing another year or two, heal up, and head to Hollywood. Fuck school.

I was glad Ms. Kefana wasn't in her office. If she had been, I would have had to think of a reason to tell her why I'd come by. Lately, she hadn't been around as much. In the last few weeks, Cody had hired five new teachers and set up another classroom in the cafeteria, and Camarin spent most of her time training them. The teachers would come to the gym from time to time, and they were . . . weird. Robotic. No time for chitchat—they got what they needed and headed back to the cafeteria, saying as little to any of us as possible.

But they said plenty to Cody, laughing at his dad jokes and telling him how smart and wonderful he was. It was as if Cody had stopped hiring teachers for their people skills and was now building a small army of sycophants. Karla, Doreen, Barry, and I figured this was because one of the original teachers had started openly criticizing Cody for our curriculum's "unacceptable lack of differentiation," and the Code Man was terrible with confrontation. Whenever someone challenged him, he'd get red and stammer as he defended his position, and we figured that after his recent "celebrity," he was tired of putting up with that crap. Tired of believing he was anything less than "the maverick of modern education," as they'd called him on TV. Better to build an army of ass-kissers. After he fired the "difficult" teacher, she went to the *Soul City Times* and they published a piece about how we were destroying the education world with our "watered down" curriculum, and Cody slipped deeper into his cowboy bullshit. Perhaps now that his fantasy of helping students was a reality, he needed more fantasies, and shit just kept getting weirder.

A little before the day was over, one of the new teachers passed by my desk, and though I said hi both on his trip to and from the bathroom, he didn't even look up. The student Karla had been coloring with also walked by, and I said bye to her, but she didn't look up either. I felt like saying, "Have a mediocre day!" to her or something, but when she got to the door, she turned and said, "Bye, Mr. S! Thanks for the candy earlier." She probably hadn't heard me when I said goodbye, and I was glad I hadn't said anything rude. It was too easy to take out aggression on kids. They were sponges for shame and abuse and anger, and they'd smile at you and try to please you, even as you were tearing them apart inside. It was something I'd had to learn over the years. To realize that even if a kid was smiling at me, it didn't mean he or she was all right. It didn't mean he or she was happy with me.

I think that was why so many parents tore into their kids. Because sometimes the more they smiled, the more we wanted them to feel the shame and misery we had felt at that age. But kids already felt that shame, and it was the job of adults to minimize and eliminate it. I started repeating, "It's never okay to be mean to kids" in my mind whenever I felt the urge to yell at one of them or to make them feel bad for failing a test or whatever. It's never okay to be mean to kids. It's never okay to be mean to kids. Repeating this lifted me up several times when I felt low enough to lash out, but I knew I had to be stronger. I knew I had to hold back the anger and understand what it was telling me, so that I could explain to the kids calmly and clearly how they, too, could understand and control their own emotions and impulses. And the more I did this, the less I was held down by the weight of all those adults who'd terrorized my childhood. Despite the muscle spasms and stiffness and soreness in my muscles and joints and my overall lack of energy, I was feeling better than ever, and each small victory—building a kid up rather than knocking them down—made me feel that hope was possible. That maybe I could make up for a lifetime of abuse by being good to kids.

But no matter how good I was to the kids, I still felt this wall between us, and I knew the only way to knock it down was to go back to Buffalo and confront the trauma that had ruined me as a kid. To confront the people who had hurt me. The people I had hurt. Why was it easy to tell a student, "Great job! I'm really proud of you," but impossible to say the same to my brothers or sisters? To tell Mom I loved her? If I was going to beat this thing, I'd have to get close to the people I'd felt isolated from growing up, and find a way to respond to them as calmly and clearly as I did to my students. Find a way to love them despite the trauma and the shame, and if that wasn't possible, to find a way to let them go. Find a way to forgive, and to apologize. If this healing thing involved peeling back the layers of an onion, I knew Buffalo was the center. I also knew that if I could confront all of this and keep my cool, that maybe I could also be the glue uniting us rather than another hammer smashing us apart. If I wanted to stop feeling like such a goddamned phony whenever I smiled and said something nice to someone, I would have to learn how to say something nice to the people who loved me—and mean it.

A parent called me about ten minutes before school ended, and she was sobbing, carrying on about her recent divorce and begging me to "help me understand! Please help me get him back! What do I say? What, what, what?" I hung up forty-five minutes later, realizing that maybe it wasn't my responsibility to get close to *everybody*. I also realized that I should probably never pick up the phone so close to the end of my shift again.

When I left school, it seemed much farther from the cliff than ever. In fact, it wasn't hanging over the edge anymore. The waves weren't shaking the school anymore either, but I only noticed this when I heard one hit the cliff but didn't feel it. On the drive back, I watched the sun set over the ocean and realized how badly I needed that perfect California climate. That I needed to be someplace where

I didn't have to worry about shoveling snow or blocking rain or wearing layers. I needed to be able to wake up and put on a button-down and pants and know I'd be okay for the day. And I knew I'd need this consistency for much longer. I'd need the consistency of Cody Cares for much longer too. I needed to be somewhere reliable and warm where I felt safe enough to allow the Darkness and horror inside of me to bubble to the surface and dissipate like the marine layer once it was hit by the California sun.

But if I stayed here too long, I would have to take more classes. I no longer had my coping mechanisms to help me get through school, so there was no way I'd be able to clear my credential. Hell, they'd probably find out sooner or later anyway that I was a phony and revoke my current credential, so why even worry about it? It's Hollywood or bust, Jay. Besides, your free time is sacred now. Now you're meeting with the Frog and shaking and sweating in bed. You're writing books and screenplays. How much longer do these assholes think they can control your life? Don't they realize it's yours now? You already gave them your entire youth. Even though Barry said his classes were online, there was no way I could manage that. I wasn't about to log into a system and allow that horrible energy to filter into my home. My safety zone. As much as I needed to remain consistent, I also needed to fly the hell out of Soul City and Cody Cares and strike it rich in Hollywood. Then I could take my money, fuck off to some remote Italian village, lock myself in my stone house and have all the consistency I needed, eating pasta and gelato all day. Drinking wine all day. Shooting smack all day.

Fuck . . . Maybe I would need Cody Cares for the rest of my life.

Chapter 23

I finally did it, and it worked, just as the Frog had said it would. My neighbor was blasting music, the bass driving right through the wall, and after about forty minutes of pacing my apartment and debating whether or not to say something, I finally decided to do it—then I spent the next half hour building up the courage. I almost chickened out, but when he cranked the volume further and the floor started pulsating, I used my frustration as a fuel to start moving. I walked outside and knocked on his door, and he answered with a "what the fuck you want?" look on his face.

"Hey, uh, I'm your neighbor and the bass is really loud. Can you turn it down and move it away from the wall? It's driving me nuts."

"Oh, yeah, sure. Sorry, it's a small system, and I didn't realize how powerful it is. Hey, you wanna beer or something?"

"Oh, no thanks."

I wandered back to my place, and even though it was quiet now, I was still flooded with anxiety. Dude, there's no going back now. You just started a war. Even though he said he was sorry, he's gonna remember this and turn up the music again someday when you need the silence the most, and you'll have used up your one hey-can-you-turn-down-the-music request, and if you ask again, he's gonna point that speaker at your head and blow out your brains. He's probably already telling all your other neighbors what a bitch you are. Half of

Sand Beach probably thinks you're a piece of shit. Your life is over, you fucking loser. *Who* does that? It's Saturday afternoon. The fuck's wrong with you, man? Don't make *your* problems other people's problems as well.

Yeah, but still, it was loud as hell. Aren't you entitled to some peace and quiet, even on a Saturday? Yeah, it's an apartment building, but doesn't that mean neighbors should be even *more* aware of the noise they're making? If any of them asked me politely to stop slamming cupboards or turn down my TV, I'd probably smile and say no problem. What's so wrong with asking someone for something you need, especially a neighbor? Why's it so hard for us to ask the world for something we need? He's probably still listening to his music, but now you aren't. It's a win-win. Just relax. Go take a walk or something and try to calm down.

I decided to give it a shot. It'd been months since I'd walked through Sand Beach during the day, and I wanted to test my progress. But I only got halfway down the main strip before I had to turn back. All the fire-breathers and bikers and punks and street kids asking for change and people looking at me as if I was still an *outsider* and wanting to fight me because of it. It was too much. I locked the door behind me when I got back and spent the rest of the day in bed.

How did you ever do this shit? You used to cruise up and down that strip high and drunk, winning fights against these clowns. Now, you shit your pants when a twelve-year-old looks at you wrong. You've fucked yourself. You've lost your armor, and there's no turning back. You can't survive in the freak show anymore, but do you really think the squares will take you in? They know you're a side-mouth-talking, wife-fucking, wallet-swiping son of a bitch. They know you have dreams bigger than their white-bread existence. They don't want you or your ripped jeans or bloodstained sneakers or scornful looks. You're all alone now, man. You're not even like Karla or Barry or Camarin. You're not like Doug anymore either. It's just you, surrounded by threats. Hostility. Screaming parents on the phone. Cute women walking right by your pleated-pants-wearin' ass. You did this to yourself. I told you to move straight to LA. Use your fire and grit to make it big, then go burn out somewhere like all the greats. That was your destiny, but you fucked it all up by saying yes to Cody. Saying yes to Dr. Tom and the Frog. Saying no to Nima and Doug. By putting off your trip to see Carolina. You've condemned yourself to a lifetime of middle-class American isolation and misery. Never in, never out. Never up, never down.

The changes inside of me also affected my perception of time and space. Whereas before, everything felt as if it were right on top of me and I needed it all NOW, NOW, NOW!, now I was slowly developing more distance between myself and things. Feeling time in more of a long-term sense. Since moving to Soul City, I'd had so many victories— sleeping through the night, keeping a job, being able to cook and clean for myself—that I felt confident enough to think beyond the present. But I went from living for the moment to living for retirement—no in-between. No next week or next month. Everything was always all or nothing, and now I saw myself trying to kill it all away so I could make it to fifty-five. Numbing myself so I could survive the bottomless depression of adult American life. Telling myself things like, okay, if you can just get through this week, there are only two more until the month is over, then there are only two more months until November, and then you'll have the month off. Then just a few weeks until winter break, and all you have to do is repeat this cycle another thirty times and you'll finally have the freedom you crave. You can take your pension and move to a remote mountain village in Nicaragua and do weird shit inside of your fortified compound, drinking rainwater you've collected in plastic buckets and cooking scorpions you've picked off the walls. No longer was I thinking of parties and bars and women I wanted to meet THAT NIGHT! Now, I'd be wrinkled and gray before I ever found love. Before I ever made it to Mexico City to meet Carolina, who would almost assuredly be married by then. By then, you'll just be the weird guy she spoke with on the Internet years ago. Jason, right? The guy who kept saying, "Yeah, I'll come next month," but never did.

But you're better off without her or anyone else. Remember

what happened with Mariposa? Remember how you'd absolutely panic the moment the stillness set in? Remember how you'd freak her out whenever you shut down during dinner and stared at the walls, refusing to speak? Remember how she worried about you at first but later, she started hanging out with her "friend" and you heard rumors about what was going on between them? Remember how, despite how much you loved her, the thought of spending even one more day with her made you want to stick your head in the oven? The same shit'll happen with Carolina. Just leave her alone. Just stay in your noisy, messy apartment. Avoid friends. The people you choose are the ones who bring you to whorehouses and back-alley bars and leave you drunk beside the dumpster out back. The people who promise you gold but hand you shit, and you eat it and tell them what great friends they are. The people who take everything you have and make you apologize for not having more. You're not ready for friends or lovers and you probably never will be. Just enjoy the silence. Enjoy the fact that they haven't brought you down yet. Enjoy the fact that you never ended up in prison. Enjoy the fact that you're not dodging bullets in Afghanistan like Tippy-Toe Timmy. "It could be worse" is your only comfort.

Now, you're on a long-term journey. There are no more blackout nights or wild road trips for you. In some ways, this was comforting. Knowing where I'd be in a month. Maybe in a year. But in other ways, thinking on a long-term scale made my OCD symptoms much worse. Obsessing over every noise the neighbors made. Demanding that I read books on economics and philosophy and politics until I knew *everything*. Worrying that I'd say or do something stupid at work. If I called some kid a whiny bitch or took a swing at a parent, I wouldn't be able to just quit and move on. In a long-term world, there were real consequences. Take a swing, and go to jail. Get sued. Lose it all.

At 4 a.m., I was woken up by a party in the building next door, and even though I knew it made me the biggest bitch alive, I numbed myself and dialed the police non-emergency number. The officer said, "Man, you're the third person who's called about them tonight," and I realized that there were other people like me out there, who were tired of being abused and were doing their best to fight back. I didn't know whether the cops ever showed or not, but that wasn't important. Just knowing that someone was taking me seriously and actually working to make the world a little quieter made me calm down enough to fall back asleep. I was now the adult calling the cops on the kids. I'd crossed a line I'd never be able to cross back over, but I'd crossed so many of those lately, what was one more?

I woke up around ten on Sunday and saw I had a missed call from my mom. I lay in bed trying think of something I could do that day, but there were too many horrors outside to leave my apartment. I thought about writing, but after the previous day's disaster with my neighbor's music, I knew that was too risky. If I started writing something, I'd get deeper and deeper into it and just when I'd made the revelation of a lifetime, he'd start blasting the bass, and I'd never be able to write again.

You were lucky enough to finish that one script. Don't push it. When it gets produced into a film and starts winning Oscars, then you can let the other story ideas come, but if you start trying now, it'll only end in insanity.

Though I hadn't done any physical exercise in months, my back was killing me. It was as if a giant had grabbed me by the shoulders and feet and twisted my upper body 180 degrees, with my shoulders perpendicular to my hips, and then shifted my left shoulder six inches above the right, and my head forward, so I was leaning in toward my chest. I tried to relax enough to straighten myself out, but I also knew this was an exercise in futility, just like the writing. Once I started relaxing enough to understand what was going on with my body, someone next door would light off fireworks or blast their music or have loud donkey sex. I had to stay tight. Had to stay wrapped up in the safety and cover of my own muscles.

I stayed in bed for about an hour, until my other neighbor started puking in her bathroom, which was on the opposite side of my bedroom wall. After, she slammed a few cupboards, and I felt trapped. I couldn't go to the right side of my apartment because of my neighbor's music and now I couldn't go to the left, and I avoided the rear wall because the people in the building next door were always screaming like idiots, so I curled into a ball in the center of my place and let the chemicals contort my body and numb me. This was where I'd have to stay for the next thirty years—in this position, wrapped in a Darkness so thick I could hardly breathe. Outside, it was a gorgeous day. People were surfing and playing beach volleyball and getting drinks with friends. People like Nima and Winston and Jadia were out there chasing their dreams. But here I was, crushed by the weight of my own misery, which filled the room like coal dust.

Eventually, I grabbed my computer and saw Carolina had posted a picture of herself with another guy. It looked as if they were at a party, and they were both smiling with their arms around each other. I started sobbing and didn't try to stop. I wanted to tap into that well of misery and let it all gush out, and I left wet spots all over the living room carpet as I paced, apologizing to Mariposa and my sisters, cursing out my father and mother, telling off that psychotic woman who'd harassed me on the phone at work, begging Carolina to wait for me—promising that I'll be whole soon and we'll walk hand in hand down the red carpet at my film's premiere. Thanking Karla and Camarin for their compassion. Asking the California Gods to give me enough inspiration to make it through this Darkness.

When the tears stopped, I felt better. I called my mom and after saying hi, I started ranting like a lunatic, telling her, "Dad doesn't have scoliosis! It's not scoliosis. It's not his back—it's his brain. Take him to the doctor. Take him to therapy. HE DOESN'T HAVE SCOLIOSIS! *NOBODY* HAS SCOLIOSIS!" I hung up, then started pacing again. I thought of that picture Carolina had posted. The guy she was with was handsome and muscular. I walked to my bathroom scale and stepped on it. For months, I'd been avoiding that scale, and when I saw I was ten pounds heavier than usual, I took off my shirt and looked in the mirror. I was losing all of the definition I'd worked a lifetime to have—just letting it go, offering it up as a sacrifice to the Gods of Healing. Who could love this? This absolute fucking mess? As bad as things were before, at least women would casually rub your arms and back. As bad as things were before, at least they'd look at you when you walked down the beach. Nobody's ever gonna look at you again. You're gonna die a big, crazy marshmallow in this noisy, dark apartment and no one's gonna come to your funeral. You shut them all out. You think anyone's ever gonna give a fuck about you again?

After pacing and cursing people and myself for most of the afternoon, I decided to start eating healthier. If I couldn't exercise, I could at least control what I was putting in my body. No more microwaved pizzas or burritos. All organic, wholegrain foods. Fruits and vegetables. Chicken breasts. Black beans. Steel-cut oats. You've got all the time in the world now to prepare food, anyway.

But when my neighbor slammed another cupboard, my fantasy of eating healthy vanished. How can I build *anything* here? I guessed California was the land of earthquakes as much as it was the land of healing. Maybe none of this was supposed to come easy. You've gotta fight for it, Jay. You can't let it win. When the panic takes over, just do what you can. Create a list of what you need to do to survive, starting with the most basic necessities, and when your brain starts shutting down, just focus on the list. Do the steps in order. And write this list when you're feeling okay, so you can think about it more clearly, and then when the world crashes down on you, just start crossing off items. Crawl through the maze. Climb over the concrete walls. You'll arrive someday. You gotta *believe*. You've been following your inner path your entire life and it's never been wrong. It's brought you to this exact spot. Trust in the process.

I decided to take the Frog's advice and see a psychiatrist. I had no idea how taking pills could stop me from running to the other side of my apartment every time I heard a neighbor burp, but it was worth a try. I'd been holding out because I'd gone over the edge on drugs a few times, and then I didn't know if *I* was me or if the drugs were. I was terrified to take something that might push me off the path that had led me to the Frog. With all the night-and-day changes, I still had no idea who I truly was. I could see it clearly sometimes—like that night I read *The Prophet*, or those times I'd traveled by bus through Mexico—but maybe if I took a pill, it would turn me into a different person. Maybe it would stop my writing and seeking and yearning to see every inch of the world. Maybe it would make me like *them*—all the fuckin' squares who spent their free time getting brunch and shopping for furniture and spending entire weekends at the mall, hoping to reinvent themselves with a swipe of their credit cards. Maybe it'd make me want to stay at Cody Cares past my expiration date, like all those lunatics who could have retired but stuck around their dead-end jobs because they had absolutely no clue what else to do with their free time. Maybe it'd round my edges and blunt my desire and turn me into a soulless, top-forty-radio-consuming shithead.

Or, maybe it'd finally be the push that sent me into eternal Darkness. After all, the only guiding light I'd had in this process was getting out of my own way and trusting my body and psyche to heal on their own. Pills were made by people, and people couldn't be trusted. If I swallowed a pill, how could I relax? How could I trust the process?

But seeing Carolina with that other dude made me realize I needed to act fast. It also made me realize how much my conception of true love had changed since I'd started seeing the Frog. Before, love had felt wild, like a drug, and I'd always felt shredded both outside and in. But the more control I felt, the more I realized that I couldn't rely on a woman to heal me. I had to heal first, and once I did that, how would love feel? Would it be bland? Tasteless? Would I feel compelled to run across deserts and over mountains and through jungles just to feel her breath on my face? Would I feel compelled to rip off her clothes and lick every inch of her body, sticking my tongue in places dark and wet, and never get enough?

Maybe not. Maybe Carolina would feel more like a friend.

Maybe I'd feel warm and safe and happy, but never rage with desire. As I entered square society, I started understanding these people a little better. I was starting to see why they would settle for a job and a house and a city and a life partner, even though it was all wrong. I could see that most people weren't like me—raging all the time. Seeking everything and nothing all at once. Living and dying to dive inside the Great River. Most were happy at brunch and at the crowded mall and being with someone who was socially competent and attractive enough to walk beside without feeling ashamed. Now I could see why they dated so many people. It was easy to toss people away when they were so interchangeable. But when I liked a woman, there was no substitute, and I couldn't imagine spending a moment away from her. I would have fought armies, traveled to distant planets, dangled my balls in fire ant hills. I didn't want to lose that. Before, there was no way I would have put off seeing Carolina. Before, I would have run down to Mexico the night I met her. Was I becoming one of *them*?

The more control I had, the easier it was to talk to women. But something about this terrified me. I don't want it to be easy! I want it to be fire and ice. I need to *believe*. To believe that true, heart-on-fire love is real. But this healing journey is taking me to a place where I can meet a woman without having to flex or chug or fight to impress her, then take her to the new ramen place downtown where we talk about our careers while checking our phones a hundred times and fake-smiling our way through the conversation, then we go back to her place, kiss in the kitchen after she opens a bottle of wine, then I get a decent hand job on the couch, leave, and we never talk again.

I want to go back to the old way. I should call up Doug. Tell him I'm sorry. Tell him to come by and let's go out tonight. Let's go drink every last drop of beer in Sand Beach and fuck every woman we see. Who cares if your wife just gave birth? It's all ME, ME, ME anyway, don't you know that? Don't you know this is California? This isn't a place of healing. It's a place of posturing. It's a place of sin. Let's dive in and never look back!

When it got dark, I headed to the least-crowded supermarket in town to buy some healthy food. Before I left my place, I noticed that I'd had to check the faucets in the bathtub and sink, and I had to lift the lid on the toilet to make sure it wasn't running even though I couldn't hear it running. Then I had to check the kitchen sink and the fridge door, then I went back to the bedroom and checked the window to be sure it was locked, then I went to the living room to be sure the lamp wasn't too close to the edge of the table where it could fall over and start a fire, then I went back to the bathroom and waved my hand underneath each faucet to be sure they weren't on, then I removed the toilet lid again and counted to seventy-six while touching the flusher handle with my left hand. I kept doing that, rushing from room to room and checking things while counting and humming and it took me about forty minutes before I could leave, and then it took me another ten minutes or so to lock the front door. Even though the knob wouldn't turn and the door wouldn't open no matter how hard I pushed on it, I still didn't believe it was locked.

I thought about all of this as I walked to the market and as obnoxious as it all was, I smiled, realizing that this was the OCD I'd buried under decades of muscle tension and fear. I'd been doing these rituals more and more over the last month or so, and they seemed to be getting worse the more I did them. It felt that, the more I did them, the less control I had over everything, but knowing that this healing process was going to be like peeling back layers of an onion, I was actually glad to have started on a new layer. But still, I knew this layer was going to be more challenging than any of the previous, and I didn't know how I was going to stop these rituals. It felt impossible.

I bought fruit, vegetables, whole-grain pasta, and chicken and started making stir-fry for dinner. I was able to chop the pepper, onion, and garlic before my neighbor started hammering something into his wall, and I was hit with a wave of Darkness. I realized that when I panicked, my whole being shut down. But I told myself, just follow your list. Finish chopping the vegetables, then cut up the chicken, put it in the pan, and let it cook. While it cooks, just relax.

Pace if you need to—and I did. While pacing, I realized that the panic had caused blackout moments in the timeline of my life. That it was the panic that had fucked up my sense of time, kept me from living beyond each agonizing moment.

But now I was better able to understand how the panic affected me and my concept of time. If I could get beyond the fear, maybe I could be like Nima and Winston and all the others who were able to make long-term plans and work toward them, little by little each day—unlike my plan to storm down to LA like a monsoon and WIN immediately, in that very moment, while I still felt the rush of confidence. I realized that this inability to see beyond the moment was causing a great deal of my depression. That I wasn't able to free my hope and let it wander, but rather, I kept it wrapped in the thick heavy blanket where it had learned long ago that it was better to lie still than fight back.

The stir-fry burned, and I microwaved a pizza instead. Hell, maybe Carolina won't care if I'm fat. Maybe I should just grow a pair and buy my fucking ticket.

So I did—after confirming the dates with her, of course. She wasn't free in November, which was one of the months I had off, so we decided on March. Yeah, it was far off, but at least now we had a plan, and now I had some more time to figure out how to stop checking every damned thing before leaving my place and going to bed.

I did the rituals again before bed and timed myself: an hour and twenty minutes of checking and counting and unplugging appliances and touching windows. Still, I had hope it would all improve soon.

"No, you don't. You absolutely do not have it under control," the Frog said, sitting on a rock in the cave.

"I dunno—I mean, it's not *that* bad," I said.

"Oh yeah? How many hours a day are you spending doing these rituals?"

"Maybe two, sometimes three."

"That's not under control."

"It feels like I just need to exorcise it all through me, ya know? Kinda like I did with the intrusive thoughts. If I just let it all come, feel it as fully as possible, then perform the rituals and understand what they're telling me, isn't that the way to get rid of it?"

"No, that's how you *feed* it. OCD is treatable, and you can put most of this behind you."

"How?"

"Stop performing your rituals, which may sound simple, but to someone like you, it seems impossible."

"Yeah, you might as well ask me to breathe underwater."

"Did you read that book I gave you, *Brain Lock*?"

"Not yet. I've been trying to get through an economics textbook, then I want to read up on philosophy and maybe government or law next."

"You planning on starting your own country or something?"

"No, it's for my writing. I wrote one script that was loosely based on my life, and I don't think I'll ever be able to write anything again unless I expand my mind. When I watch films like *12 Angry Men*, or hell, even *My Cousin Vinny*, I don't understand half of what they're talking about. How am I supposed to be a writer if I don't know anything?"

"But you do. You know about OCD and alcoholism, and due to this, you've developed a gift for understanding complex psychological issues. I'm sure you're able to write incredible characters."

"That stuff's easy for me, but trying to set a psychological story in a place like a courtroom or a police station or foreign embassy or wherever—I have no idea how to write that authentically."

"So, write what you can in the meantime, and learn as you go. You don't need to know everything about economics or philosophy to write a film. Look at *Good Will Hunting*. Those guys consulted mathematicians to make their script more authentic. You can't do it all yourself. That's your OCD talking. This *I need* or *I should* talk is the disease. You don't have to know everything there is before you can express yourself. Self-expression is a journey, not a destination."

"Yeah, I guess. But I don't think I can stop reading them. It feels like I *have* to, you know? Like, I'll start panicking if I don't."

"Jay, you're a young man. Why take on such a heavy burden? You should be out having fun with friends. Go live your life."

"I-I've gotta sacrifice my youth for this. I know it. I can't ever be young again. I already made this decision, and I'm okay with it."

"Listen to you. I should record you so you can hear yourself. This absolutism isn't serving you at all."

"It's helping me stay on the path to achieving my dreams. Maybe the OCD is a good thing. It keeps me disciplined and moving forward."

"It's got you defecating in plastic grocery bags."

"I haven't done that in a while now."

"No, listen to me. It's not fine. Think about that for a second."

I did and after a few moments I realized that maybe I didn't have anything under control. That maybe the disease made me think I was in charge as *it* called the shots. Maybe I couldn't trust my own judgment.

"Yeah, you're right. You know, all this shit—the OCD, the writing and whatever—it feels like a dry heave. I keep retching but nothing comes up, and it just kills my insides. Or, better, it's like an asymptote. I can get close but never touch. That's how I feel it is with the checking and touching and all that. It's also how I feel with the writing. I think there's a tremendous amount of creativity inside of me, but I'm not able to access it. If I could touch it, I'd be in that Great River with the others, but I'm not and probably never will be. And it fucking kills me. It hurts my brain. It feels like an actual wound. And that's how I feel with the sounds and everything at my apartment too. I can feel the sounds in my meat before I do in my brain. I start clenching up and flooding with anxiety and I can't even stop it. I rush over and put my ear to the wall whenever I hear what might sound like talking or a TV, and if I don't hear anything after a few minutes, then I'll convince myself I didn't hear anything in the first place, which is optimal because if I *do* hear something, I'm fucked for the rest of the day. I can't read or write or anything. I'll pace or curl up in a ball and cry. I talk to myself. I repeat words or nonsense phrases fifty, sixty, five hundred times. I'll say shit like 'sack lunch' over and over and over until the words lose all meaning and I feel like I'm falling into a void of sheer chaos. When I was a kid, I used to stare at myself in the mirror and after a minute or so, I'd lose all concept of reality, and soon it was as if I were in outer space looking into an alien's eyes. I'm not in control of anything. Not even in control of looking at myself in the mirror. I never know what I'm gonna see. When is this gonna stop? I need this to stop."

"You need to stop doing your rituals—"

"That's impossible. You said it yourself. It's like, if I don't lock the door, someone's gonna break in and steal all my shit—plates and spoons and forks and I won't be able to eat again, and I'll starve to death. They'll steal my computer and notebooks full of song lyrics and poems, and I won't be able to live anymore. They'll steal my work clothes and shoes and all that and I'll get fired from my job, and I'll end up shooting smack under the Sand Beach pier. That's the thing: If I don't check the stove, the end result is insanity. If I don't check the faucet, I'm gonna end up hurling my feces at people down near the beach, and the cops will beat me so badly I'll lose my sight and I'll die blind and alone in some jail infirmary. There's no fucking hope for me. I *can't* stop. I can't stop anything. Just put a fuckin' bullet in my brain right now. I can't do insanity. I've been there my whole life—right on the border. I'd rather die before I go over completely. Honestly, I'd rather die."

"I know this all seems overwhelming, but you'd benefit from medication—"

"I've thought about that, but fuck, man! The OCD is like an alien living inside of my body. I don't know which thoughts belong to me and which belong to it, and if I add any more variables into that equation, I'll just further confound my path to recovery. If I start droppin' pills, how do I know what's me and what's it and what's them? What if I can't write anymore? The only reason I haven't taken a leap of faith off that pier yet is because I haven't yet said what I need to say. I feel like everything I've ever written is a suicide note, you know? Just letting people know, hey, I was here and I tried my best and here's some shit that was important to me. Here are my thoughts. See, my life wasn't totally worthless."

"Jay, I gotta say, I'm worried about you. Try medication. You won't know until you try."

"I do know. I do. I know it won't work. God wants me in Hell. This is all punishment for some awful shit I've done in a past life. Some awful shit I've done in this one. I'm *supposed* to suffer. This is my path, screaming at neighbors and picking my skin and spending entire weeks each year checking shit. You know, I did the math the other day and figured in my youth, I used to spend about four hours a day praying and going through my rituals—which were different then—and they stopped for a bit once I started drinking, but even so, during that whole time, I still performed rituals, they just looked like real, normal human activities. I'd drink and smoke and stay in constant motion and absolutely panic if I stopped. Anyway, I ran the numbers, and I'd say I've spent a little over a year of my life just doing rituals. Just spinning my tires in the mud. Can you imagine what else I could have done in that time? Fuck, they built the Empire State Building in less time. That building's like a monument to my suffering. I can't take this anymore. I really can't. I'm gonna do something bad to myself. I try to improve my life by eating better or whatever, and then someone starts singing next door and I feel like chugging antifreeze."

"Here, take this." The Frog handed me a piece of paper with a phone number on it. "Call this number. Tell them it's an emergency."

"I'm fine."

"You're not fine."

I looked into the dark ocean. In the distance, the ships were passing again, leaving a trail of dots on the horizon. "Okay." I took the paper. "I think a lot of this has to do with sleep as well—the rituals I mean. I do them for at least an hour before bed now, and I feel that if I just screw up one thing, I won't be able to sleep, and then I'll go crazy and lose my job. The OCD began one night when I couldn't sleep, and I imagine that's probably where a lot of my problems come from. All these rituals and the OCD and everything have completely warped my sense of time and place. When I look at my bathroom sink, even though I can see that it's off and I can't hear any water, and I touch the handles and turn them as far as they'll go, the second I turn away, it's as if I can't remember that it's off. I don't trust it's off, and I have to keep checking until I've reduced my anxiety enough to walk away. But even then, I'm not fully convinced it's off. It's difficult for me to accept reality—not with everything, just certain things like with doors and windows and faucets and all that—and I don't trust my eyes or ears or fingers. Everything feels like chaos. You have no idea how exhausted I am. When I become rich and famous someday, I'm gonna sleep for a week straight. I need rest. I'm gonna completely collapse soon. I'm completely out of control."

"There, you said it. Now, call that number, and get in immediately. Tell them it's an emergency."

"Yeah, okay."

"And come back soon. You're a special person to me. I see a lot of people, but I gotta say, you're working harder than any five I've ever seen combined. I applaud your complete dedication to healing, and I know one day you'll look back at all of this and realize you're a better, stronger person as a result. Most writers never have the luck to see what you have, and someday you'll be able to use it more than you'll ever be able to use something you read in a law textbook. Call that number, and in the meantime, be good to yourself, will ya?"

Chapter 24

I saw the psychiatrist and after nodding a few times and writing some shit down, he handed me a prescription for some anxiety medication I'd never heard of. I researched the hell out of it, from when it was made to side effects to consumer reviews, and I decided to fill the prescription. I felt strange walking into my local pharmacy, knowing they had all kinds of drugs behind that counter that could help with my mind while drunks and tweakers and street kids hung out in the alley out back. That I could potentially end a lifetime of misery by paying five bucks and swallowing some pills I got from a place where I'd only ever bought condoms and beer. As much as I hoped this would work, when the pharmacist highlighted some rare but horrifying side effects, I knew I'd be keeping those pills in the cupboard until shit got so bad I had no other choice but to take them. And even if the horrible side effects didn't happen to me, what if the pills didn't work? I'd have no last resort left—just a lifetime of misery.

I walked through tweaker alley on the way home, still seeing little difference between them and myself, and wondered why no one ever told them that *these* pills would be the ones to save their lives, not *those*. I felt like telling them all to go see the Frog, but I also didn't want to make eye contact, and so I kept moving until I was locked inside of my apartment again.

After putting the pills in the cupboard, I realized I needed to do *something*, so I started reading *Brain Lock*, and almost immediately I was hit with the same feeling I'd gotten reading *The Prophet*. Reading page after page of case studies and symptoms and explanations of how OCD affects the brain, I was overwhelmed with how much it all sounded like my own life. To read about others who'd been tortured just as I had. How could anyone survive this? People taking twelve-hour showers to scrub away the contamination. Cleaning their houses for days because they left the front door open one second too long, and now the whole place was "contaminated." Now they had to scrub the walls and pull up the carpet and retile the kitchen floor and throw away their furniture and handwash their clothes while counting out certain numerical patterns and replaying songs over and over in their brains for days, weeks, months, until they felt so weak from it all that they wanted to kill themselves. People hoarding newspapers and pizza boxes and cat crap and mason jars filled with urine and so much shit all over the place they could hardly walk through it all. People who couldn't stop thinking about fucking their mothers or killing their children or crushing dogs' skulls with bricks or putting cats in microwaves, even though they'd never actually do such a thing. People who couldn't stop checking their doors and windows and stoves and faucets, because otherwise planes would fall from the sky or their families would die in a car accident or a flash flood would wipe out the entire town. The extreme guilt for simply being alive. The constant fear and doubt, never trusting your mind or senses. Everything was always doom and gloom. Fire and brimstone. The gods themselves lived within the minds of those with OCD, and if you didn't follow their exact orders, they'd make you pay. And they'd made me pay so many, many times. I had no idea how anyone with OCD could survive past twenty-two. Hell, how could *anyone* survive past twenty-two? How *did* I survive? It's a fucking miracle. And, now, maybe there was hope. The book said I could someday live a normal life: I just had to stop doing the rituals—like the Frog said. I had to retrain my brain. But as simple as it sounded, I knew it could take years, maybe even decades, to stop doing these, if ever.

As I continued reading, I had to stop several times because my eyes blurred with tears. For all the people who'd treated me as if I was broken or dirty or sinful or annoying or ungrateful, there were people out there like Dr. Schwartz, who had spent his life helping people. Taking the time to understand why people with OCD acted the way we did. Not getting angry because we forgot things easily or asked the same question a thousand different ways or flooded with panic because someone handed us the salt shaker with their left hand rather than their right.

Like when I'd read *The Prophet*, I realized that no matter how far gone and broken I felt, no matter what horrible things I'd done or felt I'd done, no matter how many times I'd thought about drinking so much I'd never wake up again, that there was a community of good people out there waiting to welcome me the moment my eyes opened for the first time, and I understood that the only way to live life was through compassion and love. Acceptance. Awareness. As many people as there were trying to destroy me, the same number were trying to help me. That I had the responsibility to do the same for others. I cried when I finished that book and could feel my brain's chemistry changing. A warm feeling took over my body and mind, and I knew I could get through this. I knew someday I'd be all right. And it both pissed me off and filled me with pride that I'd had to run thousands of miles away from home to find this out for myself. There were so many times I could have simply laid down and died, but I kept pushing and pushing, knowing there'd be an end to the suffering someday. And, now, here I was.

But my new journey was only beginning. This would take years. I wasn't going to LA anytime soon. My dreams of acting and directing would have to wait. In the meantime, I could write. I could write all of my pain into the world. I could write the cure. I could write an emotional map for others to follow, so they could overcome their own suffering. Maybe I'd grow soft and wrinkled doing it, but it had to be done. If only Kerouac had had a therapist. If only Van

Gogh had had someone like the Frog to talk to, maybe he'd have found his peace. For years, I'd turned my suffering into art. Perhaps now I could turn my healing into art as well. Don't fear it, Jay. Don't fear change. Allow the path to change you, and write down what you see and feel. Healing and writing are the same path, and that path is leading you to the Great River.

For dinner, I made a kale salad and chicken with black beans and brown rice and ate in silence at my coffee table. I usually watched shows like *The Office* or *Deadwood* during dinner, but I was still reflecting on the book and the ways I hoped to change. Before bed, I did my best to stop checking everything, but it was too hard, and I spent roughly the same amount of time as usual—a little over an hour. Though it was exhausting, I couldn't sleep. At first, I flooded with panic, but I listened to what that panic was telling me, and I understood that I'd had problems with sleeping since the OCD hit me when I was about ten, and every night, I got anxious trying to block out anything that might rob of me sleep. But that anxiety destroyed the quality of my sleep, which was why I always woke up feeling as though I'd just fought a long battle. It was why I'd had nightmares since I was a kid, waking up several times throughout the night drenched in sweat. I usually kept a towel nearby to wipe myself down and fall back asleep, but I couldn't keep that up anymore. I needed real sleep. So, rather than fight my insomnia, I didn't try to sleep. Instead, I just lay there, letting all of my thoughts race and scream at me and tell me I was gonna go crazy and lose my job and all that and even though I couldn't help but panic, I was still able to get about two hours of sleep. In the morning, I realized that my perception of time was also influenced by my poor sleep quality. That every night felt like a battle, often filling me with anxiety throughout the day, worrying about whether or not I'd be able to sleep, and each night felt as if it'd be the last of my life. But if I could improve the quality of my sleep, I could separate the night and day and get away from this one continuous day—this endless battle—where I was never quite awake and never quite asleep. As much as it terrified me to let down my defenses, possibly causing me to never sleep again, I knew I had to try, otherwise my life would never be mine, and as exhausted as I was, I pulled myself out of bed, got ready, and headed to Cody Cares.

After work, I saw the Frog again and let him know I hadn't taken the pills but that I did read the book.

"Well, you gotta start somewhere," he said.

I told him that I wanted to go the natural route with all of this and he suggested I see a Rolfer he knew, called the Knight. He said Rolfing was "like a deep-tissue massage but for your body's fascia. Listen to the Knight describe it. He says it's like giving your body more space. That guy's a genius. He can read people's muscles, and he'll say something like, 'Did your mother used to hit you here with a wooden spoon?' and they'll be like, 'How'd you know?'"

As little as I wanted anyone to touch me, I figured Rolfing was better than taking pills, so I called up the Knight and headed to his office on Saturday morning. He had a great place in Snob Beach with an ocean view, and it smelled like incense. I sat in a waiting room and a guy wearing chainmail and armor entered. "Jay, I could sense you were here. C'mon inside."

I followed him into the room, and after introductions, he asked me why I was seeing him. I let him know about my OCD and extreme muscular tension. "I don't know—it feels like a maze almost. When I relax, I can almost feel the way my muscles are pulling me out of alignment, but usually I'm so filled with anxiety that it all feels like chaos. I think if I had a month or two where I could just lie in bed and relax, I might be able to solve the puzzle and untangle myself. It almost feels as if my upper body is pulling in toward my chest and everything in my lower body is pulling in toward my groin. I just want to be hinged, you know? I gotta swing my whole body around to use my arms or legs and it's exhausting me. Whatever is in me needs to follow a maze to get out, and all the best stuff feels stuck inside, deep down where I can't access it, so I feel like I'm living at the surface of my being, and I don't have any time to think about my words or actions—everything is just a quick reaction, and usually an overreaction."

"It sounds like your body is locked in a defensive position. Once we loosen you up, you'll be amazed at what your body—and mind—can do. Both of those are so intertwined they're really the same thing."

"Yeah, to me it almost feels as if my muscles store memory, like a computer hard drive or something."

"Well, I'm looking forward to seeing what's in there. Let's begin."

I stripped down to my boxers and got on his table, and he played a CD of men with deep voices repeating, "Ohmm." He rubbed some peppermint oil on his hands and started reading my body, laughing and saying, "Ahh" a few times, almost as if he were having a conversation with my muscles. After a few moments, he dug into a knot in my back with his elbow, and it hurt like hell.

"If you need to scream, go ahead. Most people do," he said.

"No, I can take it." I wanted to feel the pain. The pain told a story, and screaming would only distract me from hearing it. As he worked down my spine, I jumped. "I'm extremely ticklish."

"It's because you're so tight. Let me try something."

He dug into a certain spot and released some tension, and I felt less sensitive. He continued working down my back and went to my hamstrings. When he dug into my left hamstring just above the knee, I wanted to scream. That was the worst pain yet, but I held it in and listened. While he applied pressure there, I could feel how my body was pulling out of alignment, but it felt so fucked up, it'd take years to untangle.

After the session, I lay on the table for a minute, trying to understand what my body was telling me, and when I got up, the Knight said, "You seem to be highly aware of your body, and I think it's fascinating that you're trying to solve this puzzle. There are a lot of people who are as tight as you, but so few ever seek help, let alone even know how badly they suffer. What's that quote by Blaise Pascal? Something about how all of the world's problems would be solved if man could just sit alone in a room with his own thoughts? I love that quote, and when we loosen you up, you'll be able to sit anywhere on Earth in peace and harmony."

He also said he could feel an enormous change inside of me and that he could sense I was going through a Saturn return. "You're becoming a man and understanding your true path in life. I feel it all over your body."

Driving home, I felt confused, almost anxious, and I kept thinking about the relapse I'd had with the chiropractor. But this felt different. My body felt vulnerable, but I realized the tension served a purpose and the Rolfing seemed to release it rather than bottle it up like the chiropractic sessions did. The tension was like fuel keeping me moving, but it was also a parasite, draining me of my energy and joy. I missed a step on my apartment staircase and banged my knee against the doorframe, and I dropped my water bottle in the kitchen. I was having a hard time thinking clearly, but after a few hours, my body seemed to settle down again, and I could think.

The next day, I felt extreme relaxation all throughout my body, a warm, heavy feeling as if the Knight actually *had* created more space inside of me. He said that after ten sessions, I'd gain an inch in height and be straighter than ever. Sitting on my futon, it occurred to me that if someone had been watching me these last few months, they'd likely think I was insane, but as shitty as I felt and as close to insanity as I'd been, all of this was *my* normal. This was the only perspective I'd ever had, and so repeating words hundreds of times and touching doorknobs and counting to a thousand while waving my hand under sink faucets wasn't strange to me. Maybe people who had schizophrenia or bipolar disorder or whatever didn't feel strange in their own minds either, and only felt that way when they interacted with the outside world. But it was also important to recognize that just because this was normal to me, that didn't mean it was healthy. I needed to listen to the Frog and the Knight. Maybe I should take those fucking pills after all.

I decided to wait until November break to take them. That way, if I freaked the fuck out, I'd have a month to chill out before school started up again.

I went down to the laundry room, where I'd left my laundry bag to reserve the machine, but the fucking asshole had put in another load. That dude was always hogging the machine, sometimes for six or seven hours, doing load after load and leaving his stuff in the dryer for up to an hour between loads. I felt like throwing his huge tighty-whities in the dumpster, but instead, I turned off both the washer and dryer, took my stuff, and locked myself in my apartment. I let a call from my mom go to voicemail. One of my cousins was getting married next month, and I hadn't RSVP'd. I knew it was rude, but I felt that if I mailed that card back marked "no," my family would denounce me as a traitor. Instead, I hoped it would all just go away. There was no way I could do a wedding. I'd drink myself under the bar before dinner. Besides, healing had no family. Healing happened alone.

I did, however, pick up when Silas called. He was still in Austin, but he was thinking of moving to LA.

"I'm about ready to take that next step, ya know?" he said.

"Yeah, I think I do know." Years ago, I would have had no idea what he meant. Things like "growth" and "evolution" and "take that next step" had meant absolutely nothing to me prior to meeting the Frog, when everything had been straight chaos.

"How's everything in Cali?" he said.

"I'm just ridin' the waves, man."

"I still can't believe you're going through all that shit. I never knew."

"Neither did I."

"I've been on my own healing journey out here. Playin' all these shows and everything, I realized I'm getting way too dependent on the bottle, ya know? I tried to stop a few times, but it was no use, so I finally decided to see a therapist. Figured if it was workin' for my best friend, it'd probably work for me too."

"Well, you've been through two tours in Iraq. That's enough to fuck anyone up."

"Hey, I'm just glad to be here and in one piece."

"Yeah, I feel the same . . ." I looked at the Michael Jordan poster hanging on my far wall. "You know, the other day, I was sitting here and I was overcome with this feeling like I never really existed. You know what I mean?"

"Yo, Horace." That was my childhood nickname. "I'mma tell you something. You're a Kirkland All-Star and don't you ever forget that. We spent thousands of hours hoopin' at that park, and that place wouldn't have been the same without you."

"I dunno, I feel like I never really fit in there, or anywhere else either."

"Look, man, you may not have been a knucklehead like some of the guys out there, sellin' drugs and holdin' up liquor stores and all that shit, but you were always one of us."

I thought about his words for a moment and said, "Yeah, yeah, you're right." I realized it for the first time; as a kid, I'd always bounced from group to group, never really feeling as if I fit in anywhere, but maybe that was how every kid felt. But at Kirkland, I was a part of something beautiful, playing basketball with all the other punks who had seen that court as an escape from the abuse they'd suffered at home. When I hung up with Silas, I created an outline for my next screenplay, which, Silas said, "Has to be called *Kirkland.*"

This script gave me new purpose—new energy—and I went to the Rite Aid near my house and bought a few three-subject notebooks, using the first subject to write any ideas that came to mind, then using the second to outline the story, and the third to come up with character descriptions and thematic material. I flipped back and forth through the sections, writing furiously, drawing pictures and creating a story loosely based on my own childhood—a childhood that was just as real as any other. Because my heroes were guys like Dylan and Kerouac and Bowie, I'd always felt that I'd missed out on something real—some real time that had come and passed long before I was born. But now I realized I'd grown up during a time of incredible music, great film, and unique style. I'd watched the NBA with Bird and Magic and later Jordan, who was as big an influence on me as Jim Morrison or John Lennon. My life was real and valuable and worth every bit as much as anyone else's. This disease didn't make me ugly or broken or anything else. It made me exist.

I kept writing well into the night and only stopped to make dinner around eleven. At one point, I looked outside and saw Mel, my jerkoff neighbor, bringing yet another load to the laundry room. I wanted to cover his screen door with dog shit, but that was the old me. Let it go, Jay. He looks like a miserable old man. Just focus on making your chicken and vegetables. Focus on your new story. This is gonna be the one to win you an Oscar. When they read this, they won't be able to say, "Jay, nothing *happens*."

Chapter 25

At school, I was getting better at dealing with angry parents, and I wasn't sweating as much every time the phone rang. That crazy mom had probably turned her wrath on some other undeserving chap, because she wasn't calling me anymore. As much as I loved Camarin, she'd kind of left me hanging with that one. I'd told her about it several times, letting her know how badly the woman was abusing me, but she'd done nothing about it. As great as she was, she did shitty things too, but I guess no one was perfect.

I spent most of my free time writing *Kirkland*, but it was taking much longer to finish than *The Silent Protest*. In fact, it'd already been a month, and I was still working on the outline. I had so much to say and wanted to pack as much as possible into the story's structure without adding anything unnecessary or redundant. November break was coming, and I hoped to finish it then.

The strategies I learned in *Brain Lock* were helping, but progress was slow. Still, I felt a profound change each time I was able to walk away from a faucet or window or car door without checking it a thousand times. I'd tell myself to let the rush of fear come, and the anxiety would work its way up my neck, and my face would twist and my jaw would click as I opened and shut my mouth, and my tongue would stick straight out and rub the edges of my lips. By doing this, I could feel the link between the mental and physical aspects of my disease. When I stopped checking something, I felt a release of pressure in my muscles—however small—and doing this gave me a better concept of time and space. Before, I was running from the bathroom to the kitchen to the stove, checking everything frantically and in no order. But now, I was able to go from the front door to the big window to the stove to the fridge to the bathroom, and that was it. It was no longer well over an hour, but now about forty minutes. Still, it was energy-draining and I wanted to kill it for good, but I left those anxiety pills in the cupboard.

The Silent Protest had placed in several writing competitions, making the quarterfinals and semifinals and being selected to a few film festivals. I decided to fly to Vancouver for one of these festivals, but the OCD punished me for it. The night before leaving, I spent at least an hour checking the handles and windows and trunk of my car, going from side to side, pulling and touching and humming "Someday" by Sugar Ray over and over. I could see the neighbors across the street watching me as they drank and bullshitted on their front porch. Those guys looked to be in their fifties, but every day they were out there, drinking and howling at the women passing by in bikinis. With their eyes on me, the OCD was worse. I couldn't focus on anything, and I kept checking while sweating and cursing at myself to hurry the fuck up! When I finally finished and went back upstairs to keep packing, I realized I'd left my phone charger in my car, and I started screaming. There was no way I could go through another hour of checking that damned car, especially not with those shitheads out there pointing and laughing at me, so I decided to cancel the trip. Besides, I wouldn't have been able to do all my rituals with a cab there waiting for me in the morning anyway.

I needed to try those pills. Instead of going to that film festival, I read the instructions that came with the prescription and did more research, and even though seizures were a rare side effect, I figured I'd give it a shot. If I had a seizure, I wouldn't be able to drive or walk upstairs or travel or take a shower. I'd have to move back to Buffalo and be a child again in that house of horrors. One seizure meant my life was over. But my life was already pretty much over. I hadn't gone out in months. I hadn't gotten laid in almost a year. I hadn't drunk or smoked or done anything to get out of my head. I was already a prisoner.

When Karla texted me, asking if I wanted to get lunch, I said sure and met her at a café off the beach. Weeks back, I'd turned twenty-eight, and I'd ignored all the birthday calls from my family and friends and eaten chicken stir-fry alone and watched *The Sopranos*, then spent the rest of the night writing my script. I needed to at least try to have a life.

Seeing Karla in her normal clothes was a little jarring. She wore a bandana in her hair and a long flowing dress, and her style fit her perfectly. In work clothes, I saw her as a teacher and a professional, but now I saw her as a beautiful woman I had no business talking to sitting at an outdoor table by the beach. Still, her face lit up when she saw me.

"Jay! Over here." She patted the seat beside her.

I wiped off some sand and sat. "Hey, sorry to keep you waiting, but, uh, some stuff came up . . ." As much as I wanted to tell her that it took me twenty minutes longer than usual to lock the door, I kept it to myself. It wasn't so much that I was worried she would try to get me fired for being crazy—it was more that I liked having a friend I could just be "normal" around. Besides, Camarin had told me a number of times how much I'd changed—"It's incredible! Not that you were bad or anything before, but you seem so much more confident and relaxed now," and I'm sure Karla picked up on it as well. In fact, when she noticed me pulling out my eyelashes right there at the table, she casually pointed it out to me without judgment or anything. I realized then I'd probably been doing that my whole life—pulling out eyelashes and eyebrows. I also picked at the skin on my fingers and bit my fingernails, and they were always red and raw and I was embarrassed to show them to anyone. But for whatever reason, I decided to listen to Karla when she told me to stop.

"So, that place is getting crazy, huh?" Karla said, of Cody Cares.

"Yeah, what the hell's going on with Cody lately? It's like he's paranoid someone will destroy his legacy."

"Sometimes people act strangely once they get a little success." She gave me a knowing smile. "I hope you won't when you make it big in Hollywood."

"Oh, I'm already plenty strange." I talked about my scripts and book, but told her, "You can't tell anyone about them."

"Wow, I gotta read these!"

"No, you don't. I think they might be a little too much info."

"Well, when your movies hit the theaters, you won't be able to stop me from going."

"We'll go together." I smiled at her, and she smiled back. She was always blushing and playing with her hair nervously and touching my arms, and as much as I wanted to ask her out, I decided against it.

We drank tea and ate chicken wraps and fruit, and for that hour and a half I felt like a regular person. But even so, I could feel the tension and chaos of the town draining my energy, and when she asked me if I wanted to get a drink on the strip, I said no and practically raced back to my place.

That night, I broke one of the pills in half and took it a few hours before bed, and then I watched Darren Aronofsky's *Pi*. By the end of the film, I was feeling mellow and warm, and when I went to bed, I was overcome by total relaxation. I felt cool and controlled and confident, almost like a movie star. But when I started thinking I should run off to Hollywood, I was overcome with a Darkness that flowed from my feet to my brain, and once it took hold, I couldn't shake it. I paced in my living room, but I got dizzy, so I sat on my futon, and I felt stoned and started laughing like a maniac and couldn't stop. The chemicals were altering the shape of my body, tightening muscles and rearranging me into a more difficult maze to solve. I got confused and furious and terrified and I couldn't think. I just kept laughing and feeling crazier than ever.

This was it. I'd finally pushed myself over the edge, and even the next morning, I still felt stoned and flooded with anxiety. It was as if someone had unscrewed my head, dumped a bucket of bleach down my neck, screwed my head back on, shaken me up, and set me on the futon.

Why the fuck would you do this to yourself? You knew not to trust anyone. You damned well knew never to trust a drug. This afternoon, you were happy. Remember how it felt sitting beside Karla and feeling the saltwater on your skin? Now you'll never feel normal again. Now I'm gonna punish you worse than ever. You think you can get away from me? I'm God. I'm the universe. I'm everything and you'll always be nothing.

I couldn't relax. I'd taken a hundred steps back and this would be too much to overcome. I waited until nightfall and practically ran to the cave.

"Look, you're okay. It's not even in your system anymore," the Frog said.

"Of course it is! It's a part of my DNA now. It's replaced my father's genetic code."

"You're okay."

"No, I'm not! You said this would help, and it royally fucked me up! I've got no hope left." I was careful not to push him too hard; if I lost him, I'd lose more than I could afford.

"You're terrified of relaxation. You've never been relaxed a day in your life, and you didn't know how to handle it."

"It was horrible. I think I need the fear as a motivation—a distraction maybe. I know how impossible it is to succeed at what I want to do, and I think the fear is preventing me from running straight down to LA and walking into some audition and being told over and over again that I'll never make it in this town, until my dreams turn to dust and I have nothing left to live for. I think the fear is keeping me from burning all my possessions and running out into the world and drinking myself into oblivion. It's distracting me from obsessing over my failures—I mean, fuck! The last time I played in a band I was twenty-two. I meant to start a new one the moment my college band broke up, but six years later, here we are. If I go straight at my dreams, I'm gonna be crushed so badly, I'll never recover. The fear is keeping me from killing myself, I think, and I can't be relaxed. Not yet, at least. I'll relax once I've finally heard my first, 'Yes! Yes, you got the part!'"

"Again, it's your absolutism. You need to recognize this is a symptom of your OCD."

"So what if it is? I can't shake it, man. It's a part of me, and it's not going anywhere anytime soon. If I let down my guard and start thinking of all the places I'd rather be, I'll never be able to work again. To support myself again. As much as I hate my job and my apartment, it's great being able to buy chicken and cook it and to have electricity and to take a hot shower and sleep in a comfortable bed. There's this force inside of me that's always screaming, 'GO, GO, GO!' and I don't want to."

"You should watch *My Dinner with Andre*. It's one of my favorite films."

"I think they made a few jokes about that on *The Simpsons*."

He started laughing. "Wouldn't surprise me. I think it would benefit you to hear those two discuss what it means to be content."

"I'll check it out."

"I think a lot of what you're talking about is learned helplessness. Throughout your life you've learned that whenever you try, people will let you down, so now you've created this psychological distraction, as you say, to prevent you from being let down again when the stakes are at their highest. You're so worried that you'll fail. What if you succeed? Watch that movie. Those two are great."

I left the cave and climbed up the cliff, and when I got back I saw that *My Dinner with Andre* was almost thirty bucks on Amazon. Still, I ordered it, and when I watched it, I understood what the Frog was talking about. I was starting to see that I could gain just as much feeling and experience from life by appreciating my chicken dinner as I could by selling all I owned, hiding away on a ship, and stealing my way across Asia and into Europe. I understood that it was okay to take off my shoes and feel the grass beneath my toes and let that fill me with as much joy as dancing in the best nightclub in Ibiza. It's okay to be relaxed. It's okay to be content with what you have.

A few days passed, and I was feeling slightly better, but that all changed when I logged into one of my social media accounts and saw a video that everyone in my Sand Beach group was commenting on. Someone had recorded me doing my rituals with the car. I remembered that day. Just before leaving work, a parent had yelled at me on the phone, and when I parked at home, the stress of going through my door- and window-checking rituals overwhelmed me so much, I considered sleeping in the car. It was hard enough doing the rituals inside the cover of my locked apartment, but every time I did them outside was agony. People would watch and laugh and say shit like, "What the fuck are you doing?" Or they'd watch me to be sure I wasn't breaking into the car. I had to wait until pedestrians passed or for neighbors to finish their cigarettes and go back inside their houses before I could get started with my touching and handle pulling and all that useless crap. All of this waiting added time to the process. It was the same at Cody Cares. I'd been five, ten, fifteen minutes late to work so many times, just because a group of people were talking on the sidewalk near the parking lot and I'd want to scream at them, "GET THE FUCK OUTTA HERE! JUST LEAVE ME THE FUCK ALONE!" The world had always been conspiring to end me, and now it was getting more aggressive.

The video had been viewed almost twenty thousand times and had thousands of likes and hundreds of comments. Most of them made jokes at my expense, but a few defended me. I felt a thousand knives stabbing me and had to shut off my computer. How could people do something so cruel to a neighbor? Was this what our society was becoming? Recording anything we found strange or amusing so we could get attention at another person's expense?

Based on the angle of the shot, I knew it had to be the shitheads across the street—the fifty-somethings. I wanted to go over there with a baseball bat, but I was also terrified to go outside.

I spent the next few days running from one side of the apartment to the other and cursing the world. After I was able to calm myself down, I tried to let all the negativity in to pass right through me. There must have been other people in Sand Beach locked in their apartments as well, and I had to show them that we could all go outside and reclaim our town together. I had to keep everything in perspective. Most of the people making those comments had probably forgotten about the video by now. They probably meant me no harm and had just been happy to get a cheap laugh. In fact, maybe it was good to see who was with me and who wasn't. If you can stand up to this kind of abuse, you can stand up to anything. Hell, if you can stand up to the gods in your own head, you can take on any of those mouth-breathing, knuckle-dragging troglodytes. Fuck them! Do your rituals. Block the assholes out. Let them stare. Let them make comments. They're the ones with the problem.

I thought about commenting on the video but instead I pulled *The Dharma Bums* off the shelf and read half the book in one sitting. I usually had to reread pages until the information stuck, but after successes with books like *The Prophet* and *Brain Lock*, I was able to read much quicker and without getting so many headaches. I finished the book the next day and felt ready to step back into the world. I hadn't logged on to my computer since watching that video, but I wanted to see if Carolina had written to me, and she had. I told her about the video and after discussing it, I shared the link with her. She watched it and said everything would be okay and for some reason, she still wanted to see me in March. After ending our conversation, I realized that maybe I *could* actually survive in this world with my disease. That the disease didn't define me. That I could separate myself from it, and that there would always be people who, no matter how often they saw the worst of me, would stick by my side. That maybe I didn't need to live in a world of absolutes. That maybe it wasn't me versus the world. I knew I was going to conquer my disease and use my knowledge to tell stories that helped people conquer their own.

I grabbed my notebook and resolved to use the rest of my break to finish writing *Kirkland*. While working on the script, I'd stop from time to time to play guitar and write songs and poems and jokes. I used to write these in my notebooks, but I decided to type them instead. I kept separate files for the poems, lyrics, story ideas, and jokes, and soon I had thirty, forty, fifty pages of each file. I'd come up with a joke or something while washing dishes or taking a shower, and I'd run to the computer and write it down. The more I wrote, the slower my thoughts moved. I realized that all of these words contributed to the chaos in my mind, and now that I had organized systems for their release, I could relax a little more. Now that I had some of the best parts of myself on the page, I could make more peace with death, and the more peace I made with death, the better quality of life I lived.

I hadn't spoken to my mother in weeks and decided to call her. She picked up and said she loved me and missed me, and as much as I knew she was sincere, I couldn't tell her about the video or my OCD or any of it. If I did, she would see that I was breaking away from her and the family, and it would crush her. But also, she'd already ignored all of this during my formative years, and so I felt as if she didn't deserve to know what I was going through now. That she, like everyone else, just needed to figure it out for herself. Plus, I was still angry, and even if she said she understood and supported me, if she were to hesitate just a moment too long or I heard any hint of doubt in her voice, I knew I would scream at her and hang up the phone, feeling more isolated than before. It was too risky, so instead I asked about my brothers and sisters and told her about the sunshine and the beach and complained about work and hung up. It was hard to tell her I loved her, even though I did. There was still such a high, thick wall between myself and humanity, and I knew it'd always be there until I was finally able to feel her love inside of me.

At work, Ms. Kefana started a program to involve parents in some of the school's decision-making processes, and it proved so popular, we knew she'd be punished for it. Cody was sinking deeper into his ego, and after seeing how the parents responded to Ms. Kefana, we knew she was in trouble. As much as he "cared," that school was Cody's legacy, and with Ms. Kefana fast becoming the face of the school, Karla, Doreen, Barry, and I knew a civil war was coming. Cody kept hiring more robots and Ms. Kefana kept trying to reprogram them into living, breathing humans, and the tension mounted. Cody spent most of his time in the cafeteria with the robots and Ms. Kefana spent her time with us in the gym, and soon a rivalry developed. The thing was, in the gym we didn't give a fuck about any rivalry, which meant we had better relationships with the parents and students, recorded higher grades, had better student attendance, and we spent more of our time laughing and enjoying each other's company. We were doing "not doing," and not because we were trying to do "not doing," but because this was our natural way of being. At one point, that had been the quality Cody looked for in his employees, but now the cafeteria teachers were working their asses off at "doing," and it threw the place off balance. Even though the school had moved about a hundred meters from the cliff's edge, we were getting rocked with waves of dissatisfaction and jealousy. We knew the kids could feel it, because all the cafeteria kids asked to switch to our classes, and all the gym kids would make comments whenever the cafeteria teachers walked through, saying things like, "Damn, did it just get colder in here?"

I was getting panic attacks again. But at least I was in the gym. At least I was with Ms. Kefana. I felt I belonged there and contributed to our weird, warm community. I needed the stability and warmth to survive my psychological journey. If I'd been in the cafeteria, there'd be no way I could continue making progress. The cafeteria was cold. The cafeteria was death. The cafeteria was Buffalo, and I was never going back there again.

Chapter 26

The months passed slowly. On days off from work, I was spending about ten to twelve hours writing, stopping to pace whenever someone slammed a cupboard or made a noise. Now that I was better able to define what was causing the sounds, I was getting slightly better at ignoring them, helping me to form a stronger barrier between myself and the noises, which made the world seem less chaotic. I called the number on a FOR RENT sign on the apartment complex next door and spoke with the manager about his tenants' constant parties, and he said he was in the process of evicting a few people and that things should quiet down soon. He said he was going to do a better job of screening applicants. A few former residents had destroyed his floors and walls and plumbing, and he was as sick of the Sand Beach party-animal bullshit as I was. Knowing he was kind of on my side set me at ease. I was still avoiding phone calls and hadn't gone out in over a year other than that one time with Karla. Socializing was physically painful. I'd strain my voice trying to keep up conversation, and I'd get dizzy and my back and knees would ache, and I'd wake up the next morning feeling hungover even if I hadn't had anything to drink. If I left my apartment, I knew I would destroy the armor that had grown around me, and I preferred to stay home and enjoy it.

Soon it was March, and I found myself taking the train to

the border, crossing, and taking a cab to the Tijuana airport. It was hundreds of dollars cheaper to fly to Mexico from TJ than from Soul City, and it was a thrill to cross that border on foot for the first time. Carolina was at work when I arrived, so she met me at my hotel. The guy at the front desk said there was a problem with my reservation and that I'd need to upgrade my room, and when he told me all they had left was the penthouse suite and that, due to the error, they'd knock twenty percent off the price, I said yes even though I knew there was no error. With the discount it was only sixty bucks a night, and the view was incredible. I hadn't been to Mexico City in years, and it was weird being there without Mariposa. We'd spent a week there just before Christmas in 2006, when the city had been lit up with red and green and yellow lights. But when I heard a knock at my door and opened it, I forgot all about her.

Carolina was even more gorgeous in person. She looked like Penelope Cruz, and the fact that she was still smiling when she hugged me made me feel like the King of Mexico. I knew I'd made the right choice not to bitch about being upsold the penthouse, and we sat on the bed and grinned as we spoke and touched each other and made plans for the week. She took me to a fancy steakhouse and told me it was on her, and she pointed around the room, letting me know that we were probably in the company of some top-level narco bosses but that you'd never know it because the smartest ones dressed like abuelo, knee-high socks and a cheap button-down and jeans.

"I can't believe I'm finally here," I said, before shoveling a piece of steak into my mouth.

"It took you long enough." She spoke perfect English.

"Yeah, I'm sorry about that. Y-you saw the video . . ."

"It's okay, we all have some form of weakness." She grabbed my hand and gave me a loving look.

"What do you mean, 'weakness'?"

"I mean, all of the strange things you do."

"It's a psychological condition. I have a brain disorder."

"Oh, I don't believe in any of that. I think the only way to get past your weakness is to work hard and stop complaining about it . . ." She went on, and right then I knew we had no chance together. As compassionate as she was, if she wasn't capable of recognizing my condition and the legitimacy of psychology, we would always be waging unconscious warfare. She'd accuse me of being "weak" when I needed to check the doors and faucets and windows, and I'd feel attacked, and we'd grow more resentful of one another by the day. I knew I'd need to push any woman I was with, questioning her from all angles until I knew—really *knew*, in my meat, mind, and memory—that I was safe with her, and I already knew Carolina would never stand up to this level of scrutiny. We'd never be able to bond at the most profound of levels. And, as much as I liked her, and as much as I wanted to live her Mexico City-penthouse existence, I knew I would always be Buffalo Jay, and if I couldn't be myself then I couldn't be around.

We went back to the hotel and practically tore each other's clothes off, and she got on top and rode me, her long wavy hair falling over her gorgeous face. The lights were off, but the windows were open and the city glow lit her body, and I tried so hard to forget what she'd said at dinner. I dropped my head over the bed's edge and looked at the city, buildings up and sky down. That was how things would always be with Carolina as well. I flipped her around and finished us both off, then minutes later, she started sucking my dick, and I pulled her to me, kissed her, rolled her onto her stomach, slid in from behind, and covered her back in cum. We took a shower, then she left because she had work in the morning. I stayed up most of the night, flipping through the channels and watching the CDMX skyline. There was so much energy on those streets it reinvigorated me. Since starting my sessions with the Frog, it was almost as if I'd forgotten who I was. But maybe I was more Mexico Jay now than Buffalo Jay.

After work the next day, Carolina took us to the zoo and Chapultepec Castle, and we got dinner at a French place in Polanco, and as much as I wanted to let myself fall in love with her, I couldn't stop wondering if she was having the same doubts about me. We went back to the hotel after dinner and took a shower together, and she left me alone again.

The next day, I started reading *The Basketball Diaries* while she was at work, and I couldn't stop. I sat by the window, feeling that raw city energy, and lived and breathed every move Jim Carroll made. It was probably the best writing I'd ever read, and as much as I loved Kerouac and Dostoevsky and Hemingway, I felt closest in spirit to Jim Carroll. Felt that he was telling *our* story, but I put it away when Carolina arrived. We saw more of the city and ate some great food, and I slept alone again and picked up where I left off with *The Basketball Diaries* in the morning. As much as I wanted to step out into that city alone, I couldn't, so I listened to what my psyche was telling me. I'd traveled so much in my life, but whenever I arrived somewhere new, I'd fill with fear and stay drunk the whole time. The chemicals would race and my muscles would lock and joints would ache, and I'd get confused and loopy and downright furious. But now that I didn't have alcohol and no longer needed the anxiety, I wanted to know why I'd needed it before. I knew it had something to do with shame. With feeling inches tall, and who was I to run off to this big city where everyone was a giant? It was easy to dream when you were locked inside your dark, smelly apartment. It was much harder to take the elevator down to the street and go out and make your dreams happen. My body and mind weren't yet ready for any of that. I was still so tense and off balance, and the fucking and talking and walking had destroyed my energy. I'd have to get away from Carolina soon, or she'd start seeing me screaming and smashing shit and staying drunk all day, and she wouldn't understand and I'd be the asshole again. It was easier to leave women before it got to that stage, when there was no happiness left in my brain. When if I said so much as one more word, I'd dissolve and filter down to Hell. I almost didn't want her to knock, and when she did, she could read the misery on my face.

We lay on the bed, my head in her lap, and said nothing for

several minutes. Maybe she did understand.

"Thank you for being so sweet to me. You have no idea how bad I feel all the time," I said, tears dripping down the sides of my face.

"Thank you for being sweet to me as well." She kissed me, and we got down again. The window was open, and I kept feeling as if everyone in the city was watching us, and they'd beat down the door and drag me off of her, and I couldn't cum. If I felt that sensation, they'd put a gun to my head, and in that moment of vulnerability, they'd put two in the back of my brain.

But I let all that fear come and continued to work her, clenching my teeth and pushing harder and harder and harder until I could feel it coming, and I allowed myself to be vulnerable. And as explosion worked through and out of my body, I felt an ecstasy and freedom I'd never felt before. I realized I'd rushed through every other orgasm in my life, terrified of letting down my guard for even a split second, but here, I relaxed and exploded all over her stomach and tits. She rubbed it into her skin, and I lay beside her and kissed her cheek. We took a shower and hit the town and soon the week was over. She came with me inside the airport and made sure I knew where I was going, and before she left, she said, "I don't think I've ever been in love," and I knew by the look on her face that she wanted to add, "until right now," but she kept it to herself just as we all so often keep the best parts of ourselves hidden away, and I said, "I have, and I don't think I ever will be again." The light went out in her eyes, and I knew it was over.

On the plane back, I realized I'd done to her the same thing I had to Mariposa and Nima, and what I'd do to the next woman who came along as well. Was I actively searching for something wrong? Or had I been so affected by my unique life experiences that I was incapable of settling for any woman? Incapable of just picking *somebody* because most somebodies wouldn't be able to understand the magnitude and complexity of the fear that haunted my life? Wouldn't be willing to travel with me through the warzone of that fear and Darkness to the places of beauty I knew were hidden so far down inside that I might never fully see them? Was this too unrealistic to expect? To want to share with her both the ugliness and the beauty inside of me, without having to qualify it, explain it, beg her to laugh or cry with me? To hold me when I felt vulnerable? Was that the meaning of true love? Or was I just putting up more walls to protect myself?

Even when you loved Mariposa, and felt kicked in the gut just watching her walk down the street, you still had your doubts. You might be too far gone, man. I mean, you should be grateful that Mariposa or Nima or Carolina even talked to you. In *your* mental state.

No, fuck that! I should never have to feel grateful that someone would talk to me. I should never have to beg for love. Love is a cool summer breeze. Love is the bright full moon over Sand Beach. Love rises and falls every day. I don't need to be grateful. I need to align myself with the rhythms of nature. I need to say no when I mean no and yes when I mean yes and never settle for a single thing and never worry about being alone, because it doesn't matter if I'm alone—as long as I can feel that summer breeze and see that full moon, I'll always have love.

Part III

The next few years moved slowly. Though I was feeling better, I only went out with friends a few times, and never to bars or parties— only to get lunch or tea, and in spots that were safe. I needed to know the layout of a restaurant or café in order to relax: where the exits and bathrooms were, how close together the tables were, if it was near a loud bar or club. I spent most of my free time in my apartment, writing, reading, pacing, or watching TV. The neighbor who puked every morning before going to his teaching job moved out, and when the new tenant moved in, I spent most of that month on the opposite side of my apartment. The new guy was younger, and he and his girlfriend were always throwing parties, blasting music, and stomping up and down the stairs. I left them a bottle of wine with a note, asking nicely that they be aware of the walls we shared, but they kept slamming doors and cupboards, playing loud video games, and taking showers at all hours of the night. That was a particularly rough time, but he moved out after only a few months, and the next guy was much better. The older woman below me was still there and every so often I'd hear her grandkids screaming and stomping. I hated sharing walls with neighbors and couldn't imagine how anyone else could be okay with this. People weren't meant to live this way. We needed space and fresh air and windows overlooking green valleys and blue skies. Somewhere along the way, we fucked up, and this was probably part of the reason why modern people had so many mental health issues. At home, I still wore earplugs and listened to the sound of water, but I also started listening to music again and would play a few albums in particular on repeat: *The Clash*, *The House of Love*, and *The Essential Roy Orbison*. I listened to these whenever I left the apartment as well, trying to block out conversations at the supermarket and gas station and at Target. I didn't want to know what people were saying. I didn't want their energy to infect me. When I'd get in the car, I'd take out the earplugs and turn off the music, but as I neared my apartment, I put them back in so I wouldn't hear any noise from down the block. When I parked, I'd spend a few minutes pumping myself up to go through the twenty minutes of rituals it took for me to be satisfied that the car doors and windows and trunk were closed and locked. No one had posted any new videos of me on social media—at least, none that I knew of—but still, I always felt as if people were watching me. When I finished with the rituals, I'd walk into my complex, check my mail, and walk upstairs while making nonsense sounds to myself to further drown out everything. I did my best to avoid my neighbors, even though a few were pretty cool. I felt bad rejecting their requests to get dinner or to come over for drinks. I knew people thought I was weird, but I didn't care. I just wanted to get back inside my apartment and lock that door ASAP. It was too risky to stand in the courtyard and talk. Anything could happen there, and I was too vulnerable. Most of the neighbors I'd asked to be quiet had moved out, but even so, I still felt as if I'd made the whole place turn on me. And once someplace had turned on me, I needed to turn on it forever. I'd probably only left four or five notes on doors and asked two or three neighbors in person, but even so, I knew we were all at war. The building's owner said she was glad I was there keeping the place quiet, but when she hired a new manager who was the loudest of everyone, I thought maybe she'd just been lying to keep me happy.

I continued to talk to Carolina online, but not like before. We only spoke once every few weeks, and she was more distant with me. I realized that I preferred being in an Internet relationship over a real one. It was too hard for me to go to dinner and parties and bars and smile and act normal. Carolina deserved someone who could be a part of her life and not a drain on it.

I hadn't heard from Nima, but her career was taking off. While checking her IMDB page one day, I started thinking that even though she was a dreamer as well, she'd never quite understood me—my creative vision or what I was doing locked in my apartment. I started thinking that maybe *that* was my power. That maybe I had a unique perspective, and I needed to develop it. I took the Frog's advice and stopped reading the government and economics textbooks, and I started reading fiction, using stories as a way to loosen my own gears and travel deeper inside. Studying and capturing my own thoughts. Trusting that the closer I got to the center of myself, the closer I'd get to universal truths I could build my stories upon. I also read books on filmmaking and screenwriting and writing in general. I knew I was too old and vulnerable to go back to school, so I studied as much as I could independently. I made it a point to watch at least three films a week, focusing on the greats: *Citizen Kane, Casablanca, Seven Samurai, The Agony and the Ecstasy, Lawrence of Arabia, A Streetcar Named Desire*. I also watched modern masterpieces like *The Diving Bell and the Butterfly*, *Before Night Falls*, and *A Prophet*. I timed them to see when the first acts ended, when protagonists bottomed out, when they came roaring back to life stronger than before. I studied dialogue—keeping captions on at all times—character development, tone, shot angles, how sound enhanced storytelling. Sometimes after watching a film, I'd read the screenplay to see how the words came to life on the screen. I felt less intimidated about going to film festivals and talking with people like Nima, who seemed to have been born knowing all this. For me, learning this was a struggle. On top of my problems with reading and the fact that I would shut down for hours every time a neighbor made noise, I also had an extremely difficult time retaining information. I figured the OCD had fucked up my ability to organize my thoughts, but the better I felt, the easier it was for me to store this information in a proper place so I could recall it later on. It was almost as if I were building shelves inside of my brain to store information, and this slowed my thoughts considerably and made it much easier to have an intelligent conversation. For most of my life, I was told down was up one day, then the next, down was down, and I didn't trust facts. I didn't trust books. I didn't trust teachers. My earliest teachers were nuns who'd filled my head with fire-and-brimstone lectures on God's wrath, and their definitions of sin and punishment had changed every day. Now, I had to learn how to distinguish fact from emotion, and I started seeing how connected everything was. How someone like Ms. Kefana could know what to say in almost any situation, even though it seemed impossible to me. Now, I understood that she had likely accessed this universal truth, allowing her to cut through the bullshit and self-doubt and communicate with people in effective and meaningful ways. I noticed that she respected people's boundaries when she spoke with them. She didn't say things like, "So, how'd everything go at the dentist's yesterday?" Instead, she'd say, "I hope everything went well at the dentist's yesterday," giving the person the choice to divulge more information or not. Little things like that made a big difference. If I could learn her people skills and continue to grow and develop as an artist, there was nothing that could stop me from achieving my dreams. There was nothing that could stop me from eating dinner with my neighbors.

Every minute, I still felt as if I was climbing a cliff, but now I could pull back my head and see several hundred meters above me. The mountaintop, however, was obscured by clouds. I knew it would still be years, maybe decades, before I felt good enough to leave my apartment and interact with people outside of professional environments like Cody Cares, where I hid behind a desk and a role and read from a corporate script, and this depressed the hell out of me. Aside from growing as an artist and a person, I didn't know what I wanted. I didn't know how to have fun. I realized that during all the parties and road trips and everything throughout my life, I was never really having *fun*. I mean, there'd been enjoyable moments here and there, but very few times when I'd ever felt content and relaxed and happy to be alive. Most of my *fun* had been duty—drink, smoke, fuck, hit the road. I hoped that my journey inward would also help me find ways to enjoy life.

I still saw the Frog regularly, only we'd moved to a café near the beach. He made some excuse about the rocks becoming unstable, but I'd passed by the cliffs a few times afterward and saw the firelight and heard other poor saps crying into the night. I think he wanted to get me back out into the world. Despite the fact that there were other people at the café, I knew some of them had seen the Frog too, so I was able to relax enough to speak with him. I was still having breakthroughs, but just as the Frog had said, they were slowing down and were less intense. In fact, I had several while teaching and rather than run off to the bathroom and feel the earth shaking beneath me, I just smiled and kept teaching.

I also saw the Knight regularly, and those sessions helped me loosen my muscles and mind. One day, I asked him if instead of digging into my muscles with his elbow, he'd simply touch me in a certain spot and keep the pressure on it until I told him to stop. It seemed there were certain spots on my body that were almost like pressure relief valves, and on the drive to see him, those spots would start speaking to me, letting me know where to begin that day. This process helped me to focus on that particular muscle long enough to understand how it was supposed to feel and operate in my body, and then release pressure from it. When he went slowly, I was able to be right there with him, and I often found myself thinking about Camarin and Karla. Though I never told them about the sessions, I felt as if they already understood what was going on, and the warmth of that connection made me feel closer to all of humanity. It affirmed my struggle and made me feel more normal. The Knight said he was going to start using the technique with other patients, and a few weeks later he told me he used it with a woman who said it changed the way she understood her body.

Because I was nearing the five-year deadline to clear my teaching credential, and I knew I wouldn't be leaving Soul City anytime soon, I enrolled at a local university and took some online classes. I panicked for nearly the entire month before the classes began, but Camarin assured me I'd be okay, and I was. The whole program was bullshit, and the lessons were busywork, and I spent more time worrying than actually getting work done. I loathed being told what to do. Loathed wasting my valuable time. I could have written and edited an entire book in the time it took me to clear my credential, but what could I do about it?

One day, Camarin left suddenly and moved to Boston. We threw her a going-away party at Barry's house, and she wouldn't tell us what happened, but she did tell us that when she put in her two weeks' notice, Cody made her leave immediately. We figured she'd either been forced out or had had enough of his bullshit, and now she was off to make Boston a brighter, warmer city. Karla left a few months after Camarin, moving to Guadalajara to work with a film production company. She said she'd thought teaching would make her happier, but once Camarin left, she knew it was time to move on. As much as I also wanted to move on, I was stuck, and seeing my best work friend leave made me realize how sick I still was.

With my two heroes gone, school felt empty. Cody hired some dipshit supermarket manager to be the new VP, but he only lasted a few months, and Cody replaced him with some failed VP from a desert middle school. The d-bag's name was Ramon Perez, and he was older, uglier, and more awkward than Cody, which made him the most qualified person for the job. Dude was the polar opposite of Camarin, and right out of the gate, he ruled with an iron fist. He didn't have the kind of emotional intelligence and finesse Camarin did, so he took everything as a threat or power struggle, and soon every aspect of our jobs was micromanaged. Barry, Doreen, and I stopped eating together, because we were told it "wasn't professional," so we sat at our desks and ate in silence.

Cody hired a robot to replace Karla, some dopey forty-something White woman who came from money but couldn't buy an ounce of respect. We all saw right through her fake smiles, and after she ratted on Barry for leaving five minutes early one day and Doreen for talking on her cell phone during her free period, we all just kind of stopped communicating and kept to ourselves. The change in culture was overwhelming and palpable, and the students often remarked how much worse things had become.

Mr. Perez's hardnosed approach made my OCD worse. He started regulating exactly when I ran my quizzes through the grading machine, when I took my lunch, what color ink I used to mark grades, how to keep my grade book, what to say when answering phone calls. It was a disaster. This new cornhole was like a granite lid sealing the pressure inside of me. I couldn't so much as yawn without being self-conscious about it. I ate lunch in my car on multiple occasions, while sweating out panic attacks.

He also made it my job to close up the gym at the end of the day, and it took me about an hour every day to close the five gym windows and lock the two doors. I had to wait until everyone had left the parking lot, so they wouldn't see me pulling on the door a thousand times and touching all of the windows, and there were days that people would stand out there talking for twenty minutes. A half hour. There were several times I drove halfway home, then turned around to spend another forty minutes touching the windows. There were times I wanted to get out of bed at 4 a.m. and drive over there to tug on the door. I would have rather scrubbed the toilets than locked up, and the thought of having to do that every day filled me with such hopelessness that I remembered why I'd spent so much of my life knowing I'd never be able to hold a professional job. I thought about asking Barry to switch duties with me—I'd take over his PTA responsibilities—but I knew Mr. Perez wouldn't have it. He'd see my request as a challenge, and he'd find several new duties for me while questioning my "Cody Cares spirit."

Like Karla, part of why I'd stayed at Cody Cares had been because of Camarin, and another part was the flexibility to manage my own schedule and routine. Now, that was gone. But I needed the job to continue with my sessions with the Frog and Knight. I needed the money so I could afford to live alone and continue to explore the depths of my mind without a roommate inviting his friends over to watch *American Idol* and eat nachos. I was stuck and I knew it. I started getting dark thoughts again. Started seeing death as my only way out.

I worked on my resumé, and even though I never sent it out, just having it ready made me feel safer.

Cody was drifting deeper up his own ass, and now he was dressing like an astronaut and telling kids to "soar to Heaven!" That sounded an awful lot like a prayer to me, and during the worst days, I thought about calling the *Soul City Times* to let them know. Barry was Barry and kept a positive attitude, but Doreen was with me. We fucking hated it there, and she didn't hide it, and soon she was gone, too.

Though most of my screenwriters' group had ripped my work to shreds, both of my scripts were doing better than any of theirs in the contest circuit. Every other week, someone from a film fest or contest would email me letting me know I'd moved on to the next round. Inviting me to the awards ceremony. Usually, I'd pass, remembering that time I'd canceled my trip to Canada, but some part of me wanted to head out there so I could size up the competition. I figured if I could conquer the demons in my head, there was no one in Hollywood who could stop me.

One of the judges of a prominent film fest called me, saying he wanted to produce *The Silent Protest*. We met for dinner, and I let him do most of the talking, knowing that if I opened my mouth I might start babbling like a lunatic. He said he was going to do the scheduling and budgeting and start looking for directors, but after a few weeks, he stopped answering my emails and calls.

Though I'd stopped reading economics and philosophy textbooks, I did buy DVDs of rhetoric and debate lectures given by an Ivy League professor. I wanted to learn more about the power of words and also how to compose logical and compelling arguments. I wanted to learn about logical fallacies and how to find the truth in my convoluted inner thoughts. I realized that knowledge truly was power, and the more I knew and the better I could present an argument, the more likely I'd be able to get what I wanted from life. The more I knew, the less I feared standing up to someone who was trying to manipulate me or control me or shame me back into my corner. I realized that even though no one in my life had given me power, I could give it to myself.

It was hard to find people to debate with, and still I had such horrible anxiety, so I decided to pick fights with people online. When some dumbass would say something about homosexuality being "a goddamned choice!" I'd ask them things like, "so, when did you make the choice to stop being gay, homie?" I made sure to call them "jako," or "shithead," or whatever else, because I was still furious at the world and all these mouth-breathing motherfuckers, and now I was gonna let 'em all have it. I'd sit by the computer eagerly awaiting their responses, just so I could sink my teeth back in and let them know they were insane to think that telling kids to "suck it up!" was good advice or that America was "the best goddamned country in the world and if you don't like it, you can just get the hell out!" I spent about a year arguing with people like this, and in the process, I better understood my own opinions and biases and exorcised considerable anger. But I realized there was no point in arguing with people who were likely exorcising their own anger as well, so I stopped.

One day when Mel had left a load of tighty-whities in the dryer for over an hour, I waited for him, and when he came down with another load, I told him it was my turn. I was sick of that shithead pushing everyone around, and even when he said, "Well, I got here first, so you're gonna have to wait," I looked him in the eyes and said, "Just because you get here first doesn't mean you can use the machine all day. You've been hogging it for years and you need to respect the fact that other people need to use it too." I didn't know where those words were coming from. It was one thing to ask someone to lower their music and then walk away; it was another thing to stand my ground and engage some prick in an argument.

"You know, you're a real jerk," he said. "Go ahead, take it, asshole, but just know you're a real selfish prick."

"I'm not the one hogging the machine," I said, as he grabbed his shit-stained undies from the dryer and walked off. I looked around the complex and saw a few people watching through their windows, including the fucking manager, but they all looked quickly away. After that, Mel started taking his clothes to a laundromat.

Now that I was feeling better, I decided to go to the dentist and doctor for the first time in years. I'd been avoiding them both, not so much because I was worried they'd tell me my body was falling apart, but more because I hated to have anyone tell me to open my mouth or hold up my arms, and this was for a few reasons: One, since I'd started with the Frog, I couldn't stand anyone telling me what to do. I realized that after being beaten down by so many tyrants throughout my life, I couldn't stand to hear someone call me lazy or whatever for not having brushed enough or not getting that mole checked out. Two, due to my muscular problems, it was hard for me to hold my mouth open or hold up my arms, and it also took me a few moments to process what people meant when they said things like "stick out your tongue." I'd have to actually think, "Okay, which one's the tongue again? Ahh, yeah, that pink thing in your mouth that licks the icy cream! But what does 'stick it out' mean?"

Since childhood, I'd been surviving on anxiety. The anxiety called the shots, and when a doctor would tell me to do something like stick out my tongue, the anxiety would race and overtake me and make me open my mouth before I even realized what was going on. Now, I realized this was because my body and mind were both so overwhelmed with the OCD, I simply couldn't process information quickly enough to keep up with the normal pace of life. The OCD destroyed my short-term memory and spatial awareness, and the second the doctor would touch me, I'd be overwhelmed with that sensation, and my brain would shut down, and I'd start saying shit that made no sense, and soon the world would know I was nuts and toss me in the loony bin.

But now it was time to open my mouth and raise my arms, and I found out that my teeth and overall health were good, though my cholesterol was elevated. This was nothing new: I'd known about the cholesterol since I was a kid, and I also knew that because my good cholesterol was so high, it skewed the numbers. The doc wanted me on statins, but I knew those were no bueno, so I decided to start exercising again. I walked every night, then started running once I felt strong enough, but after the second night of this, I fucked up my right ankle, so I stuck with the walking. I tried doing some pushups, but this gave me such bad anxiety I didn't feel right for about a month. The walking fucked me up as well, but not as much as the pushups or running, so I figured that was my thing.

I started walking along the beach, then the cliffs, then through the rich neighborhoods south of the main strip. The architecture was incredible, and some of the houses were so unique I wished I could go inside and check them out. I imagined living in them, but each had its flaw. They were either too close to a parking lot where people gathered to watch the sunset, or the neighbor in back had a deck with a table and chairs where people probably ate and talked late into the night, or they were too close to where surfers walked down the cliff-side path to the beach. I never found a spot where I'd be able to truly relax, but it didn't matter anyway because if I ever had the cash to live here, it would mean I'd made it big in LA, and by then I'd have some mansion on a remote cliff in Malibu, far away from anyone.

Soon, I had a preferred route, and I knew where I'd have to hold my breath because the air always stank of weed, and where I'd have to turn up my music and hum because people scream-talked on their porches or in parking lots as they watched the moon rise over the ocean. I did my best to find my own special Sand Beach. Yeah, those surfers and skaters and bikers and millionaires might own Sand Beach during the day, but I ruled it at night. I ruled the alleys and empty sidewalks and paths through quiet parks. While walking, I'd often get ideas for songs or poems or screenplays, and I'd stop to write these in my pocket notebook. I hoped someday my words would make me enough money to buy my own quiet slice of life. To find my people—the true believers—and spend the rest of my days creating inspired works that saved people. On those walks, I realized that I was always writing. That thinking was just as important to the process as putting words to paper.

I also decided to up my healthy eating game and bought a NutriBullet, even though the thought of making a smoothie and cleaning the cup and blades overwhelmed me, but after trying it, I realized it wasn't too bad and drank one every day. I also started drinking a tablespoon of apple cider vinegar every morning to lower my cholesterol, per the Frog's recommendation, and after about a year, I got tested again and my LDL had dropped pretty significantly. Knowing I could care for myself was such a powerful and liberating feeling, and I wanted to shout from the top of Sand Beach, "I'M GONNA BE OKAY! I'M GONNA MAKE IT! AND SOMEDAY, I'LL HELP YOU MAKE IT TOO!"

Every so often, I'd have another relapse. I'd do something or someone would give me a dirty look or a parent would ask me to change their kid's grade, and I'd go home and lie in bed for hours, feeling my body tightening and mind racing and screaming, "How could you be so stupid! You're never getting away! I fucking own you!" and in those moments, I'd realize how much progress I'd already made. Those relapses used to be my normal state of being. My everyday existence. Now, I was feeling good enough to know when I felt bad. I was able to separate the night from the day, and I tried not to panic when the night set in. I tried to relax and let time pass, and soon I'd feel all right again.

I knew I needed to get out of the apartment more, so I started going out to dinner alone or to cafés to read. Sometimes when I did things like this, leaving the house and enjoying myself, I'd realize how impossible it had once seemed, and I'd smile and eat my French onion soup and sip my chamomile tea and know that all that mattered was moving forward. That as soon as I freed myself from this internal prison, I'd never look back, and I'd forget about getting revenge against all the people who'd wronged me, and lay down my anger, panic, and disgust, and simply move toward something meaningful and good. That I could forgive and forget a lifetime of torment and just sit there and enjoy my steak frites in peace. That I could focus instead on the flavor and texture of the meat, and how well the fried potatoes complemented it. I could focus on the novel I was reading, falling deeper into the story and letting it settle into my bone, meat, and marrow.

I also started seeing films at the local art house theater, figuring it'd be a better spot to catch flicks than the popcorn-chomping, cell-phone-talking, hey-what'd-I-miss-while-I-was-taking-a-shit megaplex. It was great to watch films with only a few other people—people who likely loved and respected film as much as I did. I realized my people were out there if I just went looking. Someday I'll find them. Someday, when the pain and torment has passed through me, I'll be king. Someday, I'll learn how to control the fear and Darkness and use it to teach me lessons no DVD or textbook ever could. Lessons not even the Frog or Knight could. Someday, I'll be okay with just me, and I'll hope with everything that I have, that you'll be okay with just you too.

243

Chapter 27

On the first day of my July break in 2013, I packed up the car and headed to Big Sur. I hadn't had any plans for that break, but as it neared, the thought of wasting it by pacing around my sweltering apartment had driven me nuts, so I knew I had to do something. I found my answer when I pulled *The Dharma Bums* off my shelf and got lost staring at the cover. It'd been ages since I'd gone on a road trip, and I needed to get back out there. And what better place for a road trip than sunny California? Desert California. Mountain and redwood and sea stack California.

I rode the Pacific Coast Highway north, passing foggy ocean cliff-sides and brown and green mountains, and stopping to take pictures on my digital camera. Doug had sold me that camera—at an inflated price, of course—and every time I used it, it reminded me of the road trip we'd taken the summer of 2005. It felt strange not having him there in the passenger seat, pushing me along through everything. As shitty as it felt being around him, he understood parts of me no one else did, and I'd known something great could happen because of it.

But now it was just me. I'd left him long behind. Even so, I didn't feel lonely. I had myself now, and that was something I'd never had before. I got some clam chowder at a quaint restaurant above the sea and stared at the anchors and ropes and other fishing-related shit nailed to the walls, and as out of place as I felt, I didn't feel threatened like I'd always had in the past, stepping into strange places like this. Though it was probably obvious I'd never been on a fishing boat in my life, the bearded, captain-hat-wearing, Ernest Hemingway-looking guy who showed me to my table didn't seem to want to hurt me in any way. I relaxed and ate my chowder, licking the side of the bowl once I'd cleaned out the inside, and then I headed back up the coast. I started the journey listening to *Revolutions: The Very Best of Steve Winwood*, then switched to *Speaking in Tongues* by the Talking Heads, and when that was up, I popped in *Loaded* by the Velvet Underground. I was so relaxed by the time "I Found a Reason" started, I could have dissolved into the salty orange sunset. I imagined how incredible it would be to have someone beside me. Someone beautiful and smart and who understood everything without needing an explanation. Who knew when to laugh, when to sing, when to shut up and feel the night falling around her. I felt strong enough in that moment to deserve her company. To make her feel as special as she'd make me feel. To be the guy she'd been dreaming of since she was a little girl, just as she'd be the girl I'd been dreaming of since I was a kid. Everything would just *work*. We'd both have already survived our own personal wars, and now we'd be ready to simply cruise up the coast hand-in-hand while that warm sunset overwhelmed our senses. We'd have no more need for posturing or politics or pissing contests or trauma. We could just be more salt floating in the sea breeze.

I arrived an hour after sunset. The woman at the campsite's information center told me where the cabin was, assuring me I was the farthest away from other guests, as I'd requested. I parked in front of the tiny cabin, put earplugs and music in my ears, grabbed my things, and went inside. I dropped my bag on the bed and started the corner fan for the white noise. Even with the earplugs and music and fan, I could still hear someone laughing in a far-off cabin, and suddenly I felt trapped. I decided to take a walk through the redwoods to the nearby stream, as the woman at the desk had suggested, and

I sat on a rock and stared at the bright moon and all the stars that weren't blocked by the towering redwoods' leafy crowns. Despite the sheer magnitude of nature surrounding me, I didn't feel small, and that cool night breeze seemed to flow right through me, filling my stagnant insides with oxygen, and blowing the worry far away. It'd been so long since I'd looked up at the moon—I mean, *really* looked at it. Years probably. There'd been times over the last few years I'd wanted to, but I couldn't. You get lost staring up at that moon, and soon the thoughts come back, filling you with so much inspiration that you forget to eat and bathe and set your alarm for work, and you get lost deeper and deeper inside of songs or poems or stories.

For months, I'd felt a huge boulder inside of me begging to be studied. Begging to be rocked back and forth. To be set into motion. It was already there, I just needed to give it a push. And staring up at that bright, Big Sur moon, I couldn't deny it anymore.

I went back to the tiny cabin, and I pushed the cork inside the wine bottle the woman had given me at check-in. I hadn't had a sip of alcohol since starting my sessions with the Frog years back, but with so much time and distance between myself and all that now, I wanted to give it a try. To see if I could have a glass without the world imploding. I filled a clear plastic cup about halfway and sipped it as I sat on the bed and read the latest book the Frog had given me, *Iron John* by Robert Bly, which I was nearly done with. I didn't hear the laughter from other guests anymore and trusted in the night. Trusted that they'd gone to sleep. Trusted that those who didn't go to sleep wanted to hear the sounds of the night forest just as badly as I did, so they'd shut up and respected the urgent need for silence. I removed the earplugs and turned off my music and listened to the wind blowing through the trees. It'd been so long since I'd removed my earplugs while inside the house, and I allowed my ears to breathe. My soul to breathe.

The wine warmed me, and when I went to the bathroom, which was just a toilet and sink, I could feel the capillaries in the soles of my feet pulsating. I missed drinking. It had been such a part of my identity that it felt unnatural to go without it for so long. I missed being drunk and getting out of my head, but as much as I wanted to down that bottle, I stopped after that half cup and continued reading until I finished the book. When I turned off the lights, I realized I was building a new natural for myself. That the person growing inside of me was now strong enough to walk on his own feet. That I could trust myself not to dive head first into a bottle of whiskey and run naked into the forest, looking to climb redwoods and arm-wrestle bears.

In the morning, I realized I'd forgotten to pack boxers. In the past, this would have made me panic, but I decided to make going commando a part of my experience. I walked outside and hit the road. There was so much I wanted to see, and I started the day at Pfeiffer Beach. The wind was so strong it almost knocked me over, but I continued walking around and taking photos, then I headed north to Bixby Creek Bridge. I took some pictures there as well, then headed back south toward the Henry Miller Library. I popped in *After the Gold Rush* and when Neil Young started singing that beautiful "Tell Me Why" chorus, I couldn't imagine a better place to listen to that album than on those Big Sur roads.

When I got to the library, I looked at the books and pictures inside, trying to imagine the songs that had been sung there and the stories that had been told by guests such as Joan Baez, Jack Kerouac, and Dylan. I looked outside and imagined bands like the Red Hot Chili Peppers and the Pixies playing for intimate audiences. I walked out to the deck and saw a whiteboard with markers on an easel, where people had written quotes from songs or poems, and despite the inner voice screaming at me, "Don't do it! They're all watching you!" I picked up a marker and wrote "Johnny Sacrum Lives." I didn't know what it meant and kept walking.

Afterward, I got dinner on the back patio of a fancy restaurant overlooking the ocean. I ordered an overpriced chicken sandwich, but now that I'd moved up a few levels on the pay scale, I felt less stress about eating at a place like this. I looked at the other guests:

older White folks with that upper-middle-class boredom in their eyes. For once I didn't feel out of place. Over the last few years, I'd spent so much time working with people who could have been sitting at any of these tables that they didn't scare me anymore. Years back, when I'd taken that road trip with Doug, I'd imagined that people like this were just waiting to turn on me any chance they could, but now I knew they weren't any smarter or any better than I was. In fact, I knew that no matter how well dressed and mature they seemed, a lot of these folks would break into how-could-they-do-this-to-*me* tears if someone overcooked their steak. They'd start pounding on the bathroom door and saying, "Excuse me!" if they had to wait longer than twenty seconds. I knew these people now, and no matter how put-together they looked, they were no better than Doug or Tuyet or any of the other urchins running around Sand Beach. All that separated them from street trash was money. Most of these people had probably been in the middle of the pack in high school and college, some only passing because of the demands of powerful parents— the same parents who harassed me all the time to change their kids' grades even though Kiddo wouldn't know which direction to shit without Mommy pointing the way. Sure, some of 'em were probably smart as fuck and sophisticated and knew multiple languages and could charm you for days with stories of world travel and former lovers. But most of them were stylish cows chewing their cud.

After eating, I went for a walk, then got back in the car and headed to a bar. I bought a bottle of ale and sat on a couch and started reading *On the Road*. I'd read part of it in college, but I was always so drunk and nervous back then that I could hardly process a word, so when I started that first page, it was as if I was reading it for the first time. I felt incredible, finally on the road again myself. Finally drinking again. Finally feeling my soul rising inside of me. But I couldn't get too relaxed. That month would end soon, and I'd be back at Cody Cares, and the only way to survive there was to keep your soul locked in the closet. Buried under winter jackets and hats and only to be taken out a few times a year, like on this trip. Too much soul can kill, and it does kill every single day.

By page fifty or so, I started getting that grumble in my stomach, so I asked a server if she'd bring me some enchiladas with a side of guacamole. She was cute and smiled when she said, "Well, we don't serve guacamole here, but I'll make it happen." She brought out a plate of enchiladas verdes and a huge side of guac that she said was "on the house," and I devoured them while thinking how incredible women were. That sometimes they'd bring you guac even if it wasn't on the menu, and they'd smile and make everything feel as if it was gonna be okay. I flipped to the back of the book and wrote a poem about this server, and a few times when I looked up, our eyes met and we smiled, and I wanted to beg her to marry me on the spot. Marriage wasn't on the menu either, but maybe she could bring that too. Maybe I could feel happy and alive and believe that if I asked for something and needed it badly enough, that life would bring it to me on a colorful ceramic plate, and I could finally taste it and know life was actually life and not death, and that the world existed beyond the walls of my musty apartment and my classroom, and I had the power to step out into it at any time and know I could do anything I wanted without the herd bringing me down.

Suddenly, I knew what that boulder inside of me was. A book! Holy shit! You can write now without the world caving in on you. After writing those scripts, you know how to structure stories. You can do this quickly, man. The story is already there. You just need to give it a little push.

I ordered another bottle of ale and kept reading, and the further down that road I traveled with Kerouac, the clearer my own story became, and I practically danced out of there and drove up the coast, listening to Kris Kristofferson, and I pulled to the side of the road and kept writing and writing and almost filled half of my small notebook: poems and song lyrics and story ideas. Writing and not wanting to drive over a cliff. Writing and knowing I could write even more, days later. Writing and knowing there was no limit to the love and joy and inspiration inside of me. Big Sur, you beautiful, powerful slice of earth! Thank you for giving me this gift. For reminding me that life is still wholesome and sweet and worth living. Someday, I'll come back to you when I've published these books and produced these films, and we'll both feel as if we've returned home.

When I got back to the cabin, I read as much of *On the Road* as I could before passing out. The next day, I drove northeast and then south down the 5, then east again toward Sequoia National Park. I stopped at a gas station outside the park and bought some ice cream and ate it while staring at the mountains in the distance. The heat was oppressive, but I knew that soon I'd be up in the cool cover of mountain forest. I got stuck behind an RV on those twisting, tight roads, but it was all right. I had spectacular views all around me. When I finally arrived, I asked the woman at the gate if the huge tree nearby was a sequoia, but she said it was a redwood and, "When you see a sequoia, trust me, you'll know." When I parked, I did my rituals, then practically ran down the trail. Most of the forest was filled with average-sized trees, but when I saw my first sequoia in the distance, I couldn't believe how big it was. I kept going until I was at the trunk of the General Sherman, the world's largest tree by volume. If you hollowed out that trunk, you could live in it comfortably, with a couch and a bed and a kitchen and all of that.

I asked a tourist speaking what sounded like German to take a picture of me, and I hung out in the Giant Forest for a few hours and then hit the road again. The view of the mountains on that drive southwest through the park was almost as beautiful as any I'd ever seen. I stopped at a motel outside the park, then went to an Italian spot nearby and ate a bucket of spaghetti and meatballs at a picnic table inside. A mother and her three young kids, all dressed up like they were Mennonites or Amish, came in and ate at a far corner. My hair was wild and my face covered in road dust, but that didn't stop the oldest of those children, who looked to be about thirteen, from staring at me. There was no way to know what she was thinking, but she kept staring even when Mom scolded her to eat. Mom got busy with the baby, and girl kept staring. I wanted to go over and tell her, as soon as you can, run off into the wilderness. Find your own path and never look back.

I went back to the motel and almost finished *On the Road*. The next morning, I drove back to Soul City, and even though I could feel my soul wanting to climb back into its sarcophagus, as trained, I asked it to stay with me for a little while longer. But when my neighbor slammed a cupboard, it ran to the basement of my being again. Even still, I outlined my book in a three-subject notebook, using the same system I'd used with my scripts, and finished it in only a few days. After that, I used my new screenwriting skills to write a much more active plot than my Mexican book, focusing more on dialogue and short scene and character description than on lengthy internal monologues. I knew this book would be far more plot-driven than my previous, because it was loosely based on my time teaching in Miami, and the only way to survive there had been to get out of my head as much as possible. I used some of the ideas Ian and I had come up with when we developed our TV series, *Tropical Teaching*, and I gave it the same name, but I focused on one character instead of several, telling the story through his eyes. I knew I wanted this book to be as much about teachers helping to develop students' minds as it was about the developing minds of the young teachers, stuck in cycles of shame, which hindered their own growth and maturation. I wanted to create characters stuck in these loops, and by the end, the main character would break out of his own. I also wanted to keep the story as true to life as possible, including all the racism and dysfunction and drug- and alcohol abuse I'd witnessed while I was there. Books were worthless if they weren't honest, and we lived in an ugly-ass world.

I finished the first draft in about a week and a half, and after taking a few days off, I dove back in and edited it. I also edited my Mexican book, using my new writing skills to craft a better story, and by the time my July break was over, I had two books that were pretty much readable.

Chapter 28

Two nights before school started again in August, I got intense stomach pains, and my neck and back muscles strained beyond my control, and I realized how profoundly my body and mind were being affected by my toxic work environment. Yeah, I'd felt tense and shitty over that month off, but now I was aware of how much worse I felt having to return to work. I wanted to run back to the California wilderness, to explore every mountain, tree, and stone and write the stories and songs I knew would bring me closer to the Great River. School was just a thing to prop me up while I focused on my real work, writing myself into existence, but now I understood how much it was pulling me down. On that first day back, I could feel my soul being pushed so far down, I knew I wouldn't be seeing it again anytime soon. I wanted to share my Big Sur stories with Karla and Camarin, and without them there, the place felt so dark and heavy. Barry was still around, but we didn't talk much anymore, and I never really got into deep topics with him anyway. We were more likely to exchange jokes or funny stories than to discuss trips that changed the way we saw ourselves.

During the break, a clothing store had moved into the classroom that shared the wall behind my desk, and I could hear the music the second I walked in that first day back. It was worse than having an army of angry parents waiting for me. For all those years, none of the businesses in the classrooms had played music, and if they had, it was at dentist-waiting-room volumes, not hey-check-out-the-hip-new-store sonic blasts. During lunch, I gathered the strength to ask them to lower it, but the owner, a young guy with tattoos all over his forearms, laughed at me. I returned to my desk knowing I'd have to quit. Knowing I'd never be able to work anywhere else. Hoping that some big publisher would love my work and sell millions of copies, and I'd finally be free of this torment. That I'd be able to move to some cabin in the Mexican mountains and never have to force my soul back into hiding again.

I tried to fantasize about my escape from Cody Cares, but the music was beating me down so badly, not even my thoughts could rise up. I was glad I'd been able to write an entire book over break. There was no way I'd have been able to do that now—now that life was no longer possible. This music would be blasting behind me for the rest of my life. Jay, your best days are over. This trip was your last to the dog park. Life has a gun to the back of your head and that trigger will be clicking soon.

I thought about asking Mr. Perez to make the owner lower the music, but I couldn't do that for a few reasons: One, I loathed the idea of being vulnerable in front of him. Two, what if he started asking questions and found out I was nuts? Three, he'd probably misinterpret my sincere request as a challenge to his authority, making the situation infinitely worse. When I got home, a neighbor slammed his microwave door, and I thought about sticking an uncapped pen in my ear, then bashing the side of my head against the wall to drive that tip into my brain. This is what you get for trying to find peace in this world, dumbass. How many times do I have to teach you not to fucking try?

A high school friend sent me a text message: "Hey, I'll be in Soul City all week for a wedding. Let's hang, homie!" I thought of a few excuses, imagining which the Frog would say was best, then I responded, "Sorry, I'll be in LA all week taking meetings for this new TV series they got me working on. Maybe next time?" Keep writing yourself into existence, Jay. Don't let the noise beat you down.

My other neighbor started blasting his TV, so I grabbed *On the Road* and headed to a café about a mile from the beach where I'd been going a lot lately. It was called Elena's Café, and it had a European vibe—black-and-white checkered floor covered with small circular tables surrounded by uncomfortable wrought-iron chairs. Elena was an older woman from Romania who stalked around the place, kicking out people who overstayed their welcome or who gave off the wrong vibe. She gave me dirty looks the first few times I went there, but I think she backed off after seeing how many chai lattes I'd buy while I sat there and read. The place was always full of weirdos from all over the world, and you'd hear people speaking in Japanese, Turkish, Spanish, Italian, French. I loved the chai latte, and I also loved taking a quick trip around the world before having to go home and fight my neighbors, which is why I put up with Elena's misanthropic bullshit.

I usually sat in the far corner, minimizing the number of tables surrounding me, and I'd put in my earplugs and music. I was okay with a steady hum of conversation, but the moment someone started shrieking above that level, then I could hear every laugh, every word—even with the music—and it drove me nuts. It was just as bad if it was just one or two people talking. That shit felt like an invasion of my being. You do your thing, I'll do mine. I'll keep my music down, and you keep your voice down. Nobody wants to hear your fucking conversation.

Despite this noise, I finished *On the Road*. I wrote the date on the title page and headed to a Mexican place for dinner, then I saw a Swedish film that everyone was raving about. Though the theater was much quieter than the café, an older couple sitting a few rows ahead kept talking, and even though they weren't too loud, it pulled me right out of the picture. Once you hear one person make a single sound at the movies, the whole experience is fucked; you just sit there waiting for the next sound and then the next while getting angrier and angrier and hoping the film is a shitshow so you feel less outraged that you spent most of it thinking about committing murder.

About halfway through, the man laughed, even though someone onscreen had just died, and I walked up behind them, leaned over, and whispered, "Please stop talking. This isn't your living room." On the way back to my seat, a middle-aged guy whispered, "Thanks" to me as I passed. Even though the theater was now quiet, I couldn't pay attention. Too many adults were large wrinkled children, and it enraged me that I even needed to tell someone to shut up in a place where the main rule is to shut the fuck up. Some other clown started playing on his phone, and I wanted to tell him to put it away, but I didn't have any fight left in me.

A few months after opening, that fucking clothing shop closed down, and the new silence reminded me that at any moment the world would fuck me again. Some other asshole business would move in, and this one would last, and I'd be fucked for good, and the more I'd complain about it, the harder people would come at me. It didn't matter where I worked, there'd always be some asshole business there, violating my peace. You can't go anywhere, man. You can't fucking go anywhere.

I turned thirty-one that October. My parents and both brothers sent me cards, but I didn't pick up when any of them called. I didn't tell anybody at work it was my birthday. Doreen had always set up the celebrations, and now she was gone, and I didn't even want a cake. Eating it would have reminded me how far away she and Camarin and Karla were, and how I didn't talk with them or my family or friends anymore. I spent the night alone in my apartment watching *Deadwood* and eating a microwaved pizza.

I came up with an idea for a screenplay about a sensitive boy who grows up in a conservative household where no one listens to him, but even when he goes off to a liberal college, hoping to effect change in an unfeeling world, no one listens to him there either due to his background, and he ends up destroying himself. I called it *The*

Knockerman, and once I got the idea, the whole thing came together even faster than *Tropical Teaching*, and I had a finished draft in five days. Before I'd even typed "FADE OUT" I knew it was the best story I'd ever written. The whole script worked no matter how much you zoomed in or out, and I had hope that this would finally be the one to help me break into Hollywood. I edited it several times and submitted it to a few contests.

Around that time, the Zambulla Film Fest accepted my script *The Silent Protest* as a finalist in their 2013 screenwriting competition. This time, I felt strong enough to go. I was still performing my rituals, but I'd cut their time in half, and I had the whole process down to an orderly routine. Before, I'd jump from the stove to the sink to the door to the bathroom and back to the front door and so on, with no order to any of it. But now, I started at the door, then moved to the living room window, then to the kitchen, bathroom, and bedroom, and I could do it all in about forty minutes, which made me think that maybe I could handle a longer international trip. Also, when I'd lived in Mexico, everyone would always mention the beauty of Zambulla, a small mountain town north of Lila, but I'd never had the money to go.

The festival was in November, and I had the whole month off, so I bought my ticket and let the fest's director know I was coming. He emailed me a link to an online form asking for a headshot, bio, script synopsis, and a website link. I didn't have any of this shit, causing me to panic, so I used my old coping strategy and made a list and decided to start with the headshot. I found a guy who wanted to shoot me in his studio, but I told him it'd probably be better to do it on Sand Beach. My stories came from places like that beach. We did the session on a crowded Saturday afternoon, with people walking by and cracking jokes and talking shit, but I remembered hearing how seriously the members of the Doors used to take photo shoots, and when I tried to tap into that energy and block out the crowds, I realized their insults didn't hurt me the way I'd thought they would. If anything, they made me realize how much I'd grown from all of this bullshit, adding an extra layer of armor around me. After all, they were probably terrified of taking a single step toward their dreams—just as I used to be—and seeing anyone moving in this direction probably filled them with shame.

After the photo shoot, I focused on making a website. I didn't know shit about web design, so I looked at a few authors' websites and found one I loved. I contacted the designer, and he quoted me a good price. All was going smoothly until he asked me what domain name I wanted to use. I knew I was no longer Jay Sakovsky, but I didn't know who I was. I wrote names on printer paper and taped them to my walls: Jay Kirkland, Jay Bonnie, Jay Horace. I sat on the floor and shifted my head, looking at the names from every angle, trying to determine which one said it all. But none worked. While listening to the Smiths, I knew I was a Johnny, so I wrote Johnny Kirkland, Johnny Stone, Johnny Lily. But none of those worked either. Then, I almost shouted "Johnny Sacrum!"

I told the designer to buy johnnysacrum.com along with jonsacrum.com and johnsacrum.com. I felt incredible. Now, I had this new being to toss the best parts of myself into while Jay Sakovsky struggled. Now, any song or story or poem I wrote, I'd toss into Sacrum. Any joke or clever line or charming look, it was all Johnny S. Johnny, who didn't have any of the shame or trauma or guilt for simply being alive. Who wasn't terrified to get onstage and rock a room or bring a casting director to tears. The person growing inside of me now had a name. The Knight was always going on and on about how "the sacrum is usually the last bone to rot when people are buried, so ancient civilizations believed the whole body would be rebuilt around this bone in the afterlife, making it a symbol of reincarnation."

I'm Johnny Sacrum! But I hadn't invented myself entirely on my own. I'd been guided to Sacrum by the Frog and the Knight and Camarin and Karla and Mariposa and Silas and my parents and my childhood friends and my brothers and sisters and my teachers and the priests and nuns at my childhood church and all the movies I'd ever watched, books I'd read, songs I'd listened to. Johnny Sacrum wasn't just me. It was all of us. Everything. Stardust and dirt and light from distant planets. Now was my time to take everything I'd ever known and turn it into something beautiful.

Chapter 29

When Lou Reed died, I fell into such a depression, I didn't think I'd ever get out, but after a few days, I started to snap back to life. I thought about canceling my trip to Mexico, but I knew I had to honor my hero by having the courage to face my dreams, so I took a train to the border, crossed, and took a cab to the TJ airport. A woman from the festival was waiting for me at the Zambulla airport when I arrived.

"Johnny! Johnny Sacrum!" she said, looking at her clipboard and then up at me, but it took me a moment to realize.

"Oh, oh, yeah, I-I'm Johnny." Instantly, I imagined Doug jumping out from behind the rental car counter and pointing and laughing at me.

"How was your flight?" she said.

"Not too bad. Hey, I speak Spanish if you want to, uh . . ."

She switched to Spanish. "Oh, where did you learn?"

"I lived a few hours south of here, in Lila," I said.

"Do you know Zambulla?"

"No, this is my first time here."

We waited for a few others to arrive, and when there were enough people to fill the van, the driver took us to our hotels. I sat beside an actor from Toronto, and we discussed our favorite directors, hers being Paul Thomas Anderson and Stanley Kubrick. When she asked me mine, I felt the panic creeping up my spine. Though I loved both of those directors, I felt as if I wasn't good enough to truly appreciate them, as she did. Regardless, I said I liked them as well, and added Alfonso Cuarón and Pedro Almodóvar to the list, and when the guy to my other side said, "Damn, you two know all these obscure directors," I relaxed a little, thinking that, perhaps, I was better suited to be here than I realized.

The driver didn't speak English, so I translated for the other passengers, helping them to get to their hotels, then the driver brought me to my place, which looked to have been carved out of a fortress wall. When making my reservation, I'd asked for a room "on the top floor and with as few shared walls as possible," and they gave me the big spot in the back corner. My ID badge and swag bag were waiting on the bed. I took a quick shower and headed for the opening party. I saw Maddie, the actor from Toronto, and together we met a few others. We were all hungry, so we left the party to get some food in the town center. It was strange to be back in Mexico under these circumstances. To me, Mexico was a place of freedom and reinvention, and I felt as if that dinner was a job interview, where I had to list all of my influences and describe my story's structure and character arcs. I felt conflicted. This was the place where I'd learned how to stand up for myself. To fight back. And part of me wanted to tell these people to fuck off as I headed to the bar upstairs, got loaded, and took one of the pretty women in the crowd back to my hotel.

But I was a good boy and answered all their questions with a smile. When I got back to the hotel, I was exhausted. It was hard enough to socialize with friends, but now my voice was shot and muscles strained, and I felt a steady rush of anxiety flowing up my back. Here, I couldn't space out over dinner and simply enjoy the food and scenery. I had to force a smile and nod and laugh when someone said something moderately funny—but they were probably doing the same shit with me.

The next morning, I lay in bed for about an hour, feeling hungover even though I hadn't had anything to drink the night before. My whole body ached, and the thought of talking to more people crippled me with anxiety. I didn't know what to wear, how to speak, how to act. I'd brought my nicest clothes and hair gel and cologne. I knew I had to be ready. Maybe one of these people would tell me they knew I was a star and, "Let's make a picture together, baby! Here's a billion dollars and the keys to your new private jet." As much as I wanted to stay in that bed, I got up, showered, and got into character. It was hard telling people my name was Johnny. I felt like a fucking impostor. I tried reminding myself that some of my heroes used stage names—David Bowie, Iggy Pop, Joe Strummer—but this only made it worse. You're not David Bowie, dumbass. Just burn that suit, lose the hair gel, take a bus south to Lila, and go see your friends. Get some caguamas, get drunk, fuck Azucar the stripper, and never go back to California.

While eating lunch in the center, a man from the festival approached me and said he'd read my script. "It was brilliant. You put such fine attention to detail and character development that it was almost easy to overlook, but I saw it was there, and it made all the difference."

Hearing that made me feel better about my slicked-back hair and ironed button-down. I saw some films that afternoon, then went to a cocktail party and met a few more people, one being a director from Hollywood who had a short film doing well in the festival circuit. He was a pro and seemed at ease speaking with everyone, and I was glad he introduced me to others. Left on my own, I'd likely sit in the corner and keep an eye on the exit, but the director, Alex, made it easier for me to socialize. He said, "Meeting potential collaborators is one of the most important things to do at a festival." I passed out some business cards and collected a few dozen. After the party, we went to a bar, where I declined about a hundred offers for drinks, and soon I was back at the hotel.

At the cocktail party, I met a cute woman from Zambulla who interviewed me for an entertainment blog. She was surprised when I answered her questions in Spanish, and I think this impressed her because she said yes when I asked her to lunch the next day.

The woman, Frida, met me at a restaurant, and we spent most of the afternoon discussing film and music, but she kept bringing up something that I'd been hearing from a few other women at the festival. "Even though I have a degree from university, because I'm a woman, it's difficult for me to get a good job here. I'm worried about my future."

Frida and I went to see a block of live-action shorts, then we went back to the hotel and made out. There was so much life in her eyes, and she was so brimming with talent, I wanted to stay in that room kissing her for the rest of the week. I asked her to stay with me that night, but she said her parents would never allow it unless we were married. She left, and I got dinner in the center. When I left the restaurant, I saw Alex eating with about twenty other filmmakers at the spot next door; I tried to sneak by them, but he said, "SACRUM, COME SIDDOWN, BUDDY!"

I didn't have any energy left, so I started slipping into panic world, surviving on anxiety just like in the old days. I jumped to life whenever I saw anyone so much as look in my direction, nodding my head along and saying, "Oh, yeah, yeah, that's incredible," or "Oh, yeah, yeah, that's horrible." I repeated, "Oh wow," and, "That's insane!" and, "Oh, forget that!" There was no way I'd be able to make a joke or witty comment. To say anything even moderately intelligent. I was just a prop on their set. I probably could have written our dinner conversation from the safety of my room, but on the fly, I could hardly say my name. This reminded me of how ill-prepared I was to act, and how much longer I'd need to wait until I could even think of taking an acting lesson. I was a wooden doll, but at least I was around people who were cultured and educated and wouldn't corner me, forcing me to laugh at their racist jokes, seeing my anxiety and using it to manipulate me or stroke their egos or affirm their prejudices. No, here I was in good company, and as awkward as I felt, I was glad to be there, and I absorbed as much of it as possible. I watched how Alex controlled the conversation, how his words flowed from him effortlessly. He was witty and intelligent, and I hoped someday that would be me as well. He was in his forties, so he had at least a decade on me. Someday, I'd catch up.

I went back to my hotel, and the next day I was so beat, I skipped the films, cocktails, and parties. My brain felt like a hollow shell, and while lying in bed and flipping through business cards, for a brief moment, I had no idea who I was anymore. Frida met me for dinner, and we came back to the hotel to make out some more. This time, she took off her shirt, and she looked incredible. I got on top and made sweet love to her boobs as she held them together, and I came all over her neck and tits. It'd been years since I'd been with a woman—the last had been Carolina—and I'd almost forgotten how all this felt. But after cumming, I realized that as great as it was, it wasn't everything. That my healing journey was far more important, and that I would take a vow of celibacy if it would help me step into that Great River. Orgasms last for seconds, but music is forever.

The rest of the week passed in a blur, and soon it was over. I'd hoped *The Silent Protest* would win best script, but that went to a writer from Montreal. Still, I felt like a winner in a lot of ways: I'd gone to a film festival in a foreign country by myself, using a name and personality I'd only recently created, and as nervous and awkward as I felt, I met a lot of great people. I didn't get drunk or get into any fights or say anything stupid. A few people did, and watching them made me grateful I'd walked into the Frog's cave years ago. But as great as it felt not fucking anything up, that was a pretty low bar to set. I wanted to be like Alex, witty and charming and accomplished. His film won the international shorts category, and he gave a great speech about the beauty of Zambulla and how the US needed to respect and appreciate its neighbor to the south, and the crowd gave him a standing ovation. Someday, I'd learn how to bring people together with my words as well. Someday, I'd find a way to show people the beauty I saw in Mexico. Mexico had saved me so many, many times, and I couldn't think of a better place to give birth to Johnny Sacrum than the place that gave birth to Jay Sakovsky.

When I got back to Soul City, I imagined that when I was rich and famous, I'd build a house in the Hollywood Hills that stood alone—no shared walls or floors or anything—and I'd cover it in bricks, soundproof the walls, fill in the windows with cement blocks and soundproofing panels, fill the attic with so much insulation, no sound could ever get through, and then I'd be able to relax enough to write my true masterpiece.

But I didn't have a super-soundproofed house yet, and I'd have to make do with my shitty beach apartment. The moment I walked in the door, I was overwhelmed with my apartment's strong smell. It was like a combination of cigarette smoke and mold, but soon I couldn't smell it anymore.

I didn't talk much with Carolina anymore—just catching up every so often—but I did meet another woman on that website. That winter, she was moving from Lima, Peru, to work at a ski resort in Montana, and when she asked me to translate the list of rules her new boss had emailed her, I got such a horrible panic attack I had to step away from my computer. No outside calls, no Internet, no eating outside of dining hours, no alcohol, no smoking, no sex, no kissing, no fun, no freedom. They were going to stuff eight people per room, which meant no privacy, and apparently most of the town shut down in winter, and the only way to get around was by snowmobile. I asked her if she really wanted to do this, and she said yes.

After our conversation, I knew I had the idea for my next script. It would be about a Colombian woman making this same journey, hoping that coming to the US would help her find love and relief from her obsessive-compulsive disorder. She's got a boyfriend in California who keeps promising he'll visit her, but as the weeks pass and he never shows, her compulsions get worse, making people think she's insane. I wrote the script before the end of my November break, and called it *Lila's Adventure*.

I continued talking to Frida and another woman I'd met at the festival, and the other woman, Melissa, kept saying the same thing I'd heard other women say: "I feel like men don't respect women in my culture." The more she discussed this, the more I realized how much it sounded like a film. We did an intense brainstorming session, created a rough outline for a script, and wrote the fucker in two weeks. We shared a Google Doc, and one person would do research while the other wrote. Sometimes she wrote entire scenes by herself, and other times I wrote them, and I couldn't imagine a more perfect collaboration. Writing with Melissa was easy and inspiring, and at the end we had this beautiful story about a half-Mexican, half-American woman who returns to her hometown of Zambulla, Mexico, after she fails to make it as a dancer in New York, and she struggles to find her identity. We called it *Haz Tu Propia Casa.*

I wanted to do this full-time. To create powerful stories that helped people to better understand themselves and the worlds they inhabited. To inspire them to challenge the rules, social structures, and power dynamics of those worlds as a means to create a safer, more balanced society where all groups felt equally represented. I wanted my stories to spark rebellions, and after finishing *Haz* with Melissa, about a woman who realizes that she's strong enough to choose her own path in life, I knew I wanted to spend my life trying to effect positive change in the world. Stories can do that. People put down artists, telling them to get real jobs and all that crap, but this world was built by dreamers. Artisans. Poets. Painters. I wanted to be a part of that revolution, and it was an honor to have people like Melissa at my side.

For that two-week period, Melissa and I had written every day for about ten to twelve hours, including Christmas Eve and Day, and New Year's, and when I reread our completed script a week or two later, I realized what significant progress I'd made with my disease. While working on *Tropical Teaching, The Silent Protest,* and *Kirkland,* I'd get such bad headaches, I'd have to take days or even months off. Just looking at my computer screen would strain my eyes so badly, I had to walk away. With all the noise in my head, it was difficult for me to concentrate. I realized that one of my most powerful inner voices was always screaming at me to "GO! GET OUT OF HERE NOW! GO TO INDIA! GO TO SPAIN! GO TO HOLLYWOOD! JUST FUCKING GO, AND GO NOW!" Having this voice screaming at me while trying to work on a project that could take months or even years to finish zapped my energy. I was fighting a constant inner war because I had another voice telling me, "WRITE! WRITE NOW! WRITE AS FAST AS YOU CAN! GO NOWHERE! STAY IN YOUR CHAIR! DON'T GET UP TO PISS! FORGET ABOUT FOOD AND SLEEP! WRITE NOW! WRITE!"

I had to get away from the extremes, and when the headaches got so bad I could hardly see, I'd lie in bed and tell myself, "Just let it go. Let it all go. If you never finish the stories, then so be it. Just breathe. Relax. The only way to continue is to let it go. The only way to finish is to never start." All of this stress zapped my creativity, and it was hard for me to take detours from my outlines. If I took a single detour, I might start writing an entirely different story, so I had to be rigid, but rigidity was the death of creativity. When I was writing those stories, I always felt I could have done more. Added more. Made them more complex. Tightened up the thematic content and written more inspired dialogue. But I also had to remember the Frog's words: "I'm impressed that you're even able to write at all given what you're going through." I had to keep everything in perspective and realize that even though I wasn't where I wanted to be, if I kept moving forward, someday I'd get there. Someday, I'd be able to relax while writing and allow the story to flow through me without having to think. Someday, I'd be able to close my eyes and let my heart, mind, and fingers do their thing without me getting in the way.

I began to understand that a large reason why noises bothered me so much was that they pulled me out of my stories. They broke my concentration, and I knew that I needed infinite concentration to tell all of the stories inside of me. To finally break through that asymptote and touch the stories as all the greats had, who'd likely been able to touch their stories from the day they were born. I still needed to be born. And the successes I'd had with my latest scripts made me feel this was coming. This last one with Melissa was really something. The story felt entertaining and complex and *important*. That was something I always asked myself whenever I went to the theater or listened to a new album or saw a new painting: Is this *important*? Does it *need* to exist or is it just taking up space? I wanted to write stories and songs that *needed* to exist. Those pieces don't take up space, they *are* space, and entire universes fit perfectly inside of them. Maybe it'd take me a thousand years to write one. Maybe I'd do it after five more lifetimes. But now I was on that path.

Chapter 30

"You need to research OCD. I mean, you wrote that her bedroom was a disaster. People who are OCD are super clean and organized. Quite frankly, I find it pretty offensive that you'd write a script like this without doing research. As someone who suffers seasonal depression, I find it appalling that people have so little regard for mental illness. You should really be ashamed of yourself," said a woman from my screenwriters' group, discussing *Lila's Adventure*.

"I find it more appalling that there's *no* conflict. *Hello*? Where's the antagonist?" said the old dude who always needed to get in his zingers. "Can you even imagine *Star Wars* without Darth Vader?"

Yeah, it'd be kinda like this group without you, you fuckin' prick.

Half of them destroyed the script, but after the meeting, a few writers approached me again, letting me know this was my best screenplay yet and one of the best they'd read in the group. I hadn't noticed that they were all women until one asked me to lunch, and then I thought maybe they really weren't such fans of my work after all.

I told the Frog all about it during one of our café sessions.

"Well, every group has one jerk—or, in this case, five or six," the Frog said.

"I dunno, maybe they're right. Maybe I suck. Maybe I don't even have OCD," I said.

"Jay, remind me again why you were late today."

"Oh, 'cause I had to wait until my neighbor was done watering his plants before I could go through my door-locking rituals."

"That's not OCD to you?"

"It's just—even when I'm touching doors and pulling on handles and checking the stove and all that, there's this voice inside of me that says, everything's fine. *You* don't have a problem, other people do. The starving kids in Africa—they're the ones with the problem. You're one of the lucky ones. You were born in the USA, and there are no problems here. Yeah, I might be touching doors and all that, but it's only 'cause I'm ungrateful. Weak. Selfish. A whiny bitch. If I just *listened* to Dad or God or my teachers, I'd be fine, you know?"

"I gotta stop you there. Until you fully recognize how real this problem is, you won't be able to resolve it."

"Yeah, maybe I'm just scared, though. I mean, isn't that how most Americans get through the day? Push their problems off to Africa and pretend that everything here is great?"

"Indeed it is—maybe China too."

I laughed. "You know, there's this woman at work who goes on and on saying shit like, 'I'm sooooo OCD' whenever she organizes her desk or files paperwork or whatever, and even though she doesn't know what the fuck she's talking about, it doesn't bother me. It's almost as if her version of OCD is mine too, you know? That I'm sooooo OCD as well, and all this checking and shit is really just the same as this woman putting graded work in a red folder and ungraded work in a blue one."

"It's not the same, Jay, and you know that."

I laughed again. "Yo, that shit doesn't even make sense. How can someone *be* obsessive-compulsive disorder? I'm more offended as a writer by shitheads saying, 'I'm sooooo OCD' than I am as someone with the disease. It does bother me, though, when people say the word 'crazy.' I think I identify more with 'crazy' than 'OCD,' you know, and when people say, 'Oh, that's crazy,' it reminds me of all the times I've slipped off to loony land."

"I think you're right about all of this, Jay. People in this country don't value mental health. Hell, they don't understand it, and growing up in such a world, it's a miracle that you even walked into my cave in the first place. Like you said, we're conditioned to believe that everything is okay even when our hearts and minds are on fire, and I think that what you're doing is great. The world needs stories like the ones you're telling, and I think your work is getting so much criticism because people don't understand that, so often, the worst antagonists in our lives are our own selves. And when you present characters like this—who move toward their suffering as a means to understanding themselves and healing their inner wounds—it scares people. It makes them think, maybe *I* should be moving toward my own suffering, and then they start asking themselves terrifying questions: Did I marry the wrong woman? Do I really believe in God? Why do I still see my dad after all that's happened? Also, I think stories like these, which can involve subtle forms of conflict, often go right over people's heads. They're not paying attention to these forms of conflict in their own lives, so why would they pick up on it on the page or screen? For someone like you, getting out of a car and walking away without checking the windows and trunk is a colossal victory. Your disease has made you painfully aware of these kinds of subtle conflicts, and you don't need space aliens or ninjas or Russian mobsters to fill your stories with tension. The tension of everyday life is enough. If you're going to continue to write stories like these, you have to prepare yourself for the fact that most people won't be interested in them. In fact, a lot of people will feel threatened by them, but that doesn't mean you should stop. The world needs stories like these, no matter what people say, and if you're gonna tell these stories, you're going to need to derive your strength from within. You're moving in the right direction, Jay. I know you have your doubts about your work and your mental health, but you can't expect the world to help you find the answers you seek. You can only do that by looking inside. And when you get to that point where you know exactly who you are and what you're trying to say, you're going to be unstoppable, and you won't need anyone else's approval. True artists and visionaries stand on their own legs, and I can already see how strong yours are."

"Yeah, yeah, you're right," I said. "You know, I don't think people know how much damage they're causing by calling people ungrateful or selfish or whatever. We absolutely destroy boys in our culture. If you scream because your brother sneezed on your pillow, rather than taking you to the doctor and discovering that your fear of contamination is a symptom of OCD, they'll just beat your ass and call *you* an aggressive asshole. If you take too long in the shower because you're washing off that contamination, you're using all the hot water, you selfish jerk! If you stick around, you're lazy and leeching off of your parents, but if you move out then you're too good for everyone. In our culture, Mom and Dad are patient with girls, but they'll scream every terrible thing at boys. They'll beat your ass because *you* should know better. *You* should toughen up. I mean, I know that shit fucks up girls too, telling them to shut up and stay in their place and everything, but we're way more likely to let girls talk about how bad that shit fucks them up, even though we're really just nodding our heads along and hoping they'll stop crying. But if a guy expresses any emotion at all, we'll beat the absolute shit out of him so he thinks twice before ever speaking again. In these last few years, I've told maybe two people about my OCD. When am I gonna be allowed to actually have my fucking disease, ya know?"

"Jay, you can't expect anyone to understand or care about your disease or your artistic vision, but that doesn't mean you should let anyone take them from you. You're right. The world will beat all of the good out of you, if you let it. But *you* won't let it. And because of that, someday you *will* share that beauty inside of you with the world, and you'll inspire many of those beaten-down people to start fighting back."

I thought about his words for a moment, and then I started laughing.

"What?" the Frog said.

"I'd love to show that woman from my group a picture of my room so she can see how *organized* people with OCD are."

The Frog laughed as well. "Keep that sense of humor. It'll get you through the worst of times."

I submitted *Tropical Teaching* to a publisher specializing in books that address social issues, and they accepted it for publication. I was thrilled to have my book accepted by the first press I sent it to and started thinking maybe it really was something special. I hired a lawyer to review the contract, and we signed it and set a publication date: May 14, 2015, which was over a year away. I thought about submitting *The Saga of the Scorpion* as well, but knew that it still needed work and after having written a book and three scripts over the last seven months, I needed a break from writing.

Instead, I decided to type all of the song lyrics, poems, and story ideas from my notebooks onto a Word file that I could register a copyright for. I had fourteen notebooks filled with words, so I knew this would be a long task. I also knew that, since I was a kid, whenever I cleaned anything, I'd pick up a tissue or whatever and get lost in thought for an hour or more—remembering the time my ex handed me a tissue in home ec because I got black pepper in my eye and how I'd gone home that night and made her cookies but added a cup of baking powder instead of sugar, but I still gave them to her anyway to show her how much I cared about her, and she ate one and pretended it was good and weeks later she started dating Brian Hooper behind my back—and I knew it would be worse with these notebooks. I knew I'd get lost rereading and rewriting songs and poems. Thinking up new ones. Thinking of new stories.

While typing this file, I realized that part of why I was feeling creatively blocked was that my soul was buried under these words that never had a home or purpose. I'd been carrying these notebooks with me for years, and while most of what I'd written was pure crap, there was some inspired stuff in there that I feared losing, and the more I transferred to the computer, the better I felt. And the better I felt, the easier the words came to me. I realized that I was so full of stories, I had a hard time concentrating on a single one long enough to develop it. Somehow, my screenplays and books had snuck through this noise, but now that I was able to think more clearly, I wrote about a hundred new songs and poems over a six-month period.

I also found that by doing this, I wasn't spending nearly as much time checking the doors and windows and stove, and I realized that part of why I was so protective of that apartment was that if someone broke in or a fire started or whatever and I lost those notebooks, I wouldn't have been able to live without them. Losing those words would be like losing my heart. My liver. My guts. Also, by registering a copyright for my lyric- and poetry compilations, I had some protection against people stealing my work if I performed at an open mic or poetry reading. Yeah, I was a paranoid motherfucker, but it was a symptom of my disease, and doing all of this gave me considerable relief.

When I finished with the lyrics and poetry, I recorded the melodies of my songs and registered a copyright for them as well. If nothing else, I wanted the world to know they existed. If I was hit by a truck or fell off a cliff, at least people could search for Johnny Sacrum and know he was real. I even hired my lawyer to issue a trademark for my pseudonym. The Frog was right. You couldn't trust the world to do right by you; you had to protect yourself and your artistic vision. I took this seriously and was ready to go toe-to-toe with anyone who'd try to take on Johnny Sacrum.

Chapter 31

In early 2014, I was talking with Barry during a free period and mentioned how much I missed Camarin. I hadn't realized Mr. Perez *and* Cody were in earshot, and a few days later, they transferred me to the cafeteria. Though Camarin, Karla, and Doreen were gone, they were still a part of everything in that gymnasium, but we'd never worked together in the cafeteria. No, the cafeteria was uncharted emotional territory, and I was terrified to explore it on my own.

I spent pretty much the entire weekend before the transfer in bed, panicking and knowing that my healing journey was done. That I'd had a good run and had written a few scripts and books, but now I'd never write again. Thankfully, all I was working on at the time was transferring my songs and poems to my computer. My muscles squeezed and even though I'd been seeing the Knight regularly, I was still far from loose.

On Monday, Mr. Perez showed me to my new desk, on the far side of the cafeteria beside the freezer. On the other side was the stove area, and it was hot as hell over there, but my area was cold and I could feel the chill seeping right through me. There were three other teachers there: Mr. Bosch was a fifty-year-old grump from the San Francisco area, and he taught math near the stove. Ms. Collins taught science and sat near Mr. Bosch. She was a "socially-conscious" twenty-two-year-old, who always lectured that everyone should be vegan like her, but she was also the one who always said she was "soooooo OCD!" Mr. Sanderson taught English in the classroom next to mine. He was younger too—twenty-four—and he seemed the sanest of the lot. He was the only one who smiled at me when Mr. Perez introduced us. The others gave a sterile, "Hello, colleague," then got back to work.

As cold as it was in that cafeteria, both literally and figuratively, at least there were no walls shared with any businesses, like in the gym. I knew this move was supposed to be a punishment, but those fuckers didn't realize that maybe this was an upgrade. Hell, my friends were long gone, and Mr. Sanderson seemed like a pretty cool guy. Maybe I could talk with him, vent about shitty parents and Mr. Perez. Like me, Sanderson got nervous when angry parents confronted him. Maybe I could help him with that, teach him the lessons Camarin had taught me. Maybe I could be a leader here.

There was a different group of students in the cafeteria, so I had to get to know them and their parents. This was a rowdier crowd, and I could see why the teachers here were stricter. On that first day, one of my students threw an apple at a kid in Ms. Collins's class, and Ms. Collins wouldn't let me hear an end to it. "This isn't the gym! We have *structure* here. How dare you let a student disrespect an apple like that!" I thought about asking her if she'd feel the same had the kid launched a slab of corned beef instead, but she'd probably already emailed Mr. Perez about the apple thing, and I didn't want to give her anything else to bitch about. I knew I was encroaching on her turf—Mr. Bosch's as well, who'd give me looks as if to say, "Watch out, you hippie gym fuck!"

As miserable as he was, Mr. Bosch closed the cafeteria, not me, which was another perk of the transfer.

I survived the week, and headed to Elena's Café after work on Friday, which had become part of my weekly routine. I'd become friends with one of the baristas, Cecy. She was from Albania and had the most beautiful dark eyes and longest black hair, and every time

I looked at her, I thought, could this possibly be the most beautiful woman I've ever seen? But as beautiful as she was, she was even cooler, and we spoke about art and music and travel. I knew every guy there wanted her, but I liked to think she and I had something special. She told me she'd lived a hard life, but this was something I could see in a person almost instantly, and she had that I've-lived-a-life-of-service-but-I'm-still-smiling quality that was equal parts unpretentious and free-spirited. I knew I'd fall in love with her if I let down my guard, so I did my best to keep it up.

The place was more crowded than usual that night, and just as the woman sitting at my table in the back corner put her computer in her bag, I grabbed my chai latte and book and walked over. A guy sitting at a nearby table saw me and arrived at the table a moment before I did. But instead of sitting, he stood there giving me a confused look.

"Yes, I got here first." He spoke with a French accent and looked to be in his late thirties.

"I think this is a matter of intent over proximity." If he'd said something like, "Oh, I'm sorry, were you going to sit here?" I'd have said, "Oh, yeah, but go ahead and take it," but the fact that he'd hit me with all that "I got here first" bullshit flipped a switch, and I knew my night was ruined, because I was coming after this prick in ways I couldn't go after those pricks at work.

"I don't, uh—I was here first! See?" He touched the table.

"Look, dude, you clearly saw me coming. If you'd been nice about it, I'd say just take it, but you're acting like a little kid."

He quickly sat down. "Look, now I am sitting. Now it is my table."

"By that logic I could have sat when I first got here, and it'd be *my* table, rendering your whole 'yes, I got here first' shit worthless, right?"

"Look, I am sitting and I am drinking a coffee, too, so it is mine."

"Yeah, whatever, mate." I thought about sitting beside him and continuing to read, but I was over it. Instead, I went to a French restaurant a few blocks down. I ordered the steak frites and started with French onion soup with the cheese crusted all around the bowl, and I ate it while reading *Ask the Dust* by John Fante. Across the room, I saw the Knight eating dinner with his wife. I thought about saying hi, but he wasn't dressed in his armor, and it really upset me for some reason; he was just . . . a person. After dinner, I went to a movie but had to leave because some asshole in the audience kept laughing at all the worst shit. Other than the steak, the night was a disaster, and I had a hard time sleeping. I couldn't stop thinking about how far I was from Buffalo. About how little I spoke to my family. How I had no friends here anymore and how work was now just a job. I wanted to go back to Buffalo but I wasn't strong enough, and I'd slip right back into my old roles. I needed more time in Soul City to become Johnny Sacrum. I could go home when *he* was strong enough to talk for me. Say no for me. Say "that makes me uncomfortable" for me. Say "that was really racist" for me.

I finally fell asleep around 4 a.m., which ruined my Saturday. I spent the weekend transferring my songs and poems to my computer. I knew other people were at the beach. Other people were in the bars. Other people were camping with their families. Other people were traveling the world. But I also tried to remember that other people were living under bridges and escaping war-torn countries and begging for change by the tracks. At least I was warm. At least I had food. At least I had dry, comfortable clothes and a paid electric bill. And, like Wally talking about his electric blanket in *My Dinner with Andre*, that was enough.

At least, I tried to convince myself it was . . .

Sunday night, I saw that Carolina had updated her Facebook status to "In a Relationship," and I didn't sleep much that night either. Monday morning, I was later than usual, and I sped up the highway on my way to work. Since moving to the cafeteria, Cody Cares seemed farther away than usual, and the people driving slowly in the left lane were pissing me off. When I finally got a clearing, some prick in the right lane up ahead must not have liked how fast I was going, because he cut me off and dropped down to the speed limit. There were cars going that same speed in the two lanes to my right, so I was stuck. I honked and gave him the finger, but he just put up his hands as if to say, "What? What am I doing, hehe?"

I arrived ten minutes late and Ms. Collins gave me a dirty look, then wrote something in a notebook on her desk. The day passed slowly. Though we were in the cafeteria, none of the teachers ate lunch together. They only interacted with one another for work-related reasons, and once they finished gathering and exchanging information, they ended the conversation—no chitchat. As lonely as I felt, I knew they must have felt so much lonelier. I felt like speaking to each of them as Camarin had spoken with me all those years ago, letting them know they could feel so much better. Maybe I could use this transfer as an opportunity to spread a positive message and make their lives easier.

But you can't force people to change. Most people are happy being miserable. Camarin must have seen something in me that made her feel comfortable discussing all that stuff, and this transfer made me even more aware of how special our relationship had been. How rare.

Maybe if I can't be an emotional leader, I can be the reliable old veteran who teaches the newbies the school's culture and history.

While waiting at the copier, I casually told Mr. Bosch about our old system for sorting paperwork, and he gave me this "who the fuck do you think you are?" look.

"Sorry, I didn't mean anything by it," I said.

"No, you're right. Everything was much better in the past, long before I worked here, and it was all perfect in the gym too, right? That's what you're trying to say?"

After several failures, I decided to be the leader of myself instead and resolved to never try to get close to any of them again. I reminded myself that Cody had hired people who wouldn't question him. This was a dictatorship, and dictators didn't give a shit about improving anything other than their image, power, and bank account. No, this was just a job. A means to pay off my student loans and credit card debt. To enter my scripts in contests and to travel to film festivals where I could meet someone who says, "Damn, Johnny, you're a star! Here's a million bucks. Let's get your face on magazine covers around the world." Cody Cares was a no-growth zone, as the Frog would say, and if I didn't detach myself from it emotionally like I'd had to do in my house as a kid, it would break my spirit. All of this negativity affected how I worked with the students. It was hard to give them my best when my coworkers and bosses were waiting for me to screw up and then throw it in my face. Waiting to tell me that I'm smiling too much, or I'm too nice, or I shouldn't let the kids talk to me about their problems because this is a school, not a therapist's office! I shouldn't ask students how things are going with their football team or in soccer practice or say, "Hey, how'd your ballet recital go?" I shouldn't tell jokes or make abused kids smile because "this isn't a comedy club!" It was hard enough to teach in a supportive environment, but in this emotional tundra, I found myself snapping at the kids sometimes. I found myself criticizing them the way my coworkers criticized me. I found myself repeating, "It's never okay to be mean to kids" in my head more than ever before. I found myself cursing at people on the highway as I sped from that place each afternoon.

I updated my resumé and researched teaching jobs in LA, but after working in the Cody Cares system for all those years, I knew I wouldn't be able to handle regular teaching anymore. To go up against 150 kids each day, who were all trying to out-cool one another. I got an interview at a high school in Burbank, but I didn't go.

Instead, I focused on transferring my songs and poems to my computer. I focused on writing ideas for new scripts. I focused on attending film festivals and meeting filmmakers, as Alex advised. I focused on following up with people I'd met in Zambulla. On improving my website and joining groups like the International Screenwriters Association. My scripts kept winning awards, and every so often a producer or director would email me, asking to read one. I quit my screenwriting group, because it reminded me too much of the Cody Cares cafeteria. I was done putting myself in environments where people vied to make me their dog and walk me around their block. To say, "See, boy, see what I have over there? So much better than what you got down there, right?"

No, my message to the world was love. Hope. Compassion. I wanted to be around people who wanted to build, not destroy. People always called LA a soulless cesspool, but most of the filmmakers I'd met there were the nicest, most supportive people I'd ever known. Maybe it was time for a move.

But I need to enter LA as a writer, not a teacher. I need to enter LA as Johnny Sacrum. I need to enter it on my legs, not my knees. And if it takes me until I'm sixty, then so be it.

Alex invited me to lunch one Saturday, and I met him at a café on Beachwood Drive. A producer friend of his, from Colombia, joined us, and when she heard about *Lila's Adventure*, she said she wanted to make the film. I was ecstatic and afterward went for a walk through the Hollywood Hills. This was my favorite neighborhood in LA, and I hoped to buy a house there someday. Maybe after making this film, I'd be able to. Maybe this would be what turned my life around.

Over July break, I drove to Death Valley, blasting Iggy Pop and the Velvet Underground. For whatever reason, I associated *White Light/ White Heat* with the desert, and I replayed it once I passed Palmdale. My car was ten years old with no AC and back windows that no longer rolled down, so I was sweating my nuts off even after the sun set. But at least the speakers worked. I arrived in Stovepipe Wells around nine, checked into the hotel, and got some dinner. I ate a half-chicken with mashed potatoes and beans, then stepped into the hundred-degree night. The guy at the hotel's front desk said tomorrow was supposed to be the hottest day they'd had in years, and I was glad to be there for it.

I slept in a big comfortable bed while the AC worked hard all night. I got up around 10 a.m., ate huevos rancheros with avocado at the hotel restaurant, bought a gallon of water, and hit the road. I started at the Mesquite Flat Sand Dunes, which was a particularly important spot for me because part of *The Doors* was shot there, and that was one of my favorite films. Like with everything else, though, seeing it in real life was completely different than seeing it on film. But even in real life it was beautiful.

The day was hotter than anything I'd ever experienced, and the thermometer had shown 124 when I'd left that morning. It was probably hotter now. I was scared to wander too far from the car and my water jug, and I got lost watching someone hiking the dunes at least a kilometer from the parking lot. I asked a young guy to take my picture, and before I was ready, he snapped three quick shots. Even so, I liked them. Due to the tension in my muscles, I often contorted my face and stuck out my tongue and licked my lips to release pressure, and he snapped shots of me doing all of this, and as I scrolled through them, it came to life like a flipbook, and as ugly as it was, it was honest.

Next, I drove to Badwater Basin, which was 282 feet below sea level, making it the lowest point in North America. The ground was covered in salt left over from an evaporated lake, and it almost looked like snow. I walked across the salt and stopped to snap pictures of graffiti on the ground, and I also snapped some shots of a group of hippie twenty-somethings about two hundred yards ahead. They were running around with their arms spread and picking each other up and putting each other on their shoulders and rolling around in the salt and dancing and singing. It reminded me of the kind of freedom you only experience when you're a kid out in the vastness and beauty of nature. Being far away from your parents and seeing the world through your own eyes for the first time. Knowing that any day now, you were gonna conquer the world and spread your message of love. They'd probably get high and have a few drinks later on and tell jokes and have fun, even though deep down, they were eternally sad. But I was alone here and would probably go back to my room alone later on and watch TV or read until going to sleep. Things change, but as much as I missed all that action, I was happier now than ever before. I was still eternally sad, just as they probably were, but now, I knew there were answers in that sadness—soft, delicate whispers of truth—and I needed to be alone and still to hear them. These kids probably would have let me dance with them. Hell, when I was younger, it gave me such hope to see adults having fun that I'd wish they'd all join me crisscrossing the country and pounding beers in every bar along the way. Seeing adults dancing or singing or whatever made the future less terrifying. But it was better now to remain still.

Plus, it was hot as shit.

I went swimming at the hotel before dinner, and when I jumped in the pool, I realized it was the first time I'd swum in years. How the fuck could you let this happen? How the fuck could it be *years* now? You love swimming. Dip your head under. Feel the silence and freedom. Allow the water to take the pressure off your knees and back and neck. Allow yourself to feel good.

A few cute women were sunning themselves by the pool, and at least one gave me a look as I walked by, but I was on a solo adventure. I got some meatloaf with mashed potatoes and gravy for dinner, then watched *Titanic* before falling asleep in the hundred-degree Death Valley night.

The next day, I drove to Mount Whitney and blasted Joy Division the whole way. For some reason, I also associated Joy Division with the desert, and I replayed *Unknown Pleasures* as I sped from the lowest point in the continental US to the highest.

I drove up Whitney Portal Road, parked, and took a walk. The climate in the Sierra Nevada mountains was a relief after the desert, and I welcomed the cool, steady breeze. There were cascading streams and rugged white cliffs and big beautiful pines everywhere. I got a sandwich at a restaurant, and then headed back down the road. I stopped at a spot overlooking the valley, wondering if that was where Bogie stood in *Treasure of the Sierra Madre*, and the view was incredible. There was no sound except for the wind and the woman sitting in her car next to mine, scream-talking into her phone about her ex-husband. "No, *trust me*, he's a piece of shit. Don't believe a word he's sayin', all right? Oh, don't gimme that . . ."

The average American had so few opportunities to experience the pure silence of nature, and I felt like screaming, "SHUT THE FUCK UP! JUST SHUT THE FUCK UP FOR A FUCKING SECOND, YOU FUCKIN' UNBELIEVER!" I drove farther down the road and stopped, but even there, I could hear her going on and on about, "Oh, of *course* he'd say that . . ." so I got back in the car and searched for a motel. When I found one, I put my stuff in my room, then went to a barbeque place for some ribs. I'd forgotten it was the Fourth of July until I overheard people talking about the big fireworks show planned that night. I figured maybe I'd go too, but when I got back to the motel, I practically fell right asleep.

I returned to Soul City the next day, and like always, I had to stuff my soul away to prepare for battle at home and at work. Soul City was a place where people claimed to exalt the soul while keeping it stuffed away. A sunny purgatory that most saw as paradise, but I knew it was nothing more than a pretty place to wait. A place to reflect on your sins. And I had plenty of those, so I knew I wasn't getting out anytime soon.

Chapter 32

After playing a video for my sixth period seniors, I checked my email, and when I saw one from a big Hollywood screenwriting contest and it had "Congratulations! You've Won an Award" in the subject line, I couldn't open it fast enough. It gave some generic, "award certificates will be mailed . . ." crap, and I clicked the link with the list of winners. I searched the finalists first, then the winners in the drama category, but didn't see my name. Then, when I scrolled to the top of the page, I saw *The Knockerman* had won the Grand Jury award: the top script in the whole competition, which had over two thousand submissions. I smiled widely and couldn't stop. A few of the students noticed. "Everything cool, Mr. S?"

"Yeah, yeah, the Lakers just told me they want me to play small forward for them next season, but I turned 'em down. I wouldn't know what to do with all that money."

A few laughed, then continued watching the video. When the period ended, I went to the bathroom, locked myself in a stall, and processed what this all meant. The prize was five hundred bucks, plus a call with a real Hollywood agent. I texted Alex, and he was impressed. "You're on your way up, buddy. Well earned!"

When I exited the bathroom, Ms. Collins called me over. "Are we getting another raise or something?" She'd also noticed my unabashed smiling.

Maybe it was because I felt that I was, indeed, already on my way up—light-years away from Cody Cares and already living in my mansion in the Hollywood Hills—or maybe it was because I was tired of carrying so many secrets for so long, but either way, I typed the URL in her computer, and showed her my name, Johnny Sacrum, listed as the best of the best.

"Whoa, you're a writer?" she said.

"Yeah, I write screenplays, and this one just won first place. Maybe it'll get produced into a movie."

"That's so cool. Hey, check this out." She pulled her phone from her purse and showed me a picture of a huge tomato. "I grow them, and this is the biggest one I've ever seen."

"Oh wow, that's great."

"I know, right?"

We spoke a little more about her garden, then I sat at my desk feeling conflicted. Maybe winning this award meant something bigger than I was ready to deal with. Maybe I'd need to start taking meetings with agents and producers and talking with people who weren't as kind and supportive as Alex. Maybe I'd have to "explain your vision, Johnny," and I'd start stammering and carrying on like a lunatic, face twitching and sweating, as they called the paramedics to come take me away. Or, maybe I'd knock off everyone's socks, including my own, and now I'd have to put up or shut up. Now, with the world's eyes finally on me, I'd have to give them something as powerful and meaningful as John Lennon's *Imagine*. As Van Gogh's *Starry Night*. As Charlie Kaufman's *Adaptation*. Had I been lying to myself about my talent? Were all my they-hate-it-because-they-don't-understand-its just a shield to protect me from the penetrating questions that would expose me as a fraud? In the spotlight, I could no longer hide. I could no longer stuff my ears with earplugs and music and pace around my apartment searching for that one quiet spot where I'd be able to write my masterpiece "if those damned neighbors would just stop slamming the cupboards!" I could no longer hide my checking and touching and repeating weird phrases like "eggs and bacon make cheese!" Soon, there'd be more videos of me online where people would post comments like, "Why does he keep touching that window? He looks touched himself." But this is the price you pay for putting your dick on the table.

I was also nervous about putting my dick on Ms. Collins's desk. At this point, I knew better than to give someone like her ammo she could use against me—and I'd given her a fuckin' cannonball. At any point, she could blast my head square off. But is it so bad to trust in someone? I mean, she showed you her prized fucking tomato. In her fucked-up world, that's probably the equivalent of a dick pic. Maybe you did fuck up, but is it so wrong to try? Sure, it's obvious everyone here hates you, but maybe it's because they don't know you. Maybe this is the kind of shit that will turn things around. Hell, you're a nice guy. As nervous as you are, everyone always says you're relaxed like Barry. Easygoing. Is it so wrong to think someone like her could like you?

Yeah, Jay, yeah it is. Yeah, it fucking is. Some shit you just keep to yourself. You've learned this lesson the hard way already, and now you're gonna learn it again.

My script *The Silent Protest* was a finalist in a film festival in Santa Monica that took place that weekend, and I decided to go. That Friday, I found out *Kirkland* placed in a big contest in New York City. That Friday, I also spoke with that agent about *The Knockerman*, and he told me he'd been blown away by it. "You're well ahead of the pack. If this script doesn't get produced, I'm sure you'll get something else produced soon enough. I read it twice, and I never do that, and I wept at the end both times."

Alex came with me to the film festival, and I was glad to have him beside me. He was chatting up everyone, getting business cards, and telling people how much he loved their films, and I met a lot of people just hanging by his side. The final night, they announced *The Silent Protest* as the winner of the screenplay competition, and I gave a speech even though I had no idea what to say and probably sounded like a lunatic. And after, I walked to the ocean alone and stared at the Santa Monica Pier, all lit up with carnival lights and people smiling and alive, and I felt it for the first time: I knew with absolute certainty that my dreams would come true.

In November, I headed back to Zambulla for the film fest. Alex and a bunch of the others were there as well, and it felt like returning to summer camp. We got together for dinner on that first night, and just before my enchiladas verdes arrived, I found out that *The Knockerman* had won another big contest. The group bought my dinner to congratulate me.

They were all staying together at a hotel about a kilometer from the town center in a quiet area surrounded by rolling green hills. As big as the city was, it was surrounded by nature, and you could escape the hustle and bustle in no time. Their hotel was basically a hacienda with gardens and birds and had a library filled with books. I loved hanging out there, but it still drained me just to eat lunch with them, even though it also inspired me to be with such talented and driven people. The filmmakers here were like me. I didn't have to say, "C'mon, let's just quit our jobs and *make a fuckin' movie!*" I didn't have to beg them to dream with me—they were already dreamers themselves. One had sold her house to fund a film. Another had spent a year traveling the world researching and shooting a short film. And spending time with them at that hotel always set my soul straight, even though I knew I could never stay there myself. For every hour I spent socializing, I needed to spend three in bed, focusing on my breathing, relaxing my muscles, writhing in pain, contorting my face, sticking out my tongue. The hotel where I stayed was filled with tourists, not filmmakers, and I didn't care if any of them saw the worst of me. But if I asked a filmmaker, "Hey, would you please turn down your music?" I knew I'd be kicked out of the dreamer club forever.

I loved Zambulla. It was a small, walkable town loaded with some of the most beautiful colonial architecture in Mexico, surrounded by mountains and rivers and fields of tall green grass. Despite my need to stay hidden away from everyone else, I couldn't shake the desire to sell everything I owned, buy some farm in the countryside, and invite Alex and all the others to live with me. We could grow our own food and spend our time creating films, writing songs, telling jokes, enjoying nature. I needed to be in the country. In nature. With friends. Allies. I needed an army of people to bring my creative vision to life. And this was as good a place as any to recruit.

I met a woman at the opening night party, and we went to the cocktail party together the next day and spent most of the night making out in the corner. She came back to my hotel and we took a shower but didn't have sex. Instead, we massaged each other's bits until we both came, then she had to leave because, "My parents will worry if I don't arrive home soon."

The following day, I met a woman in the center while I was sipping tea and reading, and she came with me to the party that night. A few people said things like, "Damn, Johnny, a different girl each night, huh?" Then I realized that despite the fact that all of my energy was always pulling me inward, other people could indeed see me, and apparently, I was developing a reputation. Alex had warned me, "The film industry may seem huge, but trust me, word gets around about *every-fucking-thing*." I didn't want to be known as a d-bag, but still, I went back to the hotel with her, and we fucked like champs for half the night. If the others knew the truth—that for fifty-one weeks of the year, I spent almost all of my free time alone and writing—they wouldn't say shit like that. This was the one week I let myself feel free.

Frida, the blogger I'd met the year before, wanted to get together for dinner, but around 3 p.m. I got rocked with a horrible stomachache. I spent about four hours in the bathroom, puking a few times. I told Frida maybe we could meet tomorrow, but I knew I wasn't gonna be feeling good anytime soon. I spent that entire day and night in my hotel and felt a little better the next morning, but not by much. I went to a restaurant across from my hotel and ate yogurt with papaya, mango, and oatmeal, and by noon I was strong enough to hit the town again. I saw some films, but during a block of shorts, I had to race out to find a bathroom, just as the film by the director sitting beside me started playing. We'd been chatting between shorts and I felt like an asshole to run out like that, but I was pretty sure I had food poisoning. While in the bathroom, I could hear some friends outside making dinner plans. Everyone had such joy and strength in their voices, and mine was lower than a whimper. I got dinner with Frida and took her back to the hotel, and despite how shitty I felt, we fucked on the bed and in the shower. I spent the rest of the week with her and developed a crush. We walked everywhere hand in hand, stopping every so often to dance, or press one another against a beautiful stone building and kiss, or pretend we were an elderly couple walking around turn-of-the-century Paris or a young couple living in a giant bubble under the sea. She was as weird as I was, and I felt comfortable showing her everything about me.

Soon, the week was over, and I found myself talking more with Frida online. I asked her to visit, but she couldn't get a visa. Having her in Soul City with me would have made everything all right, but she was Brown, and Brown people weren't welcome in the US.

Once or twice a week, I'd get "Congratulations!" emails from contests and every so often someone would email me asking, "Hey, do you have any scripts for a twenty-two-year-old woman who fights vampires in Cold War Poland?" "Do you by any chance have anything for a forty-five-year old turkey farmer in the Highlands of Scotland?" I'd always say, "No, but I could write you one in about a month," and I'd never hear back. Everybody needed their shot at fame NOW, NOW, NOW! and fuck this "wait a month" bullshit.

Around March, I got a random email from a producer I'd met in Zambulla, and he said he wanted to produce *The Silent Protest*. He said he was going to do the scheduling and budgeting, and he knew of a director who'd been winning awards at all the biggest film fests around the world, and he and I spoke fairly regularly for about a month, discussing locations and possible actors and songs for certain scenes, and just like all the other times, one day, I stopped hearing from him. The Hollywood rejection is as silent as a still Death Valley night.

But at least I'd braved the heat for long enough to hear it.

I spent my breaks in November and December preparing *Tropical Teaching* for publication. Our original publication date had been May 14, 2015, but just after New Year's, my publisher bumped that to September. I was pissed, but at least it gave me more time for marketing. I bought several books on marketing and joined a writers' group in Soul City that specialized in marketing, and I studied as much as I could about having a successful book launch. Because it was a novel about teachers, I felt it had some commercial appeal and I knew I had to give this everything I had. I didn't want to regret not having contacted every bookseller nor having pitched every major newspaper. I studied and came up with a game plan that changed over the months, and soon I was querying book review bloggers and social media influencers and key figures in the education community and a lot of them responded, "Sure, send it over," but I only heard back from about 10 percent of them after my publisher mailed the advance copies. September was far away, so I decided not to burn myself out. I figured if I contacted one bookstore, one library, and five review bloggers every night, by my publication date I'd have generated a fairly decent amount of buzz. Early on, the novel received critical praise, and that trend continued as the months passed. "Authentic." "Compelling." "Hilarious." "Haunting." After months, I hadn't yet read a single negative word about the novel, and I felt that now was *my* time. Maybe it was better to have a book get bigger than a script. If a book sells well, you can bury yourself in a cave in Utah as your bank account steadily grows. But with a script, you gotta take notes and make changes and be on call if anything comes up during production and go with the crew to film festivals and all that.

I also sent it off to friends, including some of the guys I'd worked with in Miami, and they said things like, "Holy shit! I feel like I'm back there. My stomach kept churning every page, then suddenly

I'd burst out laughing. And I never knew you felt such pain. Hell, I never knew you were even a writer." "I never knew you felt such pain" was a common response, making me realize how many other people were out there, smiling and laughing as they covered up a vortex of inner misery their family and friends would never know about. It was also affirming for me that no one shamed me for having felt that pain. It was affirming that maybe I could have shared that pain with them at any time. Writing had been therapeutic for me in so many ways, and now that people were actually reading my work, I found even more value in it. Writing slowed my thoughts and helped me organize them. Writing helped me to understand my own biases and identify negative thought cycles. Writing allowed me protection as I dug deeper toward the universal truths uniting us all. Writing allowed me to feel emotions without having to feel shame. Writing allowed me to connect with people in ways I might not have been able to connect with them in person. Writing allowed me to exist.

Chapter 33

Writing also got me into trouble—at least, I think it did, because Mr. Perez called me into his office one day and grilled me, asking, "Do you even *want* to be a teacher?" I asked him what this was regarding, but he wouldn't say. Maybe all this shit would have been worth it had Ms. Collins become my friend, but she'd been giving me the silent treatment for the last few months because I didn't say "bless you" when she sneezed or some stupid crap. I wish I could say I was exaggerating. Every morning when I walked into the cafeteria, I could feel the toxicity invading me. Crushing me. These people were miserable as fuck and they liked it that way, and the more I came at them with my *Pollyanna* shit, the more miserable they tried to make me. It was better to just lower my head, play my videos, collect my quizzes, put my grades in the book, and go home, never making eye contact with anyone.

But even that wasn't good enough. If I didn't make eye contact, they'd find passive-aggressive ways of telling me I was an asshole for avoiding them. But if I did make eye contact, they'd tell me I was weird or wrong for doing so. If I kept to myself, they'd tell me I wasn't a team player, but whenever I tried to help, they told me they'd be better off without me. When I was tasked with creating the monthly calendars, one of the others would do it a week before it was due just so they could bitch that I wasn't doing my job. So they could email the boss and say, "I can't do *everything* around here."

Still, I always kept my cool. And I think this drove them nuts, but one day when Ms. Collins played a recording of the Cody Cares song on repeat all day, and I asked her if she could please use headphones, she smiled and knew she had me. She started playing the song all day, every day, and when Mr. Perez found out I'd asked her to use headphones, he said he was appalled at my "lack of Cody Cares spirit!" and gave me the "do you even *want* to be a teacher?" crap all over again. He praised Ms. Collins for her initiative and demanded we all sing the song at the beginning of each day, and I realized how far over the deep end this school had gone. At first, Cody had sung that song in a rush of inspiration. What had started out pure became routine, then law, and with law came expectation and punishment, which killed inspiration. I had made the mistake of telling Ms. Collins I had OCD and was hypersensitive to sounds, but she just turned it up louder. The stress was so bad, I'd spend hours in bed after work, shaking and sweating.

I just need to get to September! When my book is published, I'll be a millionaire, and I can finally leave this hellhole and get some peace. I'm not built for professional work, surrounded by toxic assholes with rules about when to breathe, shit, and smile. I'd be fine with Karla and Barry and Camarin, and people who'd be like, "Sure, no problem, I'll just use headphones, and you know why? Because I respect and care about you, Jay. You're special to me, and I want you to feel safe and happy in the workplace we all share, and you don't even need to give me an explanation about anything." And I'd say, "Thank you so much! I *do* feel safe here, thanks to people like you. Please let me know how I can make *you* feel safe and happy as well." And I'd buy them pizza for lunch and we'd tell jokes and have fun, even though we were responsible professionals who did the hell out of our jobs. Whenever we helped another person, we created a bond with them that enriched our own lives as well, and I could have survived until retirement working with the original Cody Cares crew.

But I couldn't survive another day in that cafeteria. The stress was affecting the way I spoke. The way I walked. The way I ate and taught. It invaded every facet of my life. But a few months later, when Ms. Collins moved to San Jose to marry some millionaire tech asshole she'd met online, I rejoiced knowing I could now make it to September. Before she left, I went over it in my brain: Don't say, "It's been a pleasure working with you!" Don't tell her you'll miss her. Just wish her good luck and walk away. I practiced it and was proud of myself when I smiled and wished her luck and didn't say anything else. I'd always been the type to forgive and forget quickly. Crush me but later flash me a smile, and I'll let it all go. But some things you can forgive but shouldn't forget. Like all the meetings I'd had with Perez because Collins had told him I was a minute late or "so weird; did you see him touching his car this morning? I mean, it was *raining*. So crazy." Shouldn't forget all her lectures about not eating meat or being socially conscious, only to later say, "I'm sooooo OCD, LOL!" even though I'd told her several times I actually had the disease. No, never tell anyone like her, "It's been a pleasure working with you!" again. Our words matter. They can both give and take power. And in a world where everyone's trying to take everything from you, you gotta give yourself as much power as you can.

Mr. Perez's stupid motherfucking ass quit to run some used car dealership or manage a gas station or some other crap he was far more suited for, but the woman who took over the position was no better. After working under Camarin and the vice principal of my school in Miami, I preferred having women bosses. Women seemed much more inclined to actually listen to what you were saying than men were, noticing the subtleties in tone and body language and knowing what you really meant even if you didn't use the proper words, but Ms. Donaldson was even more stone-eared than Perez. She had a chip on her shoulder the size of Montana, where she was from, and right from day one she came out ready to rumble. I think she could sense that I wasn't the type to back down, so she made an example of me early on, waiting until she had an audience before telling me to "organize your area *this instant.* No wonder students have been skipping your class. It's filthy!" Students hadn't been skipping my class, and it wasn't filthy. I spent all of two minutes clearing a few papers off my shelves and making sure the stapler was parallel with the edge of my desk, and soon my classroom was "up to Cody Cares's standards." I almost wished Perez would come back. At this point, I didn't have the energy to read a new person and learn just how much ass I'd need to kiss to be left the fuck alone, so I decided not to kiss any. When she came at me, I hit her back with reason and logic and stuck to the facts, but that made me "difficult," so she'd call me into her office once a month to discuss whether or not this was the correct work environment for me. I knew Cody wanted me out, but he didn't want to pay unemployment, so he had his minions make my life hell, hoping I'd decide to leave on my own. But I was a fucking cockroach, and like George Costanza, you lock me out of my office, and I'll crawl in through the vents.

Though I was relieved Ms. Collins had left, they hired some grade-A shithead to replace her. Dude's name was Ron McCormick, and like the others, he was a miserable SOB, but unlike the others, he didn't try to hide it—from us, at least. When Cody or Donaldson came by, though, he'd pucker right up, but as soon as they passed, he was brooding and irritable again. That shit reminded me of wandering the Sand Beach streets looking for fights. Reminded me that, as dysfunctional as the school was, at least I'd always felt physically safe there, and I didn't want to have to worry about throwing my fists up because I accidentally bumped into McCormick in the supply cabinet and now he was saying, "You tryin' ta touch my dick or sumpin?" That shit reminded me of Doug.

I went to Elena's Café after work one Friday and when I parked, I sat in my car feeling too overwhelmed to move. I'd had a shitty week at work and didn't have the strength for any of my rituals, so I sat in my car for half an hour thinking of all the ways I could kill myself without bothering anyone else. When I finally grabbed my copy of *A*

Confederacy of Dunces off the passenger seat and started going through my car rituals, some asshole walking by said, "*What* are you doing?"

"Minding my own goddamned business. What are *you* doing?" About a year back, I'd started using this as my standard response whenever some cockstain pressed me about my rituals, and usually it did the trick

"*Excuse* me?" he said.

"Yeah, excuse you for being a fucking asshole, and if you don't gets ta steppin' right now, I'm gonna put you through that window." I pointed at the glass door of the flower shop behind him.

"Yikes, someone has anger issues."

"Got stupid-motherfucker-won't-leave-me-alone-so-I-gotta-beat-his-ass issues, which are different. Check the DSM-5. After, flip to the page about Cockheaditis. Might be pretty enlightening for you. Remember, the first step is acceptance."

"He's sorry." His boyfriend tugged on his arm. "C'mon, Tim, you *always* do this."

"It's cool," I said to the nice one. They took off, and I finished my rituals. By now, I was used to the whole world watching me at my most vulnerable, and I hoped someday this experience would help me to become a better actor.

When I walked inside the café, the barista, Cecy, smiled.

"Hi, Jay. A little later than usual today, huh?" she said.

"So, you're keeping track?" I said.

"Six thirty, every Friday," she said.

"Yeah, I'd be very easy to assassinate."

"I can't imagine you having any enemies."

"You should talk to my coworkers. I'm sure some would love to see my head on a spike."

"How's the writing?"

"Still waiting for my big break."

"Just like the rest of us."

"I'm sure you'll replace Julia Roberts as America's Girl soon enough."

She laughed and blushed. "I dunno about that."

"All these guys do." I pointed at all the men who always gave her casual glances and smiles and asked her to dinner. "I do as well."

She blushed again and looked into my eyes for just long enough to make me think there was actually something going on beyond great customer service. Whenever she spoke to me, she seemed nervous. She'd play with her hair and fumble while trying to come up with something else to say when the conversation ran dry, and when she'd bring me my chai latte, she'd stand there a moment longer than necessary. I watched how she acted with the other guys, and she was all business: taking orders, bringing drinks, sticking to the script. I knew she was at work, and that she had to be nice, but she seemed genuinely warm with me. I'd catch her looking at me sometimes or whispering with a coworker and the coworker would give me a glance and Cecy would get red and I could see her saying, "Stop looking," and I really thought I had a chance. But still, I didn't want to make her uncomfortable, so I never brought the conversation there.

The café was packed, but I got my back-corner spot. There was only one person at each of the tables nearby, and they were all working on their computers, and one guy was even playing an electric guitar plugged into his computer, so it was the perfect situation. I hated sitting near people who were talking, and this place attracted some loud-ass people. Though I knew better, I allowed myself to relax. I felt if someone so much as touched me, I'd have a seizure. But in that back corner, I didn't have to worry about people coming up from behind, which was something I hated. At work meetings, I always sat in the back corners. On planes, I chose the last row. At restaurants, the host would say, "Sir, sir?" as I zoned out, trying to read the energy of the room and find a spot where I could relax. When I used to eat lunch with Karla and Barry and them at work, I'd always sit at the head of one side of the table because there were no student desks behind that section, and also because Karla usually sat to my left, and I preferred to turn my head to the left rather than the right. When I turned to the right, I'd flood with so much anxiety, I could hardly function. And, if I turned too quickly to the right *or* left, the same thing would happen, so I slowed myself down and would turn my whole body to speak with people, which is why I liked to lower the angle between them and myself. If I sat in the middle of a table and had to turn ninety degrees to the right or left every time someone spoke, I'd panic so badly, I'd have to go outside and sit in my car. But the back corner was great, and if anyone spoke to me, I could shift my chair and address them head-on, not having to worry about moving my head too quickly, nor that by moving positions I'd now have people sitting behind me. It was all complicated and it exhausted me to ponder and execute, but that night things seemed all right.

I read about a chapter, laughing out loud a few times—something I rarely did, unless it was Bukowski—when the woman sitting next to me got up. An older couple who looked to be Middle Eastern came in, and they were speaking extremely loudly—not yelling, but way too fucking loud. I started sending out vibes, pushing them toward one of the tables at the far end, and when the woman pointed at the empty seat beside me, I actually said to myself, "No, no, no, fuck."

When they sat, they immediately started shrieking with laughter, shooting misery through my body and piercing thousands of holes in my armor. I wanted to move to the other side of the café, but the woman was wearing a hijab, and if I moved, I'd probably be the star of another viral video—this one titled, "The Everyday Face of Hatred." I couldn't focus on my book and kept flooding with more and more frustration every time he laughed at another one of his own jokes, so I left my chai, said goodbye to Cecy, and took off.

I went to see a film, and though no one in the audience said a word, a man a few rows ahead kept shaking his damned popcorn bag, and early on, someone laughed at something onscreen that wasn't meant to be funny, and it pulled me out of the picture. I'd stopped seeing comedies because I couldn't take the laughter, especially the forced laughter, and only went to heavy dramas devoid of humor. Though this person only laughed once, it was enough to ruin it for me. I wasn't sure what it was about laughter that irritated me. In part, I think it had to do with conditioning. It was almost as if because someone else was laughing, I was supposed to laugh as well, and fuck that. Also, watching a film was an intimate thing. When you buy your ticket, you're signing a contract that says, I'm about to take an emotional journey with other people who've also temporarily removed their armor so they can better feel and experience this journey, and I need to respect that these people have the right to experience this journey in their own way without forcing my interpretations and emotions on them, so I will not make any sound at any time, which includes unwrapping candy bars and creaking my damned chair. Also, I won't be a huge cockhead and intentionally laugh as a means to "liven up this dead audience, yeah!" which would make me the worst human being who's ever existed. I understand that people are allowed to experience the profundity of life without making a peep, without shedding a tear, and I will respect that right by performing my most important duty as an audience member, SHUTTING THE FUCK UP!

That is, of course, unless I'm watching a film written by Johnny Sacrum, in which case I need to be rolling through the aisles at every joke.

As much as I wished other people would honor that contract, I also knew it was unrealistic to expect pure silence anywhere, and it was my responsibility to overcome my misophonia so that someday I'd be able to enjoy a film no matter how shitty the audience was.

When I got back to the beach, I drove along the cliffs and a cop pulled me over.

"License and registration."

"Everything okay, officer?" I handed over the documents.

He went back to his cruiser, and a few minutes later, two other cop cars had parked, and two cornholes in uniform started shining flashlights through my back windows. The head d-bag came back with my license and registration.

"What are you doing here?" he said.

"I live here."

"Your ID says you live about a mile back."

"I was taking a drive along the beach."

"That's kinda weird, isn't it?"

Due to my OCD, I did a lot of "weird" shit, and it made me furious when assholes like this made me *feel* weird because of it. I thought about giving him what he wanted—total control—explaining to him that I often took a drive along the beach to calm my nerves, laughing nervously and saying, "I know it's weird, *but* . . ." But instead, I said, "NO!" and wanted to grab him by the throat. I was tired of being made to kiss boots because people saw me as "weak." Tired of being forced to kiss ass just so others could feel powerful.

"What do you do for work?" he said.

"I'm a writer."

"Oh yeah? Whaddya write?"

"What do you care? Look, am I getting a ticket or something?"

"Your taillight is out."

"So you call in the whole squad for backup?"

He wrote me a ticket and he and the other shitbags left. Before I'd moved out here, the pigs had shot a schizophrenic man dead because he wouldn't put down a burrito when they commanded him to, and maybe they'd do the same to me if I couldn't stop touching my car windows after they told me, "Put your hands up!" I needed to get a camera for my car, or maybe a cell phone with a camera. I'd been using the same flip phone since college, but maybe now was the time to get one of those smart ones. If I was Black, maybe tonight woulda gone differently. I mean, I gave that shithead attitude, and he let me go. A Black man does the same, and he gets lumped on the head. Shot. Framed for murder. Maybe I needed to be ready to film that shit too.

That's kinda weird, isn't it?

Stupid pig motherfucker.

Chapter 34

Cody must have known I'd become friends with Mr. Sanderson, because he moved him to the gym and replaced him with a new hire, a woman in her late thirties named Salena Raju. I was surprised Cody picked her. She smiled and focused on big-picture stuff, not worrying that students signed into class in blue instead of black ink or whatever. We quickly became friends, and I didn't care to hide it. September, and bestseller status, was coming, and I wanted to have a good time until then.

Cody calmed down with all his cowboy and astronaut and sailor bullshit and started dressing like a normal, nerdy principal again. The school was doing well and continued to get good press, and enrollment numbers were steady, so he probably felt confident just to be himself, which was great, because I couldn't take any more of his sycophants dressing like cowboys and saying, "Yeehaw," and shit as well. Though there wasn't a dress code, I always felt pressured to join in, and now I could just relax and continue being a frumpy, disgruntled American teacher.

At home, I continued querying reviewers and contacting bookstores and libraries, and I kept track of everything on an Excel spreadsheet. I'd already contacted every bookstore in California, Oregon, and Washington that was listed on Google. Several book buyers requested copies, and I had my publisher ship them out.

Every time someone said yes, I could picture myself screaming in Cody's face, "I MOTHERFUCKING QUIT!" then taking a ship across the Pacific to start my worldwide adventure.

All of the reviews continued to be favorable, so I decided to go all in and hire a publicist. It was expensive, but I thought of Kevin Smith maxing out his credit cards to make *Clerks* and figured go big or go home. My publicist got interest from several large media organizations like *The Sunday Times* and *High Times* magazine, and I got interviews on a few big Midwest radio stations. As nervous as I was to do those interviews, once I started talking, I felt ready to take on the world.

But once my publicist put the book on a website where reviewers could download a copy and write a review, it got slammed for its bad language and sexual content. I thought about issuing a "there's bad motherfucking language and raw-dog boning in this book, so prudes beware" warning, but part of the reason why I wrote the book was to get under people's skin, and I figured I was accomplishing that. Regardless, reading those first few bad reviews stung like a motherfucker. I wanted to engage those reviewers in a debate, sticking with facts ("See, he *did* say it—right here on page two sixteen!"), but after spending most of the last decade teaching and absorbing criticism from parents, students, colleagues, and admins, I realized that facts wouldn't change their minds. I mean, the facts were right there on the page, and they either missed them or flat-out ignored them, so why argue? Some people just don't like the cover. Some just don't like the font. Some don't like that someone would have the audacity to write a book in the first place and put it out there in the world.

And some just don't like the story and/or how it's told.

It was best to let it be. I couldn't change people's minds. Besides, of all the negative reviews, not a single person mentioned the book being poorly written. It was always, "Why do there have to be so many curse words?" In a way, I liked seeing what people thought of me. I liked the honesty. It made me realize how often during the day people lied to my face, smiling when they wanted to tell me off. It helped me to recognize some of my own faults and biases and to better understand myself and my place in this world. I realized that part of why I'd been teaching for all these years was to prepare myself to read those negative reviews. Everything I did, all day, every single day, was preparing me to achieve my dreams. Every time I touched those windows or checked the doors or put my hand on stove burners, I was preparing to be king. The rituals, in part, were a distraction—pulling me out of *right now*. I couldn't live in *right now* because it hurt too damned much. If I lived in *right now*, I'd need to run to LA this very moment, where I'd crumple if I heard, "You'll never make it in this town. Next!" I had to wait until it was safe to live in the moment—until somebody said, "Yes, you're fucking brilliant! Yes a million times over!"—and only then could I stop distracting myself with the touching and checking and everything. It was like when I'd taken that pill years back and flipped out when it relaxed me. I needed to stay nervous. *Now* didn't exist for me, even though now was all any of us had.

My scripts kept winning awards, and I attended film fests in LA, San Diego, and Sacramento. I met a lot of people and had some fun, but no fest was even close to Zambulla. That place was everything for me, and I hoped to live there someday. I only knew that city as Johnny Sacrum and wanted to allow him to grow there as Jay Sakovsky had grown and developed in Lila. *The Knockerman* won the Grand Jury prize in a few other contests, and I knew it was special even though every so often I'd get feedback on it like, "Nothing happens! There's no conflict. You need a page one rewrite!" It was mind-numbing. People loved or hated my work, and that was the same with *Tropical Teaching*.

But their opinions didn't affect my writing. Now, I knew what I had to say, and I couldn't let anything change that. And there was nothing unique about what I was going through. Artists and inventors and scientists and whoever had been going through this shit since the beginning of time. Why waste a second feeling sorry for yourself? Put your ass back in that chair and keep writing. You got a job to do.

By publication day, I'd gotten over forty reviews for *Tropical Teaching*, and most were great. That night, I celebrated my novel's birthday by eating a microwaved pizza and watching *Breaking Bad*, stopping every so often to check the book's Amazon ranking. I figured if I could just make ten sales, or twenty bucks, per day, I could move to Mexico and spend my time writing books and scripts and songs and poems, and no matter what the Codys and Ms. Collinses and Mr. Perezes of the world said about it, I could block them all out and live the life they were too terrified to try for. I made more than a hundred sales that first day, and fifty on the second, then sixteen on the third day, and ten on the fourth, and four on the fifth, nothing on the sixth.

Fuck!

"What the fuck does that even mean? Likeable? Shit, people fucking love Tony Soprano and Walter White. Are those two *likeable* characters? It's all bullshit."

"You can't let the criticism get to you, Jay," the Frog said. We sat at an outdoor table at the café.

"I need to get out of here."

"Maybe now's not the right time."

"Yeah, you're probably right. I'm still doing all the fucking rituals. I'm still locked inside of myself. I still drop shit all the time and bump into things, and I have these preapproved ways of moving and if I don't follow the script, I get panic attacks. Like, if I move left when my body is screaming at me to move right, I get flooded with anxiety. How the fuck am I supposed to act like this? I mean, if a director tells me, 'Now raise your left hand above your head,' it'd take me a few seconds to process what he said and then actually do it, and doing it would throw me off so much that I would only have one shot to get it right before I'm shaking and sweating and back in my trailer."

"Doom and gloom."

"I'm heading to Zambulla again soon for the film festival. I see the way the actors behave there. They're fluid. Confident. They know how to work a room. I sit in the corner hoping nobody can see me. Plus, I'm already old as fuck. The other day when I went to the bathroom at the movie theater, I looked in the mirror and saw that my hairline is receding. I mean, I guess it's been doing that since high school, but that was the first time I actually recognized that shit and associated it with aging. I even saw I got a wrinkle up here. I'm gonna be thirty-three in a few weeks. What do I have to show for it? I've pissed away the last six years of my life, locked away in my shitty apartment. I drive an old, dented car. I got no girlfriend. I'm getting fat and old."

"You've got a bestselling book. You've got people interested in making your scripts into movies. You've got a lot going for you."

"Yeah, I guess so. I'm just not where I wanna be yet."

"Who is? Life's a perpetual state of becoming. Just relax. Breathe."

"Yeah, I know. I'm just bitching. I'll be fine. I just wish I could exercise without feeling the aches and pains all over and without being flooded with anxiety all the time."

"You can always try a different medication."

"Naw, I'm good. I need to get *there* first, you know?" I explained to him my idea about the OCD being a distraction preventing me from moving toward my dreams head-on.

"That's a fascinating observation. I'm impressed that you've connected those dots."

"All the dots are already connected inside. It's just a matter of clearing away enough junk to see them."

"Jay, you're doing good. Take it easy, will ya? Go to Mexico, have some fun, meet the love of your life, stay there if you want. You're more in control of all of this than you realize."

My hotel in Zambulla screwed up my reservation, and I had no place to stay, but Alex told me there was an extra room in the hotel where he and my other friends were staying, so I headed over. I'd bought a portable speaker a few months back, and used it to play the sound of a waterfall while I slept, and I hoped this would drown out any noise my friends made. At my usual hotel, I felt safe enough to pull on the door a hundred times or to give people dirty looks if they were being obnoxious, but I couldn't let my friends see me in a weakened position. But having that speaker eased some of my stress.

I got a room in the back near Alex, and I felt so much better immediately. It was filled with light and paintings from local artists. It had a ceramic tile floor and colorful tiles on the bathroom sink and in the shower, and I could feel my spirit coming alive. The festival had accepted my script *The Knockerman*, and I felt I had a chance of winning this year. I wanted to get up on that stage and give a speech in front of my friends and maybe even let them know what they all meant to me. Let them know that on that first day I stayed with them in the hotel, I didn't even worry when they sat at a table just outside my room and talked loudly. That I didn't even play my speaker or put in my earplugs. That I didn't even close the windows or door. That I was able to take a shit even though they were laughing outside. That I was able to take a shower and didn't get soap in my eyes or slip and fall and die. That I was able to hear their voices and instead of feeling anxious, I felt at home. The light in the room warmed me. In Soul City, I'd blocked out most of my windows with aluminum foil. I didn't want to see shadows passing by, because then I'd know my neighbors had come home, and I wouldn't be able to stop listening for any sound they made, even if they made none.

But now, things were all right. I realized that I'd made significant progress with things that felt impossible years ago. Hell, just to leave my house had seemed impossible years ago, when I was going through the worst of it. When I was overwhelmed with hallucinations and prolonged bouts of paranoia. When Karla and Camarin stood below me like pillars. I wished they were here with me now. I wished I could share my successes with them. Both had promised to buy my book, causing me to worry that maybe I had indeed used too many curse words. I wished they could be there in the audience when I accepted my trophy, and I'd thank them too. This year, I'd finally announce to the world that I had OCD.

Over dinner, I told Alex about it. I explained to him why I'd always stayed at that other hotel, and without going into too many details, I let him know how much I'd been suffering all these years.

"Someday, you need to make a film about all of this. It's truly remarkable," he said. "Maybe I can direct, hehe!"

After dinner, I met up with a woman named Dalila, who'd added me on Facebook after seeing me at last year's fest and asking a mutual friend whom I was. For most of the last year, we'd spoken off and on, and I'd check my new iPhone every five minutes to see if she'd written me. She was an actor from Mexico City, brilliant and talented and gorgeous, and I knew she was going places. We had tea at a jazz club near the center, and she told me how she'd gotten into acting but really wanted to direct because, "I'm tired of only being seen as candy for the eyes."

Because she was so open with me, I let her know about my OCD, going into much more detail than with Alex. She said that it was horrible what I'd been through, and even though I hit her with some pretty serious shit, she didn't leave. We kept drinking tea and listening to jazz, and with all that OCD crap out of the way, I could focus on how much I enjoyed her company. We went back to the hotel, sneaking in a side entrance so none of my friends would see, stripped down to our underwear, got under the bed's big, sheepskin blanket, and kissed late into the night. My balls were aching for release, but I was happy just to be in her company. Dalila invited me to visit her in Mexico City, and I allowed myself to feel happy. She wouldn't have said something like that if this was a one-night thing. She didn't mind the sound of the waterfall or the fact that I kept my earplugs in while we made out.

Around dawn, Dalila and I snuck back out, and I walked her to her hotel. We kissed at the entrance, and I walked back alone as the sky began to fill with oranges, reds, and blues, and the smells of

Mexico flooded my nose. Fruit juice and huevos a la mexicana and car exhaust. I knew with absolute certainty that I needed to live in this country. Mexico was the only place I'd ever felt alive, and it had saved me so many, many times. Maybe I could move to Mexico City and live with Dalila in Condesa, and we could grab lunch at a café after we'd both nailed our auditions. Maybe we could take weekend trips to Tepoztlán, and sit on a balcony and sip wine as we watched the sun set beyond the mountains. Maybe we could start a family, and I could take our son to therapy the second I saw him crying because his socks didn't fit quite right in his shoes. Maybe I didn't need the Frog anymore. Hell, I'd already stopped seeing the Knight after one session where my body kept screaming, "Don't let anyone touch you like this anymore! Go! Roam free!" After that, I'd gone through a month-long period where I panicked and squeezed with fear, but later, I felt looser than before, realizing how dependent I'd become on our sessions, and how all of that was causing me even more tightness. How I'd panic if he canceled or if the session didn't go just right. I realized that I didn't need a team of people to take care of me anymore. I could take care of myself.

And as I walked those gorgeous cobblestone streets back to the colonial hotel filled with my friends—friends whose dreams were aligned with my own and who inspired and guided me along—I felt a level of autonomy I'd never felt before. It'd be easy to say, "I felt a level of autonomy I hadn't felt in years," but that would be bullshit. I'd never felt like this. Even though I'd played sports and traveled and gone to parties and dated women, I'd never been free. I was always under *its* control. But now, I was learning how to feel and experience that freedom without fear creeping in, allowing the light to shine over me like the Mexican morning sun. I was learning what it meant to actually be free—not to lie to myself that I was free as I gulped down jugs of wine and popped pills and flew a million miles per hour down the highway. I was learning to be free and confident. To be ready to die so I could finally live.

The reviews kept coming for my book, and some of the things

people were saying thrilled the hell outta me. People were finding things in those pages I didn't even realize I'd written. Finding meaning and symbolism and all types of crap that only my unconscious had been aware of. I wrote from my gut. I didn't always understand what I was putting on the page, but afterward, I'd reread it and know there was something there. Maybe I wouldn't figure it out for weeks or maybe months or years, but I knew it was there, and other people were helping me understand myself faster than I ever could alone. Art was healing. It was also sacrifice and duty and death, and an infinite number of other things we'd never find definitions for, but one of those things certainly *was* healing, and I could feel the art all over the streets of Zambulla. I snapped some pics with my new phone, which had a camera in it that was better than any camera I'd ever owned. I could even listen to music with that thing too, and it saved so much space inside my pockets. The world was always improving, and these advances in technology made the future feel so much more possible.

After two days, I had to go back to the other hotel. The room I'd been staying in had been reserved, so I couldn't stay any longer with my friends, and when I closed my door behind me at the other hotel and stuffed up the windows with pillows to block out the street noise, I also blocked out the light that had been illuminating my future over those last few days, and suddenly I realized I never wanted to spend another minute alone in a cave, and the only place for me was in the light, surrounded by friends, brimming with love and compassion and creativity.

I went to dinner with Dalila, but later, when we met up with the others at a bar, I saw her talking with another actor, a big Mexican star, and they both kept smiling, and when she rubbed his arm I knew that was that. I didn't see her the rest of the week, and even though I wanted to ask her to marry me when I got up on that stage at the closing ceremony and accepted my award for *The Knockerman*, I couldn't find any words other than, "Uh, th-thank you to the lovely people of Zambulla for this award. T-thank—gracias."

The fest's director announced the winning feature-length film, and it took me a second to process that the director, Nima Farhad, was the same Nima who had touched my life so many years ago. Though I was thrilled for her, I couldn't help but feel that I was still in her shadow. I'd won best script, but she'd won best film, the top prize. They played a video of her acceptance speech, and I wanted to write her a message congratulating her, but she hadn't responded to my last few messages and what was the fucking point anyway? No matter what I did, I'd always be at the little kids' table, accepting my little-kid awards. Until I manned up and put in the ridiculous amount of work it took to get a feature made, I'd always just be Little Johnny Sacrum. You wanna be a champ, act like a champ, but you're writing fuckin' screenplays like a chump. This is an actor's world. A director's world. Go back to your cave and slit your wrists, you little bitch. Bash your head in with that trophy.

Chapter 35

A few weeks before Christmas, I flew to Buffalo for my older brother's wedding. He was marrying his high school sweetheart, so I couldn't refuse. This was my first trip back since moving out West years ago, and I was terrified to lose all the progress I'd made. Though my old bedroom was free, I stayed at a nearby motel and avoided the house the entire time I was in town.

I went to the rehearsal dinner and spoke to a few aunts, uncles, and cousins individually before the group took over again and I was off in the background. All these years, they'd been saying, "Don't you miss us?" but soon after arrival, I became wallpaper again. "So, how's work?" "How's the weather down there?" "They haven't made you start speakin' el Es-panish-o out there yet, have they, har har?" "You live in the land of sun and you come back looking like a snowman!"

It was strange seeing my brother get married. Strange seeing how we'd both grown up, even though I still felt like a little kid. Strange to see the family gathered for an event like this—to celebrate the passing of a member into a new level of life, yet no one gave a damn about my passage from death to life. No one asked how I was *really* doing. But, then again, Jay-boy, isn't that why you got to that point in the first place? Don't expect a fish to fly out of the ocean. Just eat your steak, be happy for your brother and new sister, try like hell to avoid dancing and drinking, and get outta here, fast! Just answer their damned questions. They didn't miss *you*; they missed the group being whole. Now that all the pieces are together, they can feel at ease with the shitty job they did at childrearing. A few did notice something, though. "You seem different. So much quieter." "You're so skinny now, and I think you grew a few inches." It was true. After my work with the Knight, I actually had grown a few inches, and now I was exactly six feet tall.

At the reception, I noticed one of my older cousins sitting alone in a dark corner, head looking as heavy as mine had always been. Everyone around him was dancing, but he just kept staring at the floor. I heard the others talking about him: "Man, he really wears his heart on his sleeve, huh?" "Serves him right for messin' with the needle." In the time I'd left Buffalo, he'd become a junky, but rather than going over and asking him if there was anything I could do to help, I left him alone and continued to sit in a different dark corner, wondering what everyone was saying about me.

On the plane back, I sat in the window seat in the last row, just as I'd done on the trip to Buffalo, and I thought about the woman who had sat in the middle seat next to me on the trip out: a fifty-something White woman with glasses and a grandma haircut. When the crew had closed the cabin door and our row's aisle seat was still open, I was thrilled that I'd get some extra space to spread out.

But fifteen minutes after takeoff, America's Grandma still hadn't moved, so I upped my game, using tricks I'd learned from the Frog.

"So, kinda nice that the aisle seat is empty. Now we can get some arm room, huh?" I said, thinking she'd get the hint and shift over.

"Oh, yes, of course." She smiled but didn't move.

I waited another few minutes before saying, "So nice that on this *long* flight, you can move over to that seat so we can both have some extra room, don't you think?"

Again, she smiled and said something like, "Yes, that's nice," but didn't move.

I started to get hot under the collar, but then she started digging in her bag, and I figured she was gonna grab it and move—but instead, she pulled out a ball of yarn and two long-ass metal needles and asked, "Would it bother you if I do some knitting?"

But before I could say, "Well, actually, yes it would . . ." she'd already gotten to work, flinging those killing sticks within inches of my eyes in post-9/11 America where if you wore the slightest thing resembling a hijab, you'd get kicked off the plane and tossed in Guantanamo, yet America's Grandma can practically impale me while everyone smiles at her and asks, "Oh, you making that for your grandchild?"

"Yes! Yes, I *do* mind. Can you please just move over a seat? You almost stabbed me a few times," I said.

But, instead of moving over, she balled up her yarn, gave me a dirty look, and said, "Fine!" as she stuffed it all back in her bag. But she didn't move.

"Look, I didn't ask you to stop knitting, I just asked if you could move over a seat," I said. "I've got a bad back and sitting like this is causing me physical pain. Can you please move over? I'll pay you. I'll give you real American paper money."

"I PUT THE YARN AWAY! I PUT IT AWAY! WHAT MORE DO YOU WANT FROM ME?"

People started staring, and, as always, America's Grandma was right, and the cocky, hotshot younger guy was the asshole.

"I just want you to move over a seat," I said. "I can't be any clearer than that."

The big, biker-looking guy in the seat ahead of me turned around. "Hey, jerk, you bothering this nice woman?"

"I just kindly asked her to move over a seat," I said.

"Oh, he's horrible! A horrible little *brat*!" she said.

One of the flight attendants came over. "You know, I think we have an open seat in first class. Why don't you come with me?" she said to America's Grandma. They both gave me a dirty look as they walked away. The shithead in the seat ahead of me reclined all the way, but at least I was able to stretch out my arms and legs.

I'd forgotten about all this until that flight back to Soul City, and I decided I'd write a short film about it called, *I Just Need Some*

Space! When you're a young person, especially a young man, and you ask an older person, especially America's Grandma, for anything—including something you absolutely need—you can expect the same treatment. She didn't listen to a single thing I said—just heard what she wanted to, and, "This ungrateful little brat whose butt I used to wipe feels okay to attack me? *Me* of all people? I go to church! I pay my taxes! I vote pro-life! I hate my gay son! I do everything I'm supposed to, and *this* is the thanks I get? This little *jerk!* See, he's even got me swearing! Oh, Lord, give me strength!"

This was the pervasive American "parenting" style, and my exchange with this woman was a perfect warm-up for returning to Buffalo, which was filled with America's Grandmothers. There was no chance of getting any personal space in that city without upsetting its tender, hyper-motherfucking-sensitive balance, and there was no chance of getting it on that flight either. If you wanted some space, you were gonna have to be cool with being the asshole, and I was proud to be an American Asshole for life.

Over winter break, I flew to Leon, Mexico, then took a cab to Guanajuato. I'd been to Guanajuato years back, and I was glad the city was as beautiful as I remembered. The cab driver dropped me off at my hotel, a castle on a hill overlooking the city, and I checked in, then hit the town. I ate dinner at a restaurant near Teatro Juarez, then found a café and got into *This Is How You Lose Her*, which was my first experience with Junot Díaz. I read up to "Flaca," then walked the narrow cobblestone streets, staring at four-hundred-year-old Spanish colonial buildings and listening to street buskers and singers who paraded in costume. It filled me with inspiration, but my body was still too broken and blocked to allow me to act or sing or play guitar with any true skill, and observing the art in motion all around me reminded me of how far I still had to go before I'd ever be free as well.

I found a rooftop bar, sat on a bench in back and sipped a Pacifico while getting back into the book. The place was packed, people dancing and celebrating. Every so often, I'd look up and see a pretty woman looking my way. I was still too broken for that as well and remained with Junot Díaz until I'd almost finished the book. The beer made me warm and loose, and as much as I feared I'd spiral out of control, I was able to stop at two drinks. I walked back to the castle about a mile away. I locked the door behind me and tried not to think about what Barry had said when I'd told him where I'd be staying. "I'll bet that place is haunted." There were two queen-size beds with royal seals on canopies above them, and the ceiling had to have been at least thirty feet high. The place was huge and had several spots where ghosts could hide.

I went to the window and looked down at the city, lit up like fallen stars. It was hard to believe I hadn't yet gone crazy since the last time I'd seen those lights. That I still had a job and health insurance and a pension. That I could go anywhere in the world I wanted so long as I had the cash and visa. That I could go anywhere I wanted alone and never worry about being lonely. I had my books and my thoughts and my pocket notebook. I had my music and the hope that pretty women all over the world would flash me glances as I sipped tea in city squares or strolled cool nighttime streets.

I thought of the Frog. Could I make it anywhere without him? Would I fall apart the moment I strayed too far from Soul City? Too far from my job and apartment? They had been like tent poles holding me up all these years, giving me shape.

But it felt as if those lights were helping to give me shape now. It felt as if Robert Plant's voice on the TV was shaping me as well. So were Junot Díaz's words. So were all of my own. Maybe I really could survive on my own someday. But, just as I'd felt when I was rushed with inspiration on those beautiful Guanajuato streets, the thought of hope and freedom flooded me with anxiety. I was glad the walls here were so thick; I couldn't hear a single one of my neighbors. I lay in bed and watched Robert Plant sing "When the World Was Young" as Jimmy Page played guitar. I'd never heard it before, and knowing those two could continue to write such powerful songs well into their later years made me feel that I still had some time to write my masterpiece. But it also made me feel that someday soon, I too would be remembering the world when it was young. Remembering all the times I'd played basketball and won trophies and rode bikes with my friends and hid beers in Buffalo snow banks. Remembering my first kiss in Dana Samson's basement while everyone was getting high in the laundry room. Remembering the times I'd mowed the lawn while listening to Led Zeppelin and Queen and Pink Floyd. Remembering all the dreams I'd once had of selling millions of albums and conquering the world. I felt stuck in this place where everything was always coming to me, yet slipping away at the same time. To live in real time was to deny the fantasies of youth that had been the tent poles that held me up through those worst of times—through the panic and fear and obsession. To lose those fantasies made me feel as if I'd soon crumple, yet all of my successes at work—helping students, showing up on time, only taking two sick days in the first five years—along with my successes writing books and screenplays: All of this now held me up as well. What to let go of? What to hold on to? I knew now that the answers didn't exist on these Mexican streets. The answers existed only within me.

I replayed "When the World Was Young" in my head all night, staring at the stars glowing over one of the most beautiful places I'd ever seen. To live there. To parade the streets in costume. To rid my body of the tension and pain and fear. To sing like Robert Plant. To play guitar like Jimmy Page. I woke the next morning just before noon in a queen-size bed in a castle on a hill overlooking Diego Rivera's birthplace, "When the World Was Young" still playing in my head. I thought about Barry. Thought about how he had kids. Thought about how if I had kids there'd be no way I could wake up so late, then stay in bed for another hour rubbing lotion all over my cock and balls until I came like royalty. My life was different than theirs. I could see it now. I could see how different I was from all of them and why it always felt so strange to be around them. They *wanted* to be there. They *chose* teaching. I chose the late nights staring down on Mexican cities from my castle window. I chose to stop on the edge of crowded sidewalks to capture the words that had popped into my head when I passed the old man selling tamales on the roadside. I chose to tell them all that I was doing laundry or cleaning or whatever else when they asked me on Monday about my weekend, even though I'd spent it shaking and sweating and writing my pain into the world. I knew they saw I was different as well, and I think this intrigued some of them. I think it also pissed a lot of them off. Plenty of people don't like it when they can't slap a label on you and stuff you in a box immediately after you first meet. I was a question mark, and question marks terrify some people, but if they were terrified, then good. That was their own damned problem. It wasn't up to me to save the world anymore. You don't like me? Fine. Fuck off. I gotta find a café and finish my book.

Which is exactly what I did, and while watching Aerosmith videos at a café near the Catedral de Guanajuato, I locked eyes with a gorgeous woman, who came over and sat with me. We spoke about the city and how she was from Guadalajara and how I'd been in Guadalajara when the Chivas won the championship in 2006, and how we both hated people who talked during movies, and she invited me to a party that night, but everything went downhill when she asked me to try her tea. There were pieces of fruit floating at the top, and, since getting food poisoning in Zambulla, I'd resolved to avoid eating anything that hadn't been cooked while in Mexico, but she wouldn't accept my, "No thanks," and kept hitting me with, "I don't understand? Just try it."

"I already explained to you why. I was sick and—"

"That's so weird. Just drink it!" She pushed the cup in front of me, and I said no again and she looked ready to cry, and I paid and took off, remembering another reason why I chose to spend so much time alone. It was better to wake up in a castle bed and jerk off than it was to wake up alongside the most beautiful woman on earth who forced you to drink her tea after you'd already told her a hundred times no. I was done drinking the world's tea.

When I walked back to the castle that night, I heard the familiar sound of sneakers screeching on a hardwood floor, and I followed it to an indoor basketball court. I stood in the door and watched two teams of younger guys playing a game. It'd been about eight years since I'd so much as dribbled a basketball. There was a time when I would have dominated that court. Now, I probably couldn't take a layup without falling over. I rubbed the fat growing on my stomach and wished for freedom. The freedom to use my body the way it was designed to be used. The freedom to rid myself of this unwanted tension. At one point, the tension had been necessary. The tension had kept me moving through the chaos of youth. It had kept me social and present and prepared. But now, I was able to be social without the chemicals pushing me along.

I spent Christmas Day eating and strolling the streets, and a few days later, I was home. The place reeked of mold and smoke, but I knew that soon this would lose its strength. Soon, the intense misery and depression I'd feel going into work that first day would lose its strength as well, and I'd be back in the machine, feeling nothing but a dull hopelessness like a sour stomach that never quite went away. Those weeks in Mexico gave me hope. They gave me life. They allowed me to plug back in for a while before I had to unplug and drain away again. I knew if I stayed unplugged for too long, I might not power up again the next time I got plugged back in. If I stayed unplugged for too long, I might be lost forever.

Chapter 36

Just when I'd become pretty good friends with Salena Raju, Cody transferred me back to the gym. At first I was excited, but on that first day back, I realized that without those special people there by my side, the gym was just a gym. Ms. Donaldson put me in the desk against the far wall where Doreen used to sit, and I think she intentionally chose this location because it was by far the noisiest spot in the school. We shared that wall with a bar/grill that blasted the fuck out of their music, and the bass obliterated any sense of peace, security, and hope I'd had. Though I knew it'd only make things worse, I begged her—literally begged her—to move me anywhere else, but she just said, "Quit whining and get back to work." After spending Christmas break in a quiet stone fortress, I knew I wouldn't be able to make it in such a noisy spot. I wanted to return to the protection those stone walls provided, but I knew I still had so far to go to become king.

Ms. Donaldson must not have known I'd become such good friends with Salena, because she moved Salena to the desk beside mine a few weeks later. I was happy to have my friend back, but I was also a little concerned. After seeing how sweet Salena was with her students, I'd started falling for her, and I didn't want to fall so hard I couldn't control my feelings. I didn't want to find myself staring or hoping she'd ask me to get drinks after work or whatever, even though I thought she might feel the same. She was always finding excuses to talk to me and she laughed at all my dumb jokes and she texted me with links to videos or songs or whatever, following up on things we'd discussed earlier in the day. She played with her hair when we talked, and she'd back away nervously and blush, and I didn't want to torment myself trying to read signs. I didn't want any of it. It was better to be alone. Hell, with those speakers blasting away my will to live, I didn't have the energy to be funny or charming or anything, anyway. I was just another miserable, workaday stooge.

I knew Cody and Donaldson were trying to break me down, but there was that little kid in me who'd fought and clawed his way through panic disorder and major depression and the screaming and hitting and smashing at home, and if that kid could survive obsessive-compulsive disorder and drug-induced psychosis, there was nothing those clowns could throw at me that I couldn't overcome. Though neurotic, I was a resilient motherfucker, and spiteful to boot. If they wanted to go head to head, I was coming out with the trophy. If they were trying to break me, I'd smile as I was coming apart inside and tell them how happy I was to be there.

But I also kept hearing the Frog's voice in my mind: "Don't let this get to you. You know you can always work at a different school, right? Why waste valuable energy fighting people who don't think twice about you?" And I knew he was right. I hated letting scumbags win, but some fights just weren't worth fighting.

But I couldn't let this one go. By now, I understood Cody's and Donaldson's perspectives. After publishing a book, which basically made me a business owner, I understood how difficult it was to keep a business running. I understood that they had to manage governmental bureaucracy and PR and advertising and student and teacher behavior and all the myriad day-to-day processes teachers didn't have to worry about. I knew Cody was shy like me, and I could empathize with his struggles to be a leader. But he didn't seem able to empathize with my struggles to maintain my health and dignity while teaching in a toxic environment. I felt the same about my coworkers. I could understand them, but they didn't care to understand me. They saw me as a lazy nuisance or whatever, not knowing nor caring about my anxieties. They probably had their own shit they were dealing with, but rather than create an environment where we could all help one another, they sought to destroy, creating a festering toxicity where everyone was playing passive-aggressive games and gathering dirt on everyone else, and I was gathering shit right along with them. I hated doing this crap, but I wasn't just fighting for my job. I was fighting for my right to exist, and I couldn't let them beat me.

I finished Anthony Kiedis's autobiography, *Scar Tissue,* at Elena's Café one Friday night, and I kept thinking about it so much that I couldn't sleep. As I lay in bed, I understood another reason why I was always so tense when I tried to sleep. Every part of me wanted to sprint down to LA and start a band and take over the world, and it all had to happen RIGHT NOW!

That voice had always been with me, screaming at me for all these years, and now it was perfectly clear. I'd never be able to silence that voice until I gave it my all with music and acting and everything else that required skillful motion and grace and control. I told the voice, "Shut the fuck up! I'm doing the best I can! Don't you see? I'll be there soon. I'm not ready—"

YOU'LL NEVER BE READY! GO NOW! LEAVE ALL THIS CRAP BEHIND! GRAB YOUR GUITAR! YOUR NOTEBOOKS . . . AND THAT COOL NEW STAINLESS-STEEL FRYING PAN YOU JUST BOUGHT—IT DISTRIBUTES THE HEAT SO EVENLY WITH THAT ALUMINUM INSERT IN THE BOTTOM! GRAB IT AND FUCKING GO ALREADY!

I didn't sleep at all that night—just kept battling within myself. There was a time I'd have abandoned everything, running out screaming into the night, chasing down my dreams with ruthless and wild passion. But now, like Wally in *My Dinner with Andre*, I also liked to feel warm and safe in my bed. I'd never felt warm or safe before, and the fact that I'd provided myself with such an environment made me feel proud and capable. That wasn't something to set on fire and run screaming from. It was something to respect and leave with care.

The following night, I was able to sleep, despite spending most of that day worrying I'd never sleep again. I couldn't let myself hope yet—hope that I could actually make it in LA. I needed something more solid under my feet. Maybe if some big producer bought one of my scripts and I had some real money in my bank account. After all, you know what happens when you don't have security, Jay. You self-destruct. You'll end up like Antoine the Swan smoking crack and shooting H in Hollywood motels. So, do what you need to do to build up that security around you, but also know that as you do this, time *is* passing—time you'll never get back. It literally all *is* happening *right now*. You can ignore that forceful voice up inside of you, but he's right, man. All the greats just pulled that trigger and went screaming toward their dreams. I know you face a set of unique challenges, but you ain't gonna get any extra time or special treatment because of it. So, take your time, but you gotta live with the consequences.

I knew I'd have to put up with Cody and Ms. Donaldson and the bar music for a lot longer. But I also knew that one day, that freedom would feel that much better knowing what I'd had to go through to get it.

But I didn't want to shut that voice up entirely. That was the voice of a king, so I decided to throw it some scraps. Instead of working on another big project, like a book or a script, that might not get me anywhere for a year or longer, I decided to write some short scripts that could maybe get produced that year. I took chapters from my books *Tropical Teaching* and *The Saga of the Scorpion* and made them into standalone stories, changing the characters and plots, and after a month, I had two new scripts. I submitted both to contests and hoped for the best.

A producer in New York City emailed me to say she wanted to turn *Lila's Adventure* into a TV series. We discussed it for hours over several phone calls, and I wrote a bible, creating a five-season arc with page-long descriptions of all the main characters and their inner/outer conflicts, but after a few months of speaking almost daily, I stopped hearing from her. The last thing she told me was, "I've got a meeting tomorrow with some investors," and I learned the New York rejection was just as silent as the Hollywood one.

Shit at work went in waves, and there were several times when I felt I was one dirty look away from a nervous breakdown, but each time I hit what felt like rock bottom, I bounced back days later. One particularly low point was the afternoon some of the robots invited me to lunch. We went to the loud bar/grill, and the music blasted apart my armor, leaving me defenseless as my coworkers pummeled me with questions:

"So, do you have a girlfriend?"

"A boyfriend, hehe?"

"What do you do for fun?"

"I hear you go to Mexico a lot. Is Tijuana really as dangerous as they say?"

"I heard a rumor that you write movies. This true?"

Normally, I'd have found ways of evading the questions, like, "Who has time for a girlfriend with all this new work they've given us, huh?" or, "I usually spend my free time creating bogus Facebook profiles so I can give the Cody Cares page as many likes as possible," so they'd back off and see me as one of them—which was what they were testing me for in the first place—but with that music infecting every part of me, I gave them real responses. "No, no girlfriend or boyfriend. It's true—I do write. I've written a few scripts and have won some awards, and I almost had a TV series made. I've only been to the airport in TJ, but every other spot I've ever been to in Mexico has been extremely safe. I've never been robbed or assaulted and the few fights I've gotten into were as much my fault as the other guy's. Don't be afraid to get out into the world. It's not as dangerous as you expect."

I figured giving them the truth would get them off my back, but I could tell from their looks that the truth was a little too raw for them. I think they preferred the dad jokes. I hated giving pieces of myself away to people who had no idea what to do with them, and who would likely use those pieces to hurt me later on. On the walk back, we arrived at the gym's double door, and even though my desk was just to the right, I turned left and walked a few yards, then turned to the left again and walked to my desk. For whatever reason, in the last month or so, I'd been feeling an overwhelming urge to turn to the left rather than the right, and even though I knew they'd probably tell Cody I was a psychopath, I'd given away so much at lunch and needed to keep something for myself. When I sat at my desk, I felt hollowed out inside, and the blasting music wasn't helping. I wanted to grab my things, and walk left out of there and never come back.

That particular time was one of the worst for me at Cody Cares. Now, I was in the heart of corporate culture. The authentic and safe environment that we'd created in the early days of Cody Cares was long gone, and there was no healing allowed here. Now, it was everyone for themselves. Even if I were to write a five-hundred-page book explaining what I was going through, rather than trying to understand my perspective, my coworkers and bosses would give it one-star reviews like all the other cornholes who said, "What does a straight White guy from the suburbs have to be so depressed about anyway? Suck it up, pussy!" Even if I told them specifically what was going on and gave them doctor's notes to prove it, they'd still deny my disease. I couldn't act weak or vulnerable here, even though acting vulnerable was often a sign of strength. The fearful and ignorant see "weakness" as weakness and "vulnerability" as vulnerability. Camarin had seen those qualities as assets. She'd praised me for having the courage to face my demons. Ms. Donaldson would burn me at the stake if she knew what went on in my head. "HE'S A MONSTER! A MONSTER, I TELL YOU!" It was a dangerous world out there for anyone trying to improve themselves in any way. As expected, Donaldson did call me to her office to discuss "peculiar behavior your coworkers have been complaining about." When I asked her specifically what she was referring to, she wouldn't respond—just got mad, as if I was *just supposed to know. Just supposed to know* that specifics didn't actually matter, that all these assholes cared about was that I didn't talk with them about the latest primetime hit on TV or the latest pop tart dominating the radio or all the trendy spots they loved. That I didn't put pictures of my wife and kids on my desk. That the wallpaper on my computer was black, because I didn't want to see any image that reminded me of life while stuck in that corporate hellhole. No shots of the Sierra Nevadas or of the Beatles or President Obama or Maui. When they saw shit like that black screen, I think they knew. I think they knew that I was just doing time there. That this wasn't the end result for me, and even though I smiled and worked hard and had a great rapport with my students and their parents, the fact that I was trying to get out meant I needed to be destroyed. The fact that I still couldn't be fit into a box made them uneasy and wary. I just wanted to be left alone—to do my time in peace, but every time I took a little longer in the bathroom to relax enough to piss or to breathe my way through anxiety, or I stepped outside to call the Frog during a free period or I took an extra minute at lunch, they'd email Ms. Donaldson, and she'd ask me, "Do you even *want* to be a teacher?" I mean, what kind of a fucking question is that? I wanted to scream at her, "WHAT THE FUCK DOES IT EVEN MATTER WHAT I WANT? I DO MY FUCKING JOB! YOU CAN HAVE MY TIME BUT YOU CAN'T HAVE MY SOUL! I WON'T BE MISERABLE LIKE THE REST OF YOU! I STILL BELIEVE! EVEN AFTER ALL THESE YEARS—AFTER ALL THAT I'VE BEEN THROUGH—I *STILL* BELIEVE. YOU'RE GONNA HAVE TO SHOOT ME TO BRING ME DOWN. SHOOT ME IN THE NECK AS I GIVE THAT OL' LUKE SMILE!"

The last few times I'd been to Mexico, I'd felt so good afterward that I realized I should start going there on all my school breaks. It was hard for me to make those kinds of simple connections. To recognize, "Hey, I feel better when I'm in Mexico, so maybe I should go there more often." I think part of the reason for this—aside from any cognitive impairments I likely suffered due to the anxiety/depression—was learned hopelessness. As a kid, I'd learned it was hopeless to try to improve my situation—to try to find ways of being happy and successful—which is why it usually gave me such anxiety to think about taking steps toward Mexico and LA. But after having been gainfully employed for so long, and after having weathered so many storms at work and inside my heart and mind, I started to feel much more stability and confidence with my living situation. I felt that time wasn't crumpled up into one big ball and weighing down on my back, and I could actually create plans, like a trip to Mexico, and after a series of uniform-length days, I could actually *be* in Mexico, and actually enjoy myself. I decided to go to Mexico that July to escape the nervous breakdown I knew was coming if I remained in Soul City.

I flew into Zambulla and took a seven-hour van ride through the mountains with Maya, a woman I'd met at the film festival the year before. She was a clothing designer and fashion model, and we sat in the backseat massaging each other's bits as the driver zoomed over huge potholes and around boulders and burros in the road, passing cars on blind turns, and after six straight hours of one sharp mountain turn after the next, I practically kissed the ground when we arrived in Zambulla Beach. We stayed in a hotel in a quiet area far enough away from the main strip to get some peace, but not so far that we couldn't walk to the center of the action, and the second the door closed, she went straight to the bathroom and came out in lingerie. I took off my shirt and jeans, and I rubbed myself on her thighs and crotch while massaging her ass and kissing her chest and cheeks. I wanted to savor the moment, kissing her and caressing her body, trying to calm my mind and to finally be at one with a moment of my life, but she took off her bra and lay on the bed, pulling me on top of her, so I removed her panties with my teeth, gave her pussy a long, slow French kiss, then I grabbed a scumbag from my backpack, rolled it on, got on top, and slid inside. Her face twisted in delight as my dick filled her tight pussy, and I worked it slow and sensual, kissing her and telling her we had all the time in the world. The door was locked, and I no longer feared someone would break in and put a gun to my head, so I was able to read her face and body, watching her and listening to what she needed. Every time I thrust, I could feel her big, firm ass slap against my groin, and it felt so good, I wanted to fill the room with cum, but I controlled myself and slowed when I needed to. When she got on top, she took control and worked my dick like a champ. I slapped and rubbed her ass, and stuck a finger inside her cornhole, and she loved it. She kept working me, hitting me in the face with her huge tits and staring directly into my eyes. Our spirits were aligned. She had the soul of a rebel. An artist. A lover. A warrior. She'd never call me weird for turning left when entering a room. She'd turn left with me, and together we'd discover the true meaning of leftness, finding a way to extract its beauty and relay it to the world. I stayed in the game long enough for her to get two as she rode my dick, then I flipped her onto her stomach, and went after mine. I fucked her like a dog, feeling my dick massaging her and letting it do all the work, and soon I pulled out, ripped off the condom, and covered her back in leche. I lay beside her, both of us panting and smiling and kissing. We took a shower, and I dropped to my knees and ate her pussy again, and she reciprocated. I came all over her face, and we toweled off, and as I dried her ass, I realized that was maybe the first time I'd ever felt sexually satisfied. That all the other times I'd been filled with fear and insecurity and suspicion that all the gods and saints and dead grandparents and great-aunts and uncles were watching me, judging me. That night, I was alone with a gorgeous woman in a quiet section of one of the most beautiful beaches in the world, and I felt drained of any worry.

I smacked her ass. "Thanks, baby."

"You should never thank a woman for sex. It makes her feel like a whore."

"I wasn't thanking you for sex. I was thanking you for spending time with me."

"Good, think of something else to say after sex."

"How about, de nada?"

She smiled and pinched my ass. "Pompis de escritor."

"Never insult an escritor, or they'll kill you in a novel someday."

We went for dinner, then came back and did it all again.

There were two beds, and she said, "I prefer to sleep alone," and I smiled and said, "So do I." She took the bed by the AC machine and I took the one by the window, though I would have preferred to switch, knowing that at any time, morning noise would blast through that window, but I was so tired, I fell right asleep.

In the morning, my body felt wrecked—punishment for the satisfaction and relaxation of the night before. Due to my muscular issues and horrible alignment/posture, I'd get terrible aches and pains throughout the day, but they were usually worst in the morning, and that morning was terrible. I wasn't used to getting exercise, and all the thrusting and traveling in that twisting and turning van had destroyed me. Any hope I'd had that she'd feel the same for me as I did for her was gone when she saw the look of pain on my face.

"Are you okay?" she said.

"Yeah, this is normal for me. I just need an hour or two to lie here, and I should be fine."

It was a lie. I usually needed half a day to get out of bed when I was in such bad shape, and sometimes I didn't even get out of bed. I'd grab my computer and write while lying down. But I didn't have that luxury now. No, here I was on vacation with a beautiful woman who could have any guy she wanted, and if I didn't perform, she'd leave me soon enough. So I dragged myself up, and the second I stood, I was overcome with dizziness and extreme anger and confusion—the way I'd felt for the majority of my pre-Frog life. It reminded me of how far I'd come, but also of why I'd never been able to keep a girlfriend. Of why I preferred to live and travel alone. Of why I still felt that life was hopeless.

While putting on her bikini, she bent over, and I hugged her from behind, pushing my crotch against her perfect ass. She pulled down her bottoms, and I grabbed another condom, and it was quick this time. I didn't have the stamina to drag this out, and I also knew she wanted to hit the beach.

We walked to the ocean, and I was overwhelmed by its beauty. Most Mexican beaches were littered with Domino's Pizzas and KFCs and Burger Kings, but this place was filled with small authentic restaurants and shops, and didn't have hawkers all over begging you to buy their crap. It was just us and the sand and palapas and mangos and papayas. We found a good spot and hit the water. Maya and I splashed and played like kids, and then she went to towel off. She took a picture of me exiting the water, and I was disgusted at how fat I'd let myself become. It was almost as if someone had taken a blowtorch to my torso—everything drooping and pasty and gross. I went back into the water and swam for a bit, trying to do some exercise. That picture was a symbol of the last six years of my life. It was a symbol of the change that had happened so insidiously, I hadn't even noticed how different I had become. I wanted to curse out the Frog for what he'd done to me, but I was feeling so much better than ever that there was no going back. I knew that if I just kept going, someday I'd be able to stand up straight and go to the gym and do squats and pushups the correct way, without feeling like I was going to fall over. Someday, I'd be able to run and play basketball without my feet and knees aching.

At dinner that night, Maya held my hand and kissed my cheeks, and we got down again at the hotel, but the next night, she was on a bus, returning to Zambulla and to work, and, "Don't worry, just stay here and enjoy the beach for a few more days. You're on vacation. I'll see you when you get back!" So, I let her go and didn't even think of such silly things as chasing after the bus as it took her away. Didn't even think to buy her flowers or slip a note into her backpack that would make her smile when she saw it later on. Didn't even blink when she told me she didn't want to be my girlfriend. I just made a joke of it, singing the lyric of some banda song popular at the time I'd lived in Mexico, calling myself just a pastime for her, which made her laugh, and then I couldn't stop laughing either—the two of us laughing in an empty Zambulla Beach bus station late on a Monday night. These were the moments of my life. As much as I lived in my head, following the breadcrumbs toward my dreams, time was passing me by, and these moments were real whether I acknowledged them or not. Someday I'd look back on this time and know that, as dead as I felt inside, I was still alive, and doing the best I could to make the most of my time. I was alive and conquering small villages around the fortress of my dreams, getting closer to finally sitting on that throne where I belonged. Sitting beside Maya and finding the energy to leave her notes and flowers and write her songs. God, why did I let her take that bus alone? Why did I just say, "Okay," when she told me to stay?

Dude, she wanted to be alone. Recognize that. Don't be some naïve kid anymore. Recognize what a woman is telling you when she says it. Don't rationalize or find alternate meanings. Women speak directly, even when they don't. Let her go. See her again when you get back to Zambulla. Try to enjoy your time alone.

But all I ever had was time alone. I missed her when I got back to the hotel, but soon I stopped smelling her everywhere, and I knew she'd fade away just like Carolina and Nima and Frida. I hardly ever thought about them anymore. Even Mariposa was a distant memory. Was this something I wanted? Did I push them all away? Was it only temporary while I was healing? Would I want someone around when I finally freed myself of all the horror and tension? Was I waiting until I was on that throne to find my queen? Did I feel unlovable? Unreliable?

No, listen to what it's telling you, Jay. You haven't found the right woman yet. When you do, you won't push her away. You're not the type who can settle. When you meet her, I promise, you'll know. Don't get down on yourself for all those other failed attempts. You're allowed casual relationships. You're allowed to do what they're doing too. Maya used you for some fun. So did most of the others. Allow yourself to be young and carefree. You're allowed to enjoy physical pleasure. Not everything has to be all or nothing. You can share love with someone you've only spent a weekend with. You can give parts of yourself away to any woman you feel connected to without having to spend a lifetime at her side.

Maybe I'd never be with only one woman, but with many women I felt a strong connection to. After all, it seemed that was what the world was coming to anyway. Why force a lifetime of service when it felt so unnatural? Just keep flowing. Flow like the waves. Don't stress. Just relax. The answers will come. Don't chase them. Don't stress or strain. Nobody's gonna put a gun to your head here.

I flew in a small *Indiana Jones*-style plane back to Zambulla, knowing I'd never be able to make that van trip through the mountains again. I waited in the airport and the pilot called me and two other people over, and we followed him to the plane outside.

"Sit wherever you'd like!" he said as he opened the door. I sat so close behind him I could have grabbed the controls. He flew us up the coast, then east over the mountains. It was one of the best mornings of my life, seeing the beauty of Mexico from a new perspective. I looked down at all the twisting and turning mountain roads I'd traveled with Maya and realized that we were on different life paths.

I was a little nervous that we wouldn't clear a particularly high peak, but the pilot got us over after joking, "I hope you have your parachutes!" Once we'd passed that mountain, Zambulla was just below. As much as I hated Cody Cares, the money they paid me got me over those mountains. Got me down to Zambulla. Paid for the hotel and all the enchiladas and huevos rancheros I ate. As far away as I was from that shithole, every cool thing I did reminded me of how much I needed Cody Cares.

I didn't see Maya for two days after I landed. "I'm busy with work, but I'll see you tomorrow!" And when we did see each other, it wasn't the same. She didn't stay with me at the hotel. "My parents won't allow me to spend the night with a man unless we're married." She'd lied to them about whom she was with in Zambulla Beach, and I guess I was lucky to have gotten that much time with her.

At dinner on my last night there, Maya told me about a protest she'd been organizing against the city's mayor, who'd failed to push the police force to find the man who'd raped and killed a young woman in a small neighboring town. Maya was the head of a feminist group, and her passion inspired me as she spoke about creating a society that was safe and equal for all women. Talking with her made me feel as if the future would be a safe place for me as well, and I felt proud knowing I was friends with people like her. That someone as special as Maya had spent some of her valuable time with me. Hell, a lot of my new friends, Alex, Salena, and others, were all intelligent, successful people, and I was feeling worthier of their friendship. Maybe I didn't fit in at work because those people weren't my crowd. At work, they thought I was lazy and difficult and ungrateful, but they didn't really spend any time getting to know me. Maya and Alex and the others could see who I was right away, and I was done struggling to win the approval of people who simply refused to see.

Before going to Mexico, I'd applied for a few teaching jobs at independent study schools in LA. I got some interviews and was even offered two separate jobs, but it was the bait and switch. They had me interview for teaching positions, but all they had were assistant positions. The one principal, however, said, "There's an eighty percent chance we'll need a full-time teacher in the fall. If you take the assistant position, there's no guarantee there will be a job for you after the summer, but there probably will be." At that school, the principal and teachers were warm and compassionate, and reminded me of the early days of Cody Cares. Though it was a risk, and it would take me away from the Frog and my apartment, where I'd been able to successfully write books and scripts, I told her I accepted. But she responded, "Actually, let's wait until the end of the summer to be sure there's a position for you. I don't want you to move here then not have a job in two months." I said okay, then I volunteered for a bunch of extra assignments at Cody Cares, knowing I'd be gone before I had to do any of the shit I'd signed up for. I figured it'd be my last fuck you to that shithole, but when the principal told me at the end of the summer, "Sorry, our enrollment isn't high enough yet to need a new teacher, but we'll definitely need someone in the spring," I almost cried. It was supposed to work out. I was supposed to move to Burbank, get a house with no shared walls at the end of a dead end with a mountain for a backyard, and I'd audition for films in free periods and on the weekends. But Soul City wasn't done with me yet.

When I got back from Zambulla in July, I bought a Total Gym and started working out with the seat on its lowest angle. I hadn't worked out in years, and after all those years of only moving in preapproved ways, I had to break myself out of that mold. I worked out for about an hour, moving slowly and imagining my body functioning correctly, and at the end, I felt weak and confused. But that night, I got rushed with that post-workout euphoria I hadn't felt in years. So, I started working out once a week, and after a few months, I felt much more energized.

But my muscles were still so locked up, I couldn't relax, and working out only made them tighter. Even after the progress I'd made with the Frog and the Knight, my back was still twisted, and my left shoulder was a few inches higher than the right and my left hip was also higher than the right and it rotated about an inch away from my body. My hamstrings and thighs and calves felt like bone, and I'd get exhausted just washing dishes or making dinner. The Frog wanted me on medication, but medication would make it impossible to write. I was going to have to suffer this for a little while longer, making incremental progress, moving closer and closer to that point where I'd healed my body and conquered my dreams. That time was coming; that was for certain.

That July break, I kept thinking about the knitting woman on my flight to Buffalo, and I built a story around it. After his brother attempts suicide a few weeks before Thanksgiving, an asshole with a heart of gold returns to Buffalo to help him, but discovers that the brother is the sanest member of the family. In the opening scene, the guy is on the flight home, and the woman next to him, America's Grandma, whips out her yarn and murder sticks and practically impales him. He kindly asks her to move over, and she loses her mind, turning everyone on the flight against him. I figured that'd set the tone perfectly, and we'd already know this is a story about young people being ruined by older people who never listen, and we can almost feel why the brother tried to kill himself before we even meet him. I wanted to make the protagonist as big an asshole as possible. Anytime you asked anyone in America for something you really needed, you were made to feel like an asshole for it, and this guy needed something big. His parents were in denial about his brother's suicide attempt, and he needed them to accept reality and help him. So, I had the protagonist getting into fights with Dad and Grandma and people driving slowly in the left lane and everyone else he came across, trying to save his brother while setting fire to the world, but soon, his brother is the one saving him from his boiling rage and self-destruction.

It all came together quickly, and soon *Hatesgiving* was winning more awards and getting me more attention than anything else I'd written. I wrote the script using lessons I'd learned from other screenwriters and had kept it short, fast-paced, easy to follow, and dramatic, with just the right amount of Hollywood sentimentality, and soon filmmakers were contacting me about producing it. All of my other scripts and books were heavy psychological dramas with elements of humor, but I'd made *Hatesgiving* as absurd and sardonic as possible, exposing the types of lies and shame that defined the modern American family. I felt I was entering a new phase in my writing and in my life.

Chapter 37

At work, the stress became so bad, I had to take two days off. I got such a bad panic attack while driving home from school that I had to pull over to the side of the highway. I lost vision in my right eye and felt as if I was detaching from reality. After about an hour of cars zooming past, I felt well enough to drive home, but when I closed the door behind me, my apartment started collapsing. I went for a walk, even though it was still bright enough for people to see me. I stayed away from the main strip and stuck to alleys and side streets and arrived at the pier. Here there weren't many people, so I walked to the end, but when I turned back, I felt my body dissolving. It began in my legs and slowly moved up through my groin and stomach and chest and arms—a loose, tingly feeling of dread and horror. The body and brain only had so much energy, and I'd drained them both. I had no idea how I'd made it this far carrying all that stress, and I was terrified to think that maybe now my body would quit on me for good. People passed, laughing and eating ice cream and pushing baby strollers. I kept my head down and continued walking, hoping they wouldn't turn on me as well.

Some punks were smoking weed under the pier, and I got a big whiff, causing me to drift off even further. If I'd taken so much as one hit, I'd probably have drifted away forever. I called the Frog.

"What's going on, Jay? Everything all right?" he said.

I waited until I was in an empty alley before saying, "No, no, nothing is all right. I'm fallin' apart here, man. I don't even feel like I'm talking to you right now. I don't feel here or there or anywhere."

"Well, just breathe and relax. You're having an anxiety attack, and it'll pass."

"This one isn't passing. I think this is the one that gets me. It's been waiting all this time—waiting for me to feel good enough to actually take something away from me."

"Look, you're safe. You're okay. This will pass."

"Everything is passing, man. I don't even know what I'm still doing here. I was supposed to be in LA years ago, but I'm still here. I never go at anything directly. I wanted to be an actor, so instead of acting, I went to school to become a teacher, so I could learn how to speak in front of crowds, which would prepare me to be an actor. But even though I see this now, I'm still stuck here. It's like, I feel like I still got all this time to burn, but it's passing and never coming back. Everything is light-years away, ya know? My dreams and all that. Nothing is right here, right now. I know how hard it is to make it out there as an actor now. As a teacher too. I couldn't survive teaching in Miami. If I leave Cody Cares, I might be jumping right back into the fire. I have nightmares about it. Like, I quit, but now I'm back at some shitty school filled with kids trying to destroy me, and I'm making half the pay, and I'm in an even more toxic environment than Cody Cares. It's like, I know too much now, ya know, so I can't move a step. I'm stuck. I get nightmares about leaving my apartment. I'm usually in a new house in a strange world that resembles this one, and I'm in a big room but I can't sleep because people are loud as fuck just outside the window. I can't leave. I need to stay here until someone pays me for one of these scripts. Maybe this new one will be the one, ya know?"

"I do know—"

"There's no fuckin' way I can go to work tomorrow. Hell, there's no way I could order a pizza tomorrow, let alone head a classroom. What if I can't work anymore? What happens? Nobody believes me when I tell them about the OCD. Just asking them to use headphones is too much. They go behind my back, trying to get me fired. I mean, how do I survive this? For forty years? How can anyone do this? It's hard enough just to get up in the morning. The actual job of teaching is cake—the kids don't bother me at all—it's just all the bullshit from the adults I work with that kills me. The politics and mind games and pissing contests. I just wanna work somewhere quiet. I'm a great teacher, but that's not good enough. They wanna own my heart and soul. Fuck, if they could see me right now, no one would help. No one would say, 'Hey, Jay, everything okay?' No, instead they'd be calling the boss and telling him to call the paramedics and bring a fucking straitjacket. Honestly, what happens if I can't work anymore? Do I end up on the streets, screaming at people and exposing myself? I'm doing the best I can. I'm really trying, but what if I break down? No one's ever helping. They see you sick and weak, and they go in for the kill."

"I'm here, Jay. I know you feel trapped right now, but all of this will pass. Stop thinking about your dreams and retirement and all that for a moment, and just focus on your breathing. Focus on the wind blowing through your hair. I know you don't feel capable right now, but you'll be strong again soon. All the beautiful, powerful thoughts you've had will all come back. Don't worry. Don't force them. Just feel that breeze. Remember that anxiety peaks and subsides. You've been through so much worse, and you'll be okay."

"I'm tired of people telling me I'm faking this. Telling me it's all in my head. I mean, it *is* in my fucking head, literally. What do I have to do to get some respect?"

"Just breathe."

"What if I can't sleep? What if I go crazy?"

"What if Steven Spielberg calls you tomorrow and wants to fly you out to Paris to help him with his next film?"

"But I don't speak French . . ."

He laughed. "Jay, just breathe."

So I did. I looked at the full moon above that Sand Beach alley, high above the apartment buildings and dumpsters and cars with trash bags for windows. There was so much beauty here, I wished I could feel it. But I could only feel it if I were present in that moment, and to be present in that moment meant to embrace the horror of existence. To feel safe enough to let down my guard.

Just look at it, Jay. Allow your mind to wander.

And while doing this, a song came to me. Something delicate and melodic and driving, and I captured it in my voice recorder.

See, Jay? Even now, in these moments of panic and vulnerability, the music lives inside of you. You just have to surrender to it. Don't force it. Don't *try* to write a song. Just feel the moment and let the words come.

I felt the anxiety subsiding. Even after everything I now knew—after all these years—every time that anxiety hit, it always felt like the end. But, every time, it went away, and I returned. Every time I felt that the music was gone forever, it came back more powerful than before. Nothing can destroy you, Jay. Don't be afraid of calling in sick to work. Who cares what anyone thinks? Take as much time as you need without feeling guilty or broken or diseased. You'll be strong again soon. You'll be joking with your students again soon. Allow yourself a brief break.

I kept walking and avoided the spots that always smelled like weed. The spots where people were always talking or watching TV loudly. I knew the neighborhood well—at night. I hadn't walked around during the day in years. I didn't have that kind of armor anymore. But at night I ruled the beach, and I knew all the quietest alleys and side streets. I knew exactly which houses were safe to live in if I ever earned a million bucks and needed to settle down. Maybe I was pissing my life away, but at least I was trying for something. Something good. That had to mean something.

By the time I got home, I was feeling better, but I knew not to push it. My neighbor had friends over, so I avoided that side of the apartment and sat in my room against the far wall. This is no way to live, Jay. Here, there, wherever, you're a prisoner everywhere you go. You gotta find the place where you feel free.

But I'll never feel free until I get these stories and songs out of my head.

But you'll never be able to get 'em out when you're this stressed out. Go somewhere you feel happy. Safe. Warm.

I arrived in Zambulla around ten the Friday night the film fest kicked off. I was still feeling sick in the head and weak in the body, but just before I'd left Soul City, the bar/grill at the school closed down, which meant I could relax a little on this trip. Even so, I dreaded my return to Cody Cares next week. It was getting harder to go back to work each time I returned from Mexico, and maybe this would be the trip I finally stayed.

But after that first and second night, even though I was hanging out with friends, including Alex and a Salvadorian director named Diosa, I still felt weak and distant from everyone, and watching the ease with which they socialized and laughed and drank and did yoga in the garden only made me feel worse. I'd decided to stay at the hacienda hotel with them, trusting in satisfying my need for companionship and light and love. Trusting in feeling the grass beneath my feet again and listening to John Lennon while swinging in hammocks. Trusting in hearing the pleasant sound of friends talking and laughing—but after those first two days, I thought maybe I was broken for good. They discussed budgets and funding and shooting schedules, and I hung out in the corner thinking I'd have to wait until I got back home to kill myself. No, you can't do it here. Mexico has always brought you life. Do it back in the country that's always brought you suffering and death.

Previously, Mexico had always saved me. Every time I'd gone there, I'd felt healed in a way I'd needed in that moment. But it wasn't working this time, and if I lost Mexico, perhaps I'd also lose myself. It was such a risk going back there for all those vacations. At any time I could have arrived at the point that was now staring me in the face: Mexico could no longer save me. I tried everything. I ate the foods I loved and drank freshly squeezed orange juice and strolled around town at night and watched the houses lit up on hills in the distance, but none of it was working. I was so tight and stressed, I felt that if someone so much as brushed against my shoulder, I'd have a seizure that liquefied my brain.

But while eating breakfast with everyone on that third day and listening to Alex discussing how Truffaut was the best of the New Wave directors, I realized how pretentious it all sounded—even though I loved Truffaut. I realized that even though I didn't share their opinions on every film, I was still entitled to have my own. I realized that, even though I didn't have as many credits or professional contacts as they did, none of that mattered. I brought my own weird perspective to that table, which qualified me to sit among them. I didn't need to try. To force. To push. I needed to let the songs come to me. I needed to let the talent and success come to me. I needed to let my vacation come to me and stop trying to *feel* everything, and just feel *something*.

So, after lunch, I took off my shoes and put my feet in the grass as I swung in the hammock and listened to the birds instead of John Lennon and felt the ants crawling up my legs and the Earth energy filling my body through my soles, and soon I felt healed in a way I'd never felt before. This was new, and I realized it was because I'd entered a new level with my journey, which meant I needed a new approach to achieve success. I had to stop trying. Controlling. And, the simple fact that I was here among friends in a place I wouldn't have had the strength to be years ago made me aware of how far I'd come. My body and mind knew how to heal me. I had to get out of their way and listen to what they were telling me. I had to try new things. Eat new foods. Meet new people.

I went to the town center later that night with Diosa and told her about it. "That's incredible! It makes me feel special that you feel so safe with us."

I told her a little about my OCD and the journey I'd been on, and she opened up, telling me that she was born in El Salvador, but her family had moved to Canada to escape the war. Normally, hearing something like this, I'd get flooded with shame, telling me, "See, you don't really have it all that bad." But I was able to shut that voice up, realizing I didn't have to diminish my own struggle simply because other people had had more difficult ones. I needed to stop rating "suffering" and "struggle" and accept that my struggle was valid, and having someone like Diosa affirm my struggle made me feel much more confident that I would overcome my OCD. This time, at the hotel, I hadn't been checking the doors or windows or anything as much, and even though we didn't have locks on our doors, I wasn't afraid that someone would rob me, beginning a chain of events leading to my eventual homelessness and insanity.

When I got back to Soul City, I found out that one of my childhood friends had recently gotten married. Though he was one of my best friends, I hadn't spoken to him in years and hadn't even known he was engaged. I thought about how friendship had healed me on my trip to Zambulla and how it had healed me when I was a kid, and I started writing a new script about a group of estranged friends who reunite to write a screenplay about a series of their own high school pranks; only to find themselves drifting apart again for the same reasons as before. While writing it, I kept thinking of my friends, hoping that they'd read the script and want to reunite, but by now, I knew that hope was futile. There was usually a reason people drifted apart, and even though I'd drifted from some of my best friends, I was drifting toward Diosa and Alex and all the others.

Chapter 38

I found a cheap round-trip flight to Lila, so I decided to head down the last week of November 2016. It was the first time I'd been back since Doug's wedding in 2009, and it was strange seeing how old my friends looked. It'd been ten years since I'd lived there, and we weren't kids anymore. Pedro picked me up from the bus station, and I flooded with panic when I saw him standing there, the same way I flooded with panic whenever I saw an old friend or family member for the first time in a long time. He drove me to my hotel, which he said was haunted. "There was a rebellion in Lila two hundred years ago, and the Spanish hanged the rebels from the trees in town. This whole city is very haunted, including the house you used to live in. I've seen three ghosts there myself." Holy fuck! Chill with that shit, man. I had issues with paranoia, and anything paranormal fucked with me hard.

We got dinner with a mutual friend, Liz, and she kept telling me, "You're so skinny now!" which made me want to wrap my body in a dark blanket and hide away in my ghost-infested hotel. Both of them had to work in the morning, so they brought me back to my hotel, and I spent the night sexting with a woman I'd met on a dating app who lived in Trinidad and Tobago. We did a video session, taking turns beating off for one another, and after, I slept like a baby, despite the fact that I could hear furniture moving around in the next room all night.

I got up around eleven the next morning and stayed in bed texting a woman from Fortaleza, Brazil, until about noon. She wanted me to visit too, but Brazil was so far. I figured maybe I could hit Trinidad, then Brazil, but I'd need some serious cash.

I stretched, took a shower, then walked around town in the tropical heat. I walked by my old house and the Club Deportivo where I used to run and work out, then headed to my friend Mica's old place where we'd partied so many hazy nights. I headed to my ex's apartment, where I'd felt safer than probably anywhere else in my entire life—for a time, at least. I walked past the language school where I'd worked, Lengua, and the air-conditioned mall where I used to hang out to escape the heat, and then to the café where Pedro told me he'd read *Tropical Teaching*, which he said made him laugh out loud a few times. I drank two chai lattes at the café while reading *Zen and the Art of Motorcycle Maintenance*, which I'd started on a cool, rainy mountain night in Zambulla, then met up with Pedro and Liz for dinner. The dollar was stronger than usual compared to the peso, and Lila was already cheap as hell, even though the price of everything had quadrupled since 2006, so I bought their dinner: two steaks and a plate of grilled chicken with drinks and appetizers for about twenty-two bucks USD total. After, Liz had to go. Though she was in her thirties, she wasn't married, so she still lived at home and had a curfew. Pedro and I went to one of the new bars along the highway. The city's population had more than doubled in the last ten years, and there were so many new bars and restaurants and housing developments everywhere. It made me sad to see.

"So how much would one of these houses go for?" I asked Pedro as we sipped bottles of Pacifico and checked out the scenery.

"Depends. You can get a house in the country with land for about ten thousand US, but one of these new houses would be more like forty thousand."

"Damn, if I saved for a few years, I could buy a house down here. I'm dying up there, man. I feel stuck, you know?"

"Yeah, I get it."

"I hate my job, but I'm scared to leave. As bad as it is there, it's nowhere near as bad as the school where I worked in Miami. There's no way I'd be able to do that shit again."

Pedro laughed. "Yes, I know about all that. Your book was so funny—especially since I knew you already."

"Thanks, man. At least I'm able to write. At least I've got money coming in and health insurance and all that. Without money, I feel like the stress would push me back to drinking."

"It sounds like you've gotten comfortable with your misery. Very American."

"Yeah. If I could just get here, I'd be happy, but I also want to head to LA and give myself a chance at getting discovered. I've been really close a few times to getting scripts turned into films, and if I can just get an agent, maybe I could work remotely and only head up there every so often for meetings or auditions or whatever."

"That's a good idea. They have direct flights from Lila to LA, you know."

"Maybe this is where I'm supposed to be." I looked at the houses lit up in the distance. If I could make one of them mine, maybe I could finally break through the misery causing the tension in my muscles and mind. Maybe if I just spent a year or two relaxing in a place where I felt I wasn't wasting my time, I'd be able to put the OCD in remission for good. I didn't feel as if I needed the Frog anymore, other than to rant to him about my problems once every month or two.

Pedro rubbed his hands together and hovered them over my knee. Though he wasn't touching me, I could feel an intense warmth.

"What are you doing?" I said.

"Reiki. I am cleaning your energy."

"I don't believe in that crap."

"What do you feel right now?"

"Warm. Happy."

"Let me do a full-body cleansing. I can sense a large blockage in you and want to help you clear it."

"Nah, I'm good." I was terrified of anyone or anything upsetting my balance, no matter how miserable I felt, which is why I always refused the Frog when he told me to try medication.

"What do you have to lose?"

"My mind, man. My mind."

"I promise it will help."

"Let's talk about something else. I see they're developing houses near El Campo. You think they'll ever build over your town?"

"Yes, in time."

"What do you think about that?"

"Well, the people who live there have been there for many generations. Everyone is like a large family, but I think when the developers start offering people money, they'll take it, and soon we'll lose our family."

"That sucks."

"That's life. Always changing. You can't fear it."

We finished our beers and Pedro took me home. I sexted with the Brazilian woman before bed and heard someone moving furniture again in the neighboring room. The next day, I asked the guy at the desk if he could switch my room due to the noise at night, and he said I could take any room I wanted, because I was the only guest staying in that entire section of the hotel. That creeped me the fuck out.

I ate some huevos a la mexicana with a side of beans and guacamole, then walked around some more. I got lunch at the spot where I'd taken Mariposa on our first date, which had been a bar at the time but was now a restaurant. I sat at a table near where we had sat together all those years ago and tried to imagine how I'd felt being with her, but I couldn't. I decided to just let it go. Instead, I thought about the book I'd written about my time living there, *The Saga of the Scorpion,* and it seemed so much more alive than my memories. I headed back to the café and went through *The Saga of the Scorpion* in my mind, deciding what to add and remove. The book was huge, so I knew a lot would have to go. But what do you cut from memory, and why? Will you then lose it forever?

I got dinner with Pedro, Liz, and a few other friends, then Pedro and I went to a burlesque/rock 'n' roll show in the center. A rock band played as sexy young women and men put on a performance. One woman had a Facebook-like symbol taped to her ass, and kept sitting on guys' laps asking them to give her a like. After, a man and woman did a dance about sexual assault. Others dry-humped to the rhythm of the music.

I couldn't keep my eyes off one of the women, but whenever she disappeared again in the small, smoky room, I focused on the guy playing guitar. He was rocking this hollow-body Gretsch, which had such a warm, strong tone that I knew I'd have to get one. At the end of the performance I thought about asking the woman for her number, but I was tired of being a cliché, so I headed out with Pedro for a beer in the center. As we sat there drinking our beers, surrounded by attractive women, I kept focusing on the architecture that I'd never noticed before. When I'd lived there years ago, I was a drunken mess. Now, I wanted to know more about the history of the town. About its culture.

The next afternoon, I let Pedro perform the energy work on me. I lay face down on my hotel bed and closed my eyes. He stood above me, and even though he wasn't touching me, I could tell where his hands were. It felt as if my energy was flowing down through my legs and out of my feet, and when Pedro later told me he was pulling my energy through my feet, cleaning it, and returning it to my head, I became a believer. I felt groggy, almost hungover, which he'd said would happen. "You're going to feel worse, but by tonight you'll feel like a new person." It was true. That night, my muscles felt more tender than ever, and I thanked him for pushing me to do the session. Dude had a supreme gift, and I could see why he'd been seeing ghosts all over town. He was in tune. I wasn't.

The days passed quickly, and soon I was on a bus to Guadalajara and a plane to Soul City. Whenever I came back from Mexico, I replayed "Down by the Seaside" by Led Zeppelin for an hour or two until I was done unpacking. Years ago, I happened to have been listening to that tune when returning from Zambulla, and now it was a ritual. Before I died, I figured all these little moments would flash before me—if I even had time to think first. Someday, all these weird little experiences would make up my life. And it made me smile.

I finished writing my script about the friends reuniting, then started editing *The Saga of the Scorpion.* It was almost 180,000 words, so it was a huge job. I spent my two-week winter break lying in bed with my computer on my chest, editing for ten to twelve hours a day, but even after about 150 hours of work, I was nowhere near done. I knew it'd take a herculean effort to get that book into the world, but I was up for the challenge.

For the next few months, I spent every weekend editing, and when I finally finished in March, I'd cut out forty thousand words and rewritten several passages. I was also exhausted. Pretty much the moment I finished editing, I lost vision in my right eye. I figured I needed to get the blood pumping, so I did a half hour on the exercise bike and my vision came back, but the next day at work, as I was typing an email, I couldn't spell the word "can't." A student kept calling my name as I struggled to remember how to spell "can't" and suddenly I lost vision in my right eye again. I got dizzy and went to Salena.

"I-I can't see right now. I can't spell. I . . ."

"Do you think you're having a stroke?"

"I dunno. Maybe."

"I'll go tell Cody—"

"No, no, I'll be fine. Don't tell him shit."

"Okay, well, go get some air; I'll watch your group. But if you don't feel better soon, I'm calling an ambulance myself."

I went outside and took a walk, and in twenty minutes I felt better. During our free period, I told Salena about my OCD and how I'd had panic attacks my whole life, but every so often the panic would hit me in a way I'd never experienced, just to remind me it was in charge, and all this blindness shit was relatively new for me.

Though I figured I'd probably worn out my brain editing my novel, I went to the ER that night to make sure it wasn't a stroke. Doctor Radhika, who was so gorgeous I was having trouble speaking again, told me there was almost no chance I'd had a stroke, given my age and family's medical history.

Though I was okay, I couldn't stop contemplating my mortality—something about sitting in the ER at midnight will do that to you. I knew my obsessive drive to write wasn't healthy, but it was getting me results. It was so difficult for me to concentrate that I needed the obsession to block out the doubts and irrational fears and wandering useless thoughts and the sounds from neighbors, but that obsession was also feeding my disease and that disease was what made it so hard to concentrate in the first place. I was stuck in a cycle, but the only way to break free was to stop writing. To spend my weekends at the beach. To have brunch with friends. To head on road trips up the coast. To live, as the Frog would say. But the thought of all that made me ill. No, I was better off with the obsession. My only shot at immortality was through these stories, and if I had to sacrifice my health to tell them, then so be it. Every book was a kamikaze mission anyway; writers had no business worrying about their health.

When I finished editing *The Saga of the Scorpion*, it was almost as if a stone lid had been pried off my creativity, and out jumped two more books I'd had no idea were growing inside of me. One was the story of my character's childhood and the other was about a road trip he took after graduating from college, but I didn't know which one to start with. I figured it made the most sense to go with the childhood one, but I wanted to write the road trip so badly, I let it win. I did what the Frog would have advised, listening to my inner voice, and it kept telling me to take another road trip.

I outlined the book, *Shitty Summer*, and wrote it over three weekends while waiting for my editor to send back *The Saga of the Scorpion*. It was short but potent, and I felt it was my best work yet. I wanted to dive right into the heart of the insanity I'd felt after graduating from college—my OCD and depression and panic disorder at their worst. I'd experienced a few bouts of psychosis around that time, but after all this time working with the Frog, I now felt enough distance to tell this story. I knew there were kids out there who were so overwhelmed with their demons that they felt that drugs, alcohol, constant motion and suicide were their only options. Kids who'd done nothing to deserve their mental pain. Kids who were doing their best to feel okay. To fit in. But they couldn't, and for good reason, and I wanted to let those kids know they weren't dirty or broken or diseased. They deserved as much love, respect, and compassion as anyone else. The smartasses and ungrateful SOBs and punks and street kids were people too, and they often suffered so much because they had huge fucking hearts that they didn't know what to do with. They suffered so much because they had such creativity that it was hard for them to live in a soulless, unimaginative, corporate world. These kids were our artists and shamans and leaders and activists, but we beat them onto the streets and lonely highways and under the Sand Beach pier, telling them to stay in the shadows and eat from the trash and to stay away from our goddamned daughters!

But these heroes deserved their voice, and now I had the courage to speak with my own.

A few months back, my buddy Silas—the one I'd grown up playing basketball with—moved to Soul City, too. Like me, he wanted to be close to LA to make his music, but he wasn't ready yet to dive into the Jungle. "I've got some shit to sort out first," he said on the phone when he told me he was coming. I was nervous when he told me. Other friends had come to Soul City over the years, but they were easy to avoid. I hit 'em with, "Oh, yeah, sorry, I'm real busy with work and everything, but maybe next time you're in town?" and they'd head back to Colorado or Virginia or wherever else they'd moved to after leaving Buffalo, and we'd "like" each other's pictures on Facebook and talk about how we couldn't wait to get together again sometime soon.

But I knew I couldn't avoid Silas—not because he'd get mad or anything, but because he was probably the best friend I'd ever had. You can deny acquaintances, but you can't deny blood. I knew if he was coming here it was because our lives were aligning again, and I couldn't fight it, which meant that I was going to have to learn how to have friends again. I was going to have to learn how to invite people into my home again. I was going to have to learn how to socialize while having OCD without apologizing for my quirks or downplaying my suffering. Without letting people turn it into a joke. And as much as that scared the shit out of me, I knew that since meeting the Frog I'd been growing in a vacuum. Over these lonely, emotional years, I'd realized that friends were the benchmarks by which we measured our progress. I'd spent these last years mostly alone, and perhaps the person I'd become was no longer compatible with the world. Hell, with all the problems I'd been having at work, maybe I really *was* becoming a monster. There was no one around me saying, "Dude, I don't mean to give you shit, but you know that thing you did yesterday? That was pretty fucked up." No one around me breaking my balls if I said or did something pretentious or idiotic. So, I had no idea how far up my own ass I'd gone. It was just me and the Darkness and the Frog. But I hadn't been seeing the Frog as much lately, and I was feeling better. Maybe now was the time to let friends into my world again.

But the first few times Silas called, I let it go to voicemail, then I'd write him a text: "Sorry, man, busy with work and the writing and all that. But let's get together soon! I'll show you around town." Had I been lying to myself about the purpose of my writing? Was it an excuse to shut out the world? I'd spent pretty much every weekend over the last six years writing, only stopping to drink a smoothie about halfway through the day and for a piss break. It was almost as if I'd structured my entire life around it. On Monday, I did my grocery shopping, making sure to walk through the aisles the same way, buying all the same shit. On Tuesday, I left my laundry bag, detergent, and a stack of quarters by the door, so all I had to do was grab them and head down to the laundry room after work. I'd obsess over it all day, picturing one of my neighbors beating me to the washer just as I got home, then taking their sweet time moving their stuff to the dryer. The machines were usually free, but when they weren't, I'd panic. I knew the stress from Monday or Tuesday could very easily domino into Saturday and Sunday, and that could domino into the following weekend until I'd lost an entire month of writing because some cornhole left their clothes in the washer for a half hour. On Thursday and Friday, I'd make sure to use all of my preapproved movements, only bending over and turning in ways that I'd established were acceptable as a means to limit my stress, and if anyone asked me to do anything that might cause me to move in the wrong way, I'd say no even if it was a sweet older woman asking me to grab a can of soup for her off of the top shelf. I knew other people would see me as an asshole, but I was okay with being an asshole if it meant I could finish my stories. If it meant someday I might get recognition for my work and a paycheck big enough to leave Soul City and Cody Cares and my OCD forever. Someday, I'd finally get on top of it all, and if that meant not turning to the right on Wednesdays after 6 p.m. for the next twenty-seven months, then there was no way I was fucking turning right. The writing felt right, but maybe it wasn't. Look at all the years I'd pissed away shaking and shivering and hallucinating, and now I was doing it again with the writing. Living in obsessions. Rituals. Hallucinations. Memory. Fantasy.

So, when I finished my final edit of *Shitty Summer* and again found myself in the emergency room, I realized that maybe I had a problem—aside from the migraines the doctor said were causing the blind spots in my vision. He told me to get away from my computer, but getting away from my computer was impossible. I was still so tight and anxious and depressed, and the only way for me to live a better life was to write it. To create it. Without the writing, I was just another lonely, sad, broken man slowly approaching middle age with nothing other than two aching knees and a growing gut. Even with all I'd written, I still hadn't achieved success. But what *was* success? By now I knew I'd never see myself sitting at a table with Paul Newman and Gore Vidal at Vidal's Italian cliffside mansion. I'd never see myself in a picture like the one I saw of them where they looked so happy, powerful, and alive sitting above the Tyrrhenian Sea. The one where it seemed they'd never grow old, just stay young and vital and relevant forever. But their time had come and passed just as my time was passing now. By my age, the Beatles had already broken up. Dylan had already written *Blood on the Tracks*. Hendrix and Jim Morrison and Brian Jones and Kurt Cobain and Duane Allman and far too many fucking others had already lived a thousand lives and died. I was in my prime. Life was supposed to be sweet. This was the time I was supposed to look back on one day and see how young and healthy and successful I looked.

But all of my photos would be of myself sitting in food-stained sweatpants and torn T-shirts as I typed on a computer in a dark room with tin foil on the windows, which stayed shut even in the Southern California summer. What would it mean for *me* to be a success? Pictures of me on cliffs above the Mediterranean? Walking hand in hand with Raquel Welch? Smiling for once? Part of me was just glad that I had pieces of artwork out in the world that my heroes could read. Maybe Bob Dylan would find a copy of my book in some Malibu dumpster and read it and smile. Maybe Kris Kristofferson would download a copy from Amazon and read it on his Kindle while on tour. It was incredible to have had a piece of art in the world at the same time as David Bowie, and I wished that could be enough success for me, but I still had bills to pay.

I got dinner with Silas one Saturday night, and it was weird sitting at a table with another person. And not just any person, but the best friend I hadn't seen since high school. I felt awkward at first, but in only a few moments we were old friends again.

"Ho-dingies, how's Cali been treatin' ya?" he said.

"I still don't know whether the answer to that question is good or bad."

"I heard that. I had enough of the bullshit in Texas and decided that I needed to head to LA. I'm tired of standin' still, ya know?"

"As good as anyone."

I'd already explained to him what I was going through, but I filled him in on more of the details, and he said, "It's funny. I consider you to be my best friend, but I never saw any of that shit in you growing up. You seemed totally normal to me." When he said that, I realized I probably knew dozens of people who looked "totally normal" who'd gone on to become heroin addicts or crackheads or who were now in jail or had killed themselves or other people. All the people I'd thought were "normal" whose brains had drifted off to the moon and back during fifth-period Spanish with Señora Sanchez. I knew why so many people went a lifetime without being diagnosed for major depression or general anxiety or Asperger's or whatever the hell else. If the people closest to us can't see it—the people who are our mirrors—how can we see it in ourselves? If "illness" is so normal it fades into the background, what chance do any of us have at noticing it?

As good as it was seeing Silas, just sitting straight up in that seat and trying to carry on a basic conversation drained me so much, I knew I'd need at least a few months to recover. If I couldn't even carry on a two-hour dinner conversation with my best friend as a grown man who had been through six years of therapy, what chance could I have had when I was young and completely overwhelmed with anxiety? Sitting there, I realized that I'd developed a lot of the tension in my face and neck as a means to communicate without slurring my words or losing my train of thought. I realized that I licked and bit my lips during conversation because I felt that if I stopped moving, I'd completely shut down due to the depression and people would think I'd gone nuts. I touched my face and my head and tapped my feet and looked around the room a thousand times whenever anyone dropped a fork or coughed or to be sure no one was watching, and processing all of this information while trying to simply eat and talk was too fucking much.

I made several excuses and didn't see Silas again for a few months. But at least I was making progress.

One Friday night at Elena's Café, I sat in the back corner, and had read about thirty pages when the man sitting next to me at his computer waved over a woman who was just coming in.

"Tom?"

"Diane?"

"Oh my god, you look just like your pictures."

There were no worse people to sit beside than those meeting for the first time in real life after meeting online. I'd thought I'd found the perfect spot. Everyone around me was alone, reading or on computers. I never sat next to people who were alone and texting or sipping a drink. Their friends would soon show up, and they'd be Southern-California scream-talking and oh-my-god-ing at one another for hours. I moved tables, and when I sat at a new spot, Cecy, the barista, gave me a smile as if to say, "I totally get you, Jay." I smiled back and kept reading, but Tinder Tom was going on and on about, "Yeah, I fly my own plane. Bought it brand new, in cash, last year," so loudly, I wanted to walk over and tell him we didn't need to know how big his sack was because he'd flown "solo to Helena, Montana, baby."

I thought maybe tonight would be the night I asked out Cecy, but when I got in line to pay for my drinks, the other barista, Angely, had replaced her at the register. Over the last few weeks, I could have sworn Angely had been flirting with me, so I wasn't too surprised when she asked me out. I grabbed the piece of paper with her number on it, and mulled it over during dinner that night. Angely was also gorgeous, but I didn't feel as connected to her as I did to Cecy, so I wasn't quite sure what to do. If I went out with Angely, there was no chance Cecy would go out with me, but if I asked out Cecy, I'd lose Angely.

After thinking about it way too fucking much, and discussing it with the Frog, I decided to text Angely. I picked a restaurant a few miles from the beach that was cool and not too formal, and I was a bit relieved when a half hour had passed and she still hadn't shown up. I remembered my dinner with Silas; if talking with a good friend could drain so much of my energy, I knew it'd be worse to eat with a beautiful woman I hardly knew. She sent me a text: "Was with my mother and I'm running late. Be there soon."

But after an hour, I left. When I got to my car she texted me again. "I'm here, where are you?"

"I left already. Have a nice dinner!"

"Are you far away? Please come back!"

So, like a chump, I went back. And we had a pretty delightful conversation. She was smart as hell and studying molecular biology. She told me about the summer she'd spent in India, her teenage years acting and modeling in LA, and her plans to record an album. She was a singer and wrote her own songs, and as much as I wanted to fall in love with her, I couldn't shake the fact that she'd shown up over an hour late and hadn't even apologized. In fact, she was pissed at *me*. "I don't understand. Why would you leave?" she said for the fortieth time, when I dropped her off at home. We made plans to see a movie that weekend, even though the theater was sacred to me, but it didn't matter anyway, because she didn't respond to any of my texts, and then she quit Elena's a week or two later. One of the other baristas said Angely had moved back to India to be with a man she'd met online. Thus went dating in the modern world.

Chapter 39

A few weeks later, I found out Cecy was married but didn't wear her ring, which was something I felt I could relate to. One thing inside and another outside.

At work, I still kept the best parts of me to myself, and one day, while listening to Mr. Omaya speaking with Ms. Taluca about the camping trip he'd taken with his kids that weekend, I realized that part of why I felt such hatred and disgust for people was that I wasn't allowed to share my stories with others as freely as Mr. Omaya was, going on and on about fishing and rafting and all that crap. I couldn't tell them about *my* weekend without them giving me dirty looks or unsolicited advice or telling me, "You need Jesus!" But then I remembered that Mr. Omaya always had that heavy look of despair in his eyes. He got flustered quickly and seemed to have difficulty remembering names or numbers or whatever, and I figured maybe he was hiding the best parts of himself as well. Maybe he didn't even realize he was hiding those parts and all this crap about camping was just one big distraction from the chaos in his soul.

Even so—even if we all did suffer—if he remained unable to understand and accept whatever problems were eating away at his peace and happiness, then he'd never be able to acknowledge them and separate himself from them and discuss them over lunch. And then, if I started openly discussing *my* problems, it would likely only make him further aware of his own repressed problems and make *him* pissed off at *me*. What separated us was a willingness to accept and understand our suffering. Once we did that, we'd all have much better success at understanding and connecting with one another.

While listening to that conversation about camping, I realized there was still so much I didn't know about myself or about other people or the world, and I was so glad I hadn't yet made a scene at work, telling people off or pushing books off their desks or storming out and slamming the door. It seemed every time I had another breakthrough, no matter how small, I realized that anger wasn't the way to handle any situation. Sure, things might have been bad at Cody Cares, but at least I still had a job. At least I still had health insurance and a pension and a roof over my head, and every time I made another breakthrough, and better understood my own behavior, I could see how other people might misinterpret this behavior as a personal attack. I could see that people were blinded by their own biases and traumatic pasts and intellectual limitations, and I could better understand now why someone might think I was an asshole because I always picked up the phone on the third ring or because I only opened doors with my left hand. They didn't realize this shit was due to my own mental issues, and they performed mental gymnastics to somehow make it all about themselves. Some people, like Karla and Camarin and Barry and Salena, didn't judge and gave everyone the benefit of the doubt, which was why I'd felt safe to stutter through our conversations. Why I felt comfortable to grow around them. Was it too much for me to expect my other coworkers to afford me the same courtesy? I didn't think so, but regardless, I wanted to continue to learn how my behavior affected other people and how their behavior affected me, because the more I knew, the less power they would have over me. I wanted to find new ways to grow, even in such a harsh and toxic environment. Hell, maybe due to that toxicity, I'd learn lessons about myself I'd never be able to learn around people like Karla. And in order to survive in such an environment, I had to push through all of those moments when I felt like flipping over my desk and saying, "Fuck this, I'm out!" because once I cooled off, I usually had a better understanding of what had pissed me off, and I could control my emotions better the next time.

At home, I tried not to think about Cody Cares. I didn't want to let any of it in. To infect me. To infect my *real* work. It was already hard enough to write, but it'd be impossible if I started imagining what my coworkers would think of how I was "wasting a beautiful weekend to write such depraved, self-indulgent drivel." Looking over my shoulders and laughing and taking pictures so they could post them to social media and make fun of the fonts I used or the fact that I was even writing at all.

Inside, there was also the broken boy still needing repair. A broken boy who had no time or energy for writing or any task other than survival. The boy who put his ear to the wall and paced around a room if he heard a cupboard slam and kept all the windows closed and earplugs in his ears and fans blasting at high speed all year round. The boy who still checked the doors and stove and faucets and shower—only for half the time now as before. The boy who floated off to crazy world whenever he smelled weed. Who wanted to fight everyone who looked at him funny. Who screamed at slow drivers to "GET THE FUCK OUTTA THE LEFT LANE, YOU SIMPLE PIECE OF SHIT!" Who wouldn't let drivers merge in front of him or people join their friends in line ahead of him at Elena's or take an extra seat at his table at restaurants because they could see he was eating alone and, "Oh, you don't need this seat, right?" That boy was sick of people pushing him around. Of people taking everything, often without asking. Of people *expecting* his kindness and generosity. Anyone who simply expected him to say, "Yes, sure, please join me at my table. Sit right on my lap and scream in my ears. Of course you can do this, because I'm an American pushover dipshit. Come, take everything. Here's my wallet. My car keys. My asshole. Just please use lube first. Oh, no lube? Okay, just be gentle." That boy wasn't having any of it.

But after all of these years of fighting battles at work and home and within myself—after all these years of screaming, "YES!" when I meant yes, and, "FUCK OFF!" when I meant no—I felt that maybe I was strong enough to start letting people merge ahead of me. Maybe I didn't have to feel the entire city of Buffalo invading my boundaries whenever I passed a beggar on the street. Maybe I could just toss him some change without tossing him my balls and beliefs as well. Maybe I could just chill the fuck out and start being Johnny Sacrum at work and Jay Sakovsky at home and not worry the cops were gonna bust down my door and haul me away at any second because I hurried down the supermarket aisle and grabbed that last loaf of bread when I saw America's Grandmother reaching for it. I was getting better at socializing in appropriate ways, but there was still so much about people that baffled me. Why did they go crazy when they found out people in other countries ate dogs, yet they had no problem eating bacon double cheeseburgers? Why did they see themselves as trustworthy enough to lead a lost child through a supermarket, but if someone else did it, that person was probably a pervert? Why was it okay for some people to take a longer lunch with their husband, but when I took an extra minute, those same assholes would email the boss about it? It seemed people had their own sense of personal reason separate from valid reason, and I had no energy to decode and understand this, so I kept my distance. If I told America's Grandmother to fuck off, they'd destroy me, but when they stick her in a home and never visit, they're still saints.

I had separate spots in my closet for work and home clothes, and I hung a piece of cardboard between the two so they wouldn't touch. I never wore the work clothes when I went to the café or movies, and I never wore my home clothes at work. If I did, they'd be tainted. If I did, maybe I'd finally tell Ms. Donaldson and all the others what I thought of them. All of it, both home and work, was games. Bullshit. Politics. And I had to learn how to play. Having lived all those years with no other goal than to survive, it made me irate that things weren't orderly or logical.

But they'd never be logical no matter how much I tried to

control everything—no matter what rituals I performed or songs I sang to push the evil spirits away—so I had to find a way to thrive within the chaos. This was something I still wasn't sure how to do, but I knew if I ever wanted to be free of the tension imprisoning my thoughts and motion, I'd have to find a way. If I ever wanted to stand at a microphone onstage and sing or have the energy to make it through an audition, I'd have to let go of the anger and confusion. If I ever wanted to win a debate at work, I'd have to accept that it'd be with cookies and not with reason. The world will never not be chaos. But my brain can still feel peace.

And it found peace when I went back to Mexico that July. I found a round-trip flight from Tijuana to Mexico City for $127, so I took the train to the border, crossed, and a few hours later I was eating dinner in Roma, celebrating my friend Javier's birthday. Javier was a director making a good living shooting commercials and music videos, but his goal was to shoot a feature film he'd been writing for the last year. Our mutual friend, Paloma, who was an actor living in Coyoacán, joined us for dinner, and it was great discussing our respective projects and dreams. After, we went to a bar for drinks, and I had a beer, loosening me up to the night.

Paloma drove me back to my hotel in Condesa, and I put in my earplugs before getting out of the car. Even though I could hear some street noise in my room, I didn't panic. Instead, I turned on the TV and played the sound of water on my portable speaker. I'd asked for a room on the top floor, like always, but they gave me one underneath a rooftop weight room, which I knew could be a disaster. If someone so much as dropped a one-gram medicine ball, I wouldn't be able to sleep, but after seeing it was only open from 8 a.m. to 10 p.m., I knew I'd be safe during the night.

The next day, I met another director friend for lunch at a café in Condesa, and we went to the Anahuacalli and Soumaya Museums and got dinner in Polanco. I spent the next day walking all over the city, from Condesa back to Polanco, heading through Chapultepec

Park, doing my best to absorb the city's beauty, and in the process ruining my back and knees. I got dinner in Polanco with a woman I'd met online, and even though things had gotten hot and heavy while sexting one another, she seemed to feel as awkward as I did sitting together. We'd sent each other tons of nudes and had done a few webcam sessions and said we were going to rip each other's clothes off the second we saw one another, but after a pretty unremarkable dinner, we went our separate ways.

I went back to the hotel and jerked off on webcam for a twenty-eight-year-old artist in Copacabana. She'd sent me a video of herself in the bath while I was eating dinner with the other woman, and wrote, "Sua vez." She wanted me to visit her, but Brazil was too far. A woman in Caracas had also been asking me to visit, but I wasn't going anywhere near Venezuela until the political situation stabilized. Sometime over the last year, I'd found myself regularly sexting with women like this. I made sure they were actually who they said they were first, but then it was game on. There was something about women watching me that turned me on. Years back, Mariposa and I had fucked in public a few times, and I think she liked it as much as I did. I wasn't sure what it was about it that I liked, but I would have been cool with a thousand or more women watching any of those sessions as well. Due to my illness, I was fucking about once or twice a year. But I was cyber-fucking once or twice a week, and had hundreds of pictures and videos women had sent me. It was hard for me to be social. Hard to date. I didn't go to bars and clubs. I spent my free time writing. So it made sense to meet women online. I could speak with them during writing breaks or while I ate dinner alone at restaurants or as I sat in cafés. At first, I was careful not to send any pics that were too revealing, but after a few women had gotten angry with me for not reciprocating, I decided, eh, what the hell. And I liked it. And it just spiraled out of control. I started getting beaver and ass shots at all hours of the day. Tits while eating dinner in my apartment. Videos while grocery shopping. I was careful not to open any of these at work for obvious reasons. I figured this was modern dating and just rolled with it. I figured all of these women were talking to fifty guys at once just as I was doing with them, so why worry? Even though I knew that any of the pics I sent could someday show up online or something, I didn't care. Who hasn't seen a dick?

I'd created some rules to make sure shit didn't get too out of control. I never showed anyone the pics or videos women sent me, and I told the senders I'd delete them if they asked—and I followed through on this. I also waited until the woman requested pics from me before sending any, so I wasn't cold-cocking anyone.

But after dinner that night, seeing a real live person and not some picture or video, I realized that I needed to cut back on this. We'd seen too much of one another too soon, and I didn't think we'd be able to salvage our friendship. When I'd met Carolina online years ago, we'd never done any of that shit, and that was probably why our relationship had felt so safe and complex. But these shallow cyber-fucks were like fast food. Gobble it up and toss away the wrapper. No chance of STDs or kids. No chance of getting shot by a jealous husband. But very little chance of making any kind of meaningful connection. It was probably best to wait until after we'd fucked in person before sending any sexy pics or videos.

I decided that the session with the Brazilian woman that night would be my last. I needed to put more effort into living in the real world rather than the world of fantasy, so when Paloma texted me late that night asking if I wanted to go to Tepoztlán the next morning, I said sure, even though waking up early caused me to tense up and usually ruined my day.

On the drive down, I told Paloma about my sexting revelation, and she couldn't stop laughing at me. Once we cleared the city and hit the cool country roads, mountains and trees and green grass everywhere, I felt cleansed of all the shit I was leaving behind. When we arrived, Paloma tricked me into hiking up to Tepozteco Pyramid. I told her about all the aches and pains I got from simply standing, and she said, "Don't worry, it's only like a ten-minute walk, and it's not even that high up." An hour later, I was sweating my ass off as we hiked a steep mountain, still nowhere near the top. Paloma laughed at me every time I took a break.

When we got to the top, I was surprised my body had been able to carry me so far. I didn't think I would have been able to accomplish such a hike in Soul City.

Paloma took a few pics of us, and we went back down and got dinner with some of her friends. After, we went to a small bar that served craft beer. I didn't want to drink, but after the hike, I felt looser. I was tired of having so many rules and once I got that beer down, I did something I hadn't done in a while: have fun. Paloma always spoke to me in English, but when she heard me speaking to her friends in Spanish, she said, "Sacrum, you speak Spanish?"

"Yeah, I told you like a thousand times I lived in Lila."

"You are the most Mexican gringo I know."

"That's the greatest compliment anyone's ever given me."

While pissing, I realized how buzzed I was from that one pint, and hearing friends laughing and enjoying one another's company made me feel warm in a way I hadn't felt in a long time. I started jonesin' for a joint. Paloma told me I could stay with her that night in Tepoz, but as loose as I felt, I knew not to push things too far. If I did, my brain would make me pay for it.

Paloma walked me to the bus station and waited with me until the bus arrived. I kept watching the fit, sexy women doing aerobics on some shitty TV show playing on a set on the far wall, and I knew I'd need to get down to South America soon. Before I got too fat or bald or went completely crazy. While watching that show, I got an email from a producer who'd read my script *Hatesgiving* and wanted to make it into a TV series. And this wasn't just any old producer, but a guy whose films had made over a billion dollars over the last fifteen years. I'd met him through a mutual friend months back, and he requested a copy of the script. I showed Paloma the email, and she hugged me, citing "the magic of Tepoz."

When the bus arrived, I hugged her again and took my seat all the way in the back. I opened the shade and stared at the Mexican countryside as we headed back to one of the world's largest cities, and even though I was between here and there, I was overwhelmed with the feeling that if I could just stay in one of those small houses we passed, I could write stories I'd never be able to write in Soul City. For years, I'd been terrified to leave my job and apartment because I'd been able to write there, but on that trip through the Mexican countryside, I suddenly felt that I could write anywhere. That I didn't need to be chained to any specific place. That I already had everything I'd ever need with me on that bus. I hadn't spoken with the Frog in a while, but I knew he was there with me as well. I could feel his words guiding me along. I could feel the Knight's, too, and Camarin's and Karla's. I could also feel my mother's and Sister Adele's and Mariposa's. I didn't need to block out certain voices anymore. I didn't need to run from voices I thought might hurt me. I was strong enough now to listen to those voices and hear what they had to say, and tell them, "I understand your point, but that simply doesn't work for me, and here's why . . ." without fearing that they could ruin me. If I could make it here, in beautiful Tepoztlán, then I could make it in Buffalo or LA or anywhere.

When I got back to the city, I went to a French restaurant near my hotel and ate beef bourguignon while finishing *Always Running* by Luis Rodriguez. A Colombian woman sent me a few messages, but I ignored them to enjoy the cool Mexico City night. I took a stroll through the streets, seeing lovers walking together and kids playing soccer in the park, and none of the sounds bothered me—at least, not until I got closer to the hotel. About a block away, I put in my earplugs, then flipped on the TV when I got to my room and fell asleep. I was exhausted after being tricked into that hike, but I was glad for it. Years back, I would have been pissed at her, but now I was happy. Not everything was a threat. Not everything was a challenge. Some things were just a friendly kick in the ass. And that was what I got every time I went to Mexico.

Maybe it was time I gave myself a kick in the ass as well. I was tired of seeing all of the people around me making a living from acting and producing and writing and directing, while I struggled to work a job I hated. I knew I was as talented as most of them, and maybe now was the time to get away. Maybe now was the time to believe in myself again.

No, maybe now was the time to believe in myself for the first time.

Chapter 40

When I got back from Mexico, I set up a press to publish my own books. I filled out the tax forms and set up a DBA, and I chose a name that I could use to produce my films and music as well, Lila Arts. Getting that tax ID number and setting up my online vendor accounts made me feel as if I was entering a new life stage. There was no way I would have had the energy and focus to have done any of this before, and now, here I was, an American business owner with a Mexican business name. It was time I started living the American Dream. With all the legal work in place, there was no reason I couldn't make millions, then buy a house in the Mexican countryside. All that was stopping me was me.

Over the last year, I'd read six or seven books about self-publishing: how to format books, how to set up an ISBN and barcode, where to sell the books, how to create print copies. I also attended writers' groups in Soul City that focused on self-publishing, and I spent far too many hours researching the hell out of every last detail online, so when August 23rd arrived, the eleven-year anniversary of the day I moved to Lila all those lifetimes ago, I was set to publish *The Saga of the Scorpion*. The sales weren't quite as good as with *Tropical Teaching*, but I figured once my TV show took off, people would want to check out my other work. The books were loosely linked, with events and character names and backstories changed around, resembling the complexity of memory. When you've spent so much time with other people, it's hard to remember who said what and who did what. Where you end and they begin. And our stories blend together as people and events flow and fade into one another, especially in a country where most people—and especially young people—have such poorly defined boundaries and weakened armor.

I was almost done preparing *Shitty Summer* for publication as well, and even though I could have gotten it out in another month or so, I pushed the publication date to February 20th, Kurt Cobain's birthday.

As exciting as things were with my books, work was getting worse. The business that took over for the bar/grill didn't play music, but Mr. Purcell did, and even though I asked him, "Would you please mind using headphones? I'd be happy to buy you lunch!" he turned that shit into a power struggle. After the seventh or eighth time of him shouting across the room, "Betcha can't hear it now, huh?" while blasting the volume, I walked to the bathroom and had a panic attack.

I was in there for about fifteen minutes, trying to calm myself and regain feeling in my extremities, and even though I had a free period at the time, Purcell told Donaldson that he was concerned about how much time I'd been taking in the bathroom, and she called me into her office to discuss it.

"Mr. Sakovsky, I've been hearing complaints from the other teachers that you're not at your post when you're supposed to be. Can you tell me what's going on?" She'd started calling our desks "posts" after hearing Cody say this at a meeting one day. She also said shit like, "Books will be issued twenty-four October," rather than "October twenty-fourth," proving she was, indeed, the worst person on Earth.

"I'm not exactly sure what you're talking about. Can you be specific?"

"I keep hearing from coworkers that you spend a lot of time away from your post and that this is hurting student performance."

"Well, my students have consistently had some of the highest grades in the school for pretty much the last nine years, so I'm not exactly sure what you're talking about. I'm always at my desk except for approved breaks or meetings, and the only time I step away is to use the bathroom."

"I'm hearing that you're spending far too much time in the bathroom."

"Are people timing me?"

"You understand that your students suffer when you're not at your post?"

I felt like shouting, "Can we just call it a fucking desk, please?" but this was Corporate America, so we needed to hide behind the protective distraction of buzzwords. "Which is why I'm ALWAYS at my desk. I don't leave early, I arrive on time, I never leave during the day to go to lunch or anything. I'm always here when I'm supposed to be, and if I'm not at my desk, it means I'm in the bathroom or at a meeting."

"Are you sure you even want to be a teacher?"

"What's going on here? I don't understand what the problem is."

"The problem is that you're never at your post . . ."

It went on like that. I usually took a little more time in the bathroom than others because I often needed a few minutes to relax enough to let the stream flow. If people were laughing and talking or if I could hear footsteps approaching, I'd freeze up, but I didn't tell Donaldson that. I just did what I'd learned to do to survive Corporate America: smile, nod, and deny. Assure her I was doing everything, "according to Cody Cares standards." Even though Mr. Purcell often took an hour-long lunch, heading to the sushi place next door, and even though he often left a half-hour early each day due to, "all that damned traffic. Better get a jump on it," he was the hero, and I was the villain. Once or twice over the last year, I'd spent ten to twenty minutes in the bathroom breathing my way through panic, but, luckily, those had been during my free period as well. Other than that, I was Old Steady—always there. Always ready for action at my fucking *post*. We weren't arguing facts, Donaldson and I,

"When my mom was a little girl, someone backed their car into her as she was riding her bike down the sidewalk. A lawyer said she could get rich suing, and my mom spent that summer in a cast, but all she wanted was a new bike. That's who I am, too. I just want to go off to some corner somewhere in my cast and get through the summer."

"Jay, there's no honor in letting yourself suffer." She sounded a lot like the Frog. "Will you let me look into all of this for you?"

"What if I sue and win so much the school closes and you lose your job?"

"Then I'll look for another."

"I'd never do that to you or the kids."

"Which is why you deserve to fight for your rights. You're not a leech on the system. You're the reason why the system was created in the first place. You never ask for anything except a little respect. Don't you deserve it?"

I didn't answer.

"Then why are you staying there?" the Frog said, as we sat on a bench overlooking the ocean.

"What else am I gonna do?" I said.

"You said that producer bought your TV series."

"Yeah, but he just optioned it for, like, a buck. You don't make shit for options anymore. Nobody values screenwriters. If he gets the series made, then I get paid, but until then, I need a job. Fuck, as shitty as this job is, I've been able to survive here for so much longer than I ever expected. As shitty as it is, it's better than Miami. I could have never survived there. But this is about more than just a job. I'm fighting for my right to exist. If I stop going in there, then they win—then they're right. I *am* too weak for this, and how do I ever come back from that? If I go to another job and they're playing music there, how will I survive? It'll be the same shit. For all these years, I've shut down my mind and just gone left-after-right toward retirement. I've killed away today to make it to tomorrow. I can't live *right now*. If I just open my eyes and look around, I get so dizzy I'll fall over.

If I go lie on the beach and relax, a tidal wave of fear will sweep me out to sea. I can't relax—not yet at least. When the cash comes through for my TV series, I'll be good. I'll move to Mexico. I'll get a house up in the mountains and stock it with food and water and not have to come back down for another month. I'll just lock myself in and write and write and write, and barricade the doors and windows with my books and scripts. I'll learn how to produce my own music, and I'll create album after album. I'll find a way to write myself into existence, you know? I just have to hang in there a little longer. I just have to make it to the finish line."

"Wow, I wish I recorded all of that so I could play it back for you. So, your dream is to destroy your health so you can someday barricade yourself in a house far away from anyone else?"

"Well, I don't mean it like that."

"That's what you said."

"I guess it sounds a little nuts."

"Jay, I'm worried about you. I think you should try medication again."

"If I take that shit, I won't be able to write. I'm writing my way to freedom. I'll be okay someday."

"You might not make it to someday. The feeling of water dripping on your skin is a symptom of elevated stress. Your body can't take much more of this."

"I wasn't supposed to live past twenty-one anyway. I'm living on borrowed time. As long as I get these stories and songs out of me, I'm good to go tomorrow."

"Do yourself a favor, all right? Go have some fun. Go relax. Hang out with your friends. Smoke some weed. Get some exercise. Your life is passing, and it's never coming back."

"When I first started all of this, I knew I'd have to sacrifice my youth to succeed. To heal and achieve my dreams. But I feel like I still got too much youth left, ya know?"

"Yeah, I do, but you can't spend your whole life in your stories. Go forward."

"I am. When I get these books out of me, I'll be able to move on.

They feel like anchors on my soul. I've got two more to write: *Kirkland,* and one about my time here in Soul City. Hell, you're gonna be a character."

"I'll need an autographed copy."

"I'll dedicate it to you."

"Dedicate some time for yourself."

"I've been thinking—I don't know if I've ever known how to have fun. Maybe when I was a little kid, you know, running around and spending time with my brothers and sisters and friends and cousins. I don't think I've ever had fun since. When I got older, I got into drugs and alcohol and even at all those parties, I don't think I ever had *fun*— not like I did as a kid. I never wanted this. To grow up. I just wanted to be young forever. In a way, I'm trying to get back to childhood— someplace safer, though, safe and warm and happy. I wanna play again. Ride my bike, go to the beach, play basketball, wake up early on Christmas morning. I hate what I've become. I told myself I'd never let this happen to me—never become some corporate stooge—yet here I am, lying on the doctor's table as he tries to find a way to cut out the tumor of misery the job has caused me. I wanna go back to life before OCD. I thought I'd be done with it by now, but it's still with me. It's still destroying me. I've made a lot of progress, but it's still in control."

"Give yourself some credit. You've come a long way. Someday, when you're able to put it in your rearview, you'll be amazed at what you're able to accomplish."

"Yeah, but what do I do in the meantime?"

"Live."

"I'm trying to figure out how to do that."

"Don't try, just live."

As I limped home, to my cramped, dark, musty apartment, I realized I was currently feeding the disease that would someday kill me, and there was nothing I could do to stop it. The Frog was right. It was time to take a weekend off, no matter how much panic that would cause me.

That Friday night, rather than go to Elena's Café, I got dinner with Silas at an Argentine steakhouse downtown. We'd been going there once a month to eat empanadas and chimichurri and discuss building our empires. He was saving cash to put together a home recording studio. That night, I realized that even in my free time, I was hustling. Was that healthy? Did spending time with other hustlers constitute as "living?" Would I ever be happy to return home and sit on the couch and exist in the presence of those who loved me, without thinking of all the ways I should be out pursuing my dreams?

I decided to call my mother the next day. I hadn't spoken with her since her birthday ten months earlier, and I knew that wasn't okay. When I first started with the Frog, I'd needed distance. I'd needed to break away from her spell. I'd needed to be furious at her and curse her name. But now that I'd done all that, I realized I also had a responsibility to repair our relationship. That I'd also caused her a lot of pain. That if she hadn't been able to create the bond between us that I'd craved as a child, maybe now as an adult, *I* would have the power to forge it. That maybe I could be the stabilizing force in my family, helping them all begin their own paths toward healing. For years, I'd been terrified that if I spoke with them, I'd slide back down the trench into a place where I was drinking and fighting and furious again. Where I was closed off and dying and creatively blocked.

But as I spoke to her that afternoon, I felt strong enough to ask her how *she* was doing. To listen to her explain what it felt like to be a grandma, and as she spoke about her grandkids, her voice was filled with the kind of love she always had when she spoke about me and my brothers and sisters. My mom wasn't perfect, and she'd turned a blind eye to a lot of horrific shit, but she also loved me and would have done anything to help me if she'd known what that anything was. She told me that my dad missed me, too, and when she passed him the phone, he said, almost instinctively, "We always knew there was sumpin wrong with you, and if I could do it again, I'd take you to a neurologist to see what was going on. Maybe you got some wires crossed, I dunno. Have you tried cognitive behavior therapy or whatever it's called? I read that was good for OCD." This was the same man who used to beat the shit out of me when I cried at night if I didn't fall asleep by 10 p.m. Who'd scream all day and night as I locked myself in my room and felt the floorboards underneath me vibrating and loosening, ready to fall away. He'd never acknowledged any of this shit until now, and when he said that, I wanted to cry and run into his arms and let him save me—but still I knew better. I knew I couldn't trust him. I knew that the reason I felt so distant from them was that I could never get close to either of them. I could tell random women I'd met online, "Te amo, hermosa!" but saying "I love you" to either of them still felt impossible. I'd rather staple my ballsack to my thigh than say those words.

All I said to him was, "I think you got some wires crossed yourself, and it's not too late to uncross 'em," and then he passed the phone back to my mom, and I said goodbye.

When I hung up, I got anxious thinking of how to spend the day. Every part of me wanted to get back to finishing the script I'd been writing so that I could start on a high-concept comedy TV series I'd come up with, but I followed the Frog's orders, and after thinking it over in my apartment, I decided to head to the beach. But just walking through town and seeing all the mutants and surfers and skaters and bikers made me uncomfortable, so instead I went to Elena's Café. It was unusually quiet, so I was able to almost finish *Hollywood* by Charles Bukowski in one sitting. Then I went to the French restaurant half a mile up the street where I'd taken a Tinder date a year back, and I got the steak frites and continued to read. After, I saw a film, and when I told an older couple to stop talking, a few people around me whispered, "Thanks," which made me so irate, I actually said to them, far too loudly, "Don't thank me, boo yourselves. Don't leave it to someone else to fight for your owned damned rights." I went back to my seat, but the film was shot after that—probably for them as well—so I left. Plus, some dude a few rows ahead kept making so much noise digging into his popcorn bag, I couldn't take it. On the way out, I told the manager they should serve popcorn in cardboard boxes so we didn't "have to hear that horrible loud bag-crinkling sound every two minutes." Heading to my car, I realized I'd become a cranky old man, complaining to managers and leaving places because people were obnoxious. Maybe I *was* entitled like they called me at work, but was it really so bad to ask people to stop talking in a fucking movie theater?

The next day, I got back into my script. I couldn't handle any more "fun," and figured I'd try to relax again once I'd completed a few more projects. I did realize, however, that I usually had fun on vacation, and that my problem might be that I didn't know how to have fun in Soul City—or America, really. So, when I found a cheap round-trip ticket to Lila in March, I figured, let's have some fun!

Chapter 41

Even after my breaks in November and December, the tingling in my legs and water drops on my skin never went away, and I was having problems even standing for more than a few minutes. I think people could sense my weakness, because Donaldson called me into her office one day and said, "You're hurting the students by staying here. Please consider working elsewhere."

When I walked out of that meeting and sat at my fucking "post," I looked around the room at all the younger, more stylish, better-groomed teachers, smiling and singing the Cody Cares tune, and I felt old for the first time—as if the skin on my face was sagging off my skull. I could see the youth and ignorance in their eyes that I'd once had. It reminded me that I used to feel happy here. Safe, for a time. I used to sing happy birthday to Doreen and Barry and Karla, and Cody would join in. I used to get so overwhelmed with the problems my students faced that I could hardly relax on the weekends, worrying about them morning, noon, and night. Worrying if they were eating. Sleeping. Studying.

Now, all I could think about was survival. Getting through the day. Heading into traffic so I could ride bumpers and scream at drivers on my way back to my shitty apartment where I'd hole myself up until waking up the next morning to do it all again. I let all those years slip past me—something I'd once sworn I would never do. I'd kill myself before that happened, I used to say. Had I been lying to myself about this "healing" journey? Was it all an excuse? Was I too afraid to take a shot at my dreams? Had I constructed this mess intentionally?

Any day, that producer could email me saying, "Welcome to the big leagues, buddy! Netflix picked up the series!" But I couldn't wait around for that shit any longer. Maybe I'd stay in Lila when I went there in March. Maybe I needed to get back in touch with that young guy who once had a head full of dreams and passion. I needed to walk those streets and dream again. If I could combine my current psychological state and writing skills with that young guy's raw energy and curiosity, there'd be nothing I couldn't write.

But I still had two months until then. I thought about Salena's suggestion to hire a lawyer, so I searched for one. I spoke to a few and they both said they couldn't help me until I disclosed my disability to HR. They also told me to set up a meeting with the Equal Employment Opportunity Commission. I called the EEOC, and the guy said, "Yes, you do have a case for discrimination." I scheduled a meeting at the Soul City office, but it wasn't for another three months. I started documenting every meeting with Donaldson. Every negative interaction with coworkers. Every dirty look someone gave me, and the file grew rapidly. I printed old emails and would email Donaldson after disciplinary meetings, trying to get "a rundown of the points we discussed," so I could build my case against her.

I did my best to survive those three months, trusting that someone would finally help me. I did my best to write through it, and I was able to finish my new script and the outline for my next book, *Kirkland.* In February 2018, *Shitty Summer* had its book-birthday, and the reviews were mixed. Both *Kirkus Reviews* and Barnes & Noble recommended it, and it made the finals in a prestigious book award competition, but some of the readers weren't so impressed. Regardless, I knew it'd find its audience, so I didn't worry too much about it.

Soon, I was back in Lila. I stayed at an Airbnb spot, a huge house in the town center with a Jacuzzi, washer and dryer, and best

Sacrum or Jay Sakovsky, I know I can't wait around for someone to create my masterpiece for me, which is isolating and depressing in a way I've never felt depressed. It's an aching, existential depression—one I'm sure a lot of adults begin to feel as they approach middle age. Knowing that these youthful, ignorant dreams are gone and never coming back. These coping mechanisms we used to get through those worst of times are no longer with us, so all we have left are those worst of times, and it's entirely on us to fix that. Our heroes can't save us. No more escape. I need to find a way to bring the magic back to my life, or I'm just gonna end up a miserable old man. I don't know how to do that, but there has to be a way. There has to be a way of staying hopeful and youthful and joyful even as I'm being a responsible adult. Maybe if I had kids or something. I mean, I love kids, and working with them has been so great, but even that's changing. I used to see them as future actors and senators and CEOs, but now I see them as hairstylists and bus drivers and teachers. They used to stress me out so much, but now they don't bother me at all. Now, it's the adults that kill me—their lack of imagination and hope. They want to make everyone as miserable as they are. I gotta get away from that. They think I'm depressed because I can't handle the job, but really I'm depressed because I have to absorb their crap energy every day."

"There's plenty of magic still out there. Magic and dreaming aren't only for kids. Dreams can change throughout our lives, but as long as you keep dreaming, you won't lose the magic. Maybe you have that magic with you right now and don't even realize it. I mean, did you realize you had it when you were a kid?"

"No, I didn't realize it until I'd lost it."

"Maybe it's with you now and you don't even know it because you haven't lost it. You're right. If you want to create a masterpiece, you're going to have to do it yourself. And maybe all this work you've been putting into your writing, rolling up your sleeves, as you said, *is* that magic. You're already working at it. Don't lose it, Jay. Stay curious and dedicated and compassionate and open to change."

"Yeah, maybe you're right. I think I should try cognitive behavioral therapy. My dad was telling me about it and I did some research, and it seems it can help me put my OCD away for good."

"That's what we've been doing here."

"Really? According to the research I did, I need to expose myself to things that make me uncomfortable in order to overcome them."

"No, no, you need to face the emotional factors that caused your OCD in the first place."

"But isn't it a brain disorder?"

"Your OCD is from your abusive childhood."

"That's not what the book you gave me said."

"Jay, you lived a traumatic childhood, causing your symptoms."

"I-I thought you gave me that book for a reason?"

I left there feeling confused and overwhelmed with doubt and outrage. Had the Frog been selling me snake oil all this time? Was my *dad* right, and not the Frog? After all, look at how that shit went down with Camarin. I felt a rebellion rising within my psyche, attacking the truths I'd been standing on all these years. All that I know is wrong, man. All of this is shit.

After a few weeks, I calmed down and recognized that the Frog had been right about so much, but maybe he also had limitations. Maybe I couldn't get everything I needed from one person, and I had to have the confidence, courage, and wisdom to know which truths to take from him and which to take from the books I'd read and from the conversations I'd had with Ms. Kefana and my parents and all the other people I'd met in my life, even shitheads like Cody and the assholes at work, who'd said some smart and useful things over the years. If I had access to those universal truths inside of myself, I wouldn't have to panic. I wouldn't have to distrust everyone. I could have myself, and that would be enough.

A few months after disclosing my disability, Cody still hadn't done much to help. I'd asked to be switched to a spot far away from the bar/grill, but instead, he asked their manager to lower the music, which only lasted about two minutes. I emailed Cody about it, but he didn't respond for two weeks. He wrote, "No one else is complaining about the music," and I responded, "While I'm glad to hear that my coworkers are able to tune out the extremely loud music that plays nearly all day every day, unfortunately, due to my OCD, which is protected by the Americans with Disabilities Act, I'm not one of these people. Can I please speak with the manager to discuss setting the music at a more appropriate volume for the classroom? As I've previously mentioned, several students have also complained about the noise, one even asking if there was an earthquake, and I assured him that no, that's just the bass from the music next door. Thanks!"

It took him another week to respond, but it was another "we'll look into it," or some other bullshit. Meanwhile, the stress from all of this had been wearing me down so thin, I was starting to feel the tingling in my legs again, and Cody's "no one else hears it" crap only made matters worse. A few days after that email, I had such a bad panic attack, I almost passed out, and even though I was normally able to still do my job during a period of elevated anxiety, I had to run to the bathroom and breathe my way through this one.

Just relax, man. Just write and publish one more book while you've still got this job, then you can start the next part of your journey. Get this last anchor out of you, and you'll be free. You can probably finish it by December, then slip on down to LA or Mexico or wherever else that voice inside of you wants you to go. But for now, just breathe.

The day of the panic attack, I went home and spent the night in bed, focusing on my breathing and letting the anxiety crash over me and recede like an ocean wave. My body was so tight and flooded with stress, I could hardly relax. How much more of this could I take? Yeah, I'd survived a childhood with infinitely more stress, but I was a kid then. How many more decades of constant stress could my adult body handle before giving up on me completely? How much more worry could my brain tolerate before wearing out?

Eventually, I got up, and even though I hadn't planned on doing my laundry, that was why it was the best time to do it. I brought my bag to the laundry room and saw that someone was using the washer, but the cycle was almost done. I left my bag and put quarters in the machine to reserve my spot. I relaxed knowing that Mel hadn't been doing his laundry at our building for years, and most people moved their stuff from the washer to the dryer pretty quickly.

But when I went back fifteen minutes later, my quarters were gone, and someone had put a new load in the machine. I opened the lid, intending to take the clothes out and put mine in, and almost immediately, I heard a voice from one of the apartments. "Oh, are, uh, these yours?" An older woman wearing a flowing nightgown walked to the laundry room.

"You took my turn," I said.

"What do you mean?"

"I mean, my bag and detergent are right here, and you stole the quarters out of the machine."

"I needed to do another load." She handed the coins over.

"So, you just skip someone in line?"

"You're a nas-nasty little JERK!" She started crying.

"And you're a fucking thief! So you see money that isn't yours and you just take it? Should I call the cops?"

"I HAD A BAD DAY! I DON'T NEED THIS!"

"So did I, but I'm not the one skipping you in line and stealing your money."

"OH, YOU'RE EVIL! YOU'RE THE DEVIL! BEGONE, SATAN!"

She slammed the lid on the machine, not even looking at me as she backed out of there mumbling to herself, "Begone, Satan. Oh, begone, begone, begone . . ."

Maybe she truly was crazy, so I let her have the machine. A few neighbors were watching, and I was relieved when one said, "Damn, that woman's nuts" instead of "damn, you're evil, Jay!"

I was so pissed, I called the building's owner, and she blew me off as I'd figured she would. But the real reason I called her was to let her know what really happened in case that crazy woman said

I'd done something "EVIL!" to her in the laundry room. The owner always told me to contact the manager on site, but that dude was as big a prick as they came, and I'd stopped talking to him. Over the last few months, whenever I passed by the kitchen vent for the unit below me, I would catch a whiff of cigarettes. It was a non-smoking building, and when I let the manager know about it, he said, "No one's smoking!" Weeks later, after I texted him again, he wrote, "She has a dirty vent, NOT CIGARETTES!" I wrote back, "Well, I doubt a dirty vent smells like cigarettes. Nothing smells like cigarettes but cigs." He didn't like that and had been giving me dirty looks for weeks; then one Saturday, as I was writing in my bedroom with the door closed, he burst inside screaming, "IT'S AN EMERGENCY! I NEED TO SEE YOUR WALL!" So I let him do his thing and he found a small water leak in a neighbor's bathroom pipe, which had been dripping into the apartment below. Apparently, the leak had been going on for weeks, but my dipshit manager couldn't be bothered to call me before barging in. I told him, "What if I was doing anal play with a bunch of friends I'd picked up off the beach?" and he signed the cross and left. I called the owner about it, and she didn't care, so I installed a chain lock on my door.

Then, one day, I saw that the woman below me was moving out, and I when I passed by to take out my trash, her apartment walls were yellow with cigarette stains. I practically ran to my manger's unit and shouted through the screen door, "Look! Look at her right now! She's smoking. You said she doesn't smoke!"

He didn't even get out of his recliner—just shouted, "I TOLD YOU SHE SMOKES! SHE SMOKES, ALL RIGHT! SHE SMOKES! AND SHE'S MOVING OUT, SO WHAT'S THE PROBLEM!"

"Holy shit, you people are all fucking nuts!" I brought my trash to the dumpster, and the old lady followed me, yelling, "THEY'RE NOT GONNA MAKE A STRAITJACKET BIG ENOUGH FOR YOU!"

I'd been breathing in secondhand smoke for all these years in my own fucking home—the place I'd thought was safe. Where I allowed myself to feel vulnerable and weak. Where I'd undergone this healing journey, and all the while this asshole had been filling it with carcinogens, as I put up my Christmas tree and watched *Ben Hur* for the first time and made love to Nima and wrote my first screenplay.

I felt violated and walked right up to her and said, "OH YEAH? WELL, THEY'RE NOT GONNA MAKE AN IRON LUNG WIDE ENOUGH FOR YOUR FAT ASS! I HOPE YOU DIE A SLOW, PAINFUL DEATH, YOU MISERABLE OLD BITCH!"

One of my neighbors said, "Damn, you roasted her ass!" and he and his boyfriend cracked up as they headed to their car. The younger people in that complex were usually pretty normal and cool, but the older people like Tighty-Whitey Mel and the Quarter-Thief and the Smoke Queen were mostly all nuts. Maybe this was what happened to people who stayed on the beach too long.

"GET OUT OF MY HOUSE! GET OUT OF MY HOUSE, OR I'LL CALL THE COPS!" She went back inside and closed the screen door.

"I'm not in your house, psycho! I'm standing in the common area."

"I'M GONNA CALL THE COPS!"

One of her sons approached me with this resigned look in his eye. "Just leave it alone, man."

So I did, but not before walking back to her screen door to say, "Will you at least tell me what brand I've been smoking for all these years? Am I a Marlboro man? Winston? Naw, too classy." I turned to her son. "What's the brand that crusty old dock-wenches smoke? Virginia Slims, right?"

"Watch it, buddy."

"Fuck you and your whole fucked-up family."

I went back upstairs, and even though I'd been working on an outline for my new book, I put it aside to check for a new place to live. I couldn't keep staying in these toxic situations. Luckily, I found a small house that had just been listed an hour earlier. I called the landlord and drove over. The house was at the end of a cul-de-sac beside Soul City's busiest highway, but to me that was a selling point. The cars and trucks whizzing by were like white noise, and I figured if I kept the doors and windows closed and ran air purifiers in each room, it should be a step up from secondhand smoking every day. The place had been built at the turn of the century and had exterior studs and wood-panel walls and looked like the kind of house Woody Guthrie might have grown up in. With the noise from the highway, I could play my guitar as loud as I wanted to without disturbing the neighbors, who were in a punk band. The other neighbor was a painter, and the landlord was the drummer in a local jam band. His wife was a former guide for Kenyan safaris. They were all cool as hell, and the spot was month-to-month and had a basement where I could record music and audiobooks, so I applied without thinking too much about it.

A few days later, they said the place was mine, and even though I wanted to save money before moving away from Soul City, I knew I needed to stop waiting for "the perfect time," so I handed over a fifteen-hundred-dollar security deposit and first month's rent, and they handed over the keys. I'd already paid for my other place, and even though there were a few weeks left in August, I didn't care. The new spot had its own washer and dryer, and fuck that smoky old shithole. I thought about asking Silas to help me move, but he'd dropped a keg on his foot at work, busting his toe up pretty bad, so I hired a cheap moving crew. I'd always prided myself on not buying too much shit for my apartment, but when I saw how many boxes we hauled out of there, I was amazed at how much I'd accumulated over the years. It was mostly books and DVDs, but I also had a lot of notebooks and loose paper, napkins, and whatever else I'd written on, along with papers that seemed important: tax documents and work contracts and all that.

By late afternoon, I was settled into my new place. I put my bed in the living room so I could make the bedroom my office, and I put up my tapestries and posters. I unpacked as much as I could, then put the rest of my crap in the basement. That first night, I went to bed without checking the windows or doors. The front and rear entrances had security doors, so I felt much safer, and the landlord, Gary, had put security locks on all the windows. Also, having him in the house nearby made me feel safe in a way I hadn't in ages. I kind of felt as if I was part of a weird little family on that cul-de-sac and knew that a lot of my anxiety and tightness were the result of being so isolated for so long. I needed to be around people I loved. I slept well that night, despite the ongoing highway noise, and I didn't even realize I hadn't worn my earplugs at all that day until I'd almost fallen asleep. I tried to sleep without them, but once I'd realized they weren't in, I couldn't do it.

I felt energized at work that Monday. I was usually a zombie the first few periods, but I joked around with the kids that morning. I was excited about my new place. Excited to do laundry in my own machine. Switching things up shifted my thoughts and emotions. For so long, I'd been terrified of moving, fearing I'd lose my mind if I left my apartment, but I felt great, which made me believe I could free myself of other self-imposed limitations as well. Also, I'd wanted to stay in the old place and fight my manager and landlord, beating them down with logic until they apologized and recognized what shitheads they were, but now I saw what a waste of energy that was. There was no sense addressing ignorant people with logic; they'd never know when they were beat. It was time to stop trying to control everything and right every wrong and make sense of every last detail, and simply take a step in a better direction. I knew I'd feel the same when I quit Cody Cares. I kept dreaming about putting in my two weeks' notice, but even with this cool new house and my endgame clearly in sight, I didn't know if I'd make it until December. The music from the new bar/grill was killing me, and the fact that Cody and Donaldson weren't helping even after I'd disclosed my disability made me realize how hopeless that situation was. They didn't know I was planning to leave—no one did, except for Salena, whom I told pretty much everything—and it depressed the hell outta me to think that they'd do this to someone who'd been there since the very beginning. If I actually cared to make this my career, I'd never last until retirement. The Man would win this fight.

But there were bigger and better things coming for me. The producer who wanted to create my TV series said one of the biggest actors in TV history had signed on, which would make it a lot easier to put the whole thing together. "He's thrilled as hell to get started," he said. "Welcome to Hollywood, Johnny." As much as I wanted to let down my guard and believe I'd "made it," like he said, I knew there were no guarantees, and I wouldn't relax until the money was in my bank account and a lawyer confirmed no one could take it back.

On a Friday night in late August, I went to a party at Diosa's in the Hollywood Hills and people congratulated me on my career. Several producers and an actor on a new HBO series spoke with me about projects they wanted me to write for them.

Diosa had a cool place with a huge patio on a hill above a curved street. They drank champagne and I drank tea, and I sat beside an actor and model from Egypt, and even though she was one of the most beautiful women I'd ever seen, she kept touching my arm and laughing at all of my jokes, and I was calm, cool, and controlled, realizing for the first time that I truly belonged here. Realizing how much I loved the Hollywood Hills. Realizing that soon I'd never think about Cody Cares or my old building manager or all my miserable coworkers and neighbors again. Realizing I'd someday have a house here, and maybe another in Mexico, and another in Spain. Realizing how glad I was that I hadn't immediately told these producers, "Uh, well, ya know, I'm working on a book right now, but I'll be free in a few months," as I'd told some in Zambulla and other festivals. Realizing it was okay to be successful. Realizing I needed to stop expecting Doug to pop out from behind a wall or to hop out of a tree and point at me and laugh, reminding me that I didn't belong here.

I gave a few people copies of my books, then walked to my Airbnb spot three blocks from Diosa's place, and I spent the night listening to Led Zeppelin and reading Kim Gordon's autobiography, *Girl in a Band*. Diosa had said I could sleep in her spare bedroom.

She knew about my OCD and the noise machine I ran at night and the earplugs and everything, but even so, I didn't want to be seen like that—especially not here. Here, in the Hollywood Hills, I wanted to be Johnny Sacrum, strong and confident.

The next day, Diosa and I got brunch at the Beachwood Café and discussed my script she was planning to direct. She told me her plan to get the money for it and let me know "it's going to happen, Johnny. Stop worrying and let yourself believe." After, we walked through the Hollywood Hills and stopped when we came to an open house at a mansion.

"What if they ask who we are?" I said.

"Then tell them you're Johnny Sacrum, and I'm Diosa. They don't have to know anything more than that. Don't pretend. *Be* successful. When they see that, they won't ask any questions. They'll just see that you're finally home."

We went inside, and I got lost staring at the Hollywood sign through the office window, imagining myself sitting there and writing scripts and books and songs that millions of people would love. I imagined the huge bedroom downstairs filled with musical instruments and recording equipment. I imagined the pool in back surrounded by family and friends, old and new. I imagined Silas laughing with Harvey Keitel, and Diosa talking with Salma Hayek as my dad walked around telling bad jokes and my nephews splashed in the water. As my mom told me how proud she was of me. Being here and feeling confident made me feel safe enough to go back to Buffalo—safe enough to walk into that house and let the door close behind me, and feel the love and warmth, and not the fear and anger.

Afterward, we drove to Malibu, and Diosa cleansed my chakras as the sun set, and as she finished, I couldn't help but laugh.

"What?" she said.

"If I told my uncles that I just had my energy cleansed on a beach in Malibu, they'd never let me hear the end of it."

"You've come a long way, Johnny."

"Yeah, I know. But as far as I've come, I'll always be Little Jay from North Buffalo, and that's okay with me."

She smiled. "Over the years I've known you, your energy has changed considerably, and I think you're ready now for what's coming. It seems that safety is very important to you, but you can feel safe here now. There are a lot of people here who love you. Let them love you."

"I love you too."

She smiled and hugged me. Everyone always said such horrible things about LA—Hollywood especially—but the people I knew here were some of the warmest I'd ever met. Diosa radiated positive energy, and I trusted her as much as I trusted Silas or my brothers. I knew there were plenty of sharks here, too, but if I built a community of love around me, it'd protect me from the worst of them. We watched the sunset, then drove through the mountains and back to Hollywood. I dropped off Diosa and then headed back to Soul City. Every time I went back there, whether from Mexico or LA or wherever, it always felt as if I was returning to a cave. Soon, I'd leave Soul City forever and never return. Soul City had served its purpose for me. It had propped me up when I couldn't stand and it had given me shape. Now, it was time for me to walk out into the world for the first time on my own legs—with no fear or alcohol or drugs to keep me upright. Now, I'd enter the world with arms open wide, absorbing everything dark and light around me, not judging, just letting it flow through me, learning what I could and moving forward, always forward.

Chapter 43

I had a great time at the Zambulla Film Fest that year. One of my friends rented a house on a hill, and we hung out there, playing piano and having a cookout. A few friends had recently gotten their big breaks as well: A screenwriter had a film coming out starring a few A-list actors, and a director had signed on to direct a film for a Hollywood studio. Others had projects going in New York and Mexico City, and the mood was relaxed and energized and aligned.

When I got back to Soul City, I worked on my new book, which still didn't have a title, and I was making great progress. Since moving to this new house, I was far more relaxed, and as a result, I was getting more work done. I'd take breaks to hang out in the yard and drink a smoothie while looking at the garden Gary had planted before I'd moved in, or I'd put a load of laundry in the machine and let it sit there for a few hours if I got in the groove, or I'd run to the Vons down the street and get spinach or bananas. Then, I'd pick up where I left off. Since moving in, I hadn't played the sound of water on my headphones, and after a few weeks, I stopped wearing earplugs at home, even when I went outside. I sat on the back porch a few nights and watched the sun set over the canyon behind my place. The window near my office desk overlooked this canyon, and every so often I'd look away from the computer and watch the squirrels running through the garden and the trees swaying in the breeze. At first, I couldn't stop smiling at those trees. For years, all I'd seen were my apartment walls and the tin foil covering my windows.

Now I had nature and freedom. I could walk outside without being surrounded by assholes. I could park my car right by my front door, which made me less concerned about checking the doors and windows. Instead of the sound of water, I played Neil Young and the Psychedelic Furs and Jake Bugg, filling my house with music for the first time since I'd moved to California. I still didn't listen to music in the car, but at least I could do it at home.

For the first few weeks, I had a hard time sleeping through the night. I'd wake up, terrified that I'd fallen asleep on a park bench or on the beach or something, but I'd relax once I remembered where I was. A few times, I had nightmares that I'd left the front door open and someone was inside, and I was so frozen with fear I couldn't move, but the dream-intruders never hurt me.

But after a few weeks, the nightmares went away, and I was waking up at eight forty on workdays, just like always. The new place was in a great neighborhood, and I walked to cafés and bars and once even ordered a beer as I read a book. Salena and I met for drinks one night, and she introduced me to her boyfriend, and to a bunch of her friends, and I spoke with them and danced as the band played, and even when the place filled with weed smoke, I stayed and sipped my beer and went home buzzed and happy at the end of the night. I imagined having friends over for a barbeque and I even bought an outdoor Foreman grill, and turned Sunday into steak and corn on the cob night.

Gary would stop by every so often, and we'd talk about music or Mexico or whatever. He invited me to jam with his band a few times, but I told him I wanted to finish my book first. I found myself playing my guitar daily, whereas at the old place, I'd only played once every few weeks. I started jumping rope in the backyard and doing pull-ups on a pull-up bar in the kitchen and I got a yoga mat and did sit-ups and pushups and slowly started to burn away the fat and grow back some muscle. I wished I'd moved sooner, which only made me more confident in my decision to get away from Cody Cares and to begin my next life adventure. I still wasn't sure what I would do when I quit, but I knew something would come to me. I needed a lot of money to survive in LA, but maybe I could do something else until I got my first paycheck for a script.

I kept writing, and even though I hoped the book would be short, it became the longest thing I'd ever written, and when I finished it, I drank a beer and got some Mexican food and watched *Shameless* and relaxed.

Though the writing was going well, spending so much time at my computer wore out my eyes, and I started getting migraines, which were worsened by the bar/grill's music at work. I didn't think I'd make it to December, but when December came, I knew nothing could stop me. At work, I'd hit the point of I-just-can't-go-on so many times over the last ten years and knew that if I could push past this period of fear and doubt, I could hit that finish line, no problem.

In early December, a big film producer from Mexico City hired me to write coverage on a dramedy script. A week or so after submitting my notes, he told me he'd been looking for someone to rewrite the script and that he was just testing me and "You passed, man. Oh, you passed." I had my lawyer review the agreement he sent me, and after some back and forth, I had no doubts letting HR know that I'd be done with Cody Cares as of winter break. Turning in that resignation letter felt so good, I did a little dance on the walk back to my fucking *post*. Salena smiled, and I spent the rest of the day cracking jokes with her and the kids, remembering what it used to feel like in the golden days of Cody Cares. I knew I'd long passed my expiration date at that job, and the longer I stayed there, the more damage I'd do to my health and reputation, and I knew I'd need to be more aware of any other expiration dates in the future.

That Friday, I got out of work early, so I went to see the Frog before heading over to Elena's Café. A few months back, I'd noticed that the Frog was no longer a frog, but a kind-looking older man, and even though I'd only ever seen him as a frog, I knew exactly who he was immediately, and it didn't even hit me until that night that he'd been a man all along.

"Wow, you're a machine," he said.

"Well, I haven't started editing yet, so that's still another solid two months of work," I said.

"I was talking about this new script for the Mexican producer, but I'm proud of you for the book as well. In the past, there's no way you would have decided to move on before finishing a project."

"I know I can write anywhere now, and I've proven that by how much I've completed at this new house."

"Moving there was one of the best decisions you've made in years. I know you wanted to stay in the other spot because it would have saved money, but this was the right thing to do."

"Yeah, it was. But I've decided to move again—this time to Mexico City. I was gonna use my security deposit and last paycheck to buy a small house in Lila, but I'm tired of playing it safe. I need to dive into Mexico City headfirst and stop worrying about ending up on the streets."

"Hey, now that's some great news! I always saw you ending up in Mexico."

"Yeah, but first I'm gonna move back to Buffalo."

"Oh yeah?"

"Yep." I tensed up, fearful of how he was going to respond. "I told Cody I'd quit if he extended my benefits a few months after leaving, and he agreed. I know it killed him, but at least he agreed. I'm g-gonna move back in with my parents and give them a chance to take care of me while I go through, uh, cognitive behavioral therapy."

"Oh . . ." He had this look in his eye as if I'd just broken up with him.

"It's just that, I found a great doctor there, and I think if I spend a few intensive months working on my OCD without having to worry about teaching, I can put it in remission before moving on to the next part of my life."

"Well, I don't know what to tell you. We've made such progress here."

"Yeah, but I'm still checking doors and moving away from people when they play music or videos on their phones at cafés or wherever—people really need to learn some fucking etiquette with those damned phones—and I wanna be done with all that. I'm sorry."

"There's nothing to apologize for. Go live your life."

"My dad emailed me a few weeks ago, apologizing for being a monster when I was little. Apologized for hitting me and screaming and ignoring my mental health issues. He said he never felt good enough for us, which is why he always yelled. I wanna give him a chance to do the right thing now. It'll be good for both of us. My mom, too. Relive my childhood a little while I have the armor of adulthood wrapped around me."

"Iron John—or should I say, Iron Johnny Sacrum?"

"I guess that makes you the Wild Man, huh? What *is* your name, by the way? I know nothing about you, and I'm ashamed for never asking."

"It's not important. The only thing that's important is that we found *your* name. Maybe someday, you'll help some other person find their name as well."

"That's the goal. You know, I think this new book's gonna be my last for a while. For all these years, I've been writing myself into existence, but now I just want to exist, catch me?"

"I do."

"I feel like this book has been an anchor inside of me for so long, and once I get it out, I'll be able to finally let go of the rest of the fear and doubt and anger and shame. I think I've been holding onto all of that so tightly because it's been a great teacher and guide and I've kept it close so I could share the secrets I've learned with others, and through this book, I'll be able to do that and won't need to hold on to any of that other stuff anymore. I can just go to the beach and lie in the sun and not have to contemplate my existence and take notes and create characters and all that. I'll just lie there, feeling warm."

"I hope I get a copy of this book."

"I dedicated it to you, Wild Man."

"You're gonna make me cry."

"Shit, you've made me cry so many times, it's time I returned the favor."

He laughed. "I've seen thousands of patients over the years, but I've always felt a strong connection to you. I wish you the best of luck with whatever comes next."

"Thanks. You, too. You know, I've imagined this moment since our first session, but it isn't how I'd pictured. I imagined myself being completely free of the tension in my muscles and free of the OCD, and I'd have a specific plan in place—a safety net below me as I jumped from one moment in my life to the next—but it's not like that. Change doesn't happen cleanly sometimes, and I'm tired of planning out every meticulous detail before making a move. I just gotta go and trust the Great River will be there to catch me should I fall."

"Now you're talking like a man with vision."

"You should come down to Mexico and visit sometime. Bring the Knight."

"He asks about you sometimes."

"Give him copies of my books for me, will ya?"

"Sure."

"Anyway, thanks for everything. I don't know what would have happened to me if I never stopped in your cave that day. I was in bad shape, and I might not still be here, or maybe I'd be on the streets or in prison."

"It's been my pleasure."

"I can't help but think of how many of these kids out here on the streets are simply overwhelmed by the beauty, power, and potential of their thoughts."

"Probably most of 'em."

"How do you save 'em all?"

"You don't."

I took a deep breath and nodded gently. "So, why a frog?"

"Well, you're a story guy, and I could see that you needed a fairy tale to ease you into reality."

I laughed. "Yeah, yeah, I guess so. Thanks."

"Right back atcha, kiddo."

We hugged and I walked away, never looking back. I was done with the beach and with the cave and with worrying I'd end up living under the pier and with asking the wrong people to love me and to help me with my problems. Done with going to the dentist if I hurt my foot. Done coming up with a million excuses not to go directly to the podiatrist to fix the real problem so I could get back on my feet again quickly. Done prolonging the pain so I could use it as an excuse to push everyone away and wallow in misery.

When I got to Elena's Café, I pulled out *A Little Life* by Hanya Yanagihara and read about thirty pages before a young couple meeting for the first time in person sat down next to me. "Oh my god, you're even prettier than in your pictures, LOLOLOL!" I put the book away, and sipped my chai latte. I was glad the book had held my attention after all those pages. My new one, which I decided to call *The Wild Men*, was about a hundred thousand words shorter than *A Little Life*, but it was still long as hell, and I wanted to see how Yanagihara was able to keep readers engaged. Sometimes, a longer length made a story more powerful, but other times, it caused it to collapse under its own weight.

I wished Cecy the barista would magically appear so I could tell her goodbye. For all those years, we'd spoken about quitting our jobs and moving on, and she had done it before I could. I hoped she was happy, wherever she was, and I hoped she felt safe to wear her wedding ring again.

That night, Elena was making the drinks, which I'd never seen her do, but there was no one else there. She'd chased so many great baristas out that door, I was surprised any new ones even applied, but maybe she would finally learn from her mistakes after finding herself alone.

Probably not.

My last day at work, my coworkers gave me a card and bought me lunch, but they didn't eat with me. Maybe they realized that leaving me alone was the best gift they could give me. Some of the kids gave me gifts, and a few told me I was the best teacher they'd ever had, but I knew they would probably forget about me in a few weeks, if not sooner. While cleaning out my desk, I found the pen set shaped like golf clubs that Cody and Camarin had given me nearly ten years ago, along with presents kids had given me over the years, and I knew now to throw it all out without thinking twice. I went for drinks with Salena and Barry that night, but something came up with Barry's kid, so he took off early.

"It's gonna be so boring without you there," Salena said.

"I'm sure Cody will replace me with someone with a great personality."

Salena snickered. "Yeah, right."

"And a large set of ass-kissing lips."

"That sounds more like it."

"You know, as much as I hated it there, I learned so much about myself, I've gotta recognize that as well. All the times I hit a wall and didn't think I'd be able to go on, somehow I kept going, learning what was keeping me down and understanding new ways of overcoming those issues in the future. Learning how to respect myself and stand up for myself despite all the negativity. Learning how to be a great teacher, leading by example, even when I felt like running out the door, screaming like a lunatic. I also learned why some people perceive me as a bad employee, and even though there's not much I can do about most of that, at least I'm aware of it and can better deal with it if it comes up again."

"That's the spirit. And you're not gonna sue?"

"Well, the EEOC said that, because they'd denied my requests for reasonable accommodations, I had grounds to sue, but those records go public, and good luck ever getting a job again. I'd be tainted forever. I think the maximum I could make for a disability suit would be, like, two hundred Gs anyway, and after the lawyers and taxman take their cut, there's not much left for someone who's just been blacklisted from professional work. These corporations pretty much have a license to treat you like shit. We need a revolution, and badly."

"That sucks."

"I also learned that, even in the shittiest of situations, even when I think no good can come of something, I can still find great friends like you."

"Aww, that's sweet."

"I still get lost wondering how I ever arrived at a time in my life where I've been able to surround myself with such talented and smart and kind-hearted people as you, and I want you to know that because of you, I'm a better person. So, thank you."

"See, now I'm crying."

A tear dripped from my eye as well. Years ago, this would have never happened. Me, crying in a bar over something other than being punched in the dick or gouged in the eyes? But emotion and life had made its way through the maze and was now at the surface, and it felt good to cry in a public place and not feel as if everyone was watching me, and not care if they were, and to be with someone who wouldn't judge me for it, but rather feel more connected to me. We had a few drinks and went our separate ways. I walked the two miles home and fell asleep quickly. For years, I'd been doing whatever I could to prepare for acting: teaching, writing books, confronting my psychological and emotion pain—everything but actually acting. Now, with all these emotions at the surface, maybe it was time to change that.

A few days later, a friend threw a release party for my novel *Kirkland* at his café downtown. When he first told me about it, I was worried no one would come, but I was wrong to worry. Silas and his brother Victor came, and so did Salena and her boyfriend, along with my landlord, Gary, and a few people I'd met at the Zambulla Film Fest. For years, I'd done everything I could to separate the different parts of my life, but here they were, mixed together in one room as I discussed the novel I'd dedicated to my best friend, sitting in front of me. It was a great night, talking about how much love I put into each of my books and sharing that love with people I loved without feeling as if I needed to hide my work identity from my writing identity from my childhood identity. As Johnny Sacrum, I'd finally brought them all together and didn't feel like an impostor. It would have been nice to have had Doug there, too—maybe. It would have been nice to have seen if I could still feel that love even with him in the room. He still lived in Soul City and had a few kids and was still with his wife, and I'd thought about looking him up a few times. I'd had several dreams about him over the years and knew he was as much a part of my story as anyone else. But it was probably best not to have him around. Some people cross that line so many times that you just can't give them another chance.

After, Silas and I went to a ramen place and had a few beers. We wished each other luck and knew we'd meet up again in LA, where he was heading "in six months, for sure, man." Our lives had kept separating and reuniting since we were kids, and I knew someday we'd be old men laughing together as our bodies and minds fell apart. I hoped that the next time we met would be in a Paris penthouse or on a yacht off the coast of Greece. As I drove home, I realized that I'd been in the Great River all along, and so was everyone else I'd seen that night.

I spent a solid two weeks cleaning out my house, throwing shit away, including all of my notebooks and loose pages I'd written songs and poems and story ideas on. They'd grown so heavy over the years, and I wanted to lighten my load. Besides, I figured I'd already used everything good in those notebooks anyway. Might as well trim the fat.

I sold most of my stuff, making about thirteen hundred bucks. I gave Gary some of the shit he wanted, and on that last day we went to the Mexican place down the block and got some enchiladas and cervezas. I told him he was by far the coolest landlord I'd ever had and that, "you're not so much a landlord as a land-liaison," which we both figured took the negative connotations out of the job title.

I filled two huge bags with the stuff I was taking with me, grabbed my guitar and backpack, and headed for the airport. On the plane back to Buffalo, I sat in the right window seat in the last row, and there was an older White woman sitting in the aisle seat with no one between us. I looked at her and she smiled, and I started laughing to myself, remembering Diosa's words: "When you imagine stronger and wider boundaries around yourself, they will automatically appear."

My parents were waiting for me at the airport, and we couldn't stop smiling when we saw each other. I hugged them both, and it felt great to be under their care again. To not have to carry my weight alone anymore. After all those lonely nights in my apartment wishing I could someday return home, I was now here.

When we got home and I stepped through that door, I didn't feel the Darkness anymore. The house was lit up with Christmas decorations, and my brothers and sisters were there, and my nephews were running around, laughing. Even with all the chaos, I couldn't help but notice one thing in particular: the grease spot near the staircase where I used to knock three times before going to sleep. The whole wall had been wallpapered except for that exact spot.

"Hey, Ma, what's the deal with that?" I pointed at it.

"Jay, you have no idea how much we've missed you."

"I love you too, Ma." I gave her a hug.

I sat at the table and we ate, and even though I fell back into my old routine, making a joke of everything, it didn't feel so heavy anymore. I knew now that all the sarcasm and anger in my humor before had just been my way of mocking the culture of shame and ignorance we'd danced around, but I didn't see that role as necessary anymore. Now, my jokes were lighter. I'd been joking with the kids at school for years and had learned how to do it in a good-natured and fun manner, and I figured why not bring some of that joy home? Nothing here could crush me anymore. If it tried, I knew how to fight back. I knew how to say, "No, that's an invasion of my personal space, and I don't accept it." I let them know about my plans to move to Mexico and how they were all invited down there.

Diosa texted me during dinner. "I'm gonna show the script to some financiers in Los Cabos, so I'd like for you to go through it again."

No, nothing here could stop me now. I was home. LA was also home. So was Mexico. So were all of my friends.

Later that night, after everyone went to bed, I sat on the couch below the grease stain and got lost remembering how I used to run around that house almost nonstop. Though my back still wasn't quite straight, I reached up and rubbed that grease spot.

Little boy, I know you're scared. I know the horrors tormenting your body and mind. I know how isolated and terrified you are. I know you feel that hope is hopeless and you'll never survive beyond the day. I know you feel that no one understands you, and because of that, you feel dirty and diseased. I know no one listens when you talk, not even God. I know better than all of them what you're suffering through. But, know this, little boy: because of this suffering, you'll go places none of them ever will. Because of this suffering, you'll know things about yourself few people will ever stop to ponder. Because of this beautiful gift, you'll find ways of connecting with the world that others will never discover. Because of this gift, you'll be able to unlock the beauty in your heart and soul and share it with others. I know you're scared, little guy, and that's okay. Don't fear your thoughts. They're a part of you and were given to you for a reason. Little boy, I know you feel you can't trust anyone, and that's okay, too. Don't worry about trusting the saints or priests or angels or gods or godparents or aunts or uncles. Don't worry about offending gods or breaking their rules. Trust in me.

Sweet little boy, *I* am your destiny.

About the Author

Jonathan LaPoma is an award-winning novelist, screenwriter, songwriter, and poet from Buffalo, NY. In 2005, he received a BA in history and a secondary education credential from the State University of New York at Geneseo, and he traveled extensively throughout the United States and Mexico after graduating. These experiences have become the inspiration for much of his writing, which often explores themes of alienation and misery as human constructions that can be overcome through self-understanding and the acceptance of suffering.

LaPoma has written five novels, thirteen screenplays, and hundreds of songs and poems. His screenplays have won over 160 awards/honors at various international screenwriting competitions, and his black comedy script *Harm for the Holidays* was optioned by Warren Zide along with Wexlfish Pictures (*American Pie, Final Destination, The Big Hit*) in July 2017.

LaPoma's novels have been recommended by *Kirkus Reviews* and Barnes and Noble (B&N Press Presents list), have hit the #1 Amazon Bestseller lists in the "Satire," "Urban Life," "Metaphysical," "Metaphysical & Visionary," and "Religious & Inspirational" Kindle categories (USA, Canada, and Australia), and have won awards/honors in the 2018 Eric Hoffer Book Award, the 2016 and 2017 Florida Authors and Publishers Association President's Awards, and the 2015 Stargazer Literary Prizes. He lives in Mexico City.

www.jonlapoma.com

Also by Jonathan LaPoma

**Hammond, The Summer of Crud, Understanding the Alacrán, Developing Minds: An American Ghost Story*, and *The Soul City Salvation* are books one-five of a loosely-linked series. Each novel can be read independently of the others.

Hammond

A group of troubled but charismatic boys in a tough Buffalo, NY neighborhood play basketball at a local park and dream winning a state high school championship.

The Summer of Crud

The summer after graduating from college, a mentally ill 22-year-old takes a cross-country US road trip with a friend, hoping to find the inspiration to reach his songwriting potential, start a band, and avoid student teaching in the fall.

Understanding the Alacrán

A 22-year-old man moves to Mexico and better understands the addiction and mental illness destroying his life.

Developing Minds: An American Ghost Story

A group of recent college graduates struggle with alienation and addiction as they try to survive a year of teaching at dysfunctional Miami public schools.

The Soul City Salvation

Not yet ready to take on Hollywood, a 26-year-old aspiring actor and writer moves to Soul City, CA and begins therapy for OCD, setting him on a ten-year healing journey that drives him to near madness as he explores the limits of his heart, creativity, and psyche.

A Noble Truth (screenplay)

Two friends set off on a road trip to explore what truths unite people in a modern America dominated by apathy and discord. It is soon clear, however, that truth is the last thing either man seeks.

www.ingramcontent.com/pod-product-compliance
Lightning Source LLC
Chambersburg PA
CBHW032112110726
47902CB00003B/562